Praise for the novels of Jill Marie Landis

Lover's Lane

"Sexy and sweet, warm and wise, Jill Marie Landis's emotional stories will stay with you long after you've finished reading."

—Kristin Hannah

Magnolia Creek

"Appealing characters and a swiftly moving pace."

—*Kirkus Reviews*

Summer Moon

A Romance Writers of America "Rita" Award Finalist

"A sure winner . . . Hardship, reality, adventure, and love combine to make this an emotional and dramatic tale."

—*Rendezvous*

"A tender, satisfying historical romance . . . A breezy, beach-blanket read, offering up well-developed characters, a compelling plotline, and a pleasing slice of Americana."

—*Publishers Weekly*

Also by Jill Marie Landis

SUMMER MOON
LOVER'S LANE

MAGNOLIA CREEK

Jill Marie Landis

IVY BOOKS • NEW YORK

This is a work of fiction. Names, places, and incidents are either a product of the author's imagination or are used fictitiously.

An Ivy Book
Published by The Random House Ballantine Publishing Group

This book contains an excerpt from the forthcoming book *Lover's Lane* by Jill Marie Landis. This excerpt has been set for this edition only and may not reflect the final content of the forthcoming edition.

www.ballantinebooks.com

ISBN 0-345-44042-0

Manufactured in the United States of America

First Hardcover Edition: August 2002
First Mass Market Edition: June 2003

OPM 10 9 8 7 6 5 4 3 2 1

Mahalo to
Shauna Summers for her insight
and to
Ken Christison and Donna Quist
for reference help.

When lovely woman stoops to folly
And finds too late that men betray,
What charm can soothe her melancholy,
What art can wash her guilt away?

OLIVER GOLDSMITH
The Vicar of Wakefield

1

Southern Kentucky
May 1866

A YOUNG WOMAN clothed in widow's weeds rode in the back of a crude farm wagon and watched the landscape roll by through a cascading ebony veil draped over the wide brim of her black hat. The misty veil not only cast the world in an ominous dark pall, but hid her auburn hair, finely drawn features, clear blue eyes, and the swelling bruise that marred her left cheek.

Her arms were wrapped around her daughter, a toddler with golden cherub curls who was bundled in a thick black shawl to protect her from a brisk afternoon breeze. Sound asleep with her head on her mother's shoulder, the little girl was as oblivious to the chill on the late spring air as she was to the utter desperation in her mother's heart.

Sara Collier Talbot had traveled for days. She had walked south from Ohio along roads shredded by war, circumvented byways stalled by downed bridges and trails clogged with foot traffic, carts full of soldiers going home and liberated Negroes heading north. Carrying her child, Sara had begged rides in carts, on the backs of crowded wagons, atop piles of straw, wedged herself between barrels of dry goods. She had sold her other clothing to help pay for the mourning ensemble.

She had no place to call home, no money, no pride, nothing but an old weathered satchel that held a fresh petticoat, two gowns for the child, a dozen saltine crackers, and the heel end of a stale loaf of bread. Her love child, Elizabeth, a child born of shame, was the only treasure she could claim.

She shifted her precious daughter higher on her shoulder, stunned that fate had brought her home to Magnolia Creek.

An unexpected breeze skimmed across the open farmland, teasing the edge of her veil as the sun raked the tops of the trees bordering the road. Behind the protective anonymity of the black veil, Sara contemplated the only other passenger besides herself and Lissybeth riding in the farmer's wagon.

An ex-soldier still dressed in tattered gray wool, the remnants of a uniform of the once proud Confederate States of America, lay curled up in the far corner of the wagon bed. Sad-eyed, defeated, he was so thin that he resembled a skeleton far more than a man. With no more than a nod to Sara when she first climbed aboard, he had promptly fallen asleep. Thankfully there would be no small talk to suffer.

A pair of scarred crutches padded with rags lay on the wagon bed beside him. He was missing his right foot. His cheeks were covered with sparse salt-and-pepper stubble, his sunken eyes surrounded by violet smudges.

Sara sighed. In one way or another, the war had made invalids of them all.

Looking away from the soldier, she stared out across the surrounding landscape: gentle rolling hills, yellow poplar, sycamore, oak, chestnut, walnut trees all gathered into woods between open fields now lying fallow.

Here and there, trails of chimney smoke snaked up from the treetops, signs of cabins hidden in the wood.

The Kentucky countryside had changed very little since she saw it last, but not so the look of the travelers along its byways.

Before the war, back roads pilgrims were mostly farmers, a few tinkers and merchants, or families on their way across the state. Now the majority were war refugees—many of them Confederate soldiers hailing from Kentucky, men banished and marked as traitors after the state legislature voted to side with the Union. A long year after surrender, those men were still making their way back home.

There were far more Negroes on the roads. Former slaves who had feasted on the first heady rush of freedom, but now wearing the same disoriented look as the white casualties of war. They wandered the rural countryside searching for a way to survive the unaccustomed liberty that had left so many displaced and starving in a world turned upside down.

Sara had spent nearly all she had to buy the black ensemble to wear while she was on the road. The South was full of widows; the North, too, if the papers were to be believed. The sight of a woman alone in drab black garb was not all that unusual and she blended in, one more casualty of the war between the states.

On the outskirts of town the wagon rattled past the old painted sign that read, *Welcome to Magnolia Creek, Home of Talbot Mill, Population three hundred and eighty-one.* Obviously no one had bothered to change the sign. Sara knew, painfully well, that there was at least one who would not be coming home.

For the most part, the town of Magnolia Creek looked the same, the streets evenly crisscrossed like a fancy piece of plaid that was a bit worn and frayed around the edges. The brick buildings along Main Street showed signs of weather and shelling, as battered as their occupants must surely feel.

Melancholy rode the air. She could feel it as she viewed wood-framed homes with peeling whitewashed siding that lined every even street.

A few of the shops and stores around Courthouse Square were still boarded up, their broken windows evidence not only of Yankee cannon fire, but the shortage of replacement glass. The courthouse still remained proud and unbattered. The Union stars and stripes flew triumphantly over the grassy park surrounding the impressive two-story building.

She remembered walking Main Street for hours the day she had first moved into town, recalled staring into storefront windows at all the bright new things. Now she barely gave those same windows a second glance as the wagon rumbled by.

The farmer finally reached his destination, pulled the team up before the dry goods store and set the brake. Sara gingerly lifted Lissybeth off the floor beside her. The exhausted soldier didn't even stir as she stepped from the back of the wagon onto the wooden porch that ran the length of the storefront. She thanked the man for the ride and when her stomach rumbled, Sara stared longingly into the store's dim interior before she turned away and started walking toward Ash Street two blocks away.

"Not far now, baby," she whispered to Lissybeth. "Not far." She prayed that she was doing the right thing, that once she reached the Talbots' fine, familiar house, a hot meal and safe haven would be waiting, even if only for a night.

Number 47 Ash Street came into view the moment she turned the corner. Set off behind a white picket fence with a wide lawn, it was still the grandest house in town.

Sometimes late at night she would lie awake and wonder if the magical time she had spent living in the Talbots' home had been real or merely a figment of her imagination. Her life before the war seemed like a dream; at fifteen she had moved in to care for Louzanna Talbot; at seventeen, after two glorious, golden weeks of a whirlwind courtship she had married Dr. Dru Talbot and thought to live happily ever after.

Five years later, it was hard to believe she had ever truly been the innocent, starry-eyed girl that he had taken for his bride.

Now she was not only Dru Talbot's widow, but a fallen woman in the eyes of the world. She was no better than a camp follower. She was a woman who had lost the man she so dearly loved to war, a woman who then put her faith and trust in the wrong man and now had nothing save the child of that union.

Sara lingered across the street from the Talbots', staring at the wide, columned porch that ran across the entire front and side of the house, and tried to make out some sign of movement behind the lace curtains at the drawing room windows. Then, mustering all the confidence she could, she shifted Lissybeth to the opposite shoulder and quickly crossed the street.

The gate in the picket fence hung lopsided on its hinges. The flower beds bordering the front of the house overflowed with tangled weeds. The same deep abiding sadness she had felt earlier lingered around the place, one that thrived beneath the eaves and lurked in the shadowed corners of the porch behind the old rockers lined up to face the street. The lace draperies at the windows, once so frothy white, hung limp and yellowed behind weather-smeared, spotted panes of glass.

A sigh of relief escaped her when she spotted a familiar quilting frame standing inside the long parlor window. An intricate bow-tie pattern made up of hundreds of small, evenly cut squares of print and checkered pieces was framed and ready to finish quilting. Louzanna Talbot's world had been reduced to fabric patches and thread that bound cotton batting between patchwork tops and backing.

Sara stared at the front door while trying to shush Lissybeth's whining. She lifted the brass knocker and stared at the black, fingerless gloves that hid the fact that she wore no wedding ring. She pounded three times, then tightened her arms beneath her little girl's bottom and waited patiently. When there was no answer, she lifted the knocker again and let it fall, wondered why Louzanna Talbot's Negro manservant, Jamie, was taking so long to answer.

A flicker of movement caught her eye. Someone was inside the house, standing near enough to brush the edges of the curtain against the window in the center of the door. Sara pressed her nose to the pane but could not make out a shape through the layers of her veil and the sheer curtain panel at the oval window.

"Hello? Is anyone home? Jamie, are you there?" She pounded on the doorframe. "Louzanna? Can you hear me?"

A recluse afraid of her own shadow, Louzanna suffered from severe bouts of hysteria. Sara resolved to stand there all evening if she had to as she pressed her forehead against the windowpane and tried to see through the curtain.

"Louzanna? Lou, *open the door,* please." She lowered her voice. "It's Sara."

Finally, a latch clicked, then another. The door creaked and slowly swung inward no more than six inches. All Sara saw of Louzanna was a set of pale, slender fingers grasping the edge of the door and thick braids of wren-brown hair pinned atop her crown.

"Louzanna, it's me. It's Sara. May I come in?" Sara knew what it cost her former sister-in-law to open the front door at all.

Dru's older sister was thirty-eight now, but her translucent skin, hardly ever touched by sunlight, was barely creased at all. Her hair was streaked with a few wisps of gray, but for the most part, it retained its fullness and soft brown hue.

Silence lengthened. The knuckles on Lou's hand whitened. Finally, in a weak, low voice, the woman on the other side whispered, "Is it *really* you, Sara? Is it really, truly you?"

Tears stung Sara's eyes. She frantically tried to blink them away. "It's really me, Louzanna. Please, let me come in."

Another pause, another dozen heartbeats of despair.

Louzanna's voice wavered. More of her braids showed, then her forehead, then pale, hazel eyes peered around the edge of the door. Those eyes went wide when they lit on the child in Sara's arms.

"Oh, Sara." Louzanna's voice was thready.

"Please, Lou."

Louzanna clung to the edge of the door, wielding it like

a shield, a barrier between herself and a world she had shut herself off from long before the war ever started.

Sara couldn't imagine Louzanna coping all alone for very long. One of the reasons she had felt she could leave Lou at all was because she knew Jamie would be there to care for her.

"Where's Jamie?" she asked.

"He's gone. Gone with the Union soldiers. They took him right after you left."

The sun was dipping low on the edge of the sky. Dusk was gathered in the thick, overgrown hedges and dense woods that ran behind the homes on Ash Street. Her desperation no longer tempered by daylight, Sara planted her thigh against the door, afraid Lou might suddenly become fretful and edge it shut.

Dear Lord, give her the courage to let me in.

Frantic, Sara spoke quickly, glancing over her shoulder toward the deserted street.

"I've come all the way from Ohio. I stopped by Collier's Ferry first, but my daddy turned me away. I've no place else to go. I'm begging you, *please* let me in. If not for me, for my child. She's innocent of everything I've done. Take pity on her and let us in, just for tonight. All I'm asking for is a meal and a place to sleep."

She remembered there was an old cabin behind the house where Jamie had lived. "We can sleep out in Jamie's old place. You won't even know we're here."

What did it matter where she slept, as long as there was a roof over her child's head?

"Lift your veil, Sara." Lou sounded edgy and fearful, her voice weak, as if unfamiliar with sound.

Slowly Sara shifted Lissybeth, grasped the edge of her veil and lifted it over the wide hat brim to reveal her face.

She smiled, but the result was weak and wobbly at best and a painful reminder of the swelling on her cheek. The image of the door wavered as it floated on her tears.

"Oh, my, Sara!" Lou gasped, shaking her head, her eyes gone wide. "What happened to your face?"

"I . . . tripped and fell." Sara avoided Lou's gaze as she mumbled around the lie. Daddy had always hit first and asked questions later. Today he had given her something to remember him by before he had turned her away from the family cabin at Collier's Ferry.

Lou backed up and disappeared momentarily. When the door swung wide enough for Sara to slip in, she moved quickly, knowing Lou's deep abiding terror of the front yard and the street beyond. Once inside, she turned to her former sister-in-law with a rush of relief that comes after finding something long sought and familiar.

Lou was dressed the way she had always dressed, much like Sara was now, in a black silk gown with black lace trim and jet buttons. A gold wedding band with an opal stone dangled from a long gold chain around Louzanna's neck. Her faded brown hair and evenly drawn features were the same as Sara remembered, save for added etching at the corners of her eyes.

Louzanna had kept her figure, her slender waist, and dignified stance despite bouts of fear and hysteria that bordered on madness. Though the cuffs and hem of her dress were worn and turned inside out and her gown was wrinkled, she didn't have a single curl out of place.

Quieted by new sights and sounds, Lissybeth laid her head in the crook of Sara's neck and sucked her fingers as she stared at Louzanna.

"I'm sorry to show up like this without word, but I truly have no place else to go," Sara apologized.

Lou was watching her closely, her gaze darting to the door and back again as if she suspected some horror had followed Sara inside.

"What are you doing all alone? What happened to the man you ran off with, Sara?"

Humiliation pierced Sara's heart. She had been such an utter, witless fool the day she had run off and left the wedding ring Dru had given her atop a note for Lou on the upstairs hall table.

Sara licked her lips, swallowed. She could lie, but she and Louzanna Talbot had lived together for nearly two years, shared Dru's letters, shared their joys and heartaches. Louzanna deserved more than lies, but Sara couldn't bear to tell the whole sordid story.

"He is out of my life for good."

Lou stared at Elizabeth, unable to take her eyes off the child. "And so you've finally come home," Lou said softly.

"Yes."

"I knew you would, eventually. I never lost hope." The edges of Lou's lips curled up into what might have been an attempt to smile. She concentrated on the little girl in Sara's arms.

"What is her name?" Lou and Lissybeth exchanged curious stares.

"Elizabeth. I call her Lissybeth," Sara said.

One of Lissybeth's little hands, fingers splayed and extended, stretched toward the lonely recluse.

Timidly, Louzanna slowly raised her hand and offered her index finger to the child. When Lissybeth's little hand closed around Louzanna's fingers, Lou closed her eyes and let out a sigh.

"Lou?" Sara was used to Louzanna's mind drifting and having to coax her around.

Startled, Louzanna looked up, met Sara's eyes, and suddenly threw her arms around Sara's neck. She held on for dear life, encompassing both Sara and Lissybeth in her embrace. When she finally drew back, her hazel eyes were shimmering with tears.

"I haven't much," Louzanna admitted softly, "but you're welcome to share it. This is still your home, Sara, if you want it. I'm so glad you've finally come back."

2

DR. DRU TALBOT stumbled on a rock in the middle of a bone-dry road and hit the ground. He tasted dust and stifled a groan. As the woods along both sides of the road came back into focus, he straightened to a sitting position and tried to shake the stars out of his head. Used up by the war, he felt as old as the dirt he was sitting in.

An old swayback mule he'd found wandering a back road blinked down at him without a lick of comprehension.

"I must be a damned terrible sight," he told the mule. "But at least we're a matched pair."

He had traveled with an odd mix of companions on the road between southern Georgia and home, but the mule was the most amiable and the easiest to suffer, by far.

After months of crossing the South on foot, searching for any rail line still running and finding none, meeting dead ends at every turn, he had finally walked across the Tennessee border and was so close to home that he could almost taste it.

His hand shook when he reached out to push himself up off the ground and a groan escaped him. There was a chill in the evening air and he found himself wishing that he hadn't lost the Irish chain quilt his sister had given him on the night he declared he was going to Tennessee to enlist in the Confederate army. Back in the early days of the war he had carried the tattered keepsake for so long it had almost become part of him, as much as an old ache in his shoulder and the long scar above his right ear. As much as his memories of home, of his sister, and most of all, of Sara, his wife.

His legs were heavy as lead but he pushed on, determined to keep moving until there was just enough light left for him to see by to make a fire. Every step he took put him another minute closer to home.

He hadn't laid eyes on Sara since the dawn after their wedding. He'd done as she had asked, left the way she had wanted him to, slipping away with no good-bye, the way he had promised her that he would go. Now he wondered if he was fooling himself thinking that after all he had been through he could slip back into his old life just as easily as he had walked out of it.

He remembered every moment of their brief but passionate love affair as if it had happened yesterday. He had met Sara two years before they married on a warm spring day, the day he had been leaving for South Carolina Medical College.

He'd first laid eyes on her aboard the ferry raft that her father and brothers ran across Magnolia Creek.

He boarded the ferry deeply lost in thought when suddenly there came a tug on his sleeve accompanied by a low, seductive female voice.

"Nickel fare, Mister. You paid yet?"

Reaching into his vest pocket for change, Dru palmed a nickel, turned around, and suddenly found himself staring into the bluest, most enchanting eyes he had ever seen. The sound of the creek lapping against the side of the huge raft, the low cough of a rheumatic old man, the babble of children crowded along the rail, everything but the girl faded from his conscience. His tongue had stuck to the roof of his mouth, and his lips, of their own volition, had curled into a smile.

Immobile, he had stood there with one hand half out of his pocket and his heart beating in his ears, unable to do anything more than gaze into eyes so captivating that he didn't even mind that they had paralyzed him.

A lovely smile broke across her features and although dirt smudges marred her cheeks, the complexion beneath them was flawless and radiantly aglow. She was tall for a woman, though not tall enough to look him in the eye; whip thin; with well-rounded breasts beneath the rough homespun fabric of a faded gray gown; and barefoot.

She blinked at him and the spell was momentarily broken, at least long enough so that his hand had come out of his pocket, almost as if it had never stopped moving at all. Once again he had become aware of the sights and sounds around them, but all he could do was stare at the bewitching girl standing before him.

"Thank you kindly, Mister . . ."

He could tell she was waiting for him to tell her his name, but he could only concentrate on her fingers as they closed around the nickel and thought, lucky, lucky coin.

He had to stall and clear his throat before he could finally remember his own name. "Talbot. Dru Talbot."

Her lashes lazed over her eyes, forcing her to peer through them. She took a step that brought her up heart-stoppingly close.

"Of the Talbot Mill Talbots?" she asked.

His grandfather had founded a sorghum mill at the old family farm, which had eventually led to the settlement of the nearby town. Farmers from all around the county brought their sorghum cane into the mill to have it processed. Dru's father, Gerald, took over running the mill when the time came and had kept the family one of the most successful and prominent in the county.

He nodded in acknowledgment. "My family used to own the mill."

She stood there squeezing the life out of the nickel and Dru found himself thrilled to have her tarry rather than move on to another passenger. Suddenly he didn't care if the ferry ever reached the opposite shore. He was content to stare into her gorgeous eyes and bask in her warm smile.

"Are you married, Dru Talbot?"

He laughed at her boldness which somehow, coming from such innocent, pouting lips, seemed perfectly natural.

"No. I'm just off to medical college."

"College? You're goin' off to college? Where?"

"South Carolina."

"So far away." She shook her head in awe. "I don't know a lick about either one. I've never been past this damn creek."

When she looked as if she was about to move on he knew a moment of unforeseen panic and before he knew it he had asked, "What's your name?"

"Sara. Sara Collier."

She said the name proudly, as if daring him to speak against it. He'd heard the name but only knew that there were lots of Colliers who lived somewhere in the bottomland along the creek. They ran the ferry, surviving off nickel fares, hunting and selling moonshine liquor.

"How old are you, Sara?" A burning need to know and a mounting desire made him ask. She looked very

young, but in many ways seemed much older than he. He found himself wondering what her lips would taste like.

"Old enough, I reckon."

"And how old would that be?"

"Just turned fifteen."

He had been almost disappointed to think that the last thing he needed was an entanglement with an uneducated, barefoot—though very tempting—backwoods girl.

"What will you study in college, Dru Talbot, that you couldn't learn right here in Kentucky?" She arched her back, accentuating her breasts, and smiled up at him so flirtatiously that he found himself captivated by her impetuosity.

"Medicine."

"My granddaddy's a healer. He taught me to be one, too. I know all about healing herbs. I know lots of charms, too."

She was charming, he'd give her that, but he doubted any girl that young knew much about healing.

A burly, slovenly dressed young man with a few days' growth of stubble over the lower half of his face was watching Sara from across the ferry. Dru had seen him loading the passengers at the landing and figured the man for a Collier, too.

He tried to look serious, as if he and Sara might be engaged in worthy discussion. "What do you mean by charms? Is he a faith healer?"

If she was worried about taking the fares back to her sibling, she didn't appear to be. "He relies on the Bible, that's for certain, but to my mind there's always a bit of magic in it. That and what Granddaddy calls the power of belief. Folks have to believe that the healing is going to take or that a charm will work. Some folks think a charm is something like a spell, but Granddaddy would never do the devil's work."

Dru shifted, steadied himself against the sway of the raft fighting the current, and watched the breeze toy with a lock of her hair. "Give me an example," he urged.

"Well, for instance, if a body has the shingles, the cure is to rub the blood of a black cat or a black hen over the troubled parts. Or . . ." She glanced up to make certain he was listening. "Shingles can be cured by thinking of the person you like best."

He bit the inside of his cheek to keep from laughing outright and risk offending her, and focused on the far side of the creek as she went on.

"Granddaddy puts polecat grease on folks with rheumatism and cures the typhoid by binding onion and fish on the soles of his feet."

"His feet or the patient's?" Dru might have dared to laugh at his joke had he not almost choked on his own breath when his gaze slammed into the near iridescence of her huge blue eyes.

"Are you teasing at me, Dru Talbot?" She reared back, acting affronted, but her warm smile and the twinkle in her eye gave her away.

"I'm starting to fear it's the other way around, Miss Collier."

"Granddaddy takes his healing serious. He's passed on a lot to me. Some of it superstition, to be sure, but I'd be willing to bet many of his herbal remedies are the same as what you'll learn at that fancy college of yours." She tipped her head and eyed him from beneath thick sable lashes. "I'd be more than willing to help you when you start your doctorin'."

"I won't be home for two years." The notion made

him suddenly sober. Two years was a long time to be gone. He wondered where Miss Sara Collier would find herself in two years' time.

"Dru Talbot?" Sara's voice slipped over him like warm fresh cream when she tugged on his sleeve again. "I'm giving you fair warning so you won't be shocked when it finally happens."

"When what happens?"

"When we get married."

The present enfolded him again as night crept through the wood, deepening shadows, tempting cicadas to sing. An owl hooted somewhere to the east. He had grown accustomed to the comforting night sounds of the woods and so shut them out as his mind lingered, as it always wanted to, on Sara.

He had returned home from medical college two years after they met to discover Sara Collier was living in his home. Dr. Maximus Porter, Magnolia Creek's only physician, a man he greatly admired, had introduced Sara to Louzanna and strongly urged Lou to hire the girl as a companion, hoping Sara could help Louzanna combat her bouts of hysteria while Dru was away.

Fate, it seemed, had wanted them together.

Now, after rounding one more bend in the road, he noticed the flickering yellow-orange glow of a low campfire and cautiously slowed his steps. Irregulars roamed the woods, men who weren't about to let the war die even though surrender was a year old. Spawned by war, there remained a deep abiding bitterness throughout the South, but he wore the right colors in this state to be insured a modicum of safety.

His uniform trousers had been reduced to rags and exchanged for inexpensive brown homespun long ago. His ragged officer's tunic of cadet gray was nothing but a sad remnant of the surgeon's coat he had once worn so proudly. The sash of green silk net that labeled him a medical officer now lashed his sword and scarred leather instrument bag to the trappings on the mule.

"Talbot, Fifth Kentucky!" he called out to identify himself to the two men seated by the fire. It wouldn't do to get himself killed this close to home.

Both men turned in his direction, looking enough alike to be brothers with their strawberry hair and wide gaps between their teeth. One called out an invitation.

"Come on up close and sit a spell, then. We're here for the night. Got a bit of roasted squirrel to offer ya."

He led the mule into the welcoming circle of firelight, nodded to each man in turn, and began to untie a bag that held a can of beans and rummaged through his things for a tin of sardines that he'd been hoarding.

"I see by that coat you're a doctor." The thinner of the two bearded men in Confederate States of America gray was in the process of chewing a mouthful of roasted squirrel, but that didn't keep him from talking.

"That I am," Dru admitted. Once, a raw recruit and fledgling doctor at the same time, he had been proud of his new profession. But pride does come before a fall, and as soon as the war had turned fierce, he had found himself feeling more helpless and overwhelmed than anything else.

He had learned to work under the most foul of conditions, no matter how spent or mentally exhausted he was feeling. Sometimes he wondered just how many lives he had really saved when he had permanently altered a man's future by removing a hand, a foot, a limb or sometimes even two, from the same man?

In the heat of his first battle, as cannon fire sounded in the distance and the injured awaiting surgery were backed up ten deep, he was just thankful that he had been given a chance to assist a country doctor for a few weeks before he returned from school in South Carolina.

There were plenty of so-called surgeons active during the first years of the war who had never even witnessed an operation let alone performed one.

Often he found himself with no time to think, acting on sheer instinct and brash bravado. There were days he would have done anything to escape the bloody theater of war and, ashamed to admit it even to himself, he had even lived a lie to keep himself away from the conflict for a few blessed months.

Settling into a quiet practice in Magnolia Creek after all he'd been through would seem to be as easy as walking through a flower garden on a warm summer day.

He offered up the sardines and the scant dinner was accompanied by sparse bursts of conversation. The young men turned out to be brothers, farm boys from the Ninth Kentucky Regiment, headed home to Daviess County.

After dinner, cups of acorn coffee sufficed. Few in the South had tasted the real thing in years. Southerners had learned to make substitutes out of just about anything they could boil.

The older brother from Daviess County bragged that he hadn't suffered a single gunshot wound and was certain that he had nine lives and he had only used a couple of them. But Dru suspected, from the look of the dense rash on the man's neck and arms, that the farm boy was suffering the second stage of gonorrhea.

Out of silkweed root, resin, and blue vitriol—all common treatments for the ailment—Dru couldn't even offer to do anything for the young man. He had treated more cases of the disease than he had war wounds. So many young boys, newly off the farm, spent as much time with whores as they did fighting, especially if they were stationed in cities where whores were plentiful. If venereal disease didn't kill them, then typhoid, or even the measles, often took their toll.

At least he would be going home to Sara clean. He hadn't touched another woman in six years. He had lived through Shiloh and Vicksburg, fought for his life when a minié ball slammed along the side of his head above his right ear, and spent hellish months on the other side of the country in Point Lookout Prisoner of War Camp in Maryland. He considered himself lucky.

The memory of the night he had spent in Sara's arms and the dream of all the nights they would one day share had kept him alive.

Later that evening, as he hunkered down in his bedroll oblivious to the hard ground and the chilly air, Dru Talbot fell asleep with the hint of a smile on his face.

After six long years, he was almost home.

3

FOR SARA, TAKING refuge inside the Talbot house was like climbing back into a cocoon where outwardly little had changed since before the war. Here in his house, it was impossible to evade memories of Dru. A soul-stirring heaviness settled into her heart the moment she had stepped inside.

She was haunted by remembrance as she fed and changed Lissybeth and then, at Lou's insistence, bedded her child down in one of the upstairs bedrooms. When it came time to eat, Louzanna insisted that they use the dining room for old times' sake.

While helping Lou set the table, Sara thought about the first meal she had ever taken in the formal dining room. Back then, everything about the house seemed part of a magical, glittering world where candlelight sparkled and danced off more pieces of crystal and silver than she could count.

In fact, everything she had encountered when she'd first moved into the Talbots' home was new to her, something out of a dream come true. Here was enchantment—a whole new world so opposite of her own that many times she felt adrift and uncertain whether or not she belonged.

In this house there was peace and quiet and genteel splendor. Here there was love and understanding, good manners, soft-spoken words. Beautiful things had always surrounded Dru and his sister, things they took for granted: fine clothes, pretty paintings on the walls, tall crystal vases filled with feathers and dried flowers. She had also seen those same vases filled with fresh spring lilacs, summer roses, delicate ferns, and winter holly.

Shelves filled with gilt-edged books lined an entire wall of the drawing room. With wealth came education, unfathomable depths of knowledge of new and exotic things. The day Doc Porter had met her at the ferry landing and asked if she would consider moving into the house to help Louzanna Talbot had been the luckiest day of her life.

Doctor Maximus Porter had delivered her right to the home of the very same handsome, dark-eyed man she had flirted with just a few days before, the man she had fallen desperately in love with at first sight. Seeing to Miss Louzanna Talbot's health was an easy task. She used combinations of herbs Granddaddy had taught her to brew into hot teas that soothed, soaked rags in vinegar for compresses for Louzanna's forehead whenever one of her jitters came on, and calmed the woman down with plain and simple talk about the garden or the weather.

In exchange, Louzanna told Sara all about Dru, his likes and dislikes, his dream of settling down and taking over Doc Porter's practice when he returned from medical school.

By the time Dru had come home from the Carolinas in the spring of '61, Sara had convinced herself that she was still head over heels in love with him and within two weeks, Dru returned that love and asked her to marry him. His love, above all else, was the real treasure she had found here at the Talbot house.

But just as quickly as their love had bloomed, the war had taken him away forever.

Sara carefully set a dinner plate down on Louzanna's damask tablecloth. The dining room was twice as big as the whole Collier cabin, large enough to hold a cherrywood table with eight matching chairs standing around it like soldiers at attention. A huge matching sideboard once weighed down with a silver tea service and chafing dishes still banked one wall.

The silver pieces were missing now. Sara recalled how she had urged Louzanna to let Jamie hide the tea service in the well hours before the Yankees came in to take over the town of Southern sympathizers. The Union soldiers found the silver anyway.

If only the silver was all they had lost to the Yankees.

Dru had been so very handsome with his dark, curly hair and soulful black eyes. He was dashing, tall, and well educated. When they had married he had been a young man on the verge of a new profession, as absorbed in his dream of becoming the town doctor as she had been in becoming his wife and working by his side.

She knew she was nothing but a backcountry gal and that some folks might not think she should have reached so high, but she had a head full of healing know-how, a heart full of love, and a longing to fit into Dru and Louzanna's world.

Tonight she and Lou sat at the very same table in the very same places where they'd sat after Dru went off to war.

One thing that had not changed since the day Sara had met Lou was the woman's wardrobe. Louzanna had donned unrelieved black and shut herself away on the day her beloved fiancé, Mason Blaylock, was thrown and killed by his horse on the way to their wedding.

"I see you're still wearing Mason's ring," Sara commented.

Lou lifted the opal, stared at the lovely pale stone. "I haven't taken it off since the tragedy." She always referred to the day Mason had died as "the tragedy" in whispered tones, and still mourned as if it had happened yesterday.

"I'm sorry there's not more for supper," Louzanna spoke in the same soft, well-modulated tones that Sara once envied. "My neighbor, Minnie Foster . . . you remember her? She brought over this little chicken yesterday. I've a habit of making things last."

Sara stared down at the meager pieces of chicken on her plate. She indeed remembered Minnie, and more especially Minnie's husband Abel Foster, although she had tried to forget what Abel had done a few days after they received word of Dru's death.

Sara eased around thoughts of the Fosters and met Lou's eyes. "How have you gotten along on your own all this time?"

The woman never left the house except to step out into the near end of the backyard to get water and use the outhouse. When Sara left, she had assumed that Louzanna's other contact with the outside world, Jamie, would always be there.

"I pay Minnie from next door to run errands and for food. Doc Porter stops by to see how I'm faring and the neighbors bring me extra when they have it. I'm careful with what supplies I have but money is hard to come by. The mill payments stopped the year Jamie left, I don't recall exactly when." She looked vague as she glanced down at the tabletop. Dru had sold the family mill and had the payments put in Lou's name so that she would be provided for.

"What happened?" Sara asked.

"The mill was burned when the Union troops pulled out to cripple the town. Mr. Newberry can't make the necessary repairs, and without parts for his mill and no way to make money, he stopped payment. I've sold and traded things for food, lots of Mama's things, porcelain figurines, silver pieces the Yankees didn't get, paintings, and whatnots." Her eyes teared up. "Last week I even traded my best Baltimore quilt for a sack of potatoes."

Knowing what every one of Lou's quilts meant to her, Sara put down her fork and folded her hands in her lap, sharing Lou's sadness. Dru had always been so close to his sister. He had taken such care of her that Sara was thankful he would never know terrible times had befallen Lou.

"I can help you now, Lou." Her thoughts tumbled into words. "The Colliers have always lived hand to mouth. If there's one thing I know it's how to make do. I can hunt as well as put out your vegetable garden the way Jamie always used to."

Lou's considering silence encouraged rather than dismayed.

"I can cook and clean," Sara went on. "I know every root and herb that grows in these parts. I can take care of all three of us—you, me, and Lissybeth."

She pictured the last rundown boardinghouse where she had stayed with its motley gathering of boarders. Going back to that life would be a last resort.

"You've welcomed me and Lissybeth into your home.

Now I'll help provide." She looked around and snatched at another thought. "What were you planning to do when you ran out of things to barter?"

Louzanna reached up, patted the neat wave of bangs at her temple, paused, and then sighed heavily. "Become thinner, I suppose."

Sara was startled until she watched Louzanna's lips tremble around a genuine smile and then she found herself smiling for the first time in weeks.

Weeks, months, years had come between her and Louzanna. Once they had been as close as sisters. They had cried together, prepared to face the enemy, wrapped bandages for the Magnolia Creek Ladies League to send across the border to the Confederate troops. Lou had tutored her and helped her read accounts in the *Sentinel.* They had been family from the beginning, before Sara had even married Dru, before her weaker side had shown itself.

It was a relief to know that Louzanna was willing to put it all behind them and start over.

Surprisingly, the small meal of chicken and bread had sufficed. Sara was used to eating next to nothing. She leaned forward and studied Louzanna as the woman carefully blotted her lips with a linen napkin.

"Your return is a blessing, Sara."

Sara folded her hands in her lap, locked her fingers tight, and took a deep breath.

"Did you ever receive any official notification of Dru's death from the Confederate army, Lou?" Before Sara had left town there had been no official word, only Hugh's firsthand account.

With a firm but gentle purpose, Louzanna set the napkin down beside her plate, then dropped her hands to her lap. For someone so outwardly fragile, she could muster tremendous strength at times. Once Louzanna's mind had latched onto something, there was no swaying it.

"Surely you know by now not to ask me such a thing. I received no official confirmation because Dru *is not* dead. I told you that I would know here," she touched her heart, "if he was gone."

"Hugh Wickham held him as he died, Lou. Keith Jackman saw him go down, too."

The Confederate Kentucky Brigade became orphaned soldiers, unable to return home until after the end of the war, but Hugh, Dru's closest friend and captain of their Confederate regiment, had risked imprisonment crossing the border into Kentucky to bring back news of Dru's death.

"I don't care what Hugh Wickham said he saw. I have yet to receive any official word, nor will I, for my brother is still *alive*. He'll be home soon, mark my words."

When the local men crossed the state line to enlist, Dru had written nearly every day from Camp Boone, Tennessee, faithfully posting letters describing his new duties as field surgeon, the disease and sickness rampant in the camp, the lives lost even before the men entered the fight. The letters slowed to one a week, then one every few weeks and finally, once the Kentucky Brigade was involved, ceased altogether. Confederate mail into Kentucky had become contraband.

Sara still had Dru's last letter to her. It had worn through along the fold lines and fallen into quarters, but every now and then she would lay the pieces out and read it over again.

A few months after all contact between them had

ceased, Hugh had come home with the terrible news; barely a wife, Sara had been widowed.

At first she, like Lou, refused to believe Dru was gone, but after a year and a half of mourning, of existing in a deep black pit, she woke up one morning terrified of becoming Louzanna, certain that she was destined to spend the rest of her life in black, stitching countless miles of thread around an endless chain of fabric pieces, dwelling on the edge of hysteria.

Lou was trembling, staring intently into Sara's eyes.

"You made a terrible mistake by running off with another man. How could you, Sara? How could you disgrace Dru's memory like that?"

Sara already knew that she had made the most grievous mistake of her life. She had let a man entice her, woo her, and bed her, let him seduce her with pretty words and false promises. She had believed him because she was lonely and hurting, mourning Dru and frightened of falling into the pattern of Louzanna's life.

Despite Lou's periods of calm sanity there was mind sickness in her sister-in-law's deep abiding fear of the outside, in the bottomless mourning that held Louzanna imprisoned. Not only was Sara reminded of Dru constantly while she lived in his house, but she had been afraid of succumbing to bouts of hysteria like Louzanna.

Out of fear and desperation, she sought comfort from a man she should never have trusted and managed to convince herself—for a while, at least—that even though she would always and forever love Dru, she could still make a place in her heart for a young man named Jonathan Smith, a charming Yankee lieutenant.

She could never tell Louzanna that it was fear of

becoming just like her that had driven Sara from the Talbots' home. She tried as best she could to explain.

"I was only eighteen, Lou. I was facing a lifetime of loneliness, carrying around the constant ache that came with losing Dru. I let a handsome man comfort and sweet-talk me. I wanted to love him. I wanted to fill the terrible, gaping wound in my heart. He promised to marry me, to show me the world." She sighed, leaned back in her chair. "I was young and foolish enough to believe him. I needed to believe him."

She had trusted Jonathan and tried to love him, and for a while even imagined that he made her happy. She supposed she had been attracted to him because he was so very different from Dru. When she had first met Jonathan, her heart knew a sense of ease. Fair-headed and blue-eyed, Jon was boisterous and exuberant and, unbeknownst to her then, a consummate liar.

No matter what anyone thought or said, the truth was etched upon her heart. Fate had brought her and Dru together and although she would love him always, death had taken him from her.

Sara glanced up, found Lou waiting for her to go on.

"Jonathan . . ." She averted her gaze and fingered the embossed pattern on the linen and damask cloth. "He wasn't what I thought. He wasn't a good man at all." Not like Dru. Not a man of honor and caring.

"You should have known that, seeing as how he was a Yankee."

"You know I didn't understand much about the war back then. My family never took sides before the fighting started. I still don't see why it had to come to all that killing when we're all Americans."

"Did he marry you?"

"No." Sara shook her head, met Lou's eyes. "He said he wanted to, but not until we had official confirmation. I wrote to you twice, to find out if you'd received it or not, and to let you know where I was staying."

"Why, I never got any letters from you at all, Sara." Lou was astounded, looking so surprised that Sara had to believe her.

The one saving grace that had come from her indiscretion was her sweet Elizabeth. Her daughter was the only part of the whole sordid episode that she would never, ever regret. Everyone in town knew that she had run off without marrying her lover. Her reputation was so tattered that her own kin had refused to take her in today.

Lou's thoughts traveled a similar path. "Oh, Sara, your poor baby's a . . . bastard," she whispered.

Sara's hand shook as she picked up her napkin and neatly refolded it, just the way Lou had taught her back when she had been less worldly and wise, a girl just out of the backwoods who had never touched a piece of real linen in her life. Without trying, Dru's pale, soft-spoken sister always made her feel like a scruffy old hen hiding in a lark's nest.

"I wish to God I could make things different, Lou. I wish I could have been what you wanted me to be, but I was a hundred years younger then. I was hurting deep in my soul and all I wanted was to make the pain go away. I had to leave because it was getting impossible to face every new day. Sometimes, for a few blessed moments after I left, I actually forgot that Dru was gone—"

"But he's *not*!" Lou stood abruptly and clutched the edge of the table, her eyes wide and wild, looking as if she were about to flee the room.

Alarmed, Sara had forgotten how easy it was to push Louzanna to the brink of hysteria.

"Are you all right, Louzanna? Should I make you up a lavender handkerchief? Or some scullcap tea?" For an instant it seemed as if no time at all had passed since she had been here calming Lou, brewing tea to relax her and helping her cope with her hysteria.

The woman lived in a dream world, shut up in the house in which she was born, content to let her life tick away. Only the changing seasons and the varied colored patterns of each new quilt she made marked the passing of time.

No matter that years had passed, no matter what she had heard, Louzanna still clung to the hope that Dru would return.

There was no sense arguing with Lou. Confrontation only upset her, so Sara changed the subject.

"I thank you for the meal, Louzanna, especially with times so hard. And I thank you for taking us in. I know that in your eyes I have betrayed Dru's memory and have sinned by living with a man outside of marriage. My daughter may be a bastard, but I'll never regret one minute of her life. She is a precious gift, the innocent one in all of this."

"She's very beautiful," Lou admitted softly.

"Thank you for that, Louzanna." Sara looked up and saw the tears in Lou's eyes.

"I wish she were Dru's." Louzanna gave a mournful shake of her head.

Sara's heart contracted, wrapped around the words, and squeezed.

So do I, she thought. *So do I.*

4

Later that evening Sara found herself in the same room where she had slept when she had first come to the Talbot house as Louzanna's companion. Lissybeth was sleeping peacefully in a low child's crib that had been both Dru's and Louzanna's. Earlier Sara had helped Lou rescue it from the attic.

Lou had outfitted the crib with some of her feed sack patchwork quilts, folding two into a thick, colorful mattress. Appliqué rosebuds adorned the pale ivory coverlet.

Sara thought it was the most comfortable, homey room in the house. Matching oil lamps with etched glass globes on intricate crocheted doilies stood like two sentries on bedside tables. The walls were still papered with vines and roses, the high poster bed covered with a pastel quilt that Lou once proudly told her was the first double wedding ring pattern she had ever completed, an award winner at the Magnolia Creek Sorghum Saturday Festival.

On her first night in this house so long ago, Sara had seen it as a good omen that she was sleeping beneath entwined wedding rings.

Once clean as a whistle, the room was dusty now, the furniture in dire need of a good waxing. The door of the armoire hung askew—nothing that a good tightening of the hinges wouldn't cure. Before the war, Louzanna had never even lifted a dust rag. Without Jamie, the house was not being cared for as it should have been.

All of the clothes that Sara had abandoned when she had run off with Jonathan were still neatly hanging in the armoire—print day dresses and one plain, pale, butter-colored silk—dresses made for her after Dru had gone off to war. Things she had left behind.

She tried on a nightgown and, although her breasts were fuller now, the loose gown still fit. She sat down at the dressing table where an ivory-backed brush engraved with Dru's mother's initials—part of a set that Lou had presented to her on the night she married Dru—still lay as if awaiting her return. She reached out and traced her finger over the yellowed ivory before she picked up the brush.

Sara avoided her reflection while she slipped out the pins and combed her waist-length hair, but finally, gathering courage, she stared back at herself. The nightgown was as pure white as driven snow, and her auburn hair was long and glossy. Its reddish tints caught the lamplight, staining it bloodred. Her image was framed with the familiar background of vines and roses trailing over the wallpaper. The ugly bruise her daddy had inflicted rode across her cheek below her left eye.

She was still young. Twenty-two was not old by anyone's measure. Her face was unlined and her skin—not as pale as Louzanna's—fairly undamaged by the sun, though she had spent time outdoors the previous summer working on a farm in Ohio.

But her eyes. Dear heaven, her eyes looked old. Old eyes in a young face. She pressed her fingertips to her lips, wondering.

What would Dru look like now, had he lived?

Would his face show the ravages of war?

Here in his house, sitting amid her old things in a room they had shared for just one night, pain slammed into her—pain and memories she had tried to bury deep in her heart where no one, not even she, could find them.

It was a lifetime ago, the spring she turned fifteen. That morning, before she met Dru, she had been lying awake in the loft, staring at the high-pitched ceiling of the old log cabin, trying to picture the man she would marry. She longed for someone tall and handsome, dark, well-spoken, maybe even a bit on the dangerous side. She hadn't thought that it was too much to ask that he had all his teeth, either.

On her birthday her daddy started trying to marry her off, but she had refused every single man he brought around, young and old alike and those in between, until her daddy swore that before autumn he would "see for damn sartin' that she was hitched."

Bound and determined to find a man on her own terms, she awoke that morning when there was still enough predawn light to cast the cabin loft in pale gray shadows. As gingerly as she could, she crouched to avoid smacking her head on the ceiling as she jockeyed around her younger brothers and sisters, who always tended to wind up sleeping in a tangle like a litter of puppies.

For what she was about to do, she needed utmost privacy, something sorely lacking in the life of a Collier. She swiftly and silently climbed down the ladder to cross the main room, slipped past the bed where Mama slept with her arm around two-year-old Arlo and where Fannie and

Kittie, four and five at the time, were wedged between Mama and Daddy.

Seconds later she carefully lifted the flour sifter Mama always hung on the doorknob every night—an old-time, surefire way to keep witches from slipping into the bread while the household slept—and crept out of the house. She ran down the old Indian footpath until the woods swallowed her and she was out of sight of the cabin.

Dew soaked the hem of her homespun dress by the time she had reached the meadow, but she paid the dampness no mind as she sought out the gnarled old trunk of a fallen oak she had seen many times before.

She walked the length of the collapsed giant, closed her eyes, and knelt down in the damp grass beside the tree. The bark was rough where she laid her hand on the solid old trunk, and upon touching it, she wished the tree's wisdom would somehow seep into her.

There was a shallow depression in the oak, a burrowed knot where a puddle of heavy dew had collected. The dew was the priceless treasure she had sought, the element she needed to set a charm in motion.

Like a supplicant at prayer, she leaned over the small pool in the gray half light. Her reflection wavered and then disappeared as she dipped both hands in and carefully cupped the precious water. Her heart was beating with anticipation. She counted the rapid beats until the sun broke over the horizon and set the east end of the woods ablaze with light. Once, twice, three times she rinsed her face to insure the charm's success.

The ritual complete, she sat back on her heels and closed her eyes.

"Wash your face in the morning dew at the crack of

dawn and no man will be able to resist you," Granddaddy had told her. "You'll meet your one, true love."

He had said that the charm was as old as time and that she should be careful how she used it. Though she didn't put much stock in all the charms Granddaddy touted, she reckoned she had nothing to lose.

She decided to work down at the ferry that day with Daddy and her half brothers—something she rarely did. The minute she had laid eyes on Dru when he boarded the ferry, the hair had stood up on her arms and a chill shot through her to her toes, one that hit with a shock stronger than the healthy swig of white lightning that her half brother Darrel had once given her while they kept watch over the still in the woods.

Dru was the handsomest man she'd ever seen, a real man dressed in a fine long jacket with a waistcoat beneath it, the hem of his straight-cut trousers brushing fine new black shoes. Dru Talbot was nothing like anyone she knew—far more than a cut above the backwoods boys who'd vied for her hand—and she was certain that he was her destiny. Why else would he be crossing the creek on the one day that she had decided to work the raft?

Her heart nearly broke when he told her he was on his way to South Carolina to go to school. Why, she had just found him and he was going to walk out of her life forever.

She fancied she'd seen regret in his eyes when the ferry reached the other side of Magnolia Creek and he bid her farewell. After all, she'd made him laugh when she told him they were going to be married someday.

"It was nice to meet you, Sara Collier," he said as he was about to depart, then he gave her another heart-stopping

smile and politely tipped his hat like a real gentleman as he gathered up his horse's reins.

"Oh, don't you worry, Dru Talbot, you'll be seeing a lot more of me." She sidled up to him as he moved toward the edge of the raft. "Don't forget we're getting married one day."

He threw back his head and laughed again, full and throaty, so joyous a sound that it wrapped around her heart and wouldn't let go. She worried her thumbnail with her teeth, dreading having to watch him walk off the ferry and out of her life.

She had given him one last smile and a cheery farewell, as if her heart didn't feel like it was squeezing out its very last beat, then she climbed up on the rail and watched him step onto the shore. He stared down at his shoes as he carefully negotiated the muddy landing, led his horse a ways off, and mounted up. Then, before he rode away, he twisted around in the saddle to look back at her.

Sara waved both arms over her head and was even so bold as to throw him a kiss as he tugged on the brim of his hat and thrust his boot in the stirrup.

He looked back twice before he rode out of sight. She took that as a sign that he would remember her, at least for a while.

"You get all the fares, Sara?"

Donnie, her other half brother, was standing at her elbow smelling of tobacco and rancid grease. She stared up at his thick neck, at his wide chin covered with a forest of distinct dark stubble, and wrinkled her nose. The difference between her half brother and Dru Talbot was truly painful.

"I got 'em." She untied the drawstring bag from around her waist and handed it over. "Every last one."

She had given Donnie all but that very last fare, for it was the nickel that Dru had handed to her. It was still in her palm, warm as her hand, warm as her heartbeat.

That night she tucked that nickel beneath her pillow, hoping to dream sweet dreams of the handsome young man she had just met, hoping that somehow, some way, fate would bring him back into her life again.

Sara sighed. Later that spring, fate came in the guise of Doc Porter, who brought her to Dru's very doorstep. She tended Louzanna, bolstered her courage and helped keep the bouts of hysteria at bay. Dru returned from college and they were together until the war—with its impartial disregard of hopes and dreams and promises—had torn them apart.

But now that she was here in Dru's house once more, he was sure to haunt her dreams just as he haunted her waking hours.

5

HE'D BE HOME before noon.

Dru bid his fellow sojourners farewell and started down the road, looking to the future—his future with Sara.

It was a perfect spring day. The early dew lay in a thick, glistening sheen on the damp ground. Along the roadside, dogwood blossoms vied with redbud, early signs of color bound to gladden even the coldest of hearts. Red and white blooms stood out against the stark branches of sugar maples, oak, and beech trees, promises of life stirring again.

Spring in Kentucky. The perfect time to begin anew, to settle down and start his medical practice and a family. He longed to fill the house with noisy children. He hoped to see Louzanna's world broaden when she became an aunt, if not actually outside the house, then within. His sister deserved whatever joy life could bring.

Sara. Again and always, Sara. He still pictured her as the woman-child he had married and wondered how much she had changed. He had left a bride holding on to the promise of the future and now, that day was near. By noon, God willing, he would be home.

The morning chill slowly dissipated and the sun rose

higher. He was thankful for the battered felt hat he'd taken off a dying corporal who wouldn't need it anymore.

After his head wound at Shiloh, he'd been transported to Maryland to languish in the prison hospital, ignorant of who he was or how he had ended up there. Even the small case of surgical knives in his pocket hadn't helped him to remember at first, but within three weeks his memory slowly returned. When it did, it proved to be more of a curse than a blessing, for thoughts of home and Sara filled his every waking hour.

He had kept the knowledge of his identity to himself, knowing full well that since he was a doctor, he would be exchanged for Union prisoners as soon as he was deemed fit. Unable to face battlefield surgery again, he pretended not to know who he was for six months, until conscience and honor got the best of him.

Once his identity was made known, he had written to Sara and to Lou, but they never wrote back. When he returned to his regiment again, he heard that his letters weren't likely to get through to Kentucky.

Frustrated, he contented himself with daydreams and composed hundreds of letters in his mind.

Even now he could still recall the way Sara had surprised him when she opened the door to his home the day he had returned from medical college.

She stood there smiling up at him, her eyes filled with excitement, hope, and definitely promise. Gone was her tattered, faded gown, her dirty face. She smelled like Louzanna's special lemon-scented soap and looked every inch a lady in a muslin gown sprinkled with embroidered flowers. A pair of pretty slippers adorned her once bare, muddy feet. In two years she had been transformed from a plucky, bright-eyed girl who had teased him about marriage into a stunning young woman.

"Surprise and welcome home, Dru." The ferry raft girl had turned into a rare beauty.

He stepped inside, dropped his bag, and doffed his hat, unable to believe his good fortune.

"To what do I owe this pleasure, Miss Collier? How have you come to be here, in my very home?"

She drew back and looked him over with a mischievous smile.

"I work for your sister now. Doc Porter set me up as a companion to your sister because she wasn't doing very well after you first left. She's right as rain now, most of the time."

Even as he fought the stirring in his blood and tried to deny his intense attraction for this young woman he barely knew, he recalled she had mentioned having some knowledge of herbals and healing.

Standing so close that he could smell lemon balm on her skin and watch the pulse jump in her lovely throat, his heart and body assured him that Sara Collier attracted him in a way no woman had ever done before or since. With her pert smile and flashing eyes, she had been as tempting as a sugarplum candy.

The next evening after dinner he made it a point to visit Doc Porter and ask about Sara.

As they sat on the front porch of Maximus's home, the old doc rubbed his hand over his grizzled gray hair and told Dru how Sara had come to be Louzanna's companion.

"Your sister didn't admit it to you, son, for she wasn't about to hold you back, but she was terrified at your leaving and certain that something horrible would hap-

pen to you. Jamie was fetching me to calm her down more times than I could count and I was at my wit's end. One day when I was making a ferry crossing and contemplating that very problem, I struck up a conversation with young Sara. I found her bright and articulate despite her upbringing and as we talked about her Granddaddy Wilkes and what she knew about healing, I knew she was exactly what Louzanna needed. She jumped at the chance to leave home, so I took her over to meet Louzanna. Well, from the moment your sister laid eyes on her, she wanted to take Sara under her wing and make a lady out of her." Doc had gone on to describe the Colliers' situation.

"Dirt poor. Live fourteen in a one-room cabin. Old Daniel Wilkes is Mrs. Collier's father. Lives there, too. Keeps to himself. He carries a Bible in one hand and superstition in the other. He conjures up home remedies and tonics along with his own brand of spiritualism to cure the backwoods folk. For years I've taken care of people on this side of the crick and left the backwoods folk to Daniel Wilkes.

"The lot of them are pretty self-sufficient. Tend to isolate themselves from any but their own kind. DeWitt Collier's the father of the brood. Mean as hell. Ornery, bad-tempered son of a bitch. His two oldest boys are by a first wife."

It had been hard to imagine someone with Sara's unspoiled spirit, someone so lighthearted and full of hope, coming out of such poverty and abuse. He found himself as grateful to Doc for getting Sara out of her home as he was for the man finding Louzanna a companion.

"I can't wait to put out the word that my protégé is back and rarin' to go so I can finally retire," Doc said.

"Don't think about quitting yet," Dru had warned him. "I told Hugh Wickham earlier today that I'd consider going along when he goes down to Camp Boone to enlist. Some of the boys have gotten a company together and already elected him captain."

"I know your views on slavery are the same as my own," Doc said. "I know the day your father died you freed Jamie. Why join the Confederates?"

"I've been hoping Kentucky would remain neutral, but the legislature voted the other way, forcing us to choose one side or the other. The men forming the Magnolia Creek Company have been as close to me as brothers. I can hardly stand by while my friends and neighbors give their lives to the Southern cause. I can't ignore the call to help, not when I've been trained to save lives. Honor compels me to do everything I can to support them, no matter my political beliefs, Doc."

He would still be living among them after the war, caring for their families. He wasn't about to stand against them. Nor could he refuse to help when Hugh had raised his own company and begged him to sign on as their doctor.

What he hadn't counted on was falling head over heels in love with Sara Collier.

She came to him in the barn the first time he ever dared to kiss her. It was a week after his return from school that he and Lou and Sara had been sitting in the drawing room after dinner. Sara had been as lighthearted and flirtatious as the day they had met on the ferry and later, while Lou quilted by lamplight, Sara was content to sit by the fire and listen as he read them the war reports in the Sentinel.

Having her so near day after day, so attentive and curi-

ous, never taking her eyes off of him, he found himself fantasizing about folding the newspaper, crossing the room, and taking her in his arms.

As soon as his sister declared herself too tired to take another stitch and had gone to bed, he quickly excused himself on the pretense of going to the barn to tend to the animals, leaving Sara in the drawing room—it was that or sit alone in the lamplight with her. Truth be told, he was so aroused, so desirous of her, that he couldn't trust himself not to take advantage of the situation.

He had planned to stay outside until the house was dark and was certain that Sara was asleep, but she slipped out to find him, testing his resolve to its limit.

"Dru?"

She surprised him, so he sounded far harsher than he intended when he asked, "What are you doing out here?"

"I wanted to talk to you."

"It's late, Sara."

"I heard what you told Louzanna in the hallway before dinner, about how you were seriously thinking about going off to war. I just couldn't bear it if anything happened to you. You don't have to go, no matter what Hugh Wickham and the others say, you know. My daddy and the older boys aren't going to fight. They're all set to sell whiskey to both sides if the armies march through. You can stay home and make money right here, too. There's always somebody getting sick or hurt and if the fighting comes close, Doc Porter will need your help."

He tried to explain that it wasn't about making money but about loyalty to his friends and neighbors, about being of service to those he had known since childhood. By joining the Magnolia Creek Regiment as its surgeon, he would be able to give back to the men who had worked at Talbot Mill and made his family wealthy.

Raised where she was, as she was, he realized she might not understand his need to give back to the community that had always been so good to his family.

"These past few days with you here have been the best of my life," she told him. "I'd hate to have you leave again. So would Louzanna."

"She's so much better with you here," he told her truthfully. Doc Porter's plan had been an inspired one.

"That doesn't mean she'll be all right if you go off to war."

"I'm going to enlist, Sara. There are things that a man has to do in order to call himself a man."

"There are things a woman has to do, too, Dru. I'd like to think I could talk you out of getting yourself killed."

He stared down into her upturned face, shaking with desire, so tempted that he was forced to turn his back on her. She sighed, touched him lightly on the arm, urged him to face her again.

"I'm sorry, Dru. I know it's only been a few days, but I feel as if I know you so well. You . . . you've come to mean so much to me already that—"

He didn't give her a chance to say any more before he pulled her into his arms and gave in to temptation. He wove his fingers through her hair until he cupped the back of her head, pulled her close, and sealed his mouth against her honeyed lips.

When he finally lifted his head and broke the kiss, they were both breathing hard, eyes locked, the only sound in the barn the ragged notes of their panting, the rhythmic racing of their hearts.

In that split second, on that night when the moon had been full and the evidence of spring everywhere upon the land, an age-old magic was at work—the kind of magic that pays no mind to circumstances of birth, that heeds no restrictions of society.

"Kiss me again," she whispered, cupping his face between her trembling hands. "That was like nothing I've ever imagined. Please, Dru, again."

She was soft and warm, innocent and oh, so tempting. He had known the moment he had tasted her sweet lips that he wanted more than this one night. He wanted forever.

As he held her in his arms, he wondered how safe a beautiful young woman like Sara would be on her own after the fighting started. What would happen if her family called her home again and the troops came through? He imagined her working a ferry loaded with soldiers or selling whiskey by the roadside.

How would she fare at Collier's Ferry if war came into Kentucky?

When he suddenly realized that he was willing to do anything to keep her safe, he understood that he was more than infatuated. He was in love.

Her smile was as innocent as it was heart-stopping, and he knew that if he kissed her again there would be no going back.

There was no way in hell he could be less than honorable toward her.

"We haven't known each other very long, but there's no way of telling what the war is going to bring. Will you marry me, Sara? Will you be my wife?"

"I know what kind of man you are, Dru. I knew it the

day we met on the ferry. I'll be your wife for always and forever. I'll be the best wife a man could ever have."

"Then we'll do it. We'll be married at the end of the week."

"Are you still going to Tennessee with Hugh?"

"I am. Does that change your mind?"

"Of course not. I love you, Dru."

His heart was light as duck down that night. How could any dark notion of war survive in the face of her shining pledge of love?

"Now that I know I'll have the most beautiful wife in all of Kentucky waiting for me, I'll be sure to whip the Yankees and be home before you even know I've been gone."

In the spring of 1861 he had been as naive as the rest of them, certain the war would end in a few months, convinced that he would be home by the holidays to celebrate their first Christmas together.

6

Louzanna loved early morning. It was her habit to rise well before dawn, go down to the conservatory, and watch the strawberry-colored dawn creep above the horizon and spread out across the land. She enjoyed being alone with the new day, sitting at the bank of windows that looked out over the backyard at the woods beyond the barn. There she would watch the seasons change.

This morning, after tossing and turning all night, she overslept and was still groggy as she pulled on a dove-gray wrapper and slipped downstairs. Sara's little Lissybeth had spent a fitful night, sometimes fussing, sometimes outright bawling. Lou had crept down the hall and heard Sara softly singing to the beautiful child who had already breathed life into the old, quiet house.

Now she stepped into the conservatory at the back of the house, a structure made nearly all of glass that Dru and Jamie had built so that Lou could enjoy her garden without going outside. Stacks of cordwood and kindling were piled up near the back door where she could get to them easily without venturing far into the yard. After Jamie left, various neighbors chopped wood and stacked it nearby, knowing that if it were up to her, Lou would sometimes rather freeze than go outside to fetch it.

Gathering what she needed in her arms, she was headed back indoors when she spotted Minnie Foster, her next-door neighbor, bustling across the backyard.

Minnie gave nothing without a price. Once the mill payments had stopped, Lou had paid Minnie for supplies and food, trading her mother's trinkets and cherished bric-a-brac. She had even bartered off a collection of paintings in exchange for food and payment to Minnie to run her errands.

Minnie's choppy, determined stride quickly carried her to the back door where she could see Lou through the side window but insisted on rapping loudly anyway. Louzanna turned the knob and stepped well back, allowing an opening barely wide enough for Minnie to slip through.

Louzanna had never particularly liked Minnie, but the woman was an excellent quilter, so Lou had invited her into her Thursday sewing circle years ago. Minnie was in her forties, married to the owner and publisher of the *Magnolia Creek Sentinel*. They had lost their only son, Arthur, to the war shortly after Dru had been reported dead and the two had mourned together.

Short and stocky with bright yellow hair, Minnie was the unofficial Magnolia Creek town crier. Minnie prided herself on hearing gossip first and was proud to pass it on.

As Minnie trailed her into the kitchen, Lou clutched the wood to her breast, hoping that Sara wouldn't come in until Minnie had gone. Unwilling to explain Sara's situation, she prayed little Elizabeth wouldn't start fussing.

"You're up early, Minnie." Lou stood very still, clutching the rough wood, wishing Minnie would leave.

Minnie's gaze roved over every surface, into each corner, and finally stopped at the open doorway into the hall.

"Where is she?"

Lou took her time setting the wood in the basket on the floor beside the stove, then she brushed off the front of her robe. Too nervous to leave her hands free, she clutched the ring on the gold chain about her neck, her talisman, her connection to a brief time when she had been happy.

"Who?" The word barely squeaked out, Lou's timidity dissolving the confident air she tried hard to posture.

Minnie marched over to the open hall door, stuck her head through to look around, then walked back into the kitchen.

"You know who. *Her.* That woman. Sara Collier."

"Her name is still Sara Talbot." Lou wanted to bite her tongue for spilling the beans.

Minnie's eyes blossomed. A smirk curled her lips. "So. She didn't remarry?"

Louzanna knew she had made a drastic tactical error but couldn't lie, so she shook her head. Her grip tightened on the ring. The cool opal pressed into her palm, offering no relief.

"No. No, she didn't. I was about to make coffee. Would you like a cup or do you have to leave?" *Please, please leave.*

"No use trying to change the subject. I saw her yesterday. Saw a woman dressed in black with a baby in her arms. Saw her march right up to your door and start knocking. Recognized her voice when she called out to you."

Lou knew better than to deny it. There wasn't much Minnie didn't see or hear on the block, not the way she haunted the windows and lingered on the edge of her porch most of the time. Let a wagon or carriage roll down the street, and Minnie was right there watching.

"You aren't going to let her stay *here*, are you?" Minnie rocked forward onto her toes as if she was about to take flight.

"She hasn't asked to stay on yet. If she wants to, though, she's more than welcome. Dru will be home soon. He'll sort everything out."

Minnie snorted. "You're goading me now, aren't you, Louzanna Talbot? I know you're a bit . . . eccentric, but even you must realize what having her here will do to your good name in this town. Why, she consorted with *Yankees*, for heaven's sake. I would think that losing your brother to those bastards–"

Lou stiffened, Minnie's words prodding her like a bolt of lightning, electrifying every delicate nerve. "I have *not* lost my brother to anyone. Dru's alive. He's coming home."

Minnie's gaze shot around the room, lighting on everything at once. She scratched her cheek, muttered something Lou couldn't hear. Then she began to fuss and straighten the cuffs of her sleeves.

"Louzanna, everyone knows that Dru is dead. When are you going to admit it?"

Never.

The word echoed like a scream inside Lou's head but she didn't make a sound. Didn't everyone know that she would never, ever admit that Dru was dead? If she did she would surely lose what was left of her mind.

No, Dru was still alive and now she saw Sara's return as an omen that he would be home soon. Sara would be here when he returned and everything would go back to the way it was before, the way it was the day of the wedding. Dru would be a doctor and Sara would be his wife. They would live here and raise their children and all of them, including Lou herself, would be part of one big family.

"Dru is just missing. He is *not* dead." She turned her back on Minnie and started to put wood into the stove.

"All right. Assuming he is alive, what do you intend to tell him when he comes home and finds that woman here? What about the fact that she's got some man's bastard now? Why, Dru will toss her out on her ear the minute he finds out. That's what any man in his right mind would do if his wife had been whoring with someone else. And a Yankee, to boot! After what I've been through, do you really expect me to live next door to *that* woman?"

Lou's heart started to flutter. She had no idea what Dru would do when he found out about Sara, absolutely no idea at all. The Fosters' loss had left Minnie bruised and bitter, but Lou didn't believe that gave her any excuse for being so coldhearted.

"You aren't the only one who's suffered, Minnie."

"I *lost a son.* Don't tell me how much I've suffered! Don't tell me about anyone else's pain." Minnie paced to the table, straightened all the chairs, walked back to the middle of the room, and stood there with her hands fisted against her skirt. "And to think I came over to offer you part of a ham." Minnie drew herself up, clearly affronted.

"Under the circumstances," Minnie went on, "you're not welcome to my ham, not if even one morsel of it is going to go to that woman. Or that little bastard."

Fraying around the edges, Lou let go of Mason's ring,

then reached up and tucked a strand of hair into the knot at her nape. Hysteria was coming on. The signs were always the same; first the shortness of breath, then her throat closed and her legs trembled. Her heart galloped at a lopsided, uneven gait as she took a deep breath and tried to hang on.

"Are you blackmailing me, Minnie?" The words came on a whisper, echoed on the cool morning air.

Minnie's eyes slowly narrowed. "The whole town will be talking about this."

"Only if you run around telling them."

"You think you can hide her for long? You've been living off of the charity of good folks in this town for years. What do you think will happen if you let her stay? You're mistaken, Louzanna Talbot, if you think anyone will help you support the likes of her and her bastard."

Bastard.

Pretty little Elizabeth with her stunning eyes that echoed Sara's, with her bright, shining blond curls and innocent smile. And Sara, with deep sad shadows beneath her eyes, that terrible bruise and look of perpetual sadness.

There were very few in town who had not lost someone to the war. Minnie was right; most would condemn Sara for what she had done. The citizens of Magnolia Creek felt betrayed enough by the Kentucky legislature for voting to become a Union state, a move that forced husbands, sons, and brothers to leave to enlist. Strong Southern sympathizers had been driven out or imprisoned when they became too vocal. Confederate soldiers had been arrested if they tried to come home before the war ended.

Yes, Minnie was right. It would take far more compassion and understanding than most people possessed to forgive Sara. But was it right to hold her accountable for a mistake she had made out of grief and loneliness? If she was guilty of anything, it was of being young and foolish and lonely.

Lou trembled fiercely. "Please leave, Minnie," she whispered, thinking of Sara, mustering courage from somewhere.

"*What* did you just say?"

"I believe you heard me. This is still my home. I still consider Sara my sister and I always will. I can make welcome whomever I want. Right now, that's not you."

Minnie's eyes narrowed. Her mouth tightened into a firm line. The heels of her shoes made tight, clipped sounds as she marched through the conservatory to the door. She paused with one hand on the knob to deliver her parting salvo.

"You'll rue the day you opened the door to that whore, Louzanna. Don't expect me to take pity on you when she robs you blind and leaves you alone again. This time you'll have no one to help you."

7

"YOU'LL RUE THE *day you opened the door to that whore . . .*"

Sara shuddered, unable to take a step. The door slammed. Silence fell like a heavy widow's veil over the house.

She pictured Lou standing on the other side of the wall, wondered where Louzanna found the strength to stand up to Minnie Foster, why she was defending her at all.

Her own shallow breath sounded loud as cannon fire in her ears. Sara walked into the kitchen, paused, and watched Louzanna open the oven door. Three years ago, her sister-in-law had no notion of how to do anything in the kitchen. Jamie had seen to the house and yard chores; a cook came in to prepare meals.

Lou started and turned wild doe eyes her way when Sara walked in. Unsure of herself, Sara paused beside the table where a sand-colored crockery bowl full of eggs sat beside the half loaf of bread they had had slices of last night.

"I heard what you told Minnie, Lou."

There was a look of incredulity in Louzanna's eyes, almost as if even she couldn't quite fathom what she had done. She smiled tremulously. "I always feel quite a bit braver whenever you are around, Sara."

Poised on the edge of long forgotten hope, Sara wanted to hear the reason Lou had defended her. "Why, Lou?"

"What do you mean?" Lou fingered the opal.

"Why did you send Minnie packing?"

"I thought . . . I thought about what you said last night. I thought about Elizabeth. She *is* the innocent one in all of this. Besides, this is my home. Mine and Dru's and yours, too, Sara."

Mine once, too, Sara thought. *I had a real place here, too.*

She realized that she couldn't risk hurting Lou's reputation by staying. She was spoiled goods now. Minnie wasn't the only one who would think so.

Lou hadn't said a word but she did appear a bit confused, as if she couldn't quite believe what she had done.

Feeling a deep, abiding sadness for what might have been, knowing that to stay might only cause Louzanna to endure more of what had just happened, Sara said, "I don't want to cause you trouble. As soon as Lissybeth wakes up and I feed her, we'll leave—"

"No! You can't go, Sara!" Lou lunged forward, grabbed hold of Sara, and held on tight.

"But, Lou—"

"No." Lou drew back, let go, and shook her head as she smiled wanly, barely in control. "She's little more than a baby. I'll not have you take off with her without any notion of where you're going to live. I won't hear any more about it. This is your home, Sara." She glanced around as if about to panic, fighting to convince Sara to stay. "Last night you . . . you offered to help hunt and garden. A promise is a promise, isn't it? You gave me your word."

"I did," Sara whispered, then louder, "I did and I intend to keep it." This time she would keep her promise. She would stay and see to Lou and earn the love her "sister" so generously showered on her.

Sara glanced at the stove. The kindling inside had begun to pop and crackle. She longed for a cup of hot coffee, real coffee, but doubted Lou had any. Her stomach growled.

While Louzanna filled a kettle of water from a bucket on the dry sink, Sara relaxed a bit, walked to the back room, and stared though the conservatory windows at the backyard.

The flower garden was a shambles, the vegetable patch nothing more than a plot of dried weeds and their new offspring. Shaggy, unkempt lawn grew all the way back to the Talbots' small barn and carriage house and the one-room cabins that backed up to the woods at the edge of the property.

Minnie's husband Abel Foster came to mind. He had printed a piece in the *Magnolia Creek Sentinel*, a retelling of Hugh Wickham's firsthand account of what happened to the Kentucky Brigade at Shiloh. The story was a beautiful tribute to the grandson of the town's founding father. So when Sara had seen Abel walking out to the back of his property, she had gone out to thank him, never suspecting what was coming until they were out beside the very barn Sara stared at now.

"You're a widow now, Sara, but you're young," Abel told her after accepting her words of gratitude. "You'll have . . . certain needs. If you ever get lonely and want someone to talk to, I know how to be discreet."

At first she couldn't believe what she was hearing, but then he made an awkward attempt to kiss her, backing her up to the barn and pawing at her breasts. His breath had been hot and frantic, his ink-stained hands damp. She had been too shocked to do anything but shove him away. The last she had seen of him before she took off running was Abel wiping his florid face with a handkerchief.

It had been one of the worst experiences of her life, and to this day she had never told a soul about it. Now it pained her to think that poor Louzanna had ever been dependent on people like the Fosters.

Beyond the barn, the forest encircled the town. The sun's rays had risen high enough to slant through the tree branches. Soft, green buds added new spring color to the quiet forest. She knew the Kentucky woods like the back of her hand, the names of all the trees, rocks, flowers, and animals that lived there. Until she left home, she had spent hours traipsing through the woods with her granddaddy.

She could hardly wait to go hunting. Sara crossed the room until she was beside Lou again.

"Would you watch Lissybeth while I go hunting?"

Louzanna's eyes sparkled with unshed tears. "You . . . you'd trust *me* to look after her?"

"I'd trust you with her life, Lou."

"But . . . I'm not always . . . dependable." Her eyes were huge with uncertainty. "You know that, Sara. What about my hysteria? What if I have an attack?"

Sara stepped over to Lou, gently laid her hands on her shoulders, and looked her square in the eye. This gentle, caring woman had not only opened her heart and her home but had defended her at great cost to her own standing in the community. For that Sara would always be grateful. She could not think of any greater way to thank her "sister" than to convince Lou that she thought of her as a viable, capable human being.

"You are as dependable as the moon and you shine just as brightly. You will not have your hysteria because you'll be enjoying yourself too much to worry about it. Now, you look after Lissybeth and I'll make certain that we have something a lot more interesting than chicken for dinner tonight."

An hour later Sara had eaten an egg and a piece of toasted bread, donned an old pair of Dru's trousers and a shirt along with one of his father's black hats, and was in the lush Kentucky woods again.

Carrying the Enfield rifle Jamie had hid in the root cellar to keep out of Yankee hands, Sara took to the woods in search of game for dinner.

Walking through the dense, silent woods was a homecoming in itself. Remembrance harkened her back to life at her childhood home at Collier's Ferry. She closed her eyes and heard the shouts and squeals of her brothers and sisters playing hide-and-seek, dodging and darting between tree trunks. The breeze seemed to carry Granddaddy Wilkes's voice to her.

She was a few hundred yards into the wood when she sensed someone moving through the trees alongside her so she stopped walking. Her hands tightened on the rifle.

A hauntingly familiar form began to materialize between the trees and shadows. A man, tall and a bit stooped. As he approached, Sara recognized the crooked slant of those wide, bony shoulders, the slow determined gait, the battered hat. A small bag was tied to a rope belt at his waist. His long arms dangled at his sides. His hands were lax. When he stepped into a shaft of sunlight, she saw his long, white beard.

There was no need to ask how he knew exactly where to find her. He always could divine things long before anyone else. He even knew certain things were going to occur long before they actually happened.

His image blurred and tears filled her eyes as she watched Granddaddy Wilkes close the distance between them.

8

"GRANDDADDY."

Daniel Wilkes heard the tremor in her voice as soon as his name passed her lips.

"Sarie." He took note of the ugly bruise marring her cheek, hesitated but a second, then opened his arms and welcomed her into his embrace.

Daniel's son-in-law, Sara's father DeWitt Collier, stubborn as a bull and twice as deadly, had his shortcomings. The day DeWitt laid down the law that Sara was never to be recognized by any God-fearing Collier again, everyone in the family promised to obey—all but Granddaddy. Daniel figured that he was a Wilkes, not a Collier, and he didn't have to abide by a damn thing DeWitt said.

He sensed that Sara, hesitant and unsure, was yearning to make amends. Her bright Collier eyes were sparkling with unshed tears. Of all his many grandchildren, she had always been his favorite. Her deep, sky-blue eyes were starless now, but once she'd held a universe in them.

Once he thought her invincible, but then she had moved to Magnolia Creek and left herself open to a world of hurt.

"I'm sorry, Granddaddy." Even choked with uncertainty, her voice still sounded as lyrical as the notes of a lark.

"Just as I'm sorry for what happened to you yesterday. I hear your daddy turned you away." He let her go and stepped back. They both knew there was nothing he could do to change either the circumstances she had made or DeWitt's edict.

"I know, Granddaddy." A shaky smile almost blossomed. A dimple appeared in her left cheek, then vanished.

"I'm sorry you ever left in the first place, but we never could give you what you thought you needed."

"Doc Porter gave me a chance to live a different life that day he offered me a job at the Talbots'. I didn't want to end up like Mama and the girls, Granddaddy. I didn't want to spend my life working from sunup to sunset. You always said that I was quick to learn. That healing was my gift. I went off to use it."

He had predicted early on that she was marked by destiny. The night she was born he walked into the cabin, took one look into her eyes, and proclaimed that all the stars there would sometimes blind her to the truth.

His Sarie was destined for a long life, if not a smooth one. He had always seen some heartbreak and trouble down the road for this gal for certain, though he hadn't known exactly what was to come.

Lives were laid out like the pieces in a fancy quilt, and it was up to God to guide the stitching. Sometimes he could look at a person and tell what was coming, but with Sara, things weren't that clear. He had always suspected she was headed for a fall. The first time he ever held her he felt it in his bones. His premonitions came true often enough to make a body take notice.

They had spent hours in the woods searching for healing

herbs, roots, and wildflowers to make tonics and cures. Now as they slipped into a silent, comfortable communion, the morning breeze sang undisturbed in the treetops until the lingering song of a cardinal broke the whispering stillness. Between the two of them, there had never been a need for words.

Where they came from, folks believed in the power of the Lord as much as they did the healing, no matter that most of them had never stepped into a church in their lives. In the hills and backwoods of Kentucky, good and evil existed side by side. A body always had to beware.

"Where are you goin' now, gal?"

He knew she was hunting. What he wanted to know was where her life was headed.

Her chin went up a notch.

"Louzanna's taken me in. I'm hunting for her and I'm going to put in a garden, too, to help put food on the table."

He had met Dru's sister the day of the wedding. An odd woman, sick in the mind. He'd been the only one from the Collier side to attend the small ceremony in Dru Talbot's fancy parlor. As out of place and uncomfortable as a thorn in a big toe, he had left without staying for the celebration supper.

After she married, Sara had visited home not more than a handful of times before he heard that she left town with a Yankee.

"You been a world away from everything and everyone you know. Folks around here are never gonna look kindly on you again."

"What else can I do? You tell me how I'm gonna feed my little girl?" She quickly fell back into the cadence of the backwoods. "I want this new start bad enough to taste it. I'll do whatever it takes to prove I'm sorry and make amends."

"Did he marry you? The Yankee?"

He saw the truth in her eyes before she even answered. "No."

"What happened to him?" He thoughtfully stroked his long beard.

"He was a mistake."

"Talbot would have wanted more for you," he said.

Sad resignation whisked through him. She had far to go yet. So much more to learn. Remembering that, he tempered his words. "When I found out you came back and your daddy sent you packing yesterday, I couldn't settle right till I came to see how you fared."

"How did you know I'd be here?"

It was no secret that she would turn to the crazy Talbot woman. It had been her only recourse. Still, he merely shrugged. "I just knew."

"Are the others all right? How did you all get along during the war?"

"Your ma lost a babe after the occupation and ain't carried one since. Your daddy and the boys had two ferries running during the war. They made plenty of money selling moonshine to both sides. You know us, we wasn't about to show preference when there was money to be made."

Daniel heard her sigh and added, "I wish I could predict your troubles are over, Sara." He reached for the bag at his waist and damned his crippled fingers as he fought with the knot in the rope.

"Here." He handed over a hemp bag the size of a fat, ripe squash. "Ground roots and seeds all wrapped separate. Some chamomile, feverfew, sarsaparilla, scullcap, black cohosh. I forget what all else. Plant 'em and you'll have a good start at a fine healing garden."

"Thanks, Granddaddy. I used up all I had in Ohio once folks got wind of what I could do." She cupped the bottom of the bag in her hand, measured the weight of it. "Will I be needing these right away?" She was testing him, to see if he had a premonition of what was to come.

He shrugged. "You never know."

"But do *you* know?"

"Nothing certain."

"I wish my life would stop whirling out of control at every turn." She sighed, struggled with something she couldn't put into words, and then finally said, "Hunt with me, Granddaddy. Stay for a meal. I'd like you to get to know Elizabeth. She is still your great-grandchild, no matter how she came to be so."

He shook his head and reminded her of what he'd said to her on her wedding day. "You've stepped into another life now. You always were after more than you needed."

Her eyes were swimming with tears that didn't fall. When she spoke, her voice was sadness itself. "Not anymore, Granddaddy. The only thing I want now is something I'll never have."

He knew without her saying it that she wished Talbot was still alive.

She crossed the short distance between them and took his hands in hers. He reckoned his gnarled knuckles felt like scarred buds on dried twigs against her young skin. He blinked back his own tears, inwardly cursed himself as a weak old man.

Sara squeezed his hands. "I don't know if folks around here will ever forgive me, but I'm going to try to make amends. And I'll keep the devil behind me, you'll see."

"Looks like you got all you need for a while, so I'd best be going." He turned in the direction of the creek, took a few steps, and paused. "Don't come back to the ferry or the cabin whenever your daddy is around."

He wondered if she could feel his regret. He was an old man now, too weak to stand up to DeWitt, but steering clear of her daddy was something Sara and all her brothers and sisters were used to. He raised his hand to wave good-bye.

"Wait! Will I see you again soon?" She ran up to him and threw her arms around his neck. Her eyes were so shadowed, so troubled, that he wanted nothing more than to lighten her heart, to offer her a splinter of joy.

"You'll see me again. Come what may, you'll see me."

"When?"

"When the time is right. You'll know."

9

APPROACHING MAGNOLIA CREEK from the south, Dru angled around to the back of Ash Street where it ran along the edge of town. When his own home came into view, the burden of the war lifted and his pace quickened to the beat of his heart. He flexed his left arm, worked his elbow back and forth, and smiled.

Almost home.

His heart skipped when he caught a flash of movement in the garden behind the house. He focused on a moving figure dressed in brown and white as he hurried across the open land and cut between low-lying hedges. He tugged the mule along, damning it for its stubborn, plodding gait.

Almost there.

Now he could make out a boy in a baggy white shirt and brown pants. Closer still, he noticed a rifle in the boy's right hand and something dangling from the other. The youth neared the back door as Dru reached the edge of the property. Something heart-stopping and familiar about the lad's graceful stride triggered recognition in Dru. Breathless, he watched the lone figure pause outside the door to take off the hat.

The sun struck a fall of long auburn hair as it tumbled down past slim shoulders, down to a trim waist.

Everything inside Dru stilled. Everything around him went silent—the breeze, the warmth of the sunlight, the sound of the birds in the nearby trees.

Sara. The "boy" was Sara, his Sara, holding a rifle and two dead rabbits by the ears.

Sara.

He tried to call her name but the sound was strangled, drowned out by a rush of emotion. Not even when his allies had fallen around him, not even when he heard wounded men screaming for death or the hiss and whine of flying bullets had he experienced such an intense surge of emotion. He was flooded with need, love, and towering relief.

"Sara!"

She wasn't even aware that he was so close. He suspected that if he'd been blind he would still have sensed her presence. His world only revolved because she was in it. She made the very air breathable.

He garnered strength from somewhere inside and began to run. The movement jarred his shoulder but he ignored the ache as her name tumbled from his lips.

"Sara!"

Her hand froze on the doorknob. She turned, dropping the rabbits on the stoop. They tumbled lifeless, staring blindly as they lay atop each other, a pile of fur. Her face blanched white as the linen shirt.

The nameless dead soldier's hat flew off Dru's head as he started sprinting in earnest.

The sound of her name floated to her on the noontime air, drifted over the yards and gardens, and instant recognition hit her with all the force of a stray bolt of lightning, nearly knocking her to her knees. Her stomach clenched. Her head swam with dizziness. The rabbits fell with a hollow thud onto the wooden step.

Dru. Alive.

In ragged clothing and a battered, holey hat, he was tearing toward her, tripping over neighbors' roses and new tomato seedlings, staggering on. He raised his hand in a salute, picked up his fallen hat, and hooted as he whipped it round and round above his head.

Dru. Alive.

Her head began to swim. She took a deep breath to keep from fainting dead away and stared in disbelief.

There were five long years of missing him, of suffering the sick betrayal of a false love she had only turned to out of desperation. None of it would have happened if Dru had but written one single letter to prove he was alive. None of it would have happened if she hadn't been so afraid. Regret, shame, and incredulity swallowed her whole as he raced toward her, buoyant with joy.

Dru.

Back from the dead, startling her battered heart to life. The man she had fallen in love with at fifteen was home. Deep in her heart, she loved him still. She had always loved him.

Will he still love me when he finds out?

Does he have it in him to forgive?

Paralyzed by betrayal and shame, she waited, growing more and more terrified until at last he was there, standing so close she could see the overwhelming joy on his face. If only she could dissolve the past and deny what she had done. If only she could delight in his homecoming.

An imposter, she waited in silence, risking a quick glance inside through the conservatory windows. Lou and Lissybeth were nowhere in sight.

Mere heartbeats before he knows.

Fate had stolen years. He deserved a few fleeting moments of joy before his illusions were shattered.

She tried to smile, but her lips only moved in a grotesque parody of one. Then he was there.

Two steps below her, he stopped to stare up into her eyes, searching her face even as he reached for her. His hands shook like a palsied old man's. He took another step closer. Nose to nose, they stared into each other's eyes. She thought that he could read her, that surely he must know what she had done, but then with a strangled cry, he enfolded her in his embrace.

His arms were the solid, warm haven that she had longed for. As she clung to him, time shifted, yawned backward until she felt whole again, protected, cherished as he dwarfed her, squeezing her tight, rocking from side to side.

He pulled away and with his hand beneath her chin, tilted her face up, and then assessed her more closely, his eyes roving over every inch of her face.

"What happened to your cheek?" he whispered, tracing the shape of the bruise without really touching it at all.

"I ran into a tree," she whispered back. Another lie, this one spoken aloud.

And then before she could say another word, his lips were on hers and he was kissing her deeply, a soul-stirring kiss that took her back to the beginning and felt so good, so right. Surely they were meant to be, no matter what she had done. Fate, with all its dark surprises, had momentarily turned its back on them as they clung, and kissed, and held each other tight. When the kiss finally ended, they both fought for breath.

Too scared to cry, afraid to open the floodgates, Sara

lingered within the circle of his arms, content to hold him, to let Dru hold her until the world stopped spinning.

If only *she* had possessed one ounce of Lou's stubborn insistence and enough fortitude to have remained steadfast in the belief that he was coming home. Somewhere inside *she* should have *known* that Dru was still alive. *She* should have been the one who never gave up hope.

Instead, only Louzanna—poor, reclusive, terrified Lou—had been right all along.

Dru slowly raised his head, drawing back far enough to stare into her eyes again. His face was thinner, but his eyes were still black as night and hot with need. There was a deep scar at his temple, which shot through his sideburn and back over his ear. Without thinking, she reached up and traced it with her fingertip, remembering Hugh's account of the battle at Shiloh.

Dru had always been quick to smile, but not now. His eyes grew shuttered, his mouth a tight line.

He ran his hands over her shoulders, down her sleeves, as if to make certain she was real. "Do I look that bad?"

She shook her head. He looked fine. Better than fine. Older, solid despite a loss of pounds. He was a man now, hard-planed, strong despite his thinness. He looked wonderful.

"I missed you, Sara. I need you as much as I need air. If not for you, I wouldn't have made it through. Life would have been hell without the thought of you."

Still so very handsome, his face now carried the identical lingering pain, shadows, etches, and lines that she had seen on the faces of so many other soldiers.

"Aren't you going to say anything?" He laughed as he continued to hold her, but an awkward uneasiness crept into his voice.

"Welcome home, Dru." She finally managed to whisper the words she never thought to say again.

Very slowly he pulled back. His smile dimmed a notch. "Are you all right, Sara?"

"We thought . . . we thought you were dead. When your letters stopped, we tried to find you. Louzanna wrote the war department, sent letters to prisons, to hospitals both North and South. Some were returned, but there was *never* any word. Not one word until Hugh Wickham was furloughed and stole through enemy lines to come home and see his new son."

"Hugh has another boy?"

She paused, unable to find the words that could ever describe what she had been through.

"He told us you were *dead*, Dru. So did Keith Jackman. Hugh held you in his arms. He believes that you died."

Dru shook his head. "I'm glad he's a lawyer and not a doctor."

"We had nothing else to believe but that you were gone."

He paused, his expression immediately sobered, as if remembering something he would rather forget. "We heard that letters weren't getting through, but I never realized . . . I woke up a prisoner with no memory. I had nothing on me but my uniform. They found my surgical knives in my coat pocket and assumed I was a surgeon, but had no idea who I was or where I was from. I was shipped to Maryland and by the time I recovered my memory and was traded in a prisoner exchange things were going so bad for the South that there was no way to get word through to you."

He kissed her forehead, her cheek, rubbed his thumb over her lips. "I'm so sorry, Sara. Can you forgive me?"

Forgive him? Shame nearly overwhelmed her.

"There's nothing for me to forgive," she said quietly, longing to frame his face with her hands, to kiss him the way she used to, to turn back time and start over. She was too terrified even to hope things could ever be the way they were before—and they certainly wouldn't be as long as the truth held her hostage.

"Something is wrong. Is it Lou? Is she all right?" He glanced toward the door, hooked his arm around her shoulder.

Quickly, Sara shook her head. "No. Lou's fine. She's inside."

He finally eased enough to smile again when she shifted the gun to cradle it in her arms. He took it from her.

"You've been hunting?"

She glanced down at the limp rabbits bleeding all over the stoop and nodded.

"Where's Jamie?" he asked.

"Gone with the Union army."

"Union. Gone North, then?" He shook his head, his disappointment clear. "I had hoped he would stay on."

"He didn't go of his own accord. He was conscripted." She took a deep breath and softly added, "There's so much to tell."

"We've got forever now." He kept her tucked beneath his arm as if unwilling to let her go.

Sara turned the knob and glanced over at the mule happily nibbling on a shock of weeds near the back door. They stepped inside the conservatory and went through to the kitchen before he stopped to look around. He set the rifle down and then slowly straightened and took a deep breath as if trying to inhale the whole room, to take everything in at once.

"There were many times I thought I'd never see this place again."

"I thought I heard you come in, Sara." Louzanna's footsteps echoed in the hallway. Sara's stomach somersaulted.

Lou wasn't halfway into the room when she laid eyes on Dru and screamed his name. He let go of Sara as Lou rushed to his arms.

"Oh, Dru! Oh, dear God in heaven! I *knew* it! I just knew it!" Louzanna clung to his neck, laughing, sobbing, squeezing him tight. Immediately he began trying to calm and comfort her.

"Shh. I'm home now, Lou. I'm home. Sara told me that you heard I'd been done in by the Yankees, but you better believe I'd never let that happen. I promised you both I'd be back and here I am. Hush, now, Louzanna. It's all right."

He was holding his sister gently, patting her on the back, all the while staring over her shoulder at Sara. The depth of desire in his eyes made her knees go weak. He opened his arm, an invitation to include her in the embrace.

She hesitated a split second too long, but it was just long enough for doubt to ebb into his eyes.

He was too intelligent, too perceptive to have been misled for very long.

Suddenly Elizabeth chose that terrible instant to come toddling into the room with her blond curls bouncing, laughing and running with her arms outstretched as if longing to embrace the world. She ran straight to Sara, threw her arms around her knees, and yelled, "Mama!"

10

MYRIAD SCENARIOS RACED through Dru's mind as the little girl tugged at Sara's pant legs, begging to be picked up.

She could very well be a foundling, an abandoned child, orphaned by the war. It would be just like Louzanna to open her heart to a war orphan—but when the child had come running into the room, his sister had gone stiff and silent, turning inside herself the way she always did whenever any conflict arose.

And Sara? Sara suddenly refused to meet his eyes.

As she bent to scoop up the little girl and settle the child on her hip with the smooth ease of practiced familiarity, his mind echoed his suspicion of the awful truth.

Hers, but not mine. Not mine.

"Mama?"

Triumphant in Sara's arms, the child laid her head on Sara's shoulder, smiling at him all the while. Her eyes were the bluest of blue, like cornflowers or a fresh washed sky on a cloudless day. Eyes the exact color as Sara's, eyes almost equal to those that had charmed him the first time he'd looked into them, which left him cotton-headed and hot with desire.

Now those eyes of Sara's were avoiding his. Without her saying a word, he *knew*. He knew she had betrayed him with another man. Suddenly he couldn't bear to look at the child.

Except for an occasional hiccuped sob, Louzanna had fallen silent. She began to move toward Sara, her mourning gown rustled in a long forgotten way, sounds of gentility and silk so foreign to Dru and where he had been. The women communicated wordlessly. Lou took the little girl into her arms. The child started fussing, struggling to get down. She stretched her arms toward Sara as Lou carried her through the doorway and into the hall.

"Mama! Mama!" The pitiful cries echoed in the narrow hallway.

When he finally had the courage to look Sara's way again, she was staring at the open doorway with one hand pressed against her throat, looking lost and confused. Her slight frame was swamped by the shirt and pants she wore. She reached for the back of a chair for support and held on tight, as if about to collapse, her face white as candle wax.

"Would you . . . would you like to sit down?" Her words to him were clipped and stilted.

"No."

She pulled out the chair and sat down heavily herself, deflating when she hit the seat. Propping one elbow on the table, she let her other hand fall lifeless to her lap. She remained silent, staring down at the tablecloth.

He had to force himself to ask the unvoiced question hanging on the still, close air between them.

"What's going on, Sara? Whose child is that?"

"She's mine, Dru."

She's mine. No excuses, no pleading, no tears. He gave her another moment to tell him that this wasn't what it sounded like. He wanted to believe none of this was happening.

"You mean you took her in?"

"No. I mean she's mine. She's my daughter."

She's mine. Two simple words that forever altered his world.

Anger hit him so hard he walked away. He slammed his open palm against the solid oak doorframe, stared into the conservatory, seeing nothing, feeling nothing but rage.

Completely unaware of the depth of his anger, Sara followed, touched his sleeve. She might just as well have shot him. He jerked, shook off her hand.

"Dru, please, let me explain."

Vigilant, guarding his battered senses, his trampled heart, he rounded on her. "Explain *what*? How you slept with another man? That's the only explanation for your having a child that young, Sara. The only way. I don't want to hear it."

"You *have* to hear—"

"Why? Why, Sara? *Not now!*"

The little girl's frantic cries from the other room added to the tension in the air. Sara was torn, glancing frantically back and forth toward the door and then at him.

Blood pounded in his ears. His hands curled into fists at his sides. She noticed, even flinched, but held her ground. Her fear only added insult to injury.

Did she honestly think he was going to *hit* her?

The little girl's cries for her mama intensified to shrill bursts. Sara's eyes brimmed with tears.

"Dru, the past is over. Please, let me explain."

Didn't she realize the past was alive and screaming in his drawing room?

"Your child needs you, Sara. I don't."

"But, Dru—"

"Leave me be." He turned his back on her again, controlled his rage by focusing on the yawning emptiness inside him. He moved like a blind man through the conservatory and opened the back door.

She trailed him, dogging his steps until he whipped around again so quickly that they almost collided.

"I mean it, Sara. Get the *hell* out of my sight!"

Helpless, Sara watched him escape the house. The door slammed behind him with such force, the conservatory windows rattled in their frames. Elizabeth was screaming.

Stunned and too shaken to cry, Sara spun around. She ran through the kitchen and down the hall to where the double doors to the drawing room were closed tight. Lissybeth was howling on the other side. Tugging the doors wide, Sara rushed inside. Lou had a grip on Elizabeth's waist, fighting to keep her from breaking away. As soon as Lou saw Sara, she let go and Elizabeth hurtled herself across the room into Sara's arms.

"Thank you, Lou." Sara gathered the sobbing baby in her arms and held her close, swaying back and forth, patting her gently.

Louzanna's eyes were huge in her pale face, red-rimmed, frantic. She sounded shaken, confused, when she asked, "Where is my brother?"

"Outside. He needed some time alone."

"What did he say about . . ." Lou fell silent and stared at Elizabeth.

Sara shook her head. "He refused to let me talk about it."

Lou's hand went to her throat and her fingers found the gold chain, fumbled down to the opal ring, and hung on.

"Maybe he just needs some time," Lou whispered.

Picturing his grim expression, the intense anger and betrayal on Dru's face, Sara doubted an eternity would be long enough.

As soon as Sara left the room, Louzanna went into the kitchen in search of Dru but found him gone.

She got as far as the back door but did not even reach for the knob. Nothing good existed outside the house, nothing but a world full of hurt and danger and death. Pacing back and forth, she lingered by the conservatory windows wondering where Dru had gone, blaming herself for what had happened.

If only he had returned a few minutes earlier, Sara would have been out of the house. She could have broken the news of Sara's betrayal to him in calm, quiet, sympathetic tones. Instead, the shock of hearing Elizabeth call Sara *Mama* had hit him without warning.

She put her hands on the back door, but her courage failed her. Normally, she went only as far as the well in the center of the backyard. Never as far as the cabins and the barn. Never. She hadn't been more than a few feet from the back door in fifteen years.

She had guarded her own safety vigilantly, ever since the day Mason had died—quiet, bookish, devoted Mason. There had been no blinding passion between them, at least not the kind Dru and Sara seemed to have once shared. Mason had taken notice of her the first time he came home with Dru, and from that moment on he had been the love of her life.

She suspected that the entire town had been surprised when Mason offered for her hand in marriage. She was sure that most folks suspected he only wanted to marry her because she was a Talbot. In Magnolia Creek, the name was synonymous with money and success.

But Mason had seen past her frailty and shyness and accepted her for who she was. He was the only suitor she had ever had, and so she had eagerly accepted. Mason courted her with diligence and even agreed to move into the Talbot house so that she might continue to nurse her invalid mother.

He read her poetry and drew copious sketches of her. He pressed wildflowers between the pages of his books and pasted them into letters filled with sunny tributes to her goodness.

She gave her heart over to him and would have been content to devote her life to his kind and gentle soul, just as she devoted her youth to her mama.

But then, on the day of their wedding, as she waited in a silken gown of ivory, lace, and pearls that had come all the way from New York, there had come a knock on the door.

Papa had been in the drawing room, bracing himself for the nuptials with bourbon. Mama was—of course—stretched out on the chaise in her room with a rag soaked in vinegar water on her forehead. Dru had come in late from managing the mill and was getting dressed. Jamie had been out back and failed to answer the front door, so it had been left to her.

The notion came to her just as she opened the door, that it was bad luck for Mason to see her in her wedding gown. It wasn't Mason at the door, but a grim-faced Doc Porter with blood spattered across his best waistcoat, his eyes heavy with consolation.

She would never forget looking beyond Doc at the wagon pulled up alongside the front fence. Inside lay Mason—broken and bleeding. Awash with sympathy,

Doc Porter tried to tell her that Mason had suffered a terrible accident, that he had fallen from his horse, was trampled and had died, but she heard nothing. Her screams, a sound that even now still reverberated in her head, swallowed his words.

She slammed the door on the terrible scene but that had not prevented the image from imprinting itself on her mind. Her courage collapsed that day the way a piece of burning paper curls beneath a flame and quickly crumbles to ash. The house became her sanctuary, caring for her mother her life's work.

After her mother died, the thread that she used to bind her quilts became the delicate thread that held her life together. The intricate patterns, changing fabrics, and colors became the focus of her life. Her world shriveled to confinement in the house, the view of her yard, her latest quilt project. Only when she shut out the turmoil of the world did she feel safe.

Even now, when Dru needed her most, she couldn't bring herself to go in search of him. She couldn't leave the house. Not even for him.

11

Numb, Dru carried the dead rabbits out behind the barn where he went about the business of dressing them. His hands moved without thought, his mind as empty as his soul.

Without Sara, suddenly deprived of the future he had dreamed of for so long, he was lost, blank as a new sheet of paper, empty as a bucket with a hole in it.

Completing the task, he went after the mule, and as he numbly led it into the empty barn, noted that a Concord buggy, nearly new when he had left, along with an old mare and a cow, were missing. Pigeons roosted in the eaves, and though the barn now held little but must, it was crowded with memories.

Hugh Wickham had tried to warn him against marrying Sara two days before the wedding when Dru had asked his friend to stand up for him. Surprise had echoed across Hugh's rugged features when Dru told him of his plan to marry.

At first glance, Hugh Wickham might not be considered handsome. His Roman nose was slightly askew, his jaw a bit too square, and his eyes a nondescript gray, but he was a man always on the move, an organizer who was charismatic, a born leader, a lawyer contemplating politics. Hugh always wore his convictions and determination on his sleeve and, as always, he had been brutally honest with Dru that day.

"Good God, Dru! You've only known her two weeks. You can't be serious. If you want to sleep with her, you ought to just get it over with. Colliers aren't the type of people we marry. Even you don't have to carry honor that far."

When everything was said and done, Dru had made Hugh swear on their friendship that he would never again say a bad word against Sara. There had been no way to explain his impulsiveness to his friend, not when he was hard-pressed to explain it to himself.

His love for Sara had come upon him with the swift surprise of a tornado and shaken him to the core. From the moment he had walked through the door after medical school, Sara had been a part of his life.

She was beautiful, smart, and never far from Louzanna's side as she took her position in the house quite seriously. With Sara at the table, meals became lively discussions. They talked not only of the war, but about things he had learned at school. She debated many of the methods he had been taught.

She often had him at a disadvantage, for she already knew everything about him. Louzanna had filled her head with stories. Sara knew that his favorite pie was apple, that he was an early riser, that he had always admired and wanted to become a doctor like Doc Porter, even though his father had made him take over running the mill first.

All he had known about Sara was what Doc had told him, and that she had a head full of healing knowledge, that she showed a genuine loving kindness toward his sister, and that she had stolen his own heart the moment she had opened his front door.

Now, as sweet spring sunlight slid in through the half-open barn door, Dru stepped back into the cool, shadowed interior, pressed his back against the wall, crossed his arms, and stared at the sliver of the house he could just make out through the opening.

Sara was in there, a few hundred yards away, in his house, with her child. The child of another man. He couldn't bring himself to go back inside yet.

The four couples invited to the wedding had departed. Louzanna, all embarrassed and aflutter, had fled to her room early the night he and Sara wed.

He took sweet Sara by the hand, led her upstairs to his room, and closed the door on the world. They were finally alone. More nervous than he ever dreamed, he stood in the middle of the room he had lived in most of his life, surrounded by things familiar, his life forever changed for the better now that he would share it with Sara. Holding both her hands in his, he looked into her eyes and whispered, "I want you more than anything I've ever wanted in my life."

"I'm your wife now, Dru. Make love to me." She looked so willing, so very sweet, so innocent, that he was suddenly scared of hurting her.

"If you aren't ready, Sara, say the word." It might kill him not to have her, but if he unwittingly hurt her he would never forgive himself.

She didn't answer in words; she simply reached up, trailed her hand down his cheek to his lips, and traced them tenderly.

A shiver swept down his spine. He put his hand beneath her chin and brought her face up to his. He lowered his lips, moving slowly, gently. Her lips parted, opened beneath his, welcomed him.

She gasped when he kissed her long and deep, and he let the tide of passion sweep through and fill him. There had been no regret, no condemnation or hesitation that night. No guilt. Only love. Only Sara and his love for her.

Her thumbs brushed his cheeks. Her tongue darted around his. Her sigh had been a song that his heart danced to as he brought her up against his arousal. She didn't appear to be frightened and he guessed that she knew exactly what would happen between them that night. Life in the backwoods was raw and blunt. She had grown up where there were no walls, no privacy, no secrets.

"I want you, Dru."

"Do you know what you're saying, Sara?"

She ran her hands down his neck, across his shirtfront to his waist. He scooped her up, carried her to his bed, and laid her upon a heavy maroon and indigo quilt that, of course, Louzanna had made especially for him.

He reached for her hair, pulled out the pins that held spirals of curls and baby rosebuds. The flowers fell one by one, showered the pillow. Her hair swept around her shoulders and his hands.

He took off her shoes and stockings first, touched her bare toes, ran his hands up her calves to her knees. Glancing up at her face, he stopped abruptly.

"Are you crying?" He reached up to wipe away her tears. Aching to have her, convinced she must have changed her mind, he was prepared to take her to her own room. All she had to do was say she wasn't ready.

"Do you still want this, Sara?"

Slowly she climbed off the bed until she was standing before him, and reached for her gown to draw it up. Her fingers trembled as she turned around.

"Can you help me with the buttons?" she whispered.

His fingers trembled as he freed her from her gown and undergarments until she was standing before him in a light muslin chemise. She slipped the straps from her shoulders, pushed the fabric down around her hips. Her breasts, high and full, nipples taut and tempting, arrested his gaze until inch by inch the thin sheath slid down her ivory body, exposing the swell of her hips, her navel, her slender waist, and then the dark triangle at the apex of her thighs. She dropped the chemise to the floor.

Her smile was heart-stopping as she offered him all, unabashed, with all the impatience of youth and daring.

He stared in wonder at Sara cloaked in candlelight and shadows, illuminated in flickering gold. His hands, his arms, his soul ached for her.

Reaching for her, he pulled her close, kissed her flat stomach and her navel, traced her thighs with his tongue. Reveled in her scent. She clutched handfuls of his hair, cried out softly.

Leaning back, he stroked his hands down her thighs, made her shiver, parted her legs so that he could touch her intimately. His fingers discovered the hot dew between her thighs; she moaned and trembled.

He was suddenly stripping off his clothing like a madman, tossing it away. Buttons flew. His collar and cuffs fell to the floor. His shirt and pants were tossed, crumpled against the library table, the washstand, the patterned woven carpet. His boots hit the floor with hollow thuds that enticed a nervous giggle from Sara.

Desperate for the taste of her, he took her in his arms

and covered her mouth with his to swallow the sound. His arms slipped behind her knees; he carried her back to the bed. He pressed her back, stroked the length of her from shoulder to ankle. She shivered, tried to pull him over her, but he resisted, for her. All for her.

Her skin was as precious as the finest silk. She had come to him from nothing, had been brought to him by fate for reasons he could not question.

He drew her beneath him, parted her thighs with a touch and a whisper. Slowly he mounted her, slowly he eased into her, met with resistance and found her virginal, innocent.

They were man and wife tonight; she would be truly his. Steeling himself, he eased through the final barrier, stretched her, filled her until she cried out and he froze.

Panting in time to her shallow, frantic breaths, he waited until she whispered his name and then urged, "Please . . ."

Only then did he begin to move inside her. When she reached her peak, cried out, and wrapped her legs about his waist, his last shred of control snapped. He plunged deep and spilled his seed with a hoarse cry.

They had become one that night, he and his Sara. When it was over she held him close and begged, "Please, don't go to Tennessee tomorrow, Dru."

He wanted nothing more than to stay right here beside her.

"I have to go," he whispered back. "I gave Hugh my word."

"I know. It's just that I love you, Dru. I love you so much I just can't bear to say good-bye."

"Then we won't say good-bye. If you like, I'll leave

without waking you and the next time you see me the war will be over."

She stared up into his eyes, memorizing his face as tears slipped along her temple and disappeared into her hair. Then she nodded.

"Do it then, if you must, Dru. Leave me without telling me good-bye. I don't think I could live through it after tonight."

He had kept his promise and the next morning he had dressed in the dark, silently so that he wouldn't wake her, for he couldn't trust himself to leave if she cried and asked him not to go again.

When he was finally dressed and ready to leave, he sat beside her; stroked her hair; tucked the covers around her shoulders; and memorized the soft rhythmic sound of her breathing, the way she smelled, and the curve of her cheek and lips. He cursed his own honor, which held him to the promise he had made his friends.

With a touch so light and gentle that she didn't even stir, he kissed her on the temple and whispered, "Until we meet again, Sara," and then he left her as the breaking dawn spilled weak light into the room, light the same color gray as the uniform that he would wear for far too long.

Dru sat in the darkened shadows of the barn, staring out into the raw spring sunshine, avoiding going back to face a woman he had so desperately longed for just two hours ago, torturing himself with erotic memories of their wedding night. He had foolishly believed that from that night onward, she would be his forever.

12

A GOOD WHILE later, when Dru finally walked into the kitchen with the clean rabbits, his sister was waiting. The air was thick with the smell of chicken soup. A pot simmered on the stove. His stomach growled and twisted as he laid the rabbits in a clean, empty dishpan.

"You must be hungry," she said.

"Not really." He had grown used to eating very little during his incarceration in Maryland. What food they were given was usually spoiled, the water they drank tainted, the ground where they camped muddy and disease-riddled. In the midst of such deplorable conditions he wished he had never been to medical college so that he might be as ignorant about disease as the rest of the men. It wasn't easy knowing more than bullets could kill a man. Still, his respite there had probably saved his sanity.

"Sit down, Dru. You need to put something in your stomach. I can hear it rumbling from here."

He doubted he could swallow past the tightness in his throat, but he sat down in front of a soup spoon and napkin on the kitchen table. He toyed with the monogrammed spoon, his mind crowded with questions he couldn't bring himself to ask.

He watched his sister ladle soup into one of his mother's china bowls and then slowly carry it across the room. Her hands trembled and the soup began to slosh, threatened to slop over the edge. As soon as she was close enough, he took the bowl from her before she dropped it in his lap.

"Thanks, Lou."

The soup turned out to be more broth than anything else, with a few shreds of chicken and onion. Bright orange bits of carrot bobbed here and there, but not many.

"I made it myself." Her pride was as evident as her insecurity.

Dru picked up the spoon, really looked around the kitchen, and found it surprisingly bare. Not only that, but the backyard was a shambles, the garden overgrown with weeds.

"Have you been here all this time without help?" He couldn't bring himself to ask if Sara ever helped out. He couldn't even bring himself to say her name. Every now and again her footsteps tapped across the floor of the room above them.

"I found someone to come in and show me how to prepare simple meals." She paused, frowned. "After a time I had to let her go."

As far as he knew, his sister had never cooked a full meal in her life before he had left. Ignoring the soup, he shifted, and the chair creaked. Lou was wringing her hands now, staring as if she'd never seen them before.

"Lou—"

She looked up, her eyes growing a bit wild. They glistened with tears. Mason Blaylock's opal hung against her breast, sparkling in the sunlight, a constant reminder of her sorrow and her frailty.

"Oh, Dru. I'm so sorry that you had to come home and find everything in such a state. I . . . I really tried to do the best I could." She burst into tears and covered her face with her hands.

He was up immediately, crossing the room, taking her in his arms. She was older than him, but her nerves were as fragile as porcelain. He had watched out for her nearly all his life.

"Shush, Lou. Don't cry."

"Everything changed during the war. You stopped writing. Hugh came by and said you were dead. Then Sara left. Jamie stayed on, even though I couldn't pay him. Then the Yankees took him and finally when the mill payments stopped—"

Shocked, he pulled away. "What do you mean, when the mill payments stopped?"

She collected herself enough to reach for a dish towel and dry her eyes. "The Yankees broke up the sorghum mills when they left, to teach the town a lesson. Without a way to get them running again, Mr. Newberry couldn't make the payments. Most of the farmers' fields are still fallow and I hear that business has slowed to a trickle around here."

He had specifically turned over the proceeds from the sale of their father's mill to Louzanna, knowing that he could always provide for himself. Not once had he ever dreamed she might be left penniless.

Then again, not once had he imagined that Sara would forget her wedding vows. For a well-educated man, he'd been a fool.

"How have you managed?" He did the only thing he could do to cope at the moment and that was try to turn his thoughts away from Sara.

Lou shrugged. "I got by. The neighbors helped. Dr. Porter stopped by quite often. It's a godsend that Sara showed up here yesterday." She glanced at the dressed rabbits in the pan.

Dru shoved his thumbs into the waistband of his pants and strode to the conservatory. After a glance at the yard, he paced back into the kitchen.

All the pieces were slowly falling into place. Sara had just come back yesterday. Perhaps Louzanna had taken her in because she needed Sara's help.

If everyone in town didn't already know that he'd been cuckolded and that Sara had a child with another man, they would soon.

"We thought you were dead." Sara's words still rang in his ears.

He had purposely paid scant attention to the child clinging to her. She might have been a year and a half, maybe two. Exactly how long had his sweet young wife waited before she got herself another man? Days? Or weeks?

It suddenly struck him that perhaps, if he had written to them when he had first recovered his memory and had not wanted to linger for a while in the peace and quiet of the prison hospital, then the letters might have gotten through.

Had his own inner turmoil cost him his wife?

Not now. Not yet. Don't think about it all yet.

"What are you going to do, Dru?" Lou was standing beside the table, her hands now clinging to the opal ring, watching him closely.

"Most men would toss her out."

"No! You can't." Her reaction was as immediate as it

was frantic. "Please, just hear her out. Try to understand. You've no idea what war did to all of us."

But he knew good and well what war had done to him. Absently, he reached up and rubbed his temple. His fingers slid along the bare spot, the scar at his hairline.

Hear her out. Listen to all the sordid details of his wife's love affair with another man.

He tried to shove aside all thought of Sara and her child, of what she had done, knowing good and well that right now he needed to concentrate on the mundane task of getting his life back in order.

"I have money in a savings account. At least I did, before the war," he told Louzanna. "We'll make do until I can set up my medical practice."

She gave him a weak, tremulous smile. "The last thing I wanted was for you to come back and have to worry about money." Her gaze roamed over his face, paused on the scar above his ear. "You've been through so much." She visibly shook herself, then said, "You haven't even tasted your soup. Please sit back down and eat."

His senses were dead. The soup tasted like water, but he spooned it down anyway. The ceiling overhead creaked, reminding him that Sara was walking around up there, tending her child.

Exhaustion slipped into the void left when his elation had been stolen away. He pushed the empty soup bowl aside and looked down at his hands, hands that could heal but couldn't hold on to his wife.

"I need a bath and a shave," he told Lou. "Is the tub still in the pantry off the conservatory?"

"I'll heat some water. Your clothes are all still in your room. I kept it just the way you left it." A fleeting smile crossed her face. "I knew you'd be home."

She seemed to calm down immediately, happy to be able to help. Her entire life had been devoted to their mother. Unlike him, Lou had never crossed their father. Her world had consisted of loving service to her family and the small circle of women friends who came to sit and sew once every other week. He didn't even know all their names.

If he found out that Sara had come back to take advantage of Lou—

His hands clenched. He forced them open, rubbed his palms against his thighs.

"If you'll start the water boiling, I'll fill the tub." He pushed away from the table and hovered there awkwardly in the middle of the kitchen, not knowing what to do next, hesitant to move around his own home because of the woman upstairs.

"Why don't you go up and pick out some clean clothes?" Lou poured more water into the kettle. "Unless you'd like me to do that for you." She was intent, focused on her task.

"I'll go." He didn't move, though.

Sara's betrayal lingered like an unspoken presence in the room. He refused to ask for any details and though his sister would never, ever volunteer them, she would tell him the truth if he asked. But he didn't want to make her any more upset than she already was.

He knew that if he was going to hear the truth, it wouldn't be from Louzanna.

The truth would have to come from Sara.

13

THE HOUSE SETTLED around Dru as he climbed the stairs. For the most part it had remained unchanged, but seemed hollow and empty now. Perhaps because his heart was no longer here.

He noticed subtle changes, things missing here and there. In the upstairs hallway, faded outlines on the wall covering disturbed him until he realized a series of paintings by Lexington artist Matthew Jouette was missing. To think that Louzanna had been forced to sell even one precious keepsake, let alone so many, made him furious.

He paused to stare at the bare wall above the wainscoting when the sound of Sara's voice accompanied by the creak of a rocking chair drifted to him from behind her closed door.

He raised his hand to knock. She had a lovely voice, clear and true, and he realized that in the short time they had spent together, he had never heard her sing a note.

There was a lot about her that he didn't know. He never suspected she had such a fickle heart, either.

Arrested by the gentle loveliness of the sound, so melodic, so soothing and foreign to everything he had experienced during the war, he closed his eyes and let the warmth of her voice flow through him.

He pictured her sitting in the chair, slowly rocking back and forth, matching the movements to the gentle rhythm of the song, her head resting on the chair back, her arms cradling another man's child.

He rapped on the door, putting an abrupt end to her singing. There was a momentary pause before Sara answered.

He thought he had steeled himself against the onslaught of emotion that barreled into him as soon as he saw her face. She was still wearing his clothes and they dwarfed her, made her appear extremely fragile. The linen shirt was a stark white against her pale ivory skin and the hideous purpled bruise below her left eye.

With the practiced eye of a physician, he assessed the bruise again. There was no abrasion. He doubted she had run into anything but a fist—and quite recently, from the look of it. Had her lover just thrown her out of his life? Is that why she had suddenly come running back to Magnolia Creek?

"We have to talk." He tried to ignore her red-rimmed, swollen eyelids, and envied her for being able to cry.

She nodded and stood aside to let him in. He halted just over the threshold, swept the room with his gaze. Again, not much had changed. The feminine room looked the same as he remembered except that a crib now stood beneath the window, a low iron-sided bed where her child lay sleeping.

Nothing had changed and everything had changed.

He crossed his arms, stood his ground, determined to wait her out if need be. She was the one with all the explaining to do. Sara backed up a few steps, put distance between them, watching him warily. Her gaze touched him, moved on until she finally met his eyes again.

"I can't take back what I have done, but with God as my witness, Dru, I honestly believed you were dead. I was out of my mind with worry when your letters stopped. Louzanna and I kept telling each other that you were all right, that in time we would hear from you. But then Hugh came home and told us you had died in his arms."

Hugh. His best friend since childhood. The man who had talked him into enlisting in the first place.

"We need you, Dru. You, more than any of us, have something really worthwhile to contribute, something besides another gun. You said you always wanted to give back to the town that made your family wealthy. Now the sons of Magnolia Creek are going off to war. Say you'll join us, Dru. Come along and help keep us alive."

Hugh. The one who had warned him against marrying Sara in the first place.

Sara glanced at the child sleeping across the room.

"When?" he asked her.

At the sound of his voice, her head whipped around.

"What?" she asked.

"When did Hugh tell you I was dead?"

"A few months after Shiloh."

A year after he left home, give or take a few weeks. He turned guilt from lingering too long in the prison hospital into anger.

"How long did you mourn, Sara? How long did you cry over me?" He looked at the crib and then quickly away. "A week? A month?"

"Dru, *don't.*"

"Was it a whole month, Sara? Did you at *least* wait a month before you jumped into another man's bed?"

He almost walked out of the room, afraid he might be

fool enough to swallow anything she said. Afraid he would get lost in her eyes and believe every damn word.

"I thought you were *dead*."

"And I thought that by marrying you I was lifting you out of your old life at Collier's Ferry, that you'd be better off here than with your family, but it looks like Hugh and the others were right. Your family is trash, Sara, and they bred you—"

"*You were dead!*" she shouted, then she covered her mouth with both her hands, her eyes huge above them.

"And I'll bet you are wishing I'd have stayed that way."

He forced himself to ignore the tears brimming in her eyes, looked away when one lone drop slowly slipped down her cheek and trailed down the back of her hand. The child in the crib whimpered and then settled. Sara dropped her hands, squared her shoulders. She took a deep breath.

"I believed Hugh. I had no reason not to. I was no longer a wife, I was a widow."

"Well, I'm resurrected now and I don't like what I see." He stepped closer, forced her to look into his eyes. "Why come back *here*? Why don't you go home to Collier's Ferry?"

"I did. My father threw me out."

"And I'm supposed to take you back?" He dropped his voice, sighed heavily. "Did you ever *really* love me, Sara?"

"I loved you, Dru. From the day I first met you, I was yours."

He shook his head, felt his lips curl into a sarcastic imitation of a smile. "I'm not the same man who went off to war five years ago. I've seen things that would make your blood run cold. There were times I almost wished I was dead, but I was stupid enough to dream of a future with you. I stayed alive because of *you*, Sara"—he pointed toward the crib—"and this is what I come home to?"

She surprised him, grabbed hold of his wrist and clung, her fingertips pressing hard against his pulse.

"I *loved* you, Dru. When I heard you were gone I nearly went insane. Lou tried to tell me that you were alive, she told anyone who would listen. She tried to convince everyone, including Hugh, that you would come back. I wore black. I mourned our lost love and cried for what might have been. We never even had a chance to begin our life together before it was over."

"Did that make it easier? Or maybe it wasn't until things got hard and the money ran out that you left."

"When I left here Louzanna was fine. She was still receiving mill payments and Jamie was here and more than capable of looking after her. I taught him to brew teas that calmed her and he knew as well as I did when she was about to get the jitters. I left her just the way you did, in the very same situation, never guessing the Yankees would burn the mill or take Jamie. I left because I couldn't stand to be here, in this place, in your home where everywhere I turned, everything I touched reminded me of you. Lou kept your room closed up like a shrine. She wouldn't let Jamie give away your clothes or touch a thing. I was only eighteen, Dru. Little more than a child. I was terrified of becoming just like Louzanna, trapped in mourning, watching the rest of my life slip away."

Heat radiated up his arm from the touch of her hands. He smelled the woods in her hair, felt the warmth of her breath, the tension radiating from her. He needed her desperately, longed to feel her next to him, to run his hands over her soft skin and bury his face in her silken hair.

"Listen to me, Dru Talbot. *Never* doubt that I loved

you. Never. If we'd have had one word from you or the war department, one shred of hope . . . but Hugh was certain. When Abel listed your name among the dead in the *Sentinel*, I was forced to believe."

"So you slept with another man to get over me. Who was he? Someone I know? Someone here in town?"

"No. No one like that. It's over, Dru. It was over a long time ago."

"Yet you have his child."

She dropped her eyes. Her fingers slipped away and she let go of his arm.

"Legally, I'm still your wife."

Everything in his gut tightened. His heart rebelled against the truth. "My wife? You thought yourself a widow, yet you didn't even marry him?"

"He wouldn't marry me. He kept finding excuses. At first he said we had to wait until there was official confirmation, but then . . . then he changed his mind." She took a step in his direction, stopped herself. "We can start over, Dru." She reached for his hand again. This time he shook her off.

"It's not as simple as that, Sara."

Absurd notion. Was she naive enough to think that he could simply forgive and forget? If he hadn't suffered, if he hadn't been so out of his mind with pain and confusion, lost in a world of forgotten memories littered with the cries of the dead and dying around him, maybe *then* he could understand and forgive. He might have hidden his identity in order to disappear for a few months, but that paled in comparison to what Sara had done.

All the time he had been fighting for his sanity, trying to regain confidence in himself and his abilities, struggling to justify going back onto the field of battle despite what was beginning to seem insurmountable odds, Sara had been sleeping with another man.

He inhaled deeply. Forcing himself to calm down, he lowered his voice. "It's not as if you burned the dinner, Sara. We can't just start over."

"Why not? We loved each other once. We shared our hopes and dreams and promises. Why can't we put the war and everything that happened behind us and start over?"

Suddenly there came a startled cry from the crib and then, "Mama?"

The blond toddler sat up and rubbed one eye with a fisted hand, staring at Dru with a curious smile.

"That's why." He pointed at the little girl with Sara's big eyes. When the child's dimples deepened, he turned away. How much did she resemble the man who had fathered her?

"How do I know her father isn't going to show up at my door in an hour wanting you both back?" he demanded.

Sara's face lost even more color. "Don't worry. He won't come looking for me."

"How can you be sure? He might not want you, but what about his daughter?"

Sara shook her head. "Please, Dru," she pleaded.

"But I don't want you anymore, Sara."

It was a lie, a lie meant to hurt, and it hit the mark. Her eyes filled with a deep hopelessness, as if she were adrift in a sinking boat on a sea of pain. He knew exactly what that felt like, for he was right there, floating along beside her.

"I'm still your wife, Dru," she whispered.

She might still be his wife, but would he ever stop picturing her in the arms of some nameless, faceless stranger?

"There is a legal way to take care of that," he said coldly.

She appeared to fold in on herself. "I love my daughter, Dru. I have her safety and welfare to think about. You can divorce me if you want, but all I ask is that you give us a chance to work things out and if you don't, that you at least give me time to find another place."

He wondered if that meant giving her time to find another man, another fool?

"I'll be a good wife if you'd only give me another chance."

He was about to tell her that he doubted every word when the window near the crib suddenly exploded. Glass shattered and fell as a rock hurtled into the room and thudded hard against the floor where it landed at Sara's feet.

She immediately ran over to the crib and scooped up the howling child, protectively pressing the little girl's cheek to her shoulder before she took cover in the hall. Dru picked up the rock and walked over to the window. He raised the frame and leaned head and shoulders outside, daring the culprit to toss another. In a sweeping glance he saw that the front yard and street were deserted. With all the well-planted lawns and overgrown shrubbery up and down the block, there were a million and one places for someone to hide. There was no use running outside in search of the culprit.

He ducked into the room again and stared at the rock in his hand as if a piece of the moon had fallen into the window. Brown paper was crudely wrapped around it and tied with a piece of nondescript twine. He pulled off the string and carefully drew off the paper and smoothed out the wrinkles. A bold, childish scrawl covered the page, with two short lines that spoke volumes.

Get out, Yankee-loving, traitor bitch.
Leave Magnolia Creek to decent, God-fearing folk.

Only a coward would throw a rock through a woman's window and run. Dru crumpled the page. The stone felt hard and cold, unforgiving and as merciless as the words on the page. There was a deep depression in the floor where it landed. If it had hit Sara's child, it could have killed her.

He left the room and found Sara in the hallway, swaying back and forth, clutching the whimpering child to her breast. Both of them turned matched pairs of frightened eyes his way.

"It seems somebody wants you out of town in a bad way," he told her.

She was terrified, so much so that her shocked expression tripped his heart despite his anger and bitterness. The instinct to protect her was still viable. If he ever found the coward who had done this, then God help the man.

He held up the note, debated before he handed it to her, then watched her face as she slowly read it.

"While I was lying in a hospital praying that I'd live through the war and make it home to your arms, were you actually sleeping with the enemy, Sara?"

It was the final insult. He turned away before she could respond, turned his back on her and her bastard, and walked to his own bedroom door. The last time he had been in this room, Sara had been asleep in his bed.

His bedroom was like a cold and silent shrine, the furniture still draped with sheets to keep dust at bay. He ripped them off the bed and side chairs, tossed them aside, and stalked over to his wardrobe. The door bounced against the wall when he opened it with too much force. Inside, nothing was missing. All of his shirts and pants hung neatly side by side.

He turned full circle, staring at his past. He had to get out of here. He would bathe and change and then head downtown. Maybe there he would find the answers he needed. Maybe he would be able to track down the coward who had defiled his home.

14

Sara swept up the broken glass and left a distraught Louzanna watching Lissybeth. She found a hammer, nails, and wood scraps in the barn; refusing to ask Dru for help, she tacked them across the broken windowpane by herself.

Afterward she washed and changed into a dark indigo paisley dress. It had fit perfectly before she left Magnolia Creek, but now the waist hung loose while the bodice strained over her full breasts. She gave her hair a cursory brushing and then went to sit on the floor where Lissybeth was contentedly playing with one of her shoes.

Sara reached out, fingered the spot on the floor where the stone had created a deep groove in the oak, and shuddered. Granddaddy always said that it didn't do a body any good to look back, but while she was looking forward, she was going to keep an eye out for danger.

She had no idea what Dru had been thinking when he walked out on her a few minutes ago. He had turned so cold and unreadable. She never realized that he possessed such a hard, threatening side and hardly recognized this battle-scarred, solemn-eyed stranger with a dangerous edge.

Lissybeth toddled over to her, offered her the shoe. Sara absently let it fall into her lap. She gave Lissybeth a hug and a noisy kiss, then got to her feet and picked up her little girl. As she passed by the mirror beside the armoire, she caught a glimpse of her own reflection, touched her sullied cheek.

Surely Dru saw changes in her. How could he not? She was no longer the girl he married, but he had loved her once, loved her through all the years of war, loved her up until a few hours ago. It wasn't that easy to stop loving someone, she knew that well. He had never, ever been out of her heart, not for one moment, not even when she had been with Jonathan.

She desperately wanted to start over and vowed to do everything she could to earn his forgiveness and recapture his love. Until then, she would fight to prove that she was still the wife he needed, the woman he thought he had married. She had made a bargain with Louzanna, too, and she meant to keep it.

Sara turned to leave the room, intent upon cooking up stewed rabbit for dinner just the way her mama used to, when her gaze caught on the wood scraps covering the broken window and her arms tightened around Lissybeth. She quickly shut the bedroom door on the ugly proof that someone wanted her gone.

Somber gray clouds had gathered, matching Dru's dark mood as he walked three blocks to Dr. Maximus Porter's home on Maple Street. He wore his hat pulled low, thankful that there were few people out and about. He wasn't in the mood to be recognized and give explanations.

Doc Porter lived in a whitewashed, two-story, wood-frame house with a wide covered porch that wrapped around to a side door where a separate office was located on the ground floor. Dru remembered coming here as a child, looking forward to Doc opening the heavy glass jar full of hard candy he kept on the corner of his desk.

Dru knocked on the office door. After a few seconds, he tried again and finally the door swung open. At first Doc could only stare, then he grabbed Dru's upper arms and pulled him into a hard bear hug.

"As I live and breathe, I never thought to see you in this life again!" Doc drew him inside the office and continued to pound him on the shoulder. "Welcome back from the dead, son. It's wonderful to see you."

Doc's old dog, Goldie, a longhaired setter of mixed heritage, ambled slowly into the room and nudged Dru's pant leg with her nose. He gave the dog's ears a rub and patted her head, which was enough to satisfy her. She dropped to the floor at his feet.

"Thank God you're alive. I was just praying I could find someone to take over doctoring in this town. Let's go into the sitting room and talk." Doc led the way. "I've already got some hot water on for tea."

Dru stepped over Goldie and followed Doc out of the office and into the drawing room of the main house. The dog slowly trailed along behind and went to lie down on a hooked rug before the front door.

The place smelled old and well settled, full of all the things a couple acquires over many years of marriage. The tabletops were littered with books and pictures, photographs, tintypes, vases, and statuettes. The walls were covered with portraits of family and landscapes.

Lacy crocheted antimacassars covered the backs and arms of two overstuffed chairs placed close to the fireplace. Copies of the *Sentinel* along with the *Louisville Journal*, a pro-Union newspaper, spilled over the landing at the foot of the stairs.

Doc Porter and his wife, Esther, were childless. The small home they had built when they first married still suited them well.

Dru stood beside a chair that was obviously Esther's favorite. A pair of spectacles was folded atop a book on the side table. A basket full of calico scraps and finished quilt blocks sat on the floor nearby. Esther had attended Louzanna's sewing circle for years. Dru glanced toward the door to the kitchen, expecting to hear Doc's wife moving around, but the house was still.

"Where's Esther?"

Maximus Porter's dark eyes grew suspiciously bright. The old man pulled off his spectacles, turned away from Dru, and made a concentrated effort of polishing the round lenses with his shirttail. Finally he cleared his throat, then carefully hooked the fragile stems around his ears before he turned around again.

"She's gone. Six months now. One day her heart just stopped."

"I'm so sorry." Words were so little comfort. Being sorry would never bring the doc's wife back, but sorrow was all Dru could offer. With her things still spread around the drawing room, it appeared that Esther had just stepped out for a moment. There was no way that he could have known.

"I'm sorry, too." Maximus waved Dru into Esther's chair. The cushioned seat was so soft, Dru sank down a mile. "I'll get you some tea," Doc said.

The last thing Dru wanted was tea, but he suspected Doc needed an excuse to leave the room and collect himself, so he sat and stared at the cold fireplace until Doc returned carrying a tray with two cups full of a strong, dark brew.

"We were married forty-seven years," Doc said without preamble, his voice unsteady. "I've never been so alone in my life. Always thought that I'd go before she would, but now I wouldn't wish this kind of immeasurable pain on anyone, especially her."

Dru sat there in silence, tried to sip the steaming tea, set it aside on the table crowded with Esther's things. He wondered if losing a wife after forty-seven years of marriage hurt worse than Sara's betrayal. It wasn't easy to measure that kind of pain.

They made quite a pair, two heartbroken men staring into their teacups, but Dru refused to let Sara keep him down this low. He told Doc Porter some of what had happened to him during the war and what had kept him away so long, but not all of it.

"I hope you're ready to take over for me," Maximus said when he was through. "You truly are an answer to my prayers. I've been looking for someone else to step into my shoes ever since I heard you were killed. Esther and I," he paused, swallowed, "we always planned to travel. She so wanted to go to Scotland, to the village where her ancestors lived." Again, his throat grew too full to speak, but after a moment he said, "God knows I need to get away from here. Everything reminds me of her."

Almost Sara's exact words. She claimed to have seen him everywhere she looked, perhaps the way Doc saw Esther's shadows here in this house.

"When do you plan to leave, Doc?"

"The sooner the better now that you can step right into my shoes. Rather than go to the expense of setting up your own office, use mine. I've still got quite a few medical supplies. It's been hard to get much of anything since the war, but things are getting better."

"I can't take over your office," Dru objected.

"Why not? It's going to be sitting here empty. I'll close up the rest of the house. You can come and go by the side entrance."

Doc Porter's offer was a godsend. Not only would he be able to start practicing right away, but he would have a place to escape Sara.

Maximus set his teacup on a footstool. Over by the front door, Goldie scratched a flea on her neck with lack-luster enthusiasm.

"That dog won't do anything anymore but sit by the door waiting for Esther." Doc glanced at the dog and then away. "I'm afraid I'm gonna have to put her down. Nobody wants a lonely old dog."

"I'll take care of it." Dru made the decision instantly, without thought. The Doc had lost enough. He shouldn't have to put down his own dog.

"Sometimes I feel as worthless as Goldie." Doc sighed and reached beneath his spectacles to rub at his eyes.

"You've got plenty of good years left, Doc."

"That's what I'm afraid of."

"I'll need your advice," Dru told him, and for the first time since he had knocked on his door, Doc smiled. Dru wondered if Maximus knew about Sara.

"There's one thing that we haven't talked about yet. Something I wish I didn't have to bring up." Dru set his own empty cup aside.

"Sara," Doc said. "I guess it's my turn to say I'm sorry. It must have been terrible to come home and find your wife gone," Doc said.

"Sara's back. Came back yesterday."

"Right before you, then."

"Yeah."

"The Lord sure works in strange ways," Doc muttered, shaking his head.

"She brought a child with her. Not mine." He felt ashamed to say it, as if the sin was somehow his own. Sitting across from him was a man who dealt with more than physical aches and pains. Doc Porter knew how to listen without condemnation. Dru felt enough at ease to add, "She seems to think I should forgive and forget and start over."

"Just like that?"

"Yeah, just like that."

"She believed you were dead, Dru. We all did."

"So I keep hearing."

"I have to warn you, if you take her back, there'll be repercussions. Some folks around here won't want to support your decision. Things were worse than bad during the war. For a short while we were as heavily occupied as any Confederate town might have been. When the Union troops finally pulled out, they burned the mill. Conscripted all the able-bodied slaves."

"They took Jamie even though I had freed him right after my father died."

"Your Sara made no bones about being seen around town with a Union soldier. You can imagine how that was thought of around here, even though it might have all been quite innocent at the time. But after the Yankees pulled out, word got around that she had gone with them."

Dru rubbed his forehead, trying to ease the pounding tension there. "Sara never really took sides before the war because her family hadn't and it wouldn't have mattered to her what color uniform the man wore. I doubt she realized that the townsfolk would see it as such a betrayal, or that it might still matter to them now that the war is over, but obviously it does."

"Esther said Louzanna was awful upset about it for a long while but she never spoke ill of Sara. Lou was adamant that you were still alive but, of course, everyone thought that was just another of her eccentric behaviors and that she simply couldn't accept the truth. I'm damned glad it turned out your sister was right."

Silence lengthened as Dru absorbed what Maximus had said.

"I don't have to tell you that times were rough in Kentucky, Dru, but I'm sure you saw far worse. Sara was probably frightened to death by what was happening. War makes people do things they would never do otherwise."

When Doc paused, Dru said, "Someone threw a rock through the upstairs window in Sara's room." He reached into his pocket and passed the note over to Maximus. The doctor read it and shook his head.

"Have any idea who might have done this?" Dru asked.

"It could be anyone in town. As I said, don't think most folks will take kindly to Sara being here, but when you judge her, try to take into consideration that she thought you weren't ever coming back. I know firsthand that loneliness is a backbreaking burden. A broken heart doesn't always let you think too clearly, either."

Silence stretched between them and then Doc asked, "What are you going to do about Sara?"

"I haven't decided what to do yet," Dru said honestly, wishing there was no decision to make.

"She's still your wife."

"She's still my wife." His stomach churned. A wife who might have just stepped out of another man's bed.

"Well, as I said," Doc told him, "be prepared. If she stays here, you might have to stand up to the whole town."

15

DRU LEFT DOC Porter's with new determination. His domestic situation was experiencing upheaval, but at least now his life had purpose. Thanks to Doc's generosity, he could start working immediately.

The sky turned to ash and it started to drizzle light, invisible rain, but as he walked along familiar streets toward the heart of town, Magnolia Creek settled around him like a familiar old coat.

Winding avenues flanked by two-story houses behind well-kept lawns led to the center of town where wood-and-brick commercial buildings edged a grassy Courthouse Square complete with a bandstand. It was a picture-perfect town, once thriving because of the sorghum mill his grandfather had established, a business that eventually drew other enterprises and hard-working, civic-minded folk.

How long would it take the town to recover? How long until folks were able to put the war behind them?

For his part, after years of waiting, he was about to become Magnolia Creek's doctor. The experience he had gained during the war had been horrific, but for a newly graduated surgeon, it had been invaluable.

His father direly predicted that he would quickly tire

of the idea and grow weary of racing out in the middle of the night to wipe up vomit or sit and watch someone die.

"What real man would want to face the future knowing he was going to be paid off in chickens and vegetables, if he gets paid at all?"

Dru's longing was one of his father's favorite topics of debate, but despite Gerald Talbot's opinion of the medical profession, Dru had made up his mind early on that he wanted to become a man of medicine, though he could never say for certain why. At sixteen, he stubbornly voiced his wishes and soon his father's anger and disappointment turned to bitterness and finally contempt, but Dru's resolve only strengthened.

Eventually the strife in the house had escalated to the point where it greatly disturbed his invalid mother and Louzanna, so Dru gave in and put aside his dreams in order to manage the mill until the day his father died of heart failure.

His mother, Mary, long confined to her bed with what Doc Porter had diagnosed as acute female problems of the nerves and a weakened constitution, followed his father in death a few weeks later.

Six weeks to the day that they buried his father, Dru sold Talbot Mill and set up the proceeds to be paid in monthly installments to his sister before he left for medical college.

Near the center of town he turned onto Main Street and immediately began to feel the astonished stares of people on the street. When folks began to recognize him, he was forced to stop half a dozen times. Finally he reached the bank, withdrew some of his savings, and gave the bank manager a cursory explanation of how he had survived. Before he reached the *Magnolia Creek Sentinel* office, his resurrection had been exclaimed over more times than he could count.

The *Sentinel* was published once a week, give or take a day or two, depending on Abel Foster's ability to drum up news. In the months preceding the war, the pages had been filled with political news of Kentucky and the nation, but in more peaceful times, the lead stories were reduced to the likes of "Addie Smith Takes Up China Painting," or "Gus Brown Grows Fifty-Pound Pumpkin," or even "Little Aimes Boy Swallows Penny and Lives!"

Dru pushed open the door to the newspaper office where a teenaged youth he didn't recognize was seated at a desk in the outer room.

"I'm Dru Talbot. Is Abel here?" He waited while the office boy jumped up and slipped into a back room that held the printing press. Within seconds the youth returned, followed by Abel Foster.

Abel stood there looking much the same as Dru remembered. He was tall and slender, with light-brown hair oiled down and just touching his collar in back. His face was long, its length accentuated by heavy muttonchop sideburns. His mouth turned down in a perpetual frown. When he extended a slim hand with ink-stained fingers, Dru pumped it in a quick shake.

"Well, well." At first Abel could only stare. "Look who's back from the dead. Let me get some paper and I'll interview you right now. I don't often get to do a firsthand story on a ghost." Abel laughed at his own joke, rummaged around in the desk until he found a sheet of paper, a pen, nibs, and a bottle of ink.

Dru didn't feel like smiling. "I came to place an advertisement. I'm going to take over Doc Porter's office."

"You don't say. How long have you been home?"

"Since around noon."

"Good. Then your story will run before too many folks hear. I can't believe Minnie didn't see you and come tell me." He paused long enough to look down his nose and say, "I hear your wife came crawling back last evening. At least now you can get rid of her. From what my wife told me, your sister was actually going to let her stay. Louzanna was so adamant about it that she threw Minnie out of the house this morning."

"Louzanna?" It was hard for Dru to imagine his sister finding the gumption to do anything of the sort. He almost smiled. Minnie Foster was one of the biggest gossips in town and if the woman hadn't changed, word of Sara's return was surely all over by now.

"How's Arthur? Did he get home safe and sound?" Dru tried to turn the conversation in another direction. The Fosters' son Arthur was older than Dru. He had gone off to enlist with the first wave of men to leave Magnolia Creek.

Abel Foster's long, hangdog face went stony. "He died at Vicksburg." He abruptly stopped speaking, as if there was more he could have said but was obviously reluctant. "When can I have that interview?"

Dru didn't think it was likely he'd ever want to open up to Abel and the whole town. Sara might have brought him enough notoriety already. The war was over. As far as Dru was concerned, his story was old news.

"I'd like to put all that behind me, Abel. Why don't you just tell me how to go about placing an advertisement?"

Abel handed him a sheet of paper, told him to write down what he wanted to say and that it would run in a fancy outlined block at the bottom of page one.

As Dru bent over the desk to pen his advertisement, Abel stood over him. "How did you feel when you walked in and found your wife living there with another man's child?"

The pen in Dru's hand skidded across the page, leaving a blob of ink and a squiggly trail. Dru went perfectly still, fighting to keep from lunging at Abel's throat.

"How do you *think* I felt, Abel?"

"Has she told you who the father is?"

"I haven't asked."

"She took up with a Yankee."

Dru grabbed a clean sheet of paper. His hand tightened around the pen as he forced himself to keep writing. *New Doctor in Town. Office Hours from Eight to Five.*

"She even tried to seduce *me* once," Abel said, rocking back on his heels. "If I were you I'd send her packing. Not a man or woman in this town would blame you. Most folks thought you were crazy for marrying a Collier in the first place."

Straightening to his full height, Dru took a step toward Abel and towered over him, intentionally trying to intimidate the man into silence. He watched Abel's smug smile quickly dissolve.

"What happens in *my* house, with *my* wife, is my business, Abel. Not yours and not anyone else's. Do you hear me loud and clear? Maybe you should keep your own wife under control."

"Sara flaunted herself in front of everybody with an entire Yankee regiment and there's not one of us who'll forget it. My boy was killed by those bastards in blue."

"You willing to take my money for this ad, Abel, or should I leave now?"

"I'll run your ad, but as long as you let that woman

abide under your roof, I wouldn't expect much business if I were you."

Dru finished writing and handed the sheet to Abel.

"I'll still be the only doctor within twenty-five miles. If folks want to go down to Hopkinsville for help, they're more than welcome to." He reached into his pocket and drew out a handful of Yankee dollars, currency that looked foreign to him now.

Abel quoted a sum. Dru handed him a dollar.

"Run it for two months," he said, anxious to leave.

"Sure thing, *Doc.*" Abel waited until Dru was almost to the door, then said, "Don't forget what I told you. No one's ever going to accept your wife again. Not after what she did."

Dru left without a backward glance. It took all his will not to slam the door. He stopped by the store and ordered some staples to be sent round to the house before he started home. With every step he took toward Ash Street, Abel Foster's words echoed in his mind.

"Sara flaunted herself in front of everybody with an entire Yankee regiment and there's not one of us who'll forget it."

One of them hadn't hesitated to throw a rock through Sara's bedroom window, either.

Sara heard the front door close and her stomach tightened as the sound carried down the hall to the kitchen where she was bathing Elizabeth in a dishpan. She had covered the table with a folded sheet and had a stack of clean towels close at hand. Louzanna had shared a bar of precious lemon-scented soap. Lissybeth was happily splashing water and singing a nonsensical song.

When Sara heard Dru's footsteps coming down the hall, her hands stilled. She let the soap drop and it quickly disappeared beneath the cloudy water. Elizabeth heard him, too, and began to wriggle and squirm, straining to see over her shoulder.

Dru paused in the doorway, his hair and shoulders damp from the light rain now falling. His black hair glistened. He stopped short when their eyes met and held Sara's stare before he turned a cool gaze on Elizabeth.

He didn't take another step into the kitchen, but even so he filled the room with his presence. Each time Sara saw him again, she was reminded of his size and physical power, yet she had never feared him the way she did her father. Dru's strength was carefully harnessed, still he never gave the appearance that he would be an easy man to cross.

"Where's Lou?" His dark-eyed gaze swung around and bored into her again.

"Upstairs reading."

His expression remained unfathomable. She expected him to turn and walk out, but he lingered there, perhaps feeling as awkward as she did in this untenable situation. With his hands on his hips, he leaned against the doorframe.

"Louzanna said you went over to see Doc Porter." She began soaping Lissybeth again, aware that he hadn't taken his eyes off of her.

"I did." He seemed determined not to make conversation easy.

"Was he home?"

He wandered a few steps farther into the kitchen and stepped into Lissybeth's line of vision. The baby squealed and slapped the water, sending a spray of soapy water into Sara's eyes. Sara snapped them shut against the sharp stinging pain, forced to let go of the slippery child with one hand as she pressed it against her eye.

Lissybeth began kicking against the side of the dish-pan, squealing and squirming as Sara struggled to hold on to her one-handed, blinded by the soap. Finally, she shut both eyes and held on to Elizabeth with both hands.

Suddenly, she sensed Dru right beside her.

"Will you please hold her for me?" Sara still couldn't open her eyes wide enough to help herself, and she didn't dare let go of Elizabeth.

He went perfectly still, but didn't move away. He was so close that when Sara moved, she brushed against his shirtfront and heard his swift intake of breath.

"If you hold still, I'll wipe your eyes," he told her.

Eyes shut tight, she turned her face toward the sound of his voice. He gently blotted her eyes with the towel, careful to avoid touching her bruised cheek. He held the cloth against her eyes and let them tear until the stinging subsided a bit.

"I think I'm all right now," she said softly.

He lifted the towel but didn't step away. Sara opened her eyes and realized how intimately close he was standing. He must have had the same thought, for when she tried to smile and softly thanked him, he quickly stepped back and tossed the damp towel on the table.

It pained her that he had refused to touch Elizabeth, but he had come to her aid. The small gesture might not have been much, but it was a start.

Dru lingered in the warmth of the kitchen, surrounded by the savory aroma of rabbit stew and the scent of Lou's lemon soap. Unwittingly Sara drew him like a magnet, able to beguile and seduce his senses without even trying, the way she had the first time he had ever laid eyes on her.

During the war, he had dwelt on every detail about her, her laugh, her smile, the way their eyes always met and held, no matter where they were. He recalled every conversation, the way she tossed her head when she flirted, the way she had always watched him from beneath lowered lashes. She wasn't flirting now, yet he was still irresistibly drawn to her.

He thought he had convinced himself that a woman's looks wouldn't matter as much as her spirit and her willingness to stand by him through thick and thin. He had wanted to marry someone with innate goodness, someone wise and tender, someone who would make a good mother—and he thought he had. Seeing how much Sara loved her child was proof that she was at least that.

There had always been something in her very essence that appealed to him on a visceral level, something that drew him to her. He couldn't deny that irresistible pull even now. Sara was no longer the girl he had left behind, but a woman with a figure far more lush and even more tempting. The bodice of her gown was damp and far too tight. Her nipples were taut, visible and enticing beneath the thin fabric.

As he watched her lift the slippery little girl out of the dishpan and begin to towel her dry, he tasted a hunger deeper than one inspired by the mouthwatering aroma of the rabbit stew. It wasn't hard to imagine how soft her skin would feel beneath his hands. While she was preoccupied with drying her daughter, he let his eyes feast on the pale curve of her neck and the tendrils of damp curls lying against her temple. Then, as if she felt his stare, Sara slowly turned her attention away from her task.

Their eyes met across the room. So close, he thought. So close to all he had wanted for so very long. And yet they were still so far away.

Their gazes held until the child grabbed the bar of soap, licked it, and started making spitting sounds. Sara distracted her by planting kisses on her nose, and then slipped the soap out of the little girl's hand.

In that instant, Dru became the outsider. He turned and walked out of the room before Sara could look his way again and perhaps capture him with a glance.

16

Throughout a tense dinner, Lou tried her best to keep a conversation going but Dru sat in stone-cold silence, wolfing down stew until Sara fled to the seclusion of the guest room.

There, surrounded by rose-papered walls, she moved Elizabeth's crib as far away from the window as she could, tucking it safely between her own bed and the opposite wall.

Once Lissybeth was asleep, Sara changed into her nightgown and brushed out her hair, but didn't try to delude herself into thinking that she would get any rest.

Sitting alongside Dru at the table had been a trying experience, one that had left her more than shaken. Casting sidelong glances, she had watched him eat, concentrating on his hands—the strong, healing hands of a surgeon, hands that had once loved her so well and so tenderly. He had touched not only her body but her soul.

So many memories of those few but precious days when they had fallen in love came back to her. On lazy afternoons when Louzanna would quilt, they walked in the woods behind the house where Sara showed Dru how to find all the herbs he had been taught to use at school. They wandered beneath canopies of sugar maple and beech. In the rich humus below she found bloodroot, bellwort, valerian, and waterleaf. They had paused beside a smattering of golden-yellow buttercup and Dru knelt and picked a handful for her—the first bouquet anyone had ever given her—and the mere touch of his hand against hers had sent chills down her spine.

Unable to relax, she began to pace. Where the floor was bare of rugs, the floorboards felt cold against her bare feet. It was still drizzling and there was a lingering chill in the air. She rubbed her upper arms, wishing her nightgown was made of something more substantial than muslin.

After making certain Lissybeth was tucked in, Sara crawled into bed and pulled the covers over her. When she heard the click of a door closing across the hall, she knew that Dru had finally gone into his bedroom.

There has to be a way to make him forgive and forget.

There has to be some way to get through to him.

She threw back the covers and walked to the mirror, ran her hands down her body, stood on tiptoe, and turned one way and then another as she pressed her hands against her abdomen. She had quickly recovered her figure after Elizabeth had been born, not by effort, but because of lack of food.

One thing was certain, before she lost Dru she had always been headstrong and determined and had never run from a challenge. Laughter had always come easily to her. So had confidence and the certainty that she could do just about anything she put her mind to.

Dru had fallen in love with a girl possessed of spunk and spark—two qualities she hadn't shown much of lately.

She thought of Dru shut up all alone and hurting in the

room down the hall and suddenly one of Granddaddy's sayings came to her.

"Love is the glue that binds folks together, more than blood, more than spoken vows."

Love is the key.

Love will surely make things right.

She ran her hands down her hair and swept it back over her shoulders, then she walked to Lissybeth's crib. The child was sleeping soundly on her back, her little hands curled into fists that rested beside her cheeks. She looked like an angel with her golden curls and pouting lips, her soft lashes brushing her cherub's cheeks.

She loved Elizabeth with all her heart. Just as much as she loved Dru. There was a place in her heart for Louzanna, too, and Granddaddy and Mama. Unless a body's heart was made of stone, there were no limits to the amount of love it could hold. At least, not so far as she could tell.

She was convinced that there were all kinds of love and that it came in limitless amounts. It was time Dru Talbot found that out.

Sara inhaled deeply and walked silently over to the door, leaving it open a crack in case Elizabeth awakened and cried out for her. Then she stepped into the hall and headed for Dru's room.

Dru stood beside the window in the dark, watching the rain sifting through the halo of light from the gas lamp on the street corner. The white picket fence around the yard needed patching. Some of the pickets were missing or had come loose and hung sideways. He made a mental note to attend to it as soon as he could and his thoughts trailed off to Jamie, for the task would have fallen to him, were he still here.

Jamie had nearly grown up alongside him and Louzanna. Dru couldn't help but wonder if Jamie had survived the war and if so, where he was now. Dru became so lost in thought that he didn't hear the door when it opened, but a draft of cool air came in from the hall. He sensed that Sara had come to him long before he looked over his shoulder and saw her standing there.

She hovered in the doorway, cloaked in a thin white nightgown and uncertainty, waiting for him to respond. His physical reaction was immediate and telling even though he fought his arousal.

He remained facing the window and tried to concentrate on the raindrops as they oozed down the outside of the pane. Drawing a deep breath, he fisted his hands. A cold sweat broke out on his forehead even though he felt flushed.

He should have told her to get out the minute she walked in, but now she was crossing the room. The floorboards protested but he remained stone cold and silent. He knew when she stopped somewhere behind him. He could feel her body's warmth.

Suddenly, without warning, she touched his shoulder, ran her hand down his sleeve to his wrist, then repeated the motion. When her warm breath brushed the back of his shirt, he nearly came undone. He took his weakness out on her, lashing out.

"Get out, Sara."

"Please, turn around, Dru."

He thought silence enough of a refusal and kept his back to her, wishing away the throbbing heat in his veins, the quickening in his loins. She knew exactly what she was doing to him by coming in here in her nightgown, by touching him in the darkness. He hated her for having such power over him.

"You loved me once, Dru. Would it be so hard to love me again?"

He longed to press his face to the cold windowpane, cool his heated skin, but he wasn't about to show her any weakness and thus give her any more power over him.

"Things are different now," he said.

He wished she would move. She was pressed up behind him, the weight of her hand on his shoulder, the intensity almost more than he could bear.

"Different? How are they so different? You loved me when you came running across the yard today. You loved me when you took me in your arms and kissed me. You loved me until you heard Elizabeth call me Mama and you realized what I had done. You can't stop loving someone in an instant, Dru. I should know."

Her voice was warm and as seductive as her touch. She didn't give him time to respond as she pressed her argument home.

"Don't tell me that you don't love me, Dru Talbot, because I'll know you're lying. Love doesn't end in a heartbeat. I learned that firsthand. I *know* it because I tried to stop loving you and I couldn't."

"You've been with another man, for Christ's sake." He shook off her touch, spun around. They were standing toe to toe. Like him, she was barefoot, but at least he was still dressed. He leaned back against the windowpane, the cool chill of the wet glass eased through his linen shirt—no great comfort at all.

"The whole town knows about it."

"When did people's opinions start to matter to you,

Dru? They certainly didn't keep you from marrying me. I'm sure there were lots of folks who thought I was beneath you, but you ignored them. What people thought didn't keep you from giving Jamie his freedom or selling the mill after your daddy died. You're a man who goes after what he wants regardless of opinion, at least you were before the war. Maybe *things* aren't different now. Maybe *you're* the one who is different."

He looked her up and down, watched her long, unbound hair sway against her waist, imagined himself entangled in it while they made love.

"You're right. I really don't understand how you can just walk in here and tell me you still love me after what you did. Didn't your lover mean anything to you at all? Was there more than one man?" He finally hit a nerve, forced her to take a step back. "How many men did you sleep with, Sara? Do you even *know* who fathered that child?"

Her hand came out of nowhere. She slapped him so hard he rocked back before he caught her wrist and pulled her up against him, so close that he felt her breasts flatten against his chest. She was no match for him and they both knew it, but it wasn't his way to hit a woman. She already believed that or she would have never dared to strike him in the first place.

Just as quickly as he had grabbed her, he let go as if her skin was as hot as a burning ember. Then exhausted by all that had happened in the past few, terrible hours, he sighed with fatigue and disillusionment.

"Go on, Sara. It was a nice try, but as I said before, I really don't want you anymore." Stepping away from the window, he started to walk past her.

She hooked his arm at the elbow, forced him to look her in the eye. "I don't believe you."

"Do you think I could ever touch you without wondering if you were thinking of him?"

"I won't be, I can guarantee you that." Her tone was bitter as the north wind.

Dru walked to the edge of the bed, then thought better of being near it and ended up behind a chair drawn up to a library table on the other side of the room. From a side window he had a view of Abel Foster's house. The place was dark except for one lamp burning in an upstairs room.

Recalling what Abel had said about Sara only solidified his resolve.

"What's going to happen to us?" Her bravado had slipped a notch and from the sound of her voice, confusion had taken its place.

He gripped the back of the chair. Instead of walking out, she crossed the room to stand too close again. Her voice touched him as surely as a caress. "I'd leave here if I had somewhere else to go, Dru, but there's no place for me now that I have Elizabeth. Believe me, I've tried to find work." There was a slight pause. He heard a catch in her voice before she added, "Thank God Lou took me in or I would have never known you were still alive."

She pressed her hands together at her waist, drawing her gown close to her body, outlining her figure. A calculated move to tempt him? He easily convinced himself it was so and tried to deny her allure.

"I promised Lou that I would help her keep up the chores," she said. "I'm going to start on the garden as soon as this rain lets up. I can help you, too, Dru. Granddaddy has given me some seeds for the kinds of herbs that you'll need. I'm willing to do whatever I can to help make you a success."

"Because of you and your reputation in this town, I may not even have a practice." His revelation cut her spirit to the quick, filled her eyes with tears.

"I'm so sorry."

"Save the apology. Just go back to your room."

She looked about to leave, even took a step toward the door, but then she stopped. Hot waves of tension snaked through him. If she lingered much longer, he wouldn't be able to resist, not when he thought of how this was to have been the night they celebrated his homecoming. The night he would finally make love to her again. His gaze wandered to the big empty bed.

Every beat of his heart encouraged him to reach out and enfold her in his arms, to take all she offered, but that would only complicate the situation. He held firm; remained silent.

"What now, Dru?" She sighed heavily. With one hand on the doorframe, she paused to look back and whispered words he could barely hear. "If you can't love me anymore, then maybe you should divorce me."

Veiled in darkness, Sara leaned against the wall outside Dru's room and tried to gather the shattered pieces of her self-respect. Not only had he turned her away, but he had just accused her of sleeping with an entire regiment of Yankees. What's more, he believed her reputation was going to ruin him.

If not for Elizabeth, she would pack up and walk out, but no one would take her on as a housekeeper or a nanny with a young child of her own, even if there was work to be had.

For now, there was no escape. But how long could she suffer Dru's contempt? How long could either of them exist this way?

He couldn't even bear to be in the same room with her. Refusing to give up, she tried to convince herself that maybe tomorrow he would start to thaw. She made herself slowly start walking down the hall, forcing herself to think past the hurt.

If the rain stopped tomorrow morning she would break ground in Lou's garden. That would keep her hands busy and, hopefully, her mind occupied. Earlier that evening she had promised Lou that she would teach her to make corn bread, too.

Life would go on one day at a time. All she had to do was stay strong and wait for Dru to see that she would make a damn fine wife or die trying.

17

As soon as he heard the door to Sara's room close, Dru sought refuge downstairs in the drawing room. He helped himself to some of the best bourbon whiskey in Kentucky. His hand shook as he half filled a cut crystal tumbler.

Fine thing. A surgeon who can't control his hands.

After a few weeks of action he had been promoted to senior surgeon and was no longer simply providing first aid. Surgical cases were routed to him in field hospitals, temporary infirmaries set up behind the lines. The wounded were hauled to him in ambulance carts, flatbed wagons, on filthy bloodstained stretchers. He had learned to operate in barns, sheds, schools, offices, homes. More than once, doors had been torn off buildings and turned into makeshift operating tables.

Toward the end of the war, while the Confederate army was losing ground on every side, he had been forced to perform delicate surgery even as the battlefield closed in and firing was intense all around.

Not once had his hands shaken. Not once had he feared for his life, though he often wondered whether he had made the right choice when he enlisted and whether he had done all he could for the wounded.

As he watched the whiskey slosh with his tremor, it came as a crushing blow to realize that his desire for Sara had more power over him than the threat of any Yankee bullet.

He kicked back the whiskey, poured another three fingers, lifted the glass, and watched the lamplight dance through the crystal facets. He made himself sip slowly this time, for it was a crime not to savor the rich smooth flavor of the expensive bourbon, but even the liquor couldn't soothe the raw, aching tear in his soul.

What had undoubtedly been the longest day of his life didn't seem to want to end. There was no way he was going to fall asleep quickly after turning Sara down.

Intent upon burying himself in his work, he dropped the front of his father's secretary desk, pulled up a chair, and sat down, ready to list the supplies he needed. Tomorrow he would find out what Doc Porter had on hand. Adjusting the page, inspecting the nib on the pen, fingering the ink bottle—the movements kept him busy, but he couldn't concentrate.

With every breath he thought of Sara. Whenever the old house creaked, his heart stopped. He remembered how she had looked coming down the stairs on their wedding day.

How long could he deny himself the one thing he had wanted most in all the world?

He took another swallow. It wasn't Sara he heard on the stairs; it was just the house nestling down for the night. He had been spared the embarrassment of breaking down and giving in to his raw desire.

As he finished the whiskey in his glass, his tension eased. He closed his eyes, stretched, heard Sara's voice in his head.

"What now, Dru?"

"Maybe you should divorce me."

What now? He could always bury himself in his work.

One thing he knew for certain was that he could never throw her out without knowing there was a safe place for her to land.

He had no idea what was involved in obtaining a divorce. No one he knew had ever done anything of the sort, but Hugh Wickham was a lawyer, and Hugh was, he hoped, still his best friend.

The way he saw it, after what had happened at Shiloh, Hugh owed him some free advice.

He walked over to the decanter of whiskey again and this time poured himself just a splash more. He hoisted the glass, swirled the ginger liquid, and toasted himself before he took a sip. Then he turned toward the empty staircase and raised the glass again.

"Welcome home, Sara," he said. "Welcome home."

Morning dawned bright and sunny, a perfect tribute to spring. Following her usual routine, Louzanna rose early and prepared to make a hearty breakfast for Dru to try to fatten him up; but she was disappointed to find he had already gone out. He had lit the stove and left a note on the kitchen table. He had gone to the Wickhams' farm to see Hugh.

Beside Dru's note lay a copy of the *Magnolia Creek Sentinel*, still folded and tied with a piece of twine. She picked it up, slipped the string off, and unfolded the creases, wondering if perhaps Minnie had left the copy on the back step as a peace offering and Dru must have brought it inside.

The issue was a scant six pages, no more or less than

usual. She flipped through, scanning the headlines until her gaze riveted on an editorial by Abel Foster entitled, "A Traitor in Our Midst."

Her heart began to pound when she quickly realized that the entire column was devoted to Sara's return. In it, Abel questioned how a woman who had a child by a man outside of marriage had the audacity to show her face in Magnolia Creek again.

Shaken, Lou read the last paragraph twice.

"It is the expressed opinion of this publisher that the Talbots are harboring a traitor in our midst. Not only has the aforementioned tainted hussy had the nerve to come waltzing back to town carrying the proof of her sordid adulterous acts in her arms, but she has somehow managed to work her wiles on the very family she so openly betrayed. God help them all."

Then Abel called upon the good citizens of Magnolia Creek to remember what happened during the war and not to be swayed by tawdry sentiment. Louzanna crumpled the pages in her hands, walked to the stove, opened the door, and quickly tossed them in. The kitchen echoed with the sound of the iron door as she slammed it shut and latched it tight. Then she covered her cheeks with her hands and stared at the stove as the offensive paper burned.

What in heaven's name were they going to do? Would Abel's article turn the whole town against them all?

If Dru saw the article, *when* he saw it—for surely someone would show it to him—there would be no telling what he would do. She furiously started pulling crocks and bowls out of the cupboards.

Today, of all days, was quilting day. Her sewing circle ladies were due to arrive at ten. She had planned to make a cream tea cake from the groceries that Dru had delivered yesterday, anxious to share the bounty with her friends. Flour was still too dearly priced for most folks to buy and she had never even bartered for it after it became a luxury. Now she wondered if any of the ladies would come over at all. Certainly she could count Minnie Foster out.

Lou's nerves were rattled to the point where she finally grabbed hold of Mason's ring and started humming disjointed tunes. She was standing next to the sideboard with the flour bin open, staring into space, when Sara walked in.

Sara had donned Dru's old clothes again, determined to turn the ground for the garden while the soil was damp and the sun was shining. The moon was growing, a good time to plant above-ground vegetables. With Lissybeth in her arms she stepped into the kitchen and found Louzanna furiously humming, with a wide-eyed, frantic look in her eyes.

"Louzanna? Are you all right?" She touched Lou's shoulder.

Dru's sister jumped, fidgeted with her skirt, and then furiously started scooping flour out of the open bin in the sideboard and hastily started dumping it into a bowl. The finely ground flour was flying everywhere.

"Yes, yes, I'm fine. Did you sleep well? I did. I surely did. Today is sewing circle day. I'm going to bake a cake for the ladies, for us, too, of course." Her voice was high and tight. She was talking far too fast, her gaze roving around the room.

When Lou brushed her hands on her black skirt, leaving flour prints behind, Sara decided there was something dreadfully wrong and hurried into the pantry where she had left Louzanna small packets of ground herbs and roots for the medicinal teas she had taught Jamie and her sister-in-law to brew.

"I'll just make up a little rosemary and scullcap tea for you, Lou. How does that sound?" Nothing calmed and soothed as well, and from the way Louzanna looked just now, Sara could see she was on the verge of panic.

Sara moved the cooking plate on the wood stove and set the kettle directly over the fire. "Are you worried about what your friends will think of me living here?"

"Ooh!" Lou jumped, sounding as if she'd been pinched. "Oh, no." She glanced at the stove and shook her head.

Knowing what the weekly meeting of friends meant to Lou, Sara hated to think that she had jeopardized Louzanna's only contact with the outside world. As she waited for Louzanna to answer, she went after the china teapot covered with delicate chintz rosebuds in the dining room.

Louzanna's voice carried to her, unusually high and tight. "If someone chooses not to come over because Dru and I have accepted you back into our home, then that *someone* was not such a good friend after all, was she?"

Sara walked back in and stood over the kettle, willing the water to boil.

"Where is Dru?" she asked, trying to sound indifferent.

"He went out to the farm to see Hugh Wickham. I can't blame him for going there first thing. Why, most of this trouble is all Hugh's fault, isn't it? If he hadn't come back insisting that Dru had died in his arms, why, none of this would have happened."

Hugh Wickham. Of course, Dru would want to see his

best friend and tell him that he had survived, but Hugh Wickham was a lawyer.

If Dru had decided to divorce her, then Hugh was just the man he would want to see.

At that point Elizabeth started waving her arms and fussing to get down. Sara kissed her cheek before she set her on the floor and tried to imagine what life would be like without her—if indeed, as Lou had said, none of this had happened.

She could bear her shame, but life without Elizabeth was unthinkable.

"Does she like cake?" Lou watched Lissybeth toddle into the conservatory, headed toward the wood box.

"I'm sure she'll like it."

"I intend to make Mama's favorite cream tea cake recipe." Over her shoulder Lou said, "There's bacon for breakfast, thanks to Dru, and we've still got some eggs."

The water was starting to simmer. Sara measured the powdered scullcap and a teaspoon of rosemary into the pot for Lou's tea. "I want you to drink a cup quickly and then sip slowly at the second."

Louzanna paused in the midst of tapping an egg against the side of a large mixing bowl to stare at Sara. "I'm fine, really."

"Just a precaution," Sara said gently. "This will help keep you calm."

Then she filled the teapot with water and set it aside to steep. Trying not to make too much of Lou's jitters, she said, "I'll just have a bite before I go out and start the garden and I'll keep Lissybeth outside with me while your friends are here." Lou was in no condition to have Elizabeth underfoot, too.

"Oh, Sara." Lou's lower lip quivered. Her eyes flushed with tears.

Sara crossed the room and slipped her arm around her sister-in-law's shoulder. "I never wanted to hurt you."

Lou's eyes widened. She tried to blink her tears away. "Please be careful outside, will you? What if whoever threw that rock at the house comes back? What will you do? Stay inside. There's no need for you to hide from my friends out there, no need at all. I won't hide that child, either." She put her hands over her eyes and took a deep breath.

"I'm not afraid of a rock-throwing coward," Sara assured her.

"At least let me watch Elizabeth for you."

"You wouldn't get much sewing accomplished." Sara laughed softly, trying to imagine her daughter around so many scissors, needles, and pins. Then she quickly sobered.

"There hasn't been another of those awful notes, has there?" She scanned the windows.

Louzanna quickly shook her head. "No. No note. Everything is fine . . . but maybe you should keep the rifle handy."

Sara grabbed both of Louzanna's hands and forced the woman to look directly at her. "Lou, listen to me, if something else has happened, I need to know."

Lou shook her head. "No. Everything is just fine."

Sara wanted to believe her, but as she gathered up the makings for breakfast and got out a skillet, she decided that Dru had left early to avoid seeing her and now Louzanna was upset.

Despite Lou's assurances, she was afraid it would be a long time, if ever, before things were fine again.

18

DRU SOLD THE mule and rented a horse at the livery stable. He'd lost a thoroughbred at the same time that he lost his memory at Shiloh and wasn't willing to part with his limited cash to buy another until he found one he really wanted.

He had hoped the ride out to Hugh's would clear his head. Meandering streams crossed a road that wound through stretches of level pasturelands, past spacious homesteads with orchards and gardens and groves of beech, walnut, and oak trees.

As Dru crossed the porch at Hugh's the sound of laughter drifted from the open windows of the Wickhams' house, a low-roofed two-story structure with a Greek Revival portico. Dru knocked and waited. Before the war, a servant would have answered, but now it was Anne Wickham herself who came to the door.

Hugh's wife looked a bit older than Dru remembered but the war had changed them all. Of medium height, with light-brown hair and hazel eyes, Anne had always been polite and charming, a woman who had never failed to let Hugh shine.

She opened the door, took one look at Dru, let out a

scream, and then clapped a hand over her mouth. At first she could only stare.

"Hello, Anne. I'm no ghost." Dru reached out and took her elbow when it appeared she might faint.

Crying and laughing at once, Anne embraced him as she drew him into the foyer. Two young boys came tumbling out of the more informal of two drawing rooms. The older boy was six years old. The other, the son that Hugh had crossed enemy lines to see, was three. Both of them were the spitting image of Hugh.

The boys ran up to their mother, the younger clinging to her skirt while the older stared up at Dru with the same curious expression he'd often seen on Hugh's face.

"Oh my word, Dru! I still can't believe it, even though I'm standing right here holding your hand." Anne was beaming. "Dear God, Hugh thought you were dead."

Dru nodded. "So I hear. Is he home? I think it's time I assured him that I'm alive and talk him out of any notion he has about becoming a doctor."

Anne laughed and squeezed his hand. "He's working, as usual, in the drawing room. I don't know how he gets anything done with both boys underfoot, but he won't have it any other way."

Dru looked down at Hugh's fine sons. "I can see why he doesn't mind having them near."

Each had Hugh's confident smile and just like their father, each assessed him carefully, as if measuring his worth. Hugh had always taken a while to make friends, but once he deemed a man worthy, he was a friend for life.

"Who's he, Mama?" the older boy asked.

Anne introduced each child. Dru already knew the oldest was Hugh Junior. She paused and laughed when she touched her youngest on the head and said, "This little scamp's name is Dru Matthew Wickham. Hugh and I named him for you."

Dru found himself balanced on the sharp edge of an emotional sword, so moved by the loving gesture that he didn't know what to say. He cleared his throat, then reached out and ruffled the boy's brown hair.

Finally he managed, "Thank you, Anne."

Her eyes were exceptionally bright with tears when she smiled up at him. "Let me take you in to see Hugh."

Attended by the Wickham entourage, Dru let her lead him into the parlor. It felt good to be away from his own house. There had always been something warm and welcoming about the Wickham farm. Hugh's parents had been older when he was born and Hugh, the youngest son, had been the coddled darling of the family. He was the only one of his brothers to stay in Magnolia Creek, the others having moved to all parts of the West. Before the war Hugh kept the farm producing tobacco and sorghum while he practiced law.

Anne and the boys entered the room first. Both of Hugh's sons ran straight over to him, each taking a different route around the huge desk where Hugh was seated.

"Daddy, Dru's here!" Hugh Junior yelled.

Hugh, with his head down, intent on the pages spread over his desk, mumbled, "I know, son. Don't torment your little brother, now, you hear?"

"Not *that* Dru, Daddy. The big Dru."

"Hugh?" Anne drew his attention as she stood there holding "the big Dru's" hand just inside the doorway.

"What, dear?" Hugh read for a second longer and then looked up at his wife. When he saw Dru, his jaw dropped. He shook his head, started to rise, and dropped back into his chair.

Dru crossed the room, laughing. It felt good to laugh, good to share his homecoming with the man who had always been as close to him as a brother.

Still in shock, Hugh Wickham was completely subdued. All the color drained from his face. The boys, thrilled to have been privy to the secret first, were whooping and clapping their hands at the sight of their father rendered speechless for one of the few times in his life.

Dru paused across the desk. "I thought I'd better get out here and let you know that I was back from the dead before you heard it from someone else."

Hugh shook his head. "How?"

"It's no great mystery, Hugh. I never died in the first place." Dru spread his arms wide. "Aren't you even going to get up and welcome me home?"

Beside him, almost imperceptibly, Anne stiffened and Dru noticed. Hugh Junior ducked behind the desk and reappeared with a pair of crutches in his hands and handed them to Hugh.

"Get up, Daddy, and welcome big Dru home."

It was Dru's turn to fall silent while he watched Hugh smile at his son and take the crutches, fit them beneath his arms, and push back the chair. He came around the desk slowly but in fine command, as if he had been using the crutches for quite a while. His left leg was missing from the knee down.

Hasty surgeries in field tents, barns, and kitchens and on back porches flashed through Dru's mind. Cries of wounded soldiers, North or South, all sounded the same. Blood still ran as fast and red no matter what color uniform a man was wearing.

When Hugh and Dru were face-to-face, Dru embraced

his friend. As the two men held each other, there was no need for words to say all that had to be said.

Finally, Dru stepped back and took a long look at Hugh.

"You look a damn sight better than I do," he said.

"Well, you *were* dead, you know." Hugh finally smiled. Anne came to his side and slipped her arm around his waist.

"Have you had breakfast, Dru?"

He almost said yes, but his stomach growled and gave him away. "A bite of something would be great."

"Let's go into the dining room." Hugh let Anne and the boys lead the way. "I was trying to get some work done before breakfast. There don't seem to be enough hours in the day anymore."

"Are you still running the farm?"

"Yes, and practicing law again. Since the war there are so many foreclosures and so much bank business to take care of, not to mention inheritance entanglements in families who have lost so many relations, that I'm working day and night to straighten things out. It'll be years before we see our way clear of what the war has wrought."

They reached the dining room. Dru stood awkwardly by, not knowing whether to help Hugh into his chair or not, but since Anne and the boys had left Hugh to fend for himself, Dru let his friend prove his independence.

They settled down at the table as Anne went in to tell their cook that there would be one more for breakfast. When she returned a short time later with cups of real coffee, Dru was astonished and grateful.

"I can't remember when I've had a real cup of coffee." He took a sip, closed his eyes, and wallowed in the heady aroma.

"Anne's aunt lives in Boston. She sent this down last month. We only use it on special occasions," Hugh told him.

"I'm glad you deem my resurrection a special occasion." Dru set his cup down and tried to smile.

Hugh's own smile faded as he leaned on the table and looked Dru square in the eye. The little boys sensed the moment had grown serious, for even they settled down.

"I would have never left you had I known you were still alive," Hugh told Dru.

"I know that. As it is, I don't have much memory of that day. Before I was hit, we had run out of stretchers. Even the men on detail bringing in the wounded were falling fast. Within a few minutes I was out of tourniquets and dressings and reduced to running from one wounded man to the next, reassuring them help was on the way, knowing full well that was a bold-faced lie. When it looked like the Yankees were going to rout us, we evacuated the tents."

"That's when we ran into each other." Hugh began to fill in the missing pieces. "We weren't four feet from each other when you were hit in the head. I got to you as quick as I could. There was smoke and gunfire all around. You were covered in blood. You looked me right in the eye and said only one word before you passed out. I couldn't feel a pulse and believe me, I tried to find one. There were shells falling everywhere. Someone shouted that the Yankees were charging again. We were forced to fall back."

Hugh shook his head, the color drained from his face as he remembered the battle scene. More than a third of the Kentucky Brigade had been lost, many of them raw recruits baptized in fire and blood who still managed to rout the Yankees. Dru knew full well what Hugh must have witnessed on the battlefield, for he had seen the handiwork of bullets and lances on his patients in the makeshift infirmaries.

"You had to leave me, Hugh."

"I would never have left if I hadn't thought you were gone."

"I don't blame you. I would have done the same."

Hugh was staring at him intently. "Somehow, I don't think so. I believe you would have stayed."

"Believe what you want. It was war, Hugh. We did what we had to." Dru shook his head and looked at Hugh's sons. "I just hope to God they'll never see anything like it in their lifetimes." Then he looked at Hugh again. "When did you lose your leg?"

"A year later."

"It appears you're adjusting," Dru commented.

When Hugh smiled over at Anne, Dru suddenly felt more alone than ever. His friend seemed to have the perfect marriage, two strapping boys, a woman who had stood beside him throughout the war. Without Hugh having to say a word, Anne was ever at his side, refilling his coffee, adding just the right amount of milk, fetching a pillow for him to slip beneath his hip. She knew his needs and his wants and made certain they were met before Hugh even voiced them. Hugh let her know with every smile and gesture that he appreciated her knowing. Through silent communication, each reassured the other that their love had survived and would survive, no matter the obstacles.

Dru envied them their loving relationship.

"I'll be a good wife."

The echo of Sara's words rocked him to the core and

filled him with an aching desire as great as his need of her flesh. Once he wanted all that Hugh had found: family, security, children, a happy home.

"Dru, are you all right?" Hugh asked.

"Yeah, I'm all right."

The cook brought in breakfast. There was more food on the table than Dru had seen served in years, so much that it almost nauseated him, but his stomach quickly settled and he joined in the feast.

"What happened after Shiloh, Dru?"

"I woke up in a Yankee prison hospital with no recollection of who I was or where I was from. They knew I was a doctor by my coat and green sash and I still had my instrument case in my pocket which is engraved, 'From Your Uncle Nathaniel,' but without my name, they couldn't add me to the wounded rolls. I . . . I lay there without any memory for . . . months. Slowly, things began to come back to me, names and places, thoughts of home. I was put to work in the hospital at the prison. Gradually, it all came back. I knew who I was and where I wanted to be and tried to contact Sara and Lou."

He couldn't help but notice the look that passed between Hugh and Anne at the mention of Sara's name. Obviously they were well aware of his wife's escapades. Dru went on as if he hadn't noticed.

"My letters never got through." He set down his fork and stared at a pile of potatoes and eggs he suddenly couldn't finish. "It took me months to get back after the surrender. Train lines are still out, shipping virtually stalled. Bridges are down. I just got home yesterday."

Hugh and Anne listened in silence. The boys were finished and fidgeting in their seats so Anne excused them, suggesting they run outside and see the new puppies in the barn. When they were out of hearing, Anne sat back and folded her hands in her lap.

"We're sorry you had to come home to bad news," she said softly. Of all his friends' wives, Anne had been the only one who had acted halfway decent to Sara on their wedding day.

"Dammit, Dru. This is all my fault." Hugh tossed his napkin on the table and gripped the arms of his chair. "*I'm* the one who told Sara and Louzanna that you were dead." He shook his head over and over. "Sara was so upset that I found myself taking back every bad thing I'd thought about her when you married her so quickly. When I was wounded and came home and heard she'd run off with a Yankee, I was glad she had already disappeared. I don't know what I'd do if we ever came face-to-face."

"She's back," Dru said softly. "She came home the night before I arrived and Lou took her in."

Hugh rolled his eyes. "So she turned up like a bad penny."

"Is she all right?" Anne wanted to know.

Leave it to her to show compassion, Dru thought. It pained him to have to tell them the rest, but he had nowhere else to turn for advice.

"She's fine. She has a child, though. A little girl." When neither Anne nor Hugh responded, Dru answered the question they couldn't ask. "The child's not mine."

"Damn it to hell again," Hugh said. "What are you going to do?"

"Is there anything *we* can do?" Anne offered.

"Actually, I need legal advice more than anything." Dru finished the last of his coffee, thanked Anne, but declined the offer for more.

"I have plenty to do this morning, so I'll leave you two alone." She gathered up the coffee service and the children's plates and set them on the tray. Then she came around the table and gave Dru a hug. "I'm so glad you're back. Everything will work out for the best, Dru, just you wait and see."

After she discreetly left the room, Dru turned to Hugh. "You'd probably like to say I told you so."

Hugh shook his head. "Not when I feel so bad for you. I wish I could change things."

"Maybe you can."

"Are you considering divorce?"

Dru nodded. "I'll be truthful, the idea doesn't sit well with me, no matter what Sara's done. I took a vow. It's hard for me to think about going back on it."

"Do you still love her?"

"I can't bring myself to touch her. I can't even look at her child." Bleakness filled his heart. He hoped it didn't show.

"But you still want her."

"Of *course* I do." Dru pushed his chair back, stretched his legs, crossed them at the ankles. The heavy meal was settling, making him lethargic. "I'd be a fool to lie to you. You know firsthand what it's like to live every day thinking of a woman and not having her, knowing that coming back to her is all you're living for."

"Did she tell you where she's been all this time?"

"I didn't ask. I didn't want to know. She's pretty tight-lipped about it all, too. She said that was behind her now and she wants to start over."

Hugh appeared skeptical. "Did you mention divorce?"

Dru ran his hand through his hair and swore under his

breath. "Hell, I've never even met anyone who's been divorced. Sara's already the talk of the town."

"Divorce isn't as rare as you may think anymore. I heard from a judge in the next county that the number of divorce cases is considerable now compared to before the war. Seems the increase of hurried alliances before the fighting started has led to dissatisfaction of both wives and husbands now that the men have come home." Hugh leaned back in his chair. "You were only married a day. We could try getting an annulment."

To lose Sara, even now, to live life devoid of her, to cast her from his world would be as traumatic as an amputation.

"I can't think about it yet. I just need to know you'll be here for me if and when I decide."

"You know I will. But let me give you a piece of advice. Don't wait too long. You know how gangrene eats away at a wound? This will kill your spirit if you let it."

Dru pushed out of the chair and waited while Hugh stood and adjusted his crutches.

"I'm tougher than that," Dru reassured him. "I came back from the dead, remember?"

"That you did."

They walked to the front door, the silence between them broken only by the hollow sound of Hugh's crutches hitting the floor.

Dru picked up his hat, opened the door, and tried to convince himself he was ready to face going back home.

"One more question." Dru watched Hugh's expression closely.

"What's that?"

"You said that before I passed out on the battlefield, I said something. Do you remember what it was?"

Hugh took a deep breath and looked past Dru, gazing out at a field being plowed and readied for tobacco.

"Sara." Hugh let go of the word grudgingly, as if it pained him. "You said, 'Sara.' "

19

Dru couldn't decide if he felt better or worse after his visit to Hugh.

Unwanted envy was part of his dark mood as he found himself dwelling on the comfortable, loving relationship Hugh had with Anne, not to mention the open admiration Hugh's sons had for their father.

Passing along the outskirts of town, he had intended to go straight to Doc Porter's, but instead he turned down a side lane and circled around behind Ash Street, drawn by a sense of longing coupled with unease.

I'll just ride by. Make certain all's well.

At least that's what he told himself, until he saw Sara working in the backyard, dressed in his old baggy pants and shirt again, hoeing in the weed-infested garden plot. The neck of her shirt—his shirt—was open, revealing her lovely throat and far too much of the gentle swell of her breasts. Whenever she bent over to yank out another weed, her borrowed pants exposed the shape of her backside.

Not far from where she stood was a formidable pile of weeds, a sign she had been at the task for a while. Dru leaned forward on the pommel of the saddle, watched her strain until more weeds finally gave way. She stumbled back a step and caught herself just as she was about to topple over.

Half-hidden in the shadows of the barn, he watched while she straightened, tossed the weed on the pile, then planted her hands at the small of her back. When she arched and stretched, the shirt outlined her breasts and an intense wave of longing surged through him. He looked away. Once he thought he was under control, he turned around again. Sara was wiping her brow with the back of her arm.

Damn stubborn woman was going to kill herself.

Sara rolled her aching shoulders, stunned by the amount of time she had already spent hoeing and weeding that morning. As she gazed down at the cursed weeds that had taken over the garden patch, she didn't think she would ever finish, but although her back was aching and her palms were blistered, she relished being outside in the open air, letting the sun soak through the back of her shirt, filling her lungs with the scent of newly turned earth.

There was something tranquil in the strenuous chopping motion. Perhaps it was the repetitive rhythm, perhaps because her hands were occupied she didn't really have to think, just watch the earth crumble beneath her blows. Her shoes were muddy, the waistband of the trousers itchy against her skin, but inside she felt as peaceful as she had been yesterday when she was walking in the woods.

She straightened and waved over at Elizabeth, who was standing at the edge of a blanket on the ground in the shade of the back porch. Just now the child was clapping her hands in time to music only she could hear, and every now and again, laughing with glee.

Sara had tied her to the trunk of a maple sapling by a long rope that was also looped around her waist in the way her own mama had taught her to tie up the young'uns at home whenever she'd been left to mind them. Sometimes two or three of them would get all tangled up and she'd have to call one of the older boys to come and help her get them unknotted.

For the time being, Elizabeth was content.

Sara gave up pulling weeds and started hoeing ground she had already cleared, but soon stopped long enough to wipe a stinging, open blister on her palm on her shirttail. A sudden movement caught her eye.

She whirled around in the direction of the barn in time to see Dru nudge a chestnut horse to a walk and ride it to the barn door, where he dismounted and tied it to a hitching post near the trough.

Her breath caught as he started across the yard toward her. Behind her, Lissybeth chose that exact second to start squealing. Dru's brows slammed into a frown as his gaze shot over to Lissybeth. He stared at her without emotion for a moment before his eyes locked on Sara's again. She dropped her shirttail and straightened. The sharp, biting pain of the raw blisters on her palms reminded her that this was no dream, that Dru was alive and nothing was the same as before.

"You were out early," she commented, not knowing where else to start.

He nodded and glanced over at Elizabeth again, because by now the child was yelling, "Hey! Hey! Hey!" at the top of her lungs.

"I rode out to see Hugh."

"That's what Louzanna told me." Her heart was thundering in her ears now and with each beat Sara's mind chanted *divorce, divorce, divorce.* She forced herself to swallow and then asked, "How is he?"

"Doing quite well. He lost his left leg below the knee, but he seems to be adjusting."

"Well, then. That's something." When she noticed he was staring down the front of her shirt, her hand quickly flew to her throat.

"Button up your shirt, Sara." Dru turned abruptly away and looked down in the direction of the weed pile. Sara's face was burning with embarrassment, her fingers fumbling with the top two shirt buttons as she glanced at the house next door, surprised that Minnie Foster's face wasn't plastered against one of the windows.

When Dru finally turned around again, Sara knew she was still blushing, but the shirt was buttoned. She wiped the back of her arm across her forehead, found her skin damp with perspiration.

Relentlessly, Dru held her gaze without a word while behind them, Lissybeth continued to clap and squeal. Sara took a deep breath and asked, "Where did you get the horse?"

"Hired it. Let me see that blister." He held his hand out.

After a moment's hesitation, she placed her hand in his. He turned her hand over and gently inspected the blisters on her palm. They were broken open, raw, red, and edged with dirt. There were old calluses beneath them and she found herself wishing she had the soft, creamy hands of a lady and not a field hand.

He let go of her hand and shook his head. "Did you really think you could do this all by yourself? I see you haven't lost a notch of stubbornness, Sara."

"I know what I want and I work for it," she said softly, "if that's what you mean. I told Lou I would put in a garden for her and I intend to keep my word. Lou has a few melon seeds she saved from last year and I've got a lot of seeds from Granddaddy to start a healing garden, too."

Elizabeth started straining against the rope, lunging toward them, then flopping back onto the blanket like a rag doll. Dru threw her a glance over his shoulder.

"Maybe you'd better tend to her before she hurts something." He let go of Sara's hand.

"She'll settle down. Why don't you go on inside? I think a few of Lou's quilting friends might still be here. They'd probably like to welcome you home."

"The last thing I need is to be fawned over by a pack of talcum-scented, hankie-sniffing old ladies."

To keep herself from saying or doing something else that would irritate him, Sara picked up the hoe and started chopping ground, moving along the width of the patch.

Dru rocked back on his heels, then stepped out of the way. Thankfully, just as Sara had predicted, Elizabeth's hollering subsided to a few grunts. Plopped down on the blanket, the child was picking at the knot in the rope, smart enough to know that it held the key to her escape.

Sara wished Dru would leave and had made little progress for all the effort she was putting into her work. Suddenly she heard him curse under his breath and looked up to see him slip off his coat and toss it on the back stoop before he marched over to her again.

He held out his hand. "Give me the hoe."

"I don't need your help."

When Dru didn't move, Sara looked at his outstretched hand, then at the hoe, then handed it over.

Without a word, he stepped around her and angrily started taking out his frustration with every swing and pull. The ground was still moist from last night's rain, the job a bit easier than it might have been if the ground was rock hard. It was a backbreaking task, but in no time at all he had almost doubled the size of the hoed area. Not only that, but he had worked up a lather.

Sara grabbed up loose weeds and tossed them into the growing pile. The silence between them was deafening. "Would you like some water?"

"No, thanks."

He ignored her, set the hoe down, unbuttoned and stripped off his shirt, then started hoeing again.

He was whipcord-thin but muscular now, far more so than she would have guessed. Before the war his body hadn't been so finely hewn—not that he had been soft—but now he had the hard lines and definition of a man, not a boy.

Since he wasn't paying her any mind she continued to stare, enjoying the play of the sunlight over his skin, the way his muscles flexed and bunched as he tilled the soil. She had never once imagined him doing manual labor, but he didn't appear to be a stranger to it.

"Somebody might mistake you for a farmer," she said, thinking out loud.

He finally paused, wiped his forehead, and shrugged. "I had to dig plenty of latrines in prison camp before my memory came back and they put me to work in the hospital."

"You're getting all dirty."

"I had intended to go over to Doc Porter's for a while. Now I'll have to wash up and change first."

Sweat glistened across his wide shoulders. She admired his upper torso, the way the crisp dark hair across his chest tapered to a slender trail that disappeared into the waistband of his trousers.

She wanted so very badly to touch him. His dark-eyed stare always had a way of setting her on fire. Once they had declared their love for each other, he used to touch her as if she were a rare treasure, to look at her the way no one in the world ever had or ever would.

She would give up anything—anything but Elizabeth—to see that look in his eyes again.

Suddenly he raised his head and caught her watching him. His eyes were black as obsidian chips and far, far from cold, but they were guarded.

Something inexplicable had happened the first time he kissed her, something so powerful and unexpected that even though it had thrilled her, it had frightened her, too. Somehow she had known that from that moment on, Dru was the only man who would ever have that kind of power over her.

Now as they stood beneath the warm Kentucky sunshine, she ached for him to take her in his arms, longed to make things right. He was still the man she had fallen in love with at fifteen, the man she had married. The man she would love forever.

"Sara!"

The sound of his voice washed over her. She started, met his assessing stare again. Obviously he had already called her name more than once.

"What is it?"

"I said, she's crying." He nodded in Elizabeth's direction.

Lissybeth was rolling on the ground, letting out pitiful

moans, pulling on a lock of her hair with her finger as she scissored her legs back and forth.

"She's probably hungry. I should take her in."

Dru looked down at his muddy shoes and sighed. "It'll take me a while to clean up. I still need to go to Doc Porter's."

"Let me put Elizabeth down. I'll take care of that mud on your shoes," she offered.

His jaw tightened. "You're trying too hard, Sara. I don't need or want your help."

She refused to let him upset her. Anything worth wanting took time to get. "Granddaddy always says a bird flies better on two wings. You helped me out here, now I'm just trying to return the favor."

She turned away quickly before he could reply, and went straight over to Lissybeth to loosen the knot in the rope. As she straightened, Abel Foster came charging around the corner of the house.

Dru stopped what he was doing, tossed down the hoe, and hurried to stand beside Sara, his expression as forbidding as hellfire. Sara felt him tense when Abel halted a few feet away from them.

"What do you want, Foster?"

Florid color flooded Abel's sallow skin. His gaze shot over to Sara, then back to Dru.

"I thought you would want to be the first to know, seeing as how he left you a note."

Dru stepped closer and in a low, tight voice said, "Go inside, Sara."

Her arms tightened around Lissybeth. Dru's tone, far more than the scowl that Abel flashed, had her edging slowly toward the back door.

"Who? And what note?" Dru sounded foreboding. He

cast a glance her way and nodded for her to go in as she lingered on the back stoop.

Abel shoved his thumbs in his vest pockets and rolled back on his heels, appearing almost delighted with himself for knowing something Dru didn't.

"Doc Porter killed himself a few minutes ago and he left a note addressed to you."

20

LOUZANNA WALKED DOWNSTAIRS and found Sara in the kitchen wiping off Dru's muddy shoes with a damp rag. Elizabeth was sitting in the middle of the floor eating crackers with one hand and mashing them into the hardwood with the other.

"Where's Dru?" Lou watched as Sara hung Dru's shirt over the back of a chair.

"Outside washing up at the pump. Said he was too dirty to go upstairs."

Lou flew to the opposite side of the kitchen and picked up the kettle. "I'll heat some water. He might want a real bath."

Sara shook her head. "He has to leave again right away."

"He just got back." Something was wrong. Lou could see it in Sara's eyes and heard it in her hesitation to say more. "What's happening?"

"Doc Porter's dead. He killed himself."

Lou's hand crept to the chain around her neck. The kitchen started to tilt and then somehow Sara was beside her, holding on to her arm, steadying her.

"Oh, my. No," Lou whispered.

"Breathe, Louzanna. Think of something else," Sara urged. "Sit down until it passes."

Lou shook her head. She had to stay on her feet. Had to keep busy. "Maybe I should fix Dru something to eat."

"He has to meet the marshal and Abel over at Doc's. They're waiting for him."

Louzanna stared at the mess on the table, tried to make the world stop spinning. Fireworks were going off in her chest. All she could do was stand there and stare at a pile of dirty plates, silverware, and a pedestal cake plate holding half a cream tea cake—one of the best she had ever made.

Dirty cups and saucers sat beside a pile of crumpled linen napkins. Only five of the nine ladies of her quilting circle had shown up but it was more than she expected. Some were convinced that she only agreed to let Sara stay because she wasn't strong enough to turn her away. Some of them assured her that it would be for the best if she ran Sara off, but one or two had argued in Sara's defense.

She hated herself for her cowardice, wished she'd had the nerve to stand up to them the way she had Minnie, but after reading the editorial that morning, she had been so desperately thankful to have anyone show up at all that she could only sew and nod, sew and nod, silent, selfishly wanting her friends to stay.

"Lou?"

Sara's voice startled her and she realized that she was still frozen beside the table, clutching the ring. When she dropped her hands and looked up, Dru walked in the back door.

"Are you all right, Lou?" He shrugged on his shirt and buttoned it up.

Dear Dru. He had enough trouble without her falling apart again. She was quaking inside, but she didn't want him to know. "I'm fine."

"Are you sure?"

Lou discreetly nodded. Sara collected Dru's shoes and handed them over to him. With his shirttail still hanging, Dru pulled out a chair and sat down to put on his shoes. Sara eyed the crackers on the floor.

"I'll get the broom," she volunteered.

The minute she went to the pantry, Elizabeth climbed to her feet and started to toddle toward Dru. She picked up speed and threw herself at him, teetering for a second before she grabbed hold of his pant leg with her cracker-coated little hand.

Dru stared in silent shock, hesitant to touch Elizabeth even though she was smacking his thigh with one hand and clinging to his wool pant leg with the other.

When it became even more painfully obvious that he wanted nothing to do with the child, Lou beat back her hysteria, ran across the room, and pulled Elizabeth away.

"Come now, Lissybeth. You're going to get Dru dirty after he's just cleaned himself up." She kept her tone even, amazed at the strength she had mustered from some hidden reserve she didn't know she possessed.

Dru stood without a word, threw Elizabeth a dark glance, and began stuffing his shirttail into his pants. Lou turned around and discovered Sara watching the scene from the doorway. She glanced over at Dru and realized her brother knew that Sara was there, too.

Elizabeth started fussing in Lou's arms.

"Please don't leave the responsibility of that child to Lou. My sister's not up to it." He took his coat off of a hook by the door and shrugged into it.

Lou spoke up quickly. "I don't mind watching her, Dru. I really don't. I enjoy it." She touched the child's golden curls. Somehow having to think outside herself kept her sane. The same thing had happened while she was living alone without anyone there to help her. Forced to manage on her own, she had established a delicate independence, but now that Dru was home and Sara was, too, it was too easy to give her emotions full rein. Caring for Elizabeth helped her hang on to some control.

Sara was staring at Dru. "Can you really hate my daughter that much for something that I've done?" Her voice sounded as fragile as glass.

Lou's stomach knotted when she saw Sara set the broom aside and walk over to Dru. "Take your anger out on me all you want, but leave my child alone."

"That's exactly what I intend to do," he shot back.

Their voices were low, restrained yet foreboding. They exchanged heated stares that tempted Louzanna to flee the room, but Elizabeth was more than a handful, squirming and reaching out to Sara. Lou was afraid to move.

By the time Dru grabbed his hat and stalked out the back door, Louzanna was quaking all over. Sara quickly took Elizabeth from her, walked over to the kitchen cabinet, picked up a wet rag, and began swabbing the mushy cracker crumbs off Elizabeth's face and hands.

"I'm sorry, Louzanna," Sara said softly. "I know how much arguing upsets you."

With short, frenetic steps, Lou hurried to the conservatory, glanced outside, and watched Dru lead a horse away from the hitching post by the barn. She hurried back to the table, pulled out a chair, and sat down heavily, ignoring the dirty cups and tea plates.

"I've done something terrible, Sara." The admission slipped out before she could call it back.

Sara was still swabbing off Lissybeth. "I find that impossible to believe, Lou."

Despondent, Lou shook her head. "This morning when I came downstairs there was a newspaper on the table all folded up. Minnie used to leave them for me to read when she was through with them and I thought it might be a peace offering that Dru found on the back stoop on his way out. I could tell he hadn't had time to read it because it was perfectly creased and laid out all nice and neat."

Lou looked up and saw that Sara had finished mopping up Elizabeth and was giving her her full attention.

"I paged through and noticed that Abel had written an editorial calling on the townsfolk to turn their backs on us for . . . for taking you in."

Sara paled. She walked to the opposite side of the table and sat down heavily. "Where is it?"

"I threw it in the stove and burned it."

"Does Dru know?"

"No, and now I'm afraid he's walking into the lion's den unaware."

By the time Dru reached Doc Porter's, the undertaker's wagon was just pulling away from the house where a small crowd had gathered in the front yard. As soon as the onlookers recognized him, they parted to let him through. He tipped his hat and nodded to those he recognized and greeted most by name, but quickly realized that his cordiality was being met with stone-cold silence.

He made his way to the porch and into the house where Marshal Damon Monroe stood alongside Abel

Foster. The marshal saw him first and then Abel looked down his nose so far he almost fell over backward.

Dru nodded to each in turn, by now aware of which way the wind was blowing. He heard a woman wailing off in the kitchen at the back of the house. Goldie lay curled up on the rug, her muzzle on her front paws, her gaze flicking back and forth from man to man.

Word of Sara's return was obviously out, and though Dru had given as much or more to the Confederate effort as any man in town, he realized his wife's indiscretion would not be soon forgotten or forgiven.

He stared beyond the men, saw the blood-smeared wall behind Doc's chair and a shotgun on the floor beside it.

"When did it happen?"

"About an hour ago now." Marshal Monroe's main qualification for his job was his size. At six-foot four the man made a formidable peacekeeper in a town with very few problems. "The maid was coming up the walk when she heard the shot. I have the feeling Doc forgot it was her day to come to work. He wouldn't have wanted her to find him."

Dru agreed. It wasn't like Doc to be insensitive, no matter how desperate he was. Abel was watching Dru so closely that Dru wouldn't have been surprised if the man had tried to pin Doc's death on him.

"Abel said that Doc left me a note." Dru purposely avoided looking at the wall spattered with blood, bone, and gray matter—nothing he hadn't seen before, but under the circumstances, the sight turned his stomach.

The marshal picked up an envelope on the table beside the very chair where Doc had sat yesterday, calmly drinking tea. Dru's name was scrawled across the front. Obviously the two men were going nowhere until he read it, so he tore it open and quickly scanned the page, slowed by Doc's terrible handwriting.

Dru,

I've decided to take a different journey. Please don't grieve for me. I'm where I want to be now, with Esther, so I leave you the house, my horse and buggy, and what little cash I have in the bank. There's a place waiting for me in the cemetery beside my dear wife, which I look forward to a hell of a lot more than freezing my ass off roaming around Scotland alone.

If there is any money left after the burial, use it to order more medical supplies. Think of me when you deliver a newborn or drop a piece of hard candy into a child's hand.

All the best to you, Dru.

Your friend,

Maximus Porter, M.D.

When the words on the page blurred, Dru handed the letter back to Damon and headed over to where Goldie lay. Hunkering down, he rubbed the dog's ears and scratched beneath her chin. Once his eyes were dry, he stood up and walked back over to Marshal Monroe, who handed the letter back for him to keep.

"Not much to say to that, is there?" Damon asked.

Dru shook his head. How could he sum up Doc's life in a few words? He wasn't about to make excuses for what the man had done, either, not since he had learned that loving a woman too much might drive a man to do anything. Folding the letter, he carefully tucked it into his pocket.

Before Monroe bid them good-bye he took Dru aside.

"There been any more rocks come through your windows today?"

"No. Are you sure you don't have any idea who might have done it?"

Monroe shrugged. "Coulda been anyone. Probably just a prank."

"I get the feeling you don't care, Marshal. Is that any way to do your sworn duty?"

"Tell you what I'll do, Talbot. I'll ride by a couple of times a day if that'll make you happy."

"It's a start." Dru bid the man good-bye. He turned and found Abel lingering across the room.

"Shouldn't you be running back to the office?" Dru asked. "This will make big news, won't it, Abel? 'Lonely Old Man Blows His Brains Out.' You can write about all the blood and brains smeared on the wall and maybe sell a few more copies."

"The paper's selling just fine. Everyone's already talking about today's editorial."

"Good for you."

"Did you read the copy I left on your doorstep?"

"I don't have the time or the inclination to read your opinion on anything."

"Too bad. Maybe your sister read it. Or that pretty little *wife* of yours."

The way the man emphasized the word set Dru's teeth on edge. "What's it to us?"

"It's about you. Doc had a copy, in case you're interested. It's right there on the ottoman." He nodded at an overstuffed footstool with tattered corners and a sagging satin fringe.

"Get out, Abel."

"With pleasure." He sidestepped Dru, shoved the old

dog away from the front door with the toe of his boot, and walked out.

Dru stared at the newspaper folded on the ottoman and decided that he wasn't about to dance to Foster's tune that easily. He walked into the kitchen where a heavyset Negro maid was seated at the table sobbing her heart out. She had her head buried on her arms. She was a young woman who appeared to be in her late twenties.

He found a pitcher of water on the sideboard, wet a dish towel, and carried it to the table. Then he put his hand on her shoulder, gently forcing her to look up.

"What's your name?"

"M . . . Mercy."

"Mercy, put this on your eyes." He pulled out the chair next to hers. "Try to take long, slow breaths."

Mercy shuddered and her shoulders heaved. He caught a glimpse of the terror in her eyes before she covered them with the wet cloth.

"Is . . . is the body g . . . gone?" she mumbled.

"Doc's gone. You can go home as soon as you feel like it."

He thought she was going to bolt out the back door then and there, but she hiccuped down a sob, dropped the rag, and looked up at him forlornly.

"Does this mean I've lost my job?"

He shook his head, wondering how long he could afford to pay her wages.

"No. You can come in and clean the place for me every other week."

"I can?"

"Yes, you can."

"Do I have to clean up the . . . the wall?"

"I'll take care of that."

He wouldn't be seeing Maximus through his final years after all. The task was the least he could do for the man who'd given him his start.

"I'm Dr. Talbot."

"Thank you kindly." She pulled herself to her feet and walked to the back door. "Thank you, Doc."

Two hours later Dru rolled down his sleeves, the gruesome task behind him. The afternoon was waning, the sun close to the treetops, as he gave the rest of the drawing room a cursory glance and noticed the newspaper on the ottoman. Damning Abel Foster, he picked up the *Magnolia Creek Sentinel* and then started to lock the main house when he realized Goldie hadn't moved. She was still lying on the rug by the front door.

"Get up, old girl."

The dog's gaze rolled mournfully over to the two empty chairs, then back up at him.

"You're an old dog, you know. Not worth anything to anyone."

Doc had obviously found it easier to do himself in than put down his dog. Dru shook his head awhile, impatiently slapping the paper against his leg.

"Come on, Goldie. Come with me."

Goldie didn't budge.

"Come on, girl." Dru tapped the old dog gently on the haunches with the paper until she stood up. "Come on."

He located some bacon in the kitchen, fed it to the dog, and set a water bowl out in the back porch. Then he found his jacket, locked the door, and pocketed the key. He led Goldie through the house to the office, which was divided into three smaller rooms, and locked that door behind them as well.

The supply list was still in his coat pocket, but the day was gone. His shoulders and back ached from hoeing and washing down the wall. He felt as exhausted as Goldie looked. There was still enough sunlight to read by, so he decided to give in to his damned curiosity. Goldie followed him out of the office and onto the porch. When Dru sat on the top step and opened the paper, she stretched out beside him with a heavy sigh.

When he finished reading the editorial he lifted his head and stared off toward the sunlight that was sifting through the tops of the trees across the street. The content of the piece clearly explained the cool reception he'd gotten earlier.

Foster's goal of turning the town against him had been easy with Sara as the catalyst.

Dru rubbed the back of his neck with his hand, then laid his palm between the dog's ears and began to stroke her head.

He thought he had finally left the turmoil of the war behind him. On the journey home he'd even convinced himself into thinking that life would be easy once he got back. Instead he already felt as if he'd been rolling a deadweight up a mountain for two days.

The longer he pondered it, the more he became convinced that that deadweight was really his heart.

21

It had been a long week since Doc Porter's funeral and Sara still had a roof over her head, even though she had heard Dru telling Louzanna that he had read Abel's editorial.

Dru kept to himself, spending most of his time at his new office while Sara spent her days in the garden pulling weeds and her nights restlessly tossing and turning. Wishing there was something she could do to make everything right, she recalled that Granddaddy often said, "If wishes were horses, then beggars would ride."

After three days of warm, dry weather the seeds she had planted were in need of water, so she filled and toted the heavy bucket around the garden.

Her thoughts had been on Granddaddy Wilkes so strongly all morning long that she had half expected to look up and see him at the edge of the woods. Instead it was Dru who came walking up the path carrying a wooden crate so full of red geraniums that only his eyes and the top of his head showed above them. His dark eyes were looking directly at her.

She put down the bucket and hurried to meet him.

He set the crate down between them, straightened, and brushed his hands together. Inside of the crate, the root balls of each of four good-sized geranium plants lay wrapped in gunnysacks. There were onion sets and fancy seed packets for head cabbage, beets, radishes, collards, and tomatoes, even some sunflower seeds.

She went down on her knees beside the crate, picking up one lovely packet after the other. Each lithograph on the face of the seed papers was prettier than the last, each a true work of art. She'd never seen anything like them.

"Oh, Dru! These must have cost you dearly."

He shrugged. "I figured you'd need something to plant."

Mama always saved seeds from her crop of string beans, sweet peas, watermelon, cantaloupe, and pumpkin. Louzanna had saved a few also and carefully wrapped them in plain paper. Sara had never imagined anything so beautiful as the new D. M. Ferry seed packets with floral illustrations. Then she stopped to admire and gently finger the soft, furry leaves of the healthy geraniums.

"I overheard the farmer's wife who brought them into the store this morning say they were hardy and bound to bloom until late fall," Dru said.

Sara looked up and caught him frowning. "I'll plant them close to the house where Louzanna can enjoy them," she told him.

He glanced back at the house and then met her eyes. "I've got to get to the office."

Sara scrambled to her feet, brushed off her skirt. "I didn't know you were going over to Main Street."

"I'm not about to let Abel Foster intimidate me and I mean to show him. If folks want to thumb their noses at me, then let them do it to my face. I've made sure I took a walk down Main Street every day."

Her cheeks began to blaze. "I'm so sorry I brought this down on you, Dru."

"It still remains to be seen just how many folks will side with Foster." He turned and headed to where he'd left Doc's horse and the old buggy rig beside the barn. Sara watched him until he was headed down the back lane toward the street. Then she lifted two of the geranium plants out of the crate. As she stared down at the delicate petals of the vibrant red blossoms, she wondered if Dru would have bought the seeds and flowers if he knew that the simple offering meant more to her than gold.

She walked the plants over to where she thought she'd put them in the ground. The first whippoorwill of the season had already hollered, a sure sign that it was time to put in beans. She would plant them alongside the sunflower seeds so that the beans could vine around the sturdy stems, thus she wouldn't have to cut poles. The melons would go in a bit later in May, when Mama had always planted hers.

Thinking of Mama and home, she sighed. With the water bucket empty, she straightened and watched the woods for some sign of Granddaddy lingering amid the walnut and maples, but he wasn't there.

Suddenly, a tap on the windowpane in the conservatory drew her attention back to the house. Louzanna was there, waving her in.

"Dru forgot his supper," Louzanna called out, holding up a covered basket. "I'll watch Elizabeth if you'll take this over to him."

Sara walked inside and Lissybeth immediately ran across the room and threw her arms around her knees.

The way Dru treated Elizabeth as if she did not even exist bothered Sara more than his coldness toward her.

She deserved it. Elizabeth didn't. She thought that maybe if he spent some time with her he would see what a sweet, good-natured child Lissybeth was and might not be so hostile toward her.

"I'll take Lissybeth with me," Sara decided. "It's such a fine day and early yet. She's not likely to start fussing."

Louzanna nodded in agreement. "There's cheese and bread and some sliced chicken in the basket. Plenty for all of you to share."

"Oh, Lou. I doubt Dru will be in a mood to picnic with us."

"I can always hope, can't I? I want things to be so different." Lou sighed.

When Sara reached over and hugged her tight, she immediately sensed Louzanna's discomfort with the spontaneous gesture and quickly let go. Then she washed her hands and face and did the same for Elizabeth before she took up the basket and grabbed her daughter's hand. Lou trailed them to the front hall but hovered in the shadows far from the door.

"I've had a change of heart," Lou called out. "I'm not so certain you should go out."

"It's only two blocks, Lou. I won't hide and give folks that satisfaction. Neither will Dru."

"What about Elizabeth? Maybe you should leave her here with me."

It was a beautiful spring morning. Birds were singing and the buds on the trees were in bloom. Sara was sure nothing would happen to them on such a lovely day.

"Elizabeth will be just fine," she assured Lou.

Lou was clutching Mason's ring tight with both hands. "Go on now, if you're going, so you can get right back."

When Elizabeth waved bye-bye, Sara thought Lou was

going to rush them, slam the door, and lock them inside, but soon they were halfway down the block, walking hand in hand to Doc Porter's old house.

When they reached the neat white house, Sara led Lissybeth across the porch, admiring the new, hand-lettered sign that read, *Dru Talbot, M.D.* She set the basket on the porch beside her, smiled down at Lissybeth, and raised her hand to knock. Her heart was pounding, and her knees trembled in anticipation. She was completely unsure of how Dru might react to seeing her there.

Dru tossed a crumpled sheet of paper into the wastebasket and leaned back on the back two legs of a chair he'd drawn up to the big oak desk in Doc's office. He still wasn't used to calling the place his and hoped he didn't have to sell it off before he'd even treated one single patient here.

He'd had his shingle hung for almost a week and not once had anyone come by for help. Magnolia Creek was either the healthiest town in the nation or folks were getting doctored someplace else.

Everything in all three rooms was dusted, catalogued, and organized. In the examination room, vials were lined up on shelves, medicines carefully labeled and stored in the small drawers of the wooden cabinet beside the window. He had polished the brass and washed his instruments, laid them out and covered them with clean white towels.

Everything was set out in readiness for his first official patient, but the more time passed, the more he became convinced that Abel's damn editorial was bound to ruin him.

For now he was content to walk into town in the

morning and then spend the afternoon reading Doc's old medical journals. It was better than going home where Sara seemed to be everywhere. If he went after a drink of water, he would find her in the kitchen teaching Lou how to cook. In the evening before he retired, he would linger in the parlor until he was certain her bedroom door was shut for the night.

In the mornings she would come down for breakfast, looking as worn as he felt. He would spend the last few minutes before he left dwelling over his coffee, staring down into the cup, trying to avoid eye contact with her.

In all, it had been one hellish week since Doc Porter was laid in his grave. Something had to change soon or he would lose his mind.

When a knock sounded on the office door he nearly toppled over backward. He dropped the front chair legs to the floor, jumped up, and yanked on the hem of his vest. He shrugged into his coat and smoothed a hand over his hair, glanced into a small mirror in the waiting room and smiled at his reflection.

He threw the door open. His hopeful smile withered when he saw Sara standing there. When his gaze dropped to the child by her side, the remnants of that smile faded entirely away, although his pulse had certainly quickened.

"Sara."

"Are you busy?"

He shook his head, unable to say anything. His hungry gaze roved over her face and he silently cursed his weakness.

"Can we come in? Louzanna sent your supper over." She reached for the basket and held it up as if it were a pass into his office.

His inclination was to take the basket and turn her away without inviting her in, not because he didn't want her there, but because he suddenly realized how very much he did.

Before he could respond, the child spotted Goldie lying beside the desk and began desperately tugging on Sara's hand, yelling, "In! In!"

The old dog lifted her head but didn't move. Dru stepped aside as Elizabeth made a beeline toward Goldie, pulling Sara along behind her.

"Does she bite?" Sara asked as they flew past him.

"You'd know that better than I would."

"I meant the dog."

"I doubt she has the energy." This time he fought the urge to smile.

Sara pulled Elizabeth back and approached Goldie first, kneeling down beside her head, gently stroking the soft fur between her ears. She patted the spot beside her, and Elizabeth sat down, too.

"It's a dog. Can you say nice doggie?" Sara's warm voice was full of tenderness as she spoke softly to the child. "Pat the nice dog very gently."

When Elizabeth touched the dog's fur and laughed in delight, so did Sara. Their combined laughter was a melodious, joyful sound that cut deep as a saber slice, painfully reminding him of all that might have been.

He picked up the basket and tried to ignore them while he peeked beneath the checkered towel. Setting the basket aside, he leaned his hip against the corner of the examination table and crossed his arms. Sara was massaging Goldie behind the ears. If she noticed his annoyance, she ignored it.

The aged dog rested her head in Sara's lap and her tail

continued to thump the floor even though Elizabeth had decided to use her for a pillow.

"Sleep, Mama. Sleep, doggie." The little girl closed her eyes, but a smile spread over her face as she pretended to sleep on Goldie's ribs.

Goldie turned her head and licked Elizabeth on the face. The little girl squealed with delight. Sara laughed and even Dru found it hard not to smile at such an exhibition of pure joy.

How long had it been since he had laughed that way? Years, he decided on the spot. Definitely years.

As Sara and Elizabeth continued to shower Goldie with affection, he stared at the back of Sara's head, at the glossy mane of long auburn hair that she had somehow skillfully twisted into a thick bun at her nape. When she moved he caught glimpses of ivory skin beneath the collar of her dress. The sun had gilded her face, teasing out a sprinkling of freckles across her nose.

He shoved his hands in his pockets and stood up, walked to the window to watch a wagon roll by. There was a rustle of fabric and before he knew it, Sara was at his elbow.

"The place looks perfect," she told him. There was a tentative quality to her tone, as if she was almost afraid to speak to him. He knew that his sour demeanor made her nervous, but hell if he knew how to act any differently under the circumstances.

"Yeah. Perfectly empty."

"It looks like you have lots of supplies and instruments and whatnot," she said, misunderstanding.

He lifted his shoulders, shrugged slightly. "Everything but patients."

"Granddaddy always says, 'Sometimes we have to take a tater and wait.' "

When he turned, he found her far too close for comfort. Her bright eyes were intent, searching his for something that he hoped didn't show. "What the hell does that mean?"

"It means you've got to wait for things to cool down. You've got to wait for folks to come around, Dru. They're going to need a doctor sooner or later. You think a man is going to let his wife or child suffer when help is right down the road?"

"I don't know, Sara. I really don't know how far folks are willing to go to prove a point."

It was exactly what he had been asking himself daily. He knew for a fact that men often did stupid things on principle, even if the innocent suffered.

The golden freckles peppered across Sara's nose were so appealing that he was tempted to pull her closer for a better look. He turned away only to be treated to the sight of Elizabeth walking around the waiting room with her arm draped over Goldie. The dog's back was nearly as high as the little girl's head, but the child wasn't in the least intimidated as Goldie shuffled along beside her. It was the first time he'd seen Goldie actually move without prodding. Her tail was wagging double time as the duo made a lap around the examination table.

Behind him, Sara sighed. "Well, we'd best get back so Louzanna won't worry."

It suddenly dawned on him that Sara had taken somewhat of a risk coming here alone. As far as he knew, it was the first time she had ventured out of the yard since her return.

"I'll walk you back."

A smile may have flickered over her lips, but he couldn't be sure. She quickly shook her head no.

"Don't be silly. We're only two blocks away. 'Sides, you waited all this time for a patient to show up, you should be here in case someone does come around."

She rounded up Elizabeth before he could argue. The child cried and wanted down when she realized they were leaving Goldie behind. Goldie trotted to the door after them but Dru grabbed the scruff of her neck to keep her from following Sara out onto the porch.

Before Sara walked down the steps, she gave him a wistful smile and shook her head. "Don't worry, Dru. Someone will be along soon enough. Just wait and see." But the doubtful look in her eyes told him she didn't believe a word of it.

He lingered in the doorway with the dog panting beside him and watched her walk away with Elizabeth waving frantically over Sara's shoulder and hollering, "Doggie! My doggie!"

Dru was forced to pulled Goldie inside before closing the door. He looked down into her mournful brown eyes and muttered, "You traitor."

22

"SARA, WHY ARE you going out again so soon? And why are you wearing those clothes?"

Lou trailed Sara down the upstairs hall, afraid that the girl was leaving again. Sara was dressed in her black gown and gloves, carrying her veiled hat in one hand and Elizabeth in her arms as she headed toward the stairs.

"I have to do something to help Dru. I can't let him be ruined before he even gets started because of me. I'm going to get to the bottom of this and try to help and if I can't, then I'm just going to have to find another town where Elizabeth and I can live." Sara sounded mad enough to chew nails.

"You can't do this!" Lou cried. She couldn't decide whether to throw herself at Sara to stop her, or else go running to her room to lock herself in.

Sara handed Elizabeth over to Lou and then plopped the oversized hat on her head. She raised her arms and worked a long, lethal-looking hatpin into the black hat and veil, anchoring it to her hair.

"Don't try to stop me, Lou. I won't rest until I do something."

"Where are you going? What are you going to do?" Lou felt her control slowly ebbing away. She couldn't even give in to the urge to wring her hands, not with the child in her arms.

"First I'm going down to see Abel Foster at the paper to set him straight. Then I'm . . . well, I'll be back before dark." She picked up her skirt and started down the stairs.

"Where else are you going that you aren't telling me?"

"I don't want Dru to get the notion that I need his help. He might feel obligated to follow me."

"I won't tell him. I promise."

Sara waited at the bottom of the stairs until Lou was beside her. Before she knew it, they had reached the entry hall and Lou tried to stop her again.

"You can't leave me here alone like this with Elizabeth. What if I faint? What if I have to go to my room?"

She yelped when Sara suddenly grabbed her by the shoulders and looked her square in the eye.

"I wouldn't dare leave Lissybeth with you if I didn't think that you could take care of her alone. You just hold on, Louzanna. I'm doing this for Dru and you will just have to pull yourself together and help me."

Louzanna was certain a crippling bout of hysteria was descending upon her but then Sara kissed Elizabeth on the cheek and before Lou knew it, Sara was at the door with her hand on the doorknob. Lou froze and flinched when the door opened and her arms involuntarily tightened around Elizabeth to protect her from all the unseen dangers outside.

"Just play with her awhile and then put her down for a nap and before you know it, I'll be back."

The last Lou saw of Sara, she was tugging the dark veil into place.

"Crazy. Crazy. Crazy," Lou mumbled low.

"Doggie?" Elizabeth patted her cheek and blinked up at her.

"No. Not doggie." Lou had heard all about Elizabeth's first encounter with the dog at Dru's office. "Crazy. I'm afraid your poor mama is as crazy as I am."

Sara hurried along Main Street in her black widow's garb, but this time with a far more determined stride than the day she had come crawling back to Magnolia Creek. A few folks turned to stare as she passed by, but the veil did its job and hid her identity.

Near the dry goods store she heard a familiar voice and stopped when she recognized Elsie Jackman, whose husband, Keith, was an old friend of Dru's. The Jackmans had attended their wedding. Sara shored up her courage and slightly raised her veil.

"Elsie?"

Except for a face that was sharply thinner and a paisley gown that was worn and water-stained around the hem, Elsie had not changed much since Sara had last seen her. A delivery boy was trailing her, toting a wooden box filled with store-bought goods.

Elsie's cool assessing gaze dropped to Sara's worn shoes and traveled up to where her face showed beneath the hem of the veil.

"Elsie, it's me, Sara. How are you? How are Keith and your children?" Sara closed the distance between them.

With her dark eyes snapping, Elsie held up her hands as if to ward Sara off. She quickly glanced around, grabbed her skirt, and began backing away.

"Sara Collier, don't you ever, ever talk to me again."

That said, Elsie turned her back on Sara and walked away without a backward glance.

Sara dropped the veil and looked around. She didn't see anyone who might have noticed the brief exchange.

She picked up her pace and hurried on, shaken but not surprised at Elsie's reaction to her. She hoped no one had seen her, for she wanted to use the element of surprise when she paid her first call.

Halfway along the right side of Main Street, she stopped at a glass-fronted shop with a sign that matched the fancy lettering across the top of the *Magnolia Creek Sentinel*.

She leaned as close to the window as her hat would allow and shaded her eyes with a gloved hand. There was an outer office with a desk and a young boy seated there. She judged him to be around fourteen, too young yet to have outgrown his sharp-beaked nose and ears that stuck out like bees' wings.

Sara straightened her hat, and as she walked in a bell over the door signaled her entry. The boy looked up. There was a great racket going on inside the room beyond the outer office.

The young man jumped to his feet, trying to see through her veil. Suddenly important, he stuck out his chest and looped a finger through one suspender.

"Can I help you, ma'am? Here to put in an obituary notice?"

"What's your name?"

"Pete, ma'am."

"Is Mr. Foster in, Pete?" Sara reminded herself not to play her cards too soon.

"He's running the press today."

"I'd like to see him," she said over the noise. "It's of the utmost importance."

Interested now, Pete's eyes widened. "He don't like to be disturbed."

"He'll be even more upset if you *don't* go get him. I'm sure he'll want to see me."

The boy scratched his temple. "Who should I say wants to talk to him?"

"Tell him it's Sara Talbot."

Pete's brows shot up to his hairline and he was gone before she had a chance to take another breath. Pete quickly walked back out and started to say, "He'll be right here."

Before young Pete could finish, Abel walked out, wearing black sleeve protectors and a visor.

"What do you want?" A blush began to spread across his frowning face.

"Is that any way to greet a neighbor, Mr. Foster? I just came by to tell you I know the real reason you printed that story about me."

"So, you read it?"

She shook her head, raised her chin a notch. "Didn't have to." She wasn't about to tell him that it was all she could do to make out simple sentences. Lou had read all of Dru's letters to her and had helped her pen her own.

"You turned the whole town against Dru because of what I did that day I shoved you off of me in our yard and spurned your advances."

Sara didn't turn around and look at Pete but she would have bet a shiny new gold piece that he was listening to every last word.

"I think you'd better leave, Mrs. Talbot."

"Not before I've had my say." Sara pointed an accusatory finger at Abel. "I came to remind you of how you tried to kiss and fondle me out by the barn after word was first out that Dru had been killed. We weren't spitting distance from your house, either, Abel Foster. Now you're calling me a traitor and trying to cast blame on Dru for not throwing me out of his house when you're no better than me. You were married back then and you're still married now. I turned you down and I think that's what's really behind that evil story you printed about the Talbots. You just wished I'd taken up with *you* back then."

"I'll thank you to shut up."

"Why? What are you scared of, Abel? Are you afraid that Minnie will find out what you tried to do?"

"She'd never believe you."

"You don't think so? I'll bet talk would surely put some doubt in her mind, though, wouldn't it?"

"Get out," he ordered.

"I'll go, but remember one thing. You aren't playing with some weak-willed ninny, Mr. Foster. You're dealing with a Collier and we don't back down. If you don't do something to turn this situation around, then I may have to do a little writing of my own. There won't be anybody in this town who hasn't heard my side of the story by the time I'm through."

"Can you deny you had a child out of wedlock?"

"Can you deny you attacked me out by the barn?"

"You have no proof I ever did any such thing."

She leaned closer and looked him square in the eye. "Can you prove you *didn't*?"

Before he could say another word she spun around and nearly collided with Pete. The boy's face was flaming red between his freckled ears. She paused long enough to beg his sympathy with her eyes before she moved on, leaving a strained silence in her wake.

She crossed her fingers for luck and headed down Main Street toward the end of town where it crossed the road leading to Collier's Ferry. There were still as many folks out traveling as there had been when she arrived, so Sara kept to herself and rarely looked at anyone.

She had almost walked the three miles to the ferry landing when she saw a tall, thickset Negro man astride a spotted mare. Upon further inspection of his strong features and ready smile, she realized it was Jamie. He would have ridden right by her if she hadn't called his name. That turned a few heads, but no one paid any mind after he rode over to her, dismounted, and politely doffed his hat.

"Do I know you, ma'am?"

Knowing what his return would mean to Dru, she was so excited to see him that she could barely speak. "It's me, Jamie." She kept her voice low, afraid someone might recognize her, and if her daddy was working the ferry, he might get wind of it. "It's Sara."

"Miss Sara! What are you doin' way out here by yourself? You goin' home to see your kinfolk?"

"Something like that."

"How's Miss Louzanna?"

There was something in the way he said Lou's name, something in his soulful dark eyes, that made Sara wonder why she hadn't noticed before that this man's deep concern for Lou was beyond ordinary.

"She's fine. In fact, she's better than fine. Dru is *alive*, Jamie. Just like Lou always claimed. He just came home."

His smile widened and he slapped his hat against his leg. "You don't say!"

"I do. He'll be so glad to see you. We've all wondered how you were doing and where you were."

He shook his head, scanned the crowd, careful to keep his voice low.

"You won't believe the things I've seen and the places I've been, Miss Sara. I been as far north as New York City."

At one time she would have envied all he had seen, but that was before she realized that all she wanted was her old life in Magnolia Creek with Dru.

"Looks like you came home, too." He smiled down at her and went on. "I always hoped you would see yourself clear of . . . well, of things."

He volunteered to accompany her, but she insisted that she was fine. He persisted until she told a white lie and said that Dru knew where she was and that she would be back shortly.

She wasn't about to go into everything that had happened since she had seen him last, so she merely bid him good-bye and told him she would see him when she got home.

After he rode away, she walked on a bit farther, turned a bend in the road, and spied the ferry landing just ahead. Her throat tightened as soon as she saw Daddy working alongside her half brothers Donnie and Darrel. Between the three of them they could literally take her apart.

Fear nearly turned her around, but this was what she wanted. With all three men working the ferry, she stood a better chance of sneaking home to visit Granddaddy Wilkes and her mama and getting away safely again.

23

SHE PAID HER nickel fare to Donnie and walked aboard; when she passed her own daddy, he didn't even recognize her. Her heart almost stopped, for he'd seen her wearing the same dress and veil before, but the ensemble was nondescript and commonplace. She held her breath nearly all the way across the creek, making certain she was in the first wave of passengers to disembark.

Fairly flying up the road to the cabin, she caught a glimpse of Arlo and her two youngest sisters, Kittie and Fannie, as the trio disappeared down the Indian track through the woods. She watched them go with tears in her eyes, but for their sake, kept her presence unknown. She hurried to the door and softly knocked, lifting her veil by the time Mama answered.

Mama pressed her hand to her lips and shook her head in disbelief as tears began to fall. She was all limbs, long arms, and knobby elbows; she had thin hands and a swan's neck upon shoulders bent from years of toil. Mama was only forty-three but some days she walked like she was seventy.

Tessa Collier's life was an endless round of chores—toting water, kneading bread when there was money for fine wheat flour, and grinding corn for meal when there wasn't. She spun her own thread, wove her own cloth, and made clothes for all of them, cutting down old pieces that were salvageable to make them do for the younger children.

Daddy preached that Eve's sin had brought nothing but trials and tribulations down on women ever since the day she tempted Adam. Mama married Daddy when she was fourteen and took over raising Donnie and Darrel after the boys' own mama had died just three days before. Nine months to the day later, Mama started having babies of her own.

Sara let Mama pull her inside and enfold her in her arms.

"Sarie? Sarie, is it really you?"

Sara nodded and reached around to wipe away hot tears as Mama held her tight and rocked her back and forth. Then Mama held her at arm's length and reached out to trace the yellow bruise staining her cheek.

"Damn him," she whispered.

"It's nothin', Mama. It's almost healed."

"How are you, Sarie? Where did you go? I been near sick to death with worry. Granddaddy said you was living with the Talbot woman again. He came down with the rheumatism right after he saw you and wasn't able to get back to see how you're doing."

Sara realized why she had been thinking of him so much.

"I knew something was wrong. Is he bad off?"

"Not too bad. Let me take you out to him 'fore DeWitt comes home." She glanced out toward the woods where her younger brood was playing in the dirt. "Any of them young'uns see you?"

Sara shook her head. "I stayed hidden."

Granddaddy's lean-to out back had been enlarged so many times that it was nearly as big as the cabin itself. It hugged the wall of the main structure, invisible from the yard in front of the ramshackle cabin. The two sections sagged together like old crippled friends unable to stand without each other.

Granddaddy hung myriad herb and flower bundles from raw, open beams. Muslin bags filled with roots and powders, smoked ham and tobacco in every stage of preservation dangled overhead.

Sara found him alone, the way he was most comfortable. She walked over to the single bed complete with a bedstead that Granddaddy carved himself, just as he had all of the furniture in the main cabin—stools, tables, benches, and her parents' bed. In his younger days, Daniel Wilkes had been a wood-carver of some renown, but for the past few years all the woodworking he ever did was to whittle poppets for the children.

As soon as she stepped into the room, Granddaddy turned to face her from where he lay on a low, narrow bed.

"Hey, Sarie." He greeted her without a hint of surprise, as if he'd been expecting her.

Sara took off her hat and veil and set them aside. When he didn't unfurl his lanky frame to stand and hug her, Sara wanted to deny his age. She walked over to the bed and sat on the edge of the lumpy corn-husk mattress, crossed her ankles, and took his hand.

"Hey, Granddaddy. I hear you've got the rheumatism."

"A touch. There's rain comin' soon and that always sets it off."

"Have you tried a plaster of bruised mullen leaves?"

"I did," he nodded.

"What about carrying a raw potato in your pocket?"

"Got one."

She thought he might be smiling beneath his beard but she couldn't tell. "Blood of a black cat?"

"I'm waiting to see if it gets worse before I go that far."

They sat in silent communion listening to the sound of the slow-moving breeze as it rustled the treetops. The sun was dancing along the heavily budded branches.

Somewhere close by a cardinal chattered to its mate. Between Sara and Granddaddy Wilkes there was no need for words. They were that close and always had been.

"What can I get you, Granddaddy?" She scanned the ceiling above her head, trying to recall other rheumatism remedies.

"Nothing you can do for me 'cept turn back time. Even you can't do that, Sarie."

She held tight to his rough old hand. "Don't say that. There has to be something. Can I make you a poppet?" She glanced over to the long shelf where he kept his candles, earthenware bowls, and spools of thread and muslin—items he needed when he set a charm or went about a healing ritual.

One of the first things he taught her was how to make a poppet—not one of the wooden dolls that children played with, but a conjure bag filled with herbs and hair or fingernail clippings tied off to resemble a small human figure. Although he took far more stock in the old superstitions than she did, she would try anything to help him fight the pain in his joints.

"No poppet. No charms this time. I know it's 'cause of the rain. This'll pass. Just sit and talk with me a spell."

She told herself to believe he would be just fine and tried not to let doubt creep into her heart or mind, for disbelief had ruined more than one cure.

"Why do some cures take when others don't, Granddaddy?"

"Sometimes it only *appears* that cures and charms don't work whenever we don't get the outcome we're looking for." He spoke very softly, a sign that she was to listen closely. "We forget it's all up to the Almighty. You remember that above all, whenever you and your man set out to heal someone, you hear?"

She nodded and leaned closer as he began speaking again.

"When a body sets out to heal, he's nothing but a go-between, the channel between God and the poor soul in misery. You can treat a body, but God's got his own plan for a man's soul. If'n his plan and your wishes go together, then to all appearances, the healin' took. Sometimes, though, God says no. Simple as pie. That in itself *is* the healin'. It's God's will at work. You understand what I'm saying, Sara?"

She understood well and good, but she didn't want to believe that it might soon be his time to give in to God's plan. "I don't want to lose you now that I'm back," she told him, thinking out loud.

"You got a long road ahead of you, Sara darlin', and a lot of work yet to do. Hard times are coming, but you'll get through them. Don't ever forget that."

Like most backwoods folk, no matter that most of them had never set foot in a church in their lives, Granddaddy believed in the power of the Lord. He believed in a righteous spirit filled with goodness who wasn't afraid to strike men down with retribution for their sins. He was just as sure that the devil was out there, too, waiting to trip the unwary and lure them into sin.

He lived the words of the Bible and took literally the

sayings in a copy of the Good Book so old that it had come over from England with the first Wilkes to cross the ocean.

In the Kentucky hills, good and evil existed side by side. A body always had to be wary.

"You didn't just come all the way out here to see me, did you?"

"I need help, Granddaddy. The whole town's turned against Dru for taking me in. I came to see if there's some way I can help lift this trouble from his shoulders."

"That husband of yours got big enough shoulders to carry this load on his own."

"Still, I'm the cause of it and I want to help."

"When the time comes, you stand by him against the odds and he'll stand by you. Always do what you know to be right and folks will come around sooner or later."

"Dru will have to forgive me before he stands by me. I don't think he'll ever be able to do that."

"Have you told him *why* you did what you did?"

"I told him I was afraid I might go crazy like his sister. I admitted I was young and scared, too."

"What about the other man, Sara? Have you and Talbot talked about him?"

"No. I can't." She looked down, shook her head.

"A man's mind is a funny thing. Until he can see what he's fightin', then he won't know how to fight it. Tell him about the man you went away with, Sara. Wonderin' will just eat away at him until you do."

"He says he doesn't want to hear." Her hands were knotted in her lap, pale white against the dark fabric of the black gown. She swallowed bitter tears.

"Make him listen. Whatever he's got pictured in his mind is probably a hell of a lot worse than the truth."

"You think so?"

"I know so."

She let out a long, heartfelt sigh and pressed her cheek against his heart. His long beard covered his shirtfront, soft as silken threads. "I don't know if I can do it."

"You can do most anything because you're special, Sarie. God gave you something uncommon in that sharp mind of yours. Set things right with your man. Be his right hand in good times and bad and the Lord will take care of the rest. You're still the woman he fell in love with."

Braced by his assurance, Sara rose and shook out her skirt before she leaned over, took his hands, and held on tight.

"I promise that as soon as I can, I'll tell Dru everything and try to put his mind at rest. Someday I'll have the two things only he can give me."

"What's that, Sarie?"

"His forgiveness and his love." She smiled down at him, her heart lighter now that it was filled with new hope. "I'll sneak back over soon and maybe we'll go coon hunting again, all right, Granddaddy?" She squeezed his hands and he squeezed hers back. Donning her hat and veil once more, Sara paused at the door, smiling at the old man on the bed, wishing she could see him whenever she wanted.

"Thanks, Granddaddy."

When he nodded, his beard moved up and down along his shirtfront. "Be careful going back. Don't let your daddy catch you."

She sobered again. "I won't."

Sara opened the door. Outside, the tree shadows had begun to lengthen. Soon the hum of cicadas would begin and gradually mount to a grand chorus. In another month the night sounds would be deafening—summer fireflies would soon dance circles around the tree trunks and dart through the ferns, their iridescence tempting old hearts to grow young again, to cast aside the fetters of age and run barefoot through the woods trying to catch a glowing spark of night magic.

She longed to catch a handful of that magic for Dru.

24

LOUZANNA SAT IN the rocker in the upstairs guest room hugging Lissybeth tight long after the child had fallen peacefully asleep. The girl's plump cheek was so soft and comforting against her shoulder that Lou let herself pretend, just for a little while, that Elizabeth was her own. Lou closed her eyes and smiled as the warmth of the little body spread through her, giving her a sense of tranquillity she rarely knew.

She smoothed her hand over Lissybeth's shining curls. Wood on wood, the rocker creaked against the floor. She glanced over at the broken windowpane Sara had crudely mended. Dru had tried to order more glass, but was told that it was still hard to come by and that it would take weeks before a new pane arrived. Perhaps the shortage was caused by the war, or perhaps the local storekeeper was making life hard for them. Dru said they would never know for certain.

Lou stopped rocking when she thought she heard a knock at the back door. Her heart immediately started hammering in her ears. Her hands were shaking by the time she carefully lowered Elizabeth into the crib, then closed the door quietly behind her before she tiptoed from the room.

At the top of the landing, a stained-glass window in a dogwood pattern scattered pale ivory petals of light across the carpet runner. Lou paused, definitely hearing a knock this time, knowing that someone besides Sara or Dru was there because either of them would have walked right in.

She reached the kitchen, peered into the conservatory, and saw a tall Negro man standing outside with his hat in his hand. When he saw her, he waved and smiled.

"Jamie!" Lou took a deep breath and swung the door open, using it as a buffer between her and the yawning outdoors.

"Come in, Jamie! Come in." Once he was inside and the door was closed tight, without thinking of anything but how happy she was to see his familiar face, Lou threw her arms around him and squeezed him tight.

"Welcome home! Oh, dear heaven, if this hasn't been a month! Why, now *everyone* has come back home to roost. I can't believe my eyes! When those Yankees marched you off, I thought I'd seen the last of you, too, but now here you are big as life, standing right here in the kitchen again."

Her arms were still locked around his broad shoulders and she was patting him on the back when she suddenly realized what she was doing. Jamie had gone as still as deep water and was barely breathing.

Abruptly, Lou let go, shot back three steps, and pressed her hands to her flaming cheeks.

"I'm *so* sorry, Jamie. I . . . I don't know what came over me. I was just so . . . relieved to see you alive and well."

As he stood there speechless, Lou dropped her gaze and focused not on him but on the front of her skirt, arrested by a stubborn piece of lint. A stray lock of her hair had escaped a cluster of curls tied atop her crown with a long black ribbon. She blew it out of her eye.

Jamie appeared huge standing there in the middle of the kitchen and for the life of her, she didn't know why she had never noticed what a striking man he was before. She then decided that until this very moment she had never allowed herself to think of him as anything more than a servant and companion. Seeing him now, so solemn, so self-possessed, she could hardly believe that she had been so unaware of him.

In a fine wool tweed jacket, new black boots, and weathered pants, he not only looked healthier than ever, but there was a new air about him, a sense of pride that came without arrogance. He appeared confident and sure of himself, as if he knew who he was and where he was going.

She decided to break the silence herself, since he wasn't about to. "The most wonderful thing has happened. Dru's alive, just like I kept telling everyone. He's home."

"That's what I hear. I saw Miss Sara on the road."

"What? You saw Sara? Today?"

"She was headed out to the ferry crossin', goin' to see her kinfolk."

"I hope she knows what she's doing. I'm quite certain that last time she was there her father cuffed her." While speaking half to herself, Lou began to pace.

Jamie shifted uncomfortably. "I offered to go with her, but she wouldn't hear of it. Said Mr. Dru knew where she was goin' and that it was all right that she was alone."

"She wouldn't tell me what she was up to, just that she had to help Dru. Her coming home has . . . well, it's led to quite a predicament." As she quickly explained, she began to wring her hands until she finally grabbed hold of Mason's engagement ring and hung on.

"Miss Louzanna, you best calm down. Miss Sara looked like she knew just what she was doing."

"Yes. You're right, of course. There's no sense in worrying . . . yet." She stopped moving and tried to focus on more immediate needs. "I'm afraid your cabin hasn't been touched since you left. I'm sure it'll need a good cleaning, but you'll have it right as rain again in no time."

He looked down at his big hands. "I'm not stayin', Miss Louzanna."

It was a few seconds before what he said sank in. "You aren't staying?"

He shook his head. "No, ma'am. Not long. I'm makin' a new life for myself in New York. I just came back to see how you were gettin' along on your own. Now that I know Mr. Dru is back and that Miss Sara is home to help you, too, I don't expect I'll stay long at all."

"But . . . you came all this way. Why?" She hadn't thought to ever see him again and now that he was here, it deeply pained her to think he would be leaving soon.

"I came back to make sure you were all right, Miss Lou."

"Oh, Jamie." She turned away, hiding her overly warm cheeks as she busied herself with the kettle, overwhelmed to think he had traveled across the country to see how she was faring.

"You want me to do that, Miss Louzanna?"

"Do what?"

"Make some tea?"

She paused and turned around. He suddenly appeared ill at ease and she quickly realized why; for years, whenever the cook wasn't around, Jamie had served her in this kitchen. She had never so much as rinsed out a teacup for herself until the Yankees conscripted him.

It had taken her ages to learn to accomplish the kitchen chores on her own, and now it seemed important for her to prove that she could do this one thing for him. She smiled and shook her head, proud of her humble accomplishments.

"I guess everything's different now, isn't it?"

"Yes, ma'am. It sure is. I've been places that are a far cry from Kentucky, Miss Louzanna. I've seen cities where a man like me can find work and live a decent life and feel like a man without being beholden to anybody."

"What are you saying, Jamie? That you felt beholden to us?"

He nodded again. "Yes, ma'am. To tell the truth, I did. When Mr. Dru first set me free, I didn't have any notion how to live my life as a free man. I was afraid that if I left here I'd get picked up and sold off to somebody else, somebody not as fair as you folks. But the slave days are gone now and I know what freedom feels like. I'm afraid if I stay here I might forget everything I've seen and done and then settle back into the old ways. That's why I don't intend to stay."

"You're welcome to stay in your cabin as long as you like."

"Thank you, ma'am. For now I'll put my things out there and my horse in the barn. I used to have a few friends around town. I'd like to see what's become of them 'fore I leave."

She didn't know what else to say. For the first time in her life she realized that Jamie had a life of his own and that there was more to him than she had ever imagined.

Neither of them said a word, and an awkward silence

settled over the room until the kettle started boiling. Just then, the back door opened and Dru walked in looking as weary as the old golden-haired dog trailing behind him.

Dru took one look at the big man standing in the kitchen, crossed the room, and offered his hand in greeting.

"Welcome home, Jamie." After a pause, Jamie accepted and Dru pumped his hand with pleasure. "Welcome home."

"Thank you, Mr. Dru. It's been a long time."

"Too long. How are you?"

"Fine. Just fine. You look good."

"I can't complain. A few scars, but other than that, I'm all right." Neither man mentioned the war or the fact that fate had arranged for them to fight on opposite sides.

"Jamie's just here for a while." Lou went to the stove where the kettle was boiling.

Dru couldn't help but notice that his sister looked particularly nervous as she stopped to watch Goldie plop down not far from the stove. The house was unusually quiet, too. There was no sign of Sara or Elizabeth, none of the usual crumbs and toys scattered around the kitchen floor.

He'd expected to see her in the garden and when he hadn't, he'd experienced a surprisingly sharp stab of disappointment that he didn't want to admit.

"Where did you get that dog, Dru?" Louzanna asked.

He shrugged and looked down at Goldie. "She was Doc's."

Lou knelt down to pet the dog on the head. "So this is Goldie. I recall Esther talking about her." As she got to her feet again Lou said, "Well then, I guess she's ours now."

"Where's Sara?" Dru tried to sound nonchalant, as if he didn't really care as the ominous quiet unnerved him.

Louzanna appeared to be concentrating a bit too hard on pouring hot water into a chipped teapot and didn't answer. She reached for a third cup from the cupboard, then quickly began to open and close doors and drawers, growing more flustered with every passing moment until Jamie walked over, reached around her, and pulled a battered silver tea canister out from behind a tall white pottery pitcher.

"Thank you," she mumbled.

It suddenly dawned on Dru that Lou was avoiding his question, so he asked again. "Where *is* Sara?"

When Lou failed to respond, Dru impatiently turned to Jamie. "Do you know what's going on?"

"I saw Miss Sara on the road, headed down to the ferry."

Panic slammed into Dru hard. He wrapped his hand around the top rung of the chair and pinned his sister with a stare. "Louzanna, please turn around."

When Lou finally turned, all color had drained from her face. "I warned her not to go," she whispered, shaking her head.

Dru needed to pull out the chair and sit down, but his arms and legs had turned to molasses and he couldn't move a hair. Louzanna was talking, but his mind had already spiraled down another road.

She's gone again. Walked out and left you.

She gave you a chance but you didn't even give her an inkling of hope.

He shut off his own thoughts, forced himself to listen to what his sister was saying.

". . . don't know what she was planning, but she said

she had to do something to help the situation . . . since it was all her fault." Lou was trembling, waiting for him to say or do something.

"*What* was all her fault?"

"Abel's editorial. The way folks have turned against you. I told her not to go, but she had her mind set on it. She *promised* she would be home before dark."

He dragged his hand through his hair. His heart settled into place and his blood started to flow again. "She didn't move out?"

Louzanna shook her head. "Heavens, no. Whatever gave you that idea? Besides, Elizabeth is upstairs sound asleep. Sara would never leave her behind."

So Sara hadn't left again, but was off on some crazy notion of helping turn the tide of public opinion. Just how, he couldn't fathom to guess, but knowing Sara, she would go about it with all the stubborn zeal of a crusader and no thought to the consequences.

"Why was she going to the ferry?" Dru wondered aloud.

"Said she was going to see her family," Jamie told him.

Louzanna spoke on the tail end of Jamie's declaration. "The last time she was there, her father hit her."

Dru let go of the chair, headed for the door. He scooped his hat off the rack as he walked by. He had convinced himself that her former lover had hit her, but if it had been her father, and she was on her way back to Collier's Ferry, then she was putting herself in danger again.

"You know that he did it for certain?"

Lou nodded. "She never said as much, but the day she returned and asked me to take her in, she had that horrible red welt on the side of her cheek. It looked fresh to me and though she didn't admit it, I was fairly sure her father had hit her because she had just come from seeing him."

Dru grabbed the rifle out of the corner and headed toward the door. Goldie lifted her head but didn't budge from the warmth of the stove.

"Where are you going?" Lou raced across the room and grabbed his arm, staring in horror at the weapon in his hand. "Dru, please stay here. She'll come back. She promised. She'll be fine."

"Let go, Louzanna."

Her bottom lip began to tremble but she hung on tight.

Dru lowered his voice, softened his tone. "Please, Lou."

Her hand slipped away from his coat sleeve. Jamie stepped up beside her, took her by the elbow, and nodded to Dru.

"Miss Louzanna, come sit down and I'll bring you some tea. Mr. Dru came back from the war in one piece. He's not gonna let any Collier bring him down."

25

Instead of cooling, the air grew warmer and more humid as the sunlight faded. Dru followed the main road toward the ferry, scanning the faces of the folks passing by. If Sara intended to be home by sundown, then she had to be traveling among them already, for twilight was gathering.

A farmer with a wagonload of children drove by, nodded, and tipped a frayed hat in greeting. Dru stopped him and asked if he'd seen a woman alone, dressed all in black, but the man was no help. Dru continued on toward the end of the road, stopping strangers now and again to describe Sara and ask if they'd seen her, but apparently no one had. Lou's words came back to haunt him.

"She had to do something . . . since it was all her fault."

He stopped to lift his hat and wipe his brow as he rounded the last bend. Flickering torches lined the ferry landing, giving an eerie glow to the gathering gloaming. The empty raft was halfway across Magnolia Creek, headed back to his side.

Where in the hell are you, Sara?

What made you think you need to fight my battle for me?

Since it was nearly dark, he reckoned this was the last load of the day. Riding up to the landing, he noticed there were only four people left waiting to cross over to the Collier side. A young man wearing the remnants of a Confederate uniform stood with a woman and two little children, a boy and a girl, huddled against him. Dru nodded to them and dismounted.

When the ferry touched the bank and the passengers disembarked, Dru waited until the soldier and his family boarded before he spoke to the burly young man taking fares who announced that this was indeed the last trip of the day. As far as Dru could tell by torchlight, the raft operator appeared to be in his late twenties. His clothes were a mismatched combination of baggy wool and homespun, his heavy jowls peppered with dark stubble. A full moustache hid his upper lip.

"Are you a Collier?" Dru asked.

"Who wants to know?" The man scratched behind his ear as if he actually had to contemplate a spell before he answered.

"I'm Dru Talbot. I'm looking for Sara, my wife."

The ferryman turned and hollered, "Pa!"

An older version of the heavyset young man quickly came lumbering across the raft moving with surprising speed for a man his size. He was also a good head shorter than Dru, but had formidable muscles and girth. The idea that this man might have taken a hand to Sara set Dru's teeth on edge. He tried to harness his anger.

"This is Talbot," the younger one informed his father. "The one who married Sara."

The older man swung his gaze back around and his eyes narrowed. He craned his thick neck to look into Dru's face.

"I'm DeWitt Collier. What the hell you want, Talbot?"

"I'm looking for Sara. Have you seen her?"

DeWitt dipped his right shoulder and spit a stream of cloudy saliva before he slapped at a mosquito on his forearm.

"Yeah. I ran her off a good two weeks ago. She won't be showin' her face around here anytime soon." He rocked back on his heels and scratched at a bug bite on his arm. "Heard you died." Again he scratched himself, this time on his grimy neck beneath his ear. "I hope you had the good sense to throw her out, too."

"Have you seen her today, or not?"

"Hell no." DeWitt turned surly, spit again, and looked at his son. "You seen her, Darrel?"

"Nah."

Dru had no idea whether or not to believe either of them. If he took the last ferry over to their side he wouldn't be able to get back home without going miles and miles around to another crossing. The air was still and heavy with pending rain, thick with mosquitoes and the acrid smell of the pitch-coated torches as they burned.

"We're pullin' out," DeWitt told him. "You comin' aboard, or not?"

Dru's horse started backing away from the ferry. The reins tugged in his hand. He gazed across the dark, fast-moving water of Magnolia Creek. Sara had promised Louzanna she would be home by now. She had left her child behind and nothing short of a disaster would keep her from going back to the house.

Instantly, he made a decision to turn back and look for her on the road instead of crossing, but he couldn't bring himself to leave before getting the truth out of Collier.

"Did you hit my wife when she came to you for help,

Mr. Collier?" The minute he referred to Sara as his wife again without thinking, the word hit him with a jolt.

DeWitt Collier's mouth curled into a parody of a smile that narrowed his piggy eyes. In the flickering torchlight, his face became a grotesque mask.

"Hell yes, I hit her. She had it comin'. She—"

Dru's fist connected with DeWitt Collier's jaw with a satisfying sound. The man stumbled back, his arms flailing like a jerking windmill, his legs wobbling like two busted springs before he hit the raft with a hollow thud.

Darrel charged forward, took one look at Dru's face, and backed off. His head sawed back and forth from his father's prone body to Dru and he looked as if he couldn't believe his father was really down and out.

Dru stared Darrel down. "If anything happens to Sara, I'm holding your whole family responsible."

He issued his parting shot, and swung up into the saddle. All the way back he tried to assure himself that by now Sara was probably safe and sound at home.

Sara let the forest close protectively around her as she took the shortcut through the woods that led to the back of town, the one Granddaddy had used when he had come to see her. Lost in thought, she folded back her veil and picked her way along the narrow trail. She worried over Granddaddy's health and also thought of Abel Foster and the way she had threatened him. As she carefully walked along the overgrown path, she smiled and recalled the flustered look on Abel's face when she left his office.

She meant what she'd told him; she wouldn't hesitate to tell Minnie what he had done to her if he didn't do something to help turn the tide in Dru's favor.

The drone of a pesky mosquito near her ear was so irritating, she started fanning it away when suddenly the toe of her shoe caught beneath an exposed hickory root. She lost her balance and fell hard to her knees, scraping her hands on the rocky ground. Wincing, she sucked at a cut on her palm and when she finally rose to her feet, her legs were trembling. As she tried to brush off her skirt and was straightening her hat, she heard something scraping along behind her.

Whirling as fast as she could, hampered by her full skirt and petticoat, she let go a sigh of relief when she made out the silhouette of a huge raccoon lumbering along a tree limb.

She felt around the forest floor until she found a sturdy stick about four feet long and picked it up. Heading on, it seemed like forever before she eventually caught the glimmer of lights through the trees.

It wasn't long until she reached the edge of woods bordering the yards behind Ash Street. Finally she breathed a sigh of relief when she saw the welcoming light from the Talbots' house blazing through the windows of Louzanna's conservatory.

Sara stepped out of the woods and was about to round the corner of the barn when out of nowhere a dark figure rushed her. Without thinking she raised the walking stick, swung hard. There was a dull thud and shock reverberated up her arm. She heard a muffled groan. She started to run, lost her hat, and got tangled in her skirt. Before she had gone three strides, something struck her on the side of the head. She staggered back and almost fell; in that same instant, searing pain tore through her shoulder. Yet another blow sent her reeling into the side of the barn where she hit the wall so hard that her head whipped back and smacked against it with a hollow thud.

Stars whirled before her eyes as she slid down the rough planks of the outer wall. Two images came to her through the fog gathering in her mind. The first was that of Elizabeth's smiling face. The second was Dru's.

26

DRU GAVE UP trying not to pace. Again and again he strode from the kitchen through the house and on out to the front porch where he had stationed Jamie to watch for Sara. A moderate, steady rain was finally falling, but it did nothing to relieve the heat.

Dru checked his pocket watch on his umpteenth return to the kitchen—a room in chaos.

Lou was at the stove crying silently, tears streaming down her face as she hovered over two of three pots that were bubbling away. In one, potatoes boiled so hard that froth was weeping over the edge. In another, turnips had been transformed to a watery mush. In the third, the water had boiled away, leaving an exposed chicken stuck on the bottom of the pan like a pale oasis in a ring of charred carrots.

Sara's child was tumbling around on the floor, chasing Goldie back and forth beneath the table. Just as Dru turned to walk out of the room again, the little girl ran into the edge of the table, smacked her forehead, and started screaming.

Goldie started licking Elizabeth, but the little girl continued to howl. Louzanna buried her face in a dish towel.

Dru uttered the crudest of obscenities and his sister heard it.

"Dru Talbot! Not in this house!" she wailed.

He shrugged. At least the curse had gotten her to take the damn dish towel off her face.

The toddler was still bellowing so hard that he finally bent over and looked under the table to make certain that she wasn't bleeding to death. Lou was incapable of helping at the moment, and Goldie's ministrations certainly weren't working. He gave up and picked up Elizabeth himself.

The minute he touched her, she started kicking furiously, a whirlwind of hard shoes and petticoat ruffles. She howled at the top of her lungs, which set Goldie off, too. Jamie appeared in the kitchen doorway, took one look, shook his head, and quickly disappeared again.

Dru pulled out a kitchen chair and sat down, determined to calm Elizabeth. He held her gently but firmly and kept repeating, "Hush, now. You're all right."

Slowly she simmered down to a whimper and an occasional dramatic sob. The crying bout exhausted, she laid her head back against his arm, sniffling and tapping one foot up and down as she stared at him. Dru stared back into eyes the same intense color as Sara's. He gingerly brushed aside the curls matted against her forehead and examined a small goose egg.

"Mama?" She reached for his mouth. He stiffened until he realized she only wanted to touch his lips with her fingertips, so he let her. She seemed to fit perfectly in the crook of his arm, quiet and content even though he had rarely paid any attention to her.

Satisfied with her inspection of his mouth, she sighed,

tapped her foot up and down some more, then looked over at Louzanna. "Mama?"

Lou covered her face with the towel again, her shoulders heaving with silent sobs.

"Mama's coming," Dru whispered to the child. "In just a minute, Mama will be home."

"I can't do this!" Lou stared wildly about the kitchen. "Something's happened. I *feel* it. I have to go upstairs!"

Dru was about to tell her to take Elizabeth along, hoping a dose of responsibility would help calm his sister, but just then something hit the back door with a loud, dense thud. He shot off the chair, handing the child to Lou as he ran past. When he whipped the door open, not only did the rain sift in, but Sara's limp form fell over the threshold.

Clothed in ebony, she lay like a broken shadow draped half in and half out. The shoulder of her gown was ripped from the neck to the seam of the sleeve. Blood pooled on the floor beneath her.

"Is she dead?" Lou screamed.

"Jesus Christ!" he whispered. His heart was pounding in his throat; his hands had gone ice cold. Seeing her lying there like a broken, discarded memory, he experienced a new kind of panic that had never once, even through all the war years, hit him so hard.

He gathered Sara in his arms, unmindful of her wet hair and clothes. Her shoes and the lower half of her gown were coated with mud, twigs, and leaves, but it was the sight of crushed red geranium blossoms clinging to her skirt that nearly undid him.

He scooped her up and rushed into the kitchen, forgetting that Lou stood not two feet away with Elizabeth in her arms. His sister took one look at Sara's battered, bleeding form, went blank, and started moaning. Her eyes were rolling up in her head just as Jamie cleared the kitchen door. He grabbed Elizabeth in one arm and caught Lou on her way down with the other.

"I can manage," Jamie called out as he lowered Louzanna to the floor. Elizabeth cried, "Mama!" and clapped her hands. Dru ignored them all and raced out of the room.

Even soaking wet, Sara weighed next to nothing. He took the stairs two at a time and pounded down the hall to her room. Her door was ajar so he kicked it all the way open. Lou had already lit the lamp on the bedstead. He threw back a pink patchwork quilt and sheet and laid her down, staining Lou's fine linens with blood and mud.

Over and over he cursed DeWitt Collier as his fingers fumbled with the row of buttons down the front of Sara's dress. Finally, too frustrated to fit the fabric-covered knobs through the wet loops, he tore the front of her gown open, then widened the rip along her shoulder seam, exposing the wound.

Someone had sliced into her shoulder, narrowly missing her jugular. Her temple was so swollen she had to have been hit on the side of the head as well. There was a bruise across her shoulder blades and a good-sized lump on the back of her head.

Her hands were caked with dirt, the front of her gown so soiled with mud it appeared she had dragged herself to the back door.

He looked down into her still, perfect features, praying she would suddenly awaken and smile at him. He would assure her that everything would be fine. He would tell her that he would try harder to forget what she'd done. The moment he had seen her lying all battered and broken on the doorstep, he wished the last two weeks had been a bad dream.

He chafed her cold hands. "Open your eyes, Sara."

But she didn't open her eyes. She needed more than his words right now if she was going to pull through. She needed his expertise and for him to act like a doctor and not a man terrified of losing what he had once held most dear in all the world.

Instinct and experience immediately took over. Raw emotion shut down and he began to do what had to be done. He gathered towels from the washstand, pressed one to the slash across her shoulder, and held it tight until the bleeding slowed. When it looked to be under control, he stripped her of her wet clothes. Her skin was pale and cold beneath the fabric, so he bathed her with a washcloth. By the time he was finished, his hands were shaking as he gently drew the covers to her shoulder.

There was commotion in the hall—the sound of Louzanna's hysterical moans, the child babbling, Goldie panting heavily as she padded up and down the long passageway. Dru ignored it all and soon things quieted down. When he finally looked up, Jamie was standing in the doorway watching him.

"I got Miss Louzanna to her room and locked the baby and the dog in there with her. What can I do to help you?" Concern was written all over Jamie's face.

"My medical bag is in the drawing room beside the double doors. Bring it up along with some whiskey and glasses and more clean towels."

Dru washed the wound. When Jamie walked back into the room with his arms full, Dru asked him to stay. The medical bag held not only bandages, needles, and thread, but a chloroform inhaler and bottle of chloroform.

Quickly he explained how Jamie should hold the inhaler and how to align the nose pieces beneath Sara's nostrils and carefully drip chloroform into the small sieve on top of the tiny rectangular device.

Jamie remained steady and sure while Dru closed the edges of the wound, trying to make the tiniest, most precise stitches he had ever made so that Sara's scar would be minimal. As he worked he spoke quietly to Jamie to keep his own mind off of the fact that this was Sara, torn, bruised, and bleeding, lying beneath his hands.

He gently pulled dark thread through the edges of the wound and gradually closed it as she slept peacefully. Chloroform had been in short supply in the South and the small inhaler invented by a Confederate surgeon allowed doctors to use it more sparingly than dripping the liquid on a sponge.

Finally finished, he tied off the knot as he bandaged Sara's shoulder, reminding himself that the worst wasn't over yet. After any surgery, no matter how extensive or minor, lockjaw, putrefaction, even gangrene could set in. He had lost as many soldiers to the aftereffects as to the wounds themselves.

It wasn't until he pulled the sheet up over Sara's bare shoulders that his hands started shaking so hard he was forced to clasp them together between his knees. He leaned forward, elbows on his thighs, and hung his head.

"We gonna give her the whiskey?" Jamie piled bloody towels near the basin of red-stained water.

Whiskey kept a patient from slipping into shock, but Sara was already unconscious. Dru lifted his head and wondered when the ringing in his ears would stop.

"I think maybe I need it more than she does right now. Will you join me?"

Dru poured a healthy shot into each tumbler that Jamie had brought upstairs. They downed the whiskey, then he sent Jamie to see what was going on in Lou's room.

When Jamie walked out, Sara's eyes were still closed. She was so pale, the fine network of veins on the backs of her eyelids appeared thin as indigo thread. He reached out and smoothed the back of his hand along her cheek, traced her thick lashes with his fingertip.

He carried the rocker over to the bedside, sat down, picked up her hand and covered it with his own, and then he did something he had felt like doing since he had walked through the back door and found out what Sara had done.

He pressed his forehead to the back of her hand, and wept.

27

ONCE DRU PULLED himself together, he walked down the hall to see how Louzanna fared. When he opened the door to his sister's room, he nearly tripped over Elizabeth, who was sound asleep on the floor with one arm draped around Goldie. Tear streaks were dried on her cheeks. The dog opened one eye, looked up at him, then went back to sleep.

The room was overly warm but Lou was in the high tester bed buried beneath a mound of quilts. He heard her muttering over and over, "Just like Mason. Just like Mason."

With his hands anchored at his waist, he stared down at his sister and for the first time in all the years she had suffered hysteria, he lost patience and wanted to shake her. Instead, he calmed himself and reached for her wrist. Her pulse was rapid but strong.

"Lou, let me help you sit up."

The air in the room was so close it was stifling. Dru leaned over her and forced her to sit against the pillows. Once she was settled, he sat down beside her.

"Lou, Sara is going to be fine." Even as he said it, he wished he sounded more reassuring. He had no idea whether Sara's wound would fester. Any one of a number of things could still go wrong, but at this point he was hopeful.

Lou blinked and stared up at him as if she had no idea who he was or what he was saying.

He leaned close. "Louzanna, it's me. Dru."

"I know that," she said weakly. "You're lying to me, aren't you? Sara's dead, isn't she?"

"No. She's going to be fine."

She covered her face with her hands. "But . . . so much blood."

"I have her all bandaged up and she looks good as new." He pictured Sara lying down the hall as pale as the sheets, a sleeping beauty with her hair spread over her pillow like auburn silk.

For the first time in his life he understood how fear could work its wiles on Louzanna. He realized how easily it could settle in and eat away at a person's mind. He had a taste of it himself when he opened the back door and saw Sara lying there.

His sister's head lolled back on the pillow. She stared at the ceiling with haunted eyes.

"Lou, you never once gave up on me, did you? If you could believe I was alive all those years, then you have to believe that Sara will be just fine."

"I don't know . . . so much blood." She shook her head, her eyes wild and uncertain.

"Lou, it's too hot in here. Why don't I open a window and take some of these covers off of you?"

"No!" She clutched at the pile of quilts, preferring to roast herself alive.

He watched her for a moment longer and then said, "I'll be right back."

As he left the room, he heard her whimper pitifully. Soon he returned with a tumbler half full of amber liquid and said, "I brought you some new medicine."

She raised her head, eyeing the glass suspiciously. "What is it?"

"It's called tincture of zegonia. It'll settle your nerves and help you sleep."

"I've never heard of it."

"It's an old war curative."

She took the glass, sniffed at it, and wrinkled her nose. "It smells awful."

"Drink it down." He put his hand beneath the glass, helped her tip it up.

She sputtered and coughed on the first sip and then slowly drained it all. "It must work. It tastes awful."

He smiled, remembering. There wasn't a soldier among the wounded who wasn't convinced that medicine had to taste terrible in order for it to work. "You'll be much better come morning."

"It feels like it's going all through me."

"That's good."

"Are you certain one dose is enough?"

"For now." He bit the inside of his cheek, trying not to smile. His sister had just downed a half glass of whiskey and was asking for more. "That elixir has already put the roses back in your cheeks."

"Thank you, Dru."

"Sleep well, Louzanna."

He realized that he couldn't leave Elizabeth sleeping on the floor with the dog all night long, so he hunkered down on his haunches and stared at the little girl who was snoring softly with her cheek pressed against the oak planks. She was sweating from the heat in the room.

Gently, so as not to awaken her, Dru picked her up. The minute he put her head on his shoulder, she reared back and stared at him.

"Mama?" She gently tapped his cheek with her palm.

"Mama's all right," he whispered. "Mama's asleep."

"Mama's asleep." She nodded sagely. "See, Mama?"

He carried her into the hall and waited for Goldie to shuffle after them before he closed Louzanna's door. He shifted Elizabeth higher on his shoulder. Her eyes were huge, round, and very serious.

"You can see your mama, but you have to be very, very quiet." He pressed his finger to his lips and said, "Shh. Quiet."

She pressed her tiny finger to her pouting lips and imitated him. "Shh."

"That's right. No talking. Mama's asleep."

As he walked into Sara's room with Elizabeth riding on his shoulder and her arm draped around his neck, he wondered what kind of man could turn his back on such a lovely child. How could anyone have walked away from Elizabeth? Or Sara, for that matter?

He sat down in the rocking chair beside the bed with Elizabeth in his lap. Goldie stretched out beside them with a soft snort.

"Mama sleep," Elizabeth whispered, the sound no louder than angel's wings.

"That's right," he whispered back. "Mama's asleep." He leaned back, pressed Elizabeth's head against his shoulder, and gently began to rock the old chair.

Sara was lost in a thick fog before she was able to see clearly again. Relief washed over her when she recognized the rose and ivy wallpaper in the guest room and tried to lift her head. The minute she did, she saw stars. It took a while for the throbbing to ebb and for her to remember that she had been attacked on the way home from Collier's Ferry.

The room was bathed in the soft glow of a lamp turned low. She tried to move her shoulder but it pained her so that she left that alone, too. She was naked beneath the bedding.

Someone had come upon her in the dark, had hit her, stabbed her with something sharp, then knocked her against the barn. She recalled waking up in the rain, touching her shoulder, and having her fingers come away covered with warm blood.

Unable to stand, she had finally started crawling across the yard toward the well-lit conservatory. Through the falling rain, she caught glimpses of Dru and Louzanna moving around inside and tried to call out to them, but the rain poured down harder and it was all she could do to crawl.

She tried to move again and could only turn her head on the pillow. Then what she saw brought tears to her eyes.

Dru was sound asleep in the rocking chair beside the bed with Elizabeth sprawled across his chest. Her daughter was sound asleep with her arms wrapped around his neck. Dru's cheek was pressed against the crown of Lissybeth's head.

Relief and exhaustion overtook her and Sara drifted off to sleep again, but this time with a smile on her face.

28

THE NEXT MORNING when Sara awoke she saw that although Dru was still sleeping in the rocker, Elizabeth was gone. Birds were singing outside the open window and the tempting aroma of bacon filled the house. The seeming ordinariness of it all struck her as odd in light of what had happened to her last night.

Dru's chair was cast in a stream of sunshine, but he slept on with his arms folded in his lap, his wrists crossed, his big hands lifeless. She had always loved his strong, tapered hands. The hands of a healer. He hadn't shaved, that much was obvious from the dark growth of stubble over the lower half of his face.

Surely he must care a little. Surely a man who hated her would not have gone out of his way to watch over her all night long.

He is a doctor. It's his duty to care for the sick.

He would have done the same for a stranger.

As if her thoughts woke him, his eyes slowly opened and found hers. For a split second he looked at her the way he used to, the way he had back when he loved her. Then just as quickly, the look disappeared, fading to one of deep concern. She liked to think that his expression still held more warmth and worry than the impartial concern of a doctor.

He slowly straightened and moved stiffly to her side. He reached for her wrist, felt her pulse, and gently let go.

"How do you feel?" His voice sounded tight, almost rusty.

She had to lick her lips before she could answer. "Fine, I think. A bit groggy."

She felt a tickle of remembrance and the same swell of hope that had surfaced the previous night, when she'd seen him asleep with Elizabeth in his arms. Or had she only been dreaming?

"I'd like to look at that wound and change the dressing, if you don't mind." He was guarding his emotions again; his expression remained closed.

"Of course." He had seen her naked, perhaps he had even been the one to remove all her clothes himself; still, her cheeks grew fiery hot and she looked away.

He sat down on the side of the bed, paused before he finally reached for a sheet to draw it down to the top of her breasts, exposing the bandage wrapped over her shoulder. She tried to lift her arm, but a sharp pain forced her to cry out.

"I'm sorry." He focused everywhere but on her eyes. "Let me rest your arm against a pillow." He rearranged the pillows and made her comfortable before unwinding the bandage. She drew her head back and tried to survey the damage. When she caught sight of a row of neat black stitches like a dress seam along her shoulder, a wave of dizziness assailed her and she closed her eyes.

"Are you all right?"

"How is Lissybeth? Where is she?"

"She's just fine. She's downstairs eating breakfast. Jamie is with her. How are you feeling?"

"A little dizzy is all. Is it bad?" She couldn't look.

His hands stilled. "An inch closer to your throat and it could have been fatal." Dru set aside the soiled bandage and went after his medical bag on the washstand.

"Did you use a spiderweb to stop the bleeding?" That would have been Granddaddy's first choice.

He paused and looked over at her as if she were delirious. "No."

"Chimney soot and lard?"

"No, Sara. I applied pressure and stitched it up."

"Granddaddy would have sealed it first."

"To cure you or kill you?"

He paused and then was soon back at her side, bag in hand. "If you want me to, I'll go find you a spiderweb, but I don't recommend it," he said softly.

As soon as he made the offer, her eyes smarted. When his image began to swim and she knew tears were giving her away, she turned her head, unwilling to let him see just how vulnerable she was right now. He sat down beside her again and reached into his bag for another roll of clean, white bandage material.

He began to wrap the wound again. "What happened, Sara? Can you talk about it?"

She looked up into his eyes and found a tense urgency there. She knew that he would feel it his duty to track down her attacker. "I don't want you involved."

"You don't need to fight my battles for me. That's what got you into this mess in the first place."

She fell silent until he took hold of her hand and pressed it between his. A warmth and comfort the likes of which she hadn't known in a long, long time filled her.

"I'm sorry, Sara. It's just, seeing you here like this, knowing you went out alone to help me—it's hard to take."

"I wanted to fix things."

"You fixed things, all right. Tell me what happened."

She told him about her visit to her grandfather, of the shortcut through the woods and how she thought she would be safer than on the open road. "And I *was* safe in the woods," she concluded. "Someone came out of nowhere and attacked me beside the barn."

"Did you see who it was?"

She shook her head. "No, but I was carrying a walking stick and when I swung I hit something." She frowned, remembering. "I heard a groan. I *definitely* remember hearing a groan. Then I felt the sharp blow to my shoulder and fell against the side of the barn. It must have been a while later that I came to. It was raining then but I could still see the house. I was afraid to make a sound."

His hands tightened over hers encouragingly.

"I crawled to the back door and then blacked out again."

"Your father." He speculated out loud.

"What?"

"It had to be your father."

She frowned. Daddy had hit her on more than one occasion. He cuffed all his children when the spirit moved him, but he would never have tried to kill her. She shook her head with certainty. "It wasn't Daddy."

"Can you be sure?"

"Dru, if he had wanted to kill me, I'd be dead. He doesn't want me at home, but that doesn't mean he'd kill me." When Dru looked about to argue and then hesitated, she wanted to know, "What is it?"

"I may have given him a reason."

"What?"

"When Jamie told me he saw you on the road, I went to find you. I got all the way to the ferry. Your father and I exchanged words and I punched him." He shrugged. There wasn't an ounce of apology in his tone.

"You *punched* him?"

"Actually, I knocked him unconscious."

"You knocked him *out*?"

"Right after he admitted he was the one who hit you the day you came back to Magnolia Creek. Lou had suspected as much. I put the question to him and he was so damn proud of himself that I thought I ought to teach him a lesson."

"Oh, Dru." Overwhelmed, she bit her lips to keep them from trembling. Not only had he gone off in search of her, but he had stood up to her father.

He was still watching her closely. "You haven't told me everything. How did you think your grandfather could help my situation?"

"Granddaddy knows some powerful charms."

"You were going to use a *charm* to turn things around for me?" He shook his head. "Do you truly believe in those old-time superstitions?"

"Not the way Granddaddy does, but I was desperate."

"This is more than a rock throwing, Sara. This is serious business."

She swallowed. "It looks that way."

"Where else did you go?" When she hesitated, he quickly asked, "Is Elizabeth's father around here somewhere? Could he have done this?"

"Dear God, no!" She could see that he wasn't about to stop questioning her until he had the truth. "I went to see Abel Foster. I knew his piece in the paper was the reason no one has come to your office for help. I couldn't bear the thought of you sitting there day after day waiting for patients to show up. I had to do something. I . . . I have something on Abel that I thought would make him take it all back."

Dru went perfectly still. With the dark shadow over the lower half of his face and his brows pulled together, he looked so intimidating that she was afraid to tell him the rest, fearing he would go after Foster the way he had her father.

"You have something on Abel? What is it?"

"Dru, I don't think—"

"What *is* it, Sara?"

She pulled her hand away and pressed her hands together. "After we received word that you were dead, it wasn't but a few weeks later that Abel approached me out by the barn. He . . . he tried to kiss me. He grabbed me and fondled me and told me that I'd have needs that he could satisfy. He said that when I was ready, I should come to him. I told him to take his hands off of me, that he'd be the last man on earth I'd turn to."

Dru's mouth tightened. His hands clenched. He looked mad enough to take Abel apart and put him back together again. Without thinking, she reached for his hands and held tight.

"Dru, please. Calm down."

"Don't ask me to calm down, Sara. He could have killed you."

"You don't *know* that it was Abel."

"You threatened him. Who else would have reason?"

She knew that a man with the honor the depth of Dru's would want to avenge her. She reminded herself that she should have thought of that before she brewed up a new batch of trouble.

She wasn't aware that she was crying until he thumbed the tears off her cheeks and gently pulled her into his arms.

"Sara, don't." He held her tight without hurting her. "You're trembling."

"*Promise* me you won't do anything rash, Dru."

"I can't."

"Promise."

"I won't do anything rash," he mumbled grudgingly.

"What do you consider rash?"

He didn't answer. She let him hold her and gave in to the need to be comforted. It had been so long since anyone had stood up for her, so long since she had felt like anyone really cared, that she wanted to treasure the feeling a bit longer.

Now, if only he could forgive. If only he could ever love her again.

29

DRU HELD SARA fast, tried to absorb some of her fear. She was still trembling, her tears staining his shirtfront; but even as he tried to comfort her, he silently damned Abel Foster.

How dare that self-righteous prig preach to the community about her being a traitor when he was really upset about her spurning his advances?

Holding Sara in his arms only intensified Dru's yearning. Running his hands up and down her spine, he pressed his cheek against her hair and closed his eyes.

Intent on giving her something else to think about, he said softly, "Someone wants to see you." He let go and lowered her to the pillow. "Dry those eyes and I'll be right back."

He found Elizabeth in the kitchen with Jamie. There was as much cornmeal mush all over one end of the table as there was Elizabeth's face. Dru found a dish towel, wet a corner of it, and wiped off the child's face and hair. She leaned as far away from him as she could to avoid the cloth.

"Mama wants to see you," he said. The notion distracted her for an instant.

"Mama?"

"Yes, Mama." He scooped her up and she settled against his hip all too easily. The warm, familiar feel of having her there troubled him. His heart was still too raw to open itself to new, more critical wounds.

"How is Miss Sara?" Jamie was still swabbing up mush.

"As well as can be expected. I think she might be a bit feverish. Have you looked in on Louzanna?"

"Still sleeping."

"Thanks. It's just as well we let her settle down some on her own."

Dru left Jamie in the kitchen and carried Elizabeth up the stairs with Goldie on his heels. When he walked into the room, Sara's eyes began to shimmer with tears the moment she saw Elizabeth.

"Mama!" the child shrieked happily and draped herself over Dru's arm, reaching down for Sara.

Sara looked up at him, then at Elizabeth, and her face crumpled. Dru rushed to the bedside. "Are you in pain?"

She wiped her eyes and tried to smile. "It's a good one. Please, let me hold her."

"She might hurt you."

"Please," Sara begged.

He lowered Elizabeth to her lap but stayed close, ready to grab her back again if need be.

"Mama?"

"What, sweetie?"

"Doggie."

"I see the doggie." Sara looked down at Goldie, who had rested her muzzle on the edge of the bed. The old dog stared adoringly at Elizabeth.

When Sara turned her gaze on Dru, he saw stars in her eyes.

"You brought the dog home."

Caught between the way it used to be and the way things were now, he wished he hadn't noticed how she was looking at him. He shrugged.

"No use leaving Goldie alone at Doc's."

"Hurt, Mama?" Elizabeth spoke around her fingers as she frowned at Sara's bandage.

"No. I'm fine."

"Kiss it?" Lissybeth offered, pursing her lips for a kiss.

Dru reached for her and kept her from leaning toward Sara, suddenly feeling like an ogre. "No kissing. She shouldn't touch it."

Elizabeth pointed to the bump on her own forehead. "Hurt me. Kiss it, Mama."

Sara put her hand gently over the goose egg, her eyes fraught with concern. "What happened to her?"

"A little run-in with the underside of the kitchen table. She and Goldie were playing tag last night."

Sara relaxed and leaned forward to tenderly kiss Elizabeth's bump and then wrapped her arm around the child's sturdy body. Elizabeth rested her head on Sara's good shoulder and lay there sucking on her fingers. It was such a private moment between the two of them that an intense wave of loneliness swept through Dru. The outsider, he walked to the broken window, wishing things were different, wondering if they ever could be.

Outside the sky was a clear, bright summer blue. His gaze raked over the front lawn sorely in need of trimming. When he looked to the left he saw the corner of Abel Foster's house, which reminded him what Sara had told him, and his blood ran cold.

He walked back over to Sara's bedside where she and Elizabeth were playing peekaboo. Elizabeth hid her eyes, then peeked out at him through splayed fingers and giggled.

He reached for her as if he had been doing it all of her life. "It's time your mama got some sleep."

"So soon?" Sara sounded disappointed, even though she looked exhausted.

"You need to rest in order to heal." He prayed she wasn't able to read him well enough to know that he was only placating her so that he could leave.

He needed to make a pressing call on a certain newspaper publisher on Main Street.

Dru stormed into the *Magnolia Creek Sentinel* office with the fury of Sherman marching into Atlanta, slamming the door so hard the glass panes in the front window rattled and the office boy dove beneath the front desk. Abel came charging out of the back room. His jaw went slack when Dru crossed the room with all the finesse of a bull in a ladies' tea shop.

Dru didn't stop until they were nose to nose. He towered over Abel, well satisfied when the man actually cowered. Dru looked him over, searching for any injury Sara might have inflicted with her walking stick, but unfortunately, Abel looked perfectly fine.

"Where were you last night, Foster?"

"What makes that any business of yours?"

Dru reached out with both hands, grabbed him by the shirtfront, and lifted him off his feet. "I'm making it my business."

Abel's face turned red as he hung from his collar. He sputtered and grabbed hold of Dru's wrists.

"I . . . was . . . here . . ." he choked out.

"How long?" Dru noticed Abel's face was fading from

red to a nice shade of violet, so he let go. Abel sagged against the corner of the front desk. From beneath it, his young assistant stared up at Dru as if seeing a madman.

Dru took a deep breath and tried again. "What time did you leave here last night?"

"After midnight."

"Were you here alone?"

Abel shook his head and pointed at the freckle-faced youngster, pale as newsprint. "Pete was here, too."

"That right, son?" Dru reached down, offered the boy his hand, and pulled him to his feet.

Pete nodded furiously. "The . . . press broke down."

Dru swung his gaze to Foster again. "How do I know he wouldn't lie for you?"

"I wouldn't lie for anybody, sir!" Pete threw back his shoulders, speaking up for himself before Abel could open his mouth.

"Witham Spalding was here, too." Abel was a bit more composed as he straightened the front of his jacket and adjusted his collar. He was livid, staring holes through Dru, but managed to keep his tone civil.

"The whole time?" Dru asked.

"All of the time," Abel assured him. "You can ask Spalding."

Dru had known Witham Spalding his whole life, as had most everybody in Magnolia Creek. The old codger spent his days at the general store swapping stories with the other old men in town. He was known to look for any warm, friendly place to light rather than go home to an empty house.

"Don't think I won't ask him, just as soon as I leave here."

Abel put space between them by stepping around to the far side of the desk. "What's this all about?"

"Oh, I think you already know more than you're saying, Abel. In fact, I just found out that there's a whole other side to you that most folks don't know about."

"If you're talking about that cockamamy story your wife is telling—"

Dru cut him off. "After last night, I think I have good reason to believe her."

Abel paled and massaged his temples. "What . . . what happened?"

"Someone attacked Sara sometime just after sundown. Slashed her shoulder open, but I suspect he was aiming for her throat. Left her for dead behind the house. Since one of the only people she spoke to yesterday was you, and since she threatened you with the truth about what you did to her, I reckon the only one in town who would most benefit by her death is you, Abel."

Foster held up both hands defensively. "You can't be serious, Talbot. If you want to accuse me of murder, you'll need proof. I was here until twelve and at the time you mentioned, Pete, Witham, and I were having dinner. Minnie brought a dinner basket over to us around four but we didn't eat until much later."

Dru didn't let his disappointment show. He would have liked nothing better than to see Abel locked up where he belonged.

"Sara hit her attacker during the scuffle. You have any injuries you're hiding beneath your coat?"

"Injuries?" Abel's face drained of color. He appeared shaken for an instant, then quickly recovered. "No, I don't. I'll take off my shirt to prove it if you insist, but you're barking up the wrong tree, Talbot."

By now, Dru was certain that he was wrong, too, but he didn't want Abel to think that he was in the clear yet. Dru pulled himself together, ran his hand down his shirt-front, straightened the cuffs of his sleeves.

"I'm going to report the attack to Damon Monroe and if I see one word about any of this in the paper, I'll be back."

"Are you threatening me?"

"Take it any way you like."

Without another word, he walked out of the office and left Abel staring in his wake. He wasn't but a few yards down the street, headed straight for the marshal's office, when Foster's fiery-haired office boy caught up to him.

"Doc Talbot? Can I talk to you a minute?"

Dru stopped, looked Pete up and down. He was a tall boy, trim but sturdy.

"Did you ever throw a rock through one of my windows?" Dru asked him.

The boy's face paled until his freckles stood out against the white. "No, sir!"

Dru tried not to jump to conclusions just because the boy worked for Foster. "What is it?"

"Mr. Foster *was* at the shop last night, just like he said. Don't think I'd lie for him, either, 'cause I don't even like him all that much."

Dru glanced around the street. There were a few folks out already; a woman carrying an empty basket quickly scooted into the general store after giving him a cool once-over. A farmer rode by on a buckboard with a squeaking wheel, churning up the muddy street.

"Thanks for telling me, son."

"That's all right, sir. One more thing before you go."

"What's that?" Dru rubbed the back of his neck and

rolled his head from side to side. The long night spent sitting up in the rocking chair had caught up with him. Exhaustion and disappointment after his confrontation with Abel left him dragging.

"My ma's been doing real poorly lately. I was wonderin' if you'd mind comin' by to see her. Maybe you got somethin' that will fix her up."

Dru stared at Pete for a moment, realizing it was either the boy's depth of courage or sheer desperation that had driven him to ask the town pariah for help.

"I'd be privileged to see her, son."

"Let me tell her that you're comin' first. How about late this afternoon, after I'm off work? I'll be through around four o'clock."

Thinking of Sara and all the upheaval at home, Dru gauged the time. "Four should be fine."

Pete gave him directions, then ran back to the *Sentinel* office. Instead of being elated, anticipating his first real patient, Dru was disappointed that he was no closer to finding Sara's attacker. As he walked to the marshal's office, a room no bigger than a pantry in the jailhouse behind Courthouse Square, worry settled over him.

Whoever was out to do Sara harm was still a nameless, faceless threat.

30

SARA WAS AWAKE when Dru returned. Her wound ached and her shoulder was immobile, but the pain was overridden by relief the moment he walked through the door. She smiled his way, expecting him to sit in the chair beside the bed, but instead he paced over to the broken window.

"It wasn't Abel." He sounded both frustrated and exhausted as he explained. "He was at the office until midnight. There were two other people who can vouch for him."

"I'm sorry, Dru. Sorry for your worry. Sorry that I brought this down on you."

He walked to the end of the bed where she could admire the width of his shoulders, the cut of his strong features. His shirtfront was wrinkled and smeared with flecks of mud where it showed beneath his coat. He still hadn't shaved. Her heart ached with the knowledge that the longer she stayed, the more she might be putting him in jeopardy.

"Can you be absolutely certain you weren't attacked by your father or one of your half brothers? Are you covering for them out of some misguided notion of protecting me?"

"Of course not." She shook her head and tried to sound convincing. "I don't think any of them would have had time to catch up to me after making a trip to the Collier side of the creek and back."

Pain shot through her shoulder. When she winced, Dru was at her side in an instant. Guardedly, he lowered himself to the bed and reached for her hand.

"Are you all right?"

"It hurts some," she grudgingly admitted.

He drew a corner of the bandage down and inspected the wound. "It's not bleeding." Then he measured her pulse. When he was satisfied, he sat back down but didn't leave her as she had expected. Nor had he let go of her hand. He held it tenderly, lightly.

Sara's heart tightened as a peaceful warmth suffused her. Despite his fatigue, Dru smiled.

"I do have some good news, too," he said softly.

"I could sure use some."

"I'm seeing my first patient at four."

"Oh, Dru. That's wonderful. Who is it?"

"Foster's office boy's mother. It seems she's been doing poorly for a while. He stopped me after I left the *Sentinel* office."

Sara couldn't help smiling. "He overheard me talking to Abel, too." She laid her hand over her heart and laughed softly, daring to believe. "Maybe it's already working, Dru. Maybe I've done some good after all."

"It's not that simple, Sara."

She wouldn't let him diminish her hope. "Why not? Why *can't* it be that simple? Surely when word gets out that you are a fine doctor, folks will start to come around."

"You really do think that's all it will take, don't you?"

"Granddaddy always says belief is half the cure."

She looked down at their hands, so loosely entwined, but more of a beginning than she had the right to hope for. Granddaddy's advice came back to her.

She swallowed, tasting shame and fear, took a deep breath, and closed her fingers over Dru's hand. He met her eyes, took a while to study her face. For a heartbeat she thought he was going to pull away, but he didn't.

"I want to tell you everything, Dru."

"Can't you leave well enough alone for now? You could have died last night—"

"Even more reason to tell you what really happened while I have the chance."

"So you can ease *your* mind? Is that it, Sara?"

"So I can ease yours," she said softly.

He shook his head in disbelief. "You think my knowing all about you and your lovers will make it any better?"

"Lovers?" Granddaddy was right. The truth wouldn't be half as bad as what he might imagine. He tried to pull away but she held on tight. "Please, Dru," she whispered. "It's time I explained."

Dru's first inclination was to bolt out of the room. The mere touch of her hand, coupled with his own need, was already driving him crazy. Sitting close to her fueled temptation he didn't want or need. Sara was so beautiful to him that even bruised and battered, the sight of her made him ache all over.

Did she truly think revealing all the sordid details of her life with another man would make things better? Did she really believe that knowing all would make it easier for him to forget?

While the warmth of her hand coursed through him, he couldn't deny her. "You should be sleeping."

"I don't want to sleep. I want this over with."

"But Sara—"

She reached up with her free hand and touched her fingers to his lips to quiet him. "I'm still your wife, Dru. I'm still here. If there's any chance," she looked down, paused as if gathering courage, ". . . if there's *any* chance of saving even a small part of what the future once held for us, I have to take it."

He closed his eyes. They'd had two weeks together, an impulsive, head-over-heels falling in love experience, a hasty wedding and blissful wedding night. But every moment had been filled with such promise, such hope.

He gathered what few shreds of self-control he possessed, ready to listen because Sara had her mind made up to tell him.

"Go ahead then. Tell me."

She started out so softly that he had to lean closer just to hear. Suddenly the overly warm room, the sound of Elizabeth's laughter drifting up from downstairs, the birdsong from the maple in the front yard—everything faded away except the sound of Sara's voice. Through the detailed picture she painted, he began not only to hear, but to imagine exactly what had happened.

"A little over a year after we heard you'd been killed I had been feeling so low that I offered to do some errands intended for Jamie. Walking down Main Street, I ran smack into a Yankee lieutenant outside of the butcher shop. When we collided I dropped my grocery basket. We bumped heads trying to pick things up off the walk. He smiled politely and asked my name.

"He told me that he was from a small town in Ohio,

that he was mighty homesick and that he'd appreciate it if I'd let him walk me home. He offered to carry my basket and as it was heavy, I didn't see the harm. Walking beside him, all I could think of was you, of how, like him, you had been so far from home and must have felt lonely, too. That you were gone and never coming home hit me so hard that I began to cry. When he saw the tears in my eyes, he gave me his kerchief."

Dru shifted his weight on the edge of the bed. Loneliness had been his constant companion during the war. That same lingering loneliness still ate at him now that they were estranged.

"What was his name?" He needed to hear her say it, wanted to gauge the depth of feeling she still carried for the man.

"Jonathan. Jonathan Smith." She sounded little more than matter-of-fact as she gazed into his eyes. "He was fair-haired, blue-eyed. Not as tall as you, of medium build. Some would say he was handsome." She shrugged. "I suppose he was, but not in the same way that you are. He wasn't as tall or as rugged." Sara paused to lick her lips.

"Do you need water?" he asked.

She shook her head and went on. "It wasn't long before word was all over town that I had been seen walking home with him. No doubt Minnie Foster was to thank for that, but I didn't care. I'd done nothing to be ashamed of."

She sat up a bit straighter. The sheet slipped below her shoulders, banded the tops of her breasts. Sara hadn't noticed, but he certainly did. It was all he could do to keep from pulling the sheet back up to her neck.

"For the first time since Hugh brought us the terrible

news I felt myself waking up, coming back to life myself. Instead of living in a nightmare I actually began to look forward to each new day. I found myself walking downtown more often, I suppose hoping I might run into Lieutenant Smith again, although at the time I wouldn't let myself think that was the reason I went out. The Yankees had set up a staff office next door to the bank. Jonathan was there and he introduced me to some of his friends and invited me to go on a picnic.

"At first I refused, but he was very persuasive. He told me that he understood—with my being a new widow and all—that he knew I wasn't looking for a romance, but he couldn't see the harm in a little companionship. He teased and flirted and finally wore me down and I agreed to go.

"I wasn't about to sneak behind Louzanna's back, so I explained where I was going and with whom. Naturally, she was upset, insisting that you were still alive, but I went on a picnic with Jonathan anyway and as it turned out, he wanted to kiss me. I told him no and so he didn't press me, but he was so courteous and kind all afternoon, so attentive that by the time he brought me home again, I . . . I had changed my mind."

"So you let him kiss you." Dru hadn't realized he was squeezing her hand until she winced and he let her go. He tried to imagine some fair-haired Yankee taking advantage of Sara's grief and loneliness and her being none the wiser.

Sara was beet red to the hairline. "I did. I was afraid that Louzanna would know what I'd done just by looking at me. I was furious at myself for kissing Jonathan, but I kept reminding myself that I had done nothing wrong, that you were never coming back." She reached out and cupped his cheek, let the warmth of her palm linger. "You can't even imagine what it was like, knowing that I would never hear your voice or see your face again. To know you were never going to touch me again." Her hand dropped to her side again as she continued.

"I began to see Jonathan for a little while each day. We walked around the square, sometimes went on picnics. Eventually word came that the Union troops were pulling out and he begged me to go along, to pack up and leave. I told him that there was no way I could leave Louzanna, not to mention the fact that we weren't married. He proposed, said that he wanted nothing more than to make me his wife, but until official confirmation of your death arrived, we had to wait."

Even her lover had the good sense to wait to see if I was still alive.

"But you left with him anyway."

"What would *you* have believed, Dru? Louzanna's ravings, or Hugh's story of how he held you in his arms and watched you die?"

He knew that in her place, he would no doubt have taken Hugh's word over Louzanna's histrionics.

"Go on," he urged, needing it over and done with, wondering what might have happened had he not hidden his identity until he could face going back to the front again. What might have happened if he had written in time to get a letter through to her? Everything could have been different.

"What finally convinced you to leave Lou?"

"Jonathan said that as long as I lived in your home, with your sister, that the past would never be over, that I would never be able to move on. The idea that I might spend my life in mourning like Lou terrified me. She was doing much better, taking her teas religiously, concentrating on her quilting. Jamie was here to watch over her. Jonathan offered me a chance at a new life, a new beginning. Although my feelings for him were not as strong as they had been for you, I enjoyed his company and he made me laugh. I decided that since I had lost you, there was nothing left to lose, and so I grabbed at the chance at happiness.

"I left most everything I owned behind and wrote a note to Louzanna. Jonathan made arrangements for me to travel to Illinois where he was to be stationed. He paid for a room in a boardinghouse in a small river town and he would come to me there when he was off duty.

"Over and over he assured me that he was anxious to get married, but that we had to wait. I wrote to Lou again and told her where to write to me when she received news from the Confederate War Department, but I never heard from her."

So she'd lived with her lover, this faceless Jonathan Smith in Illinois, a kept woman, sleeping with the man, sharing her sweet body with him. Dru wanted her to stop, but curiosity, or perhaps perversion, made him hold his tongue.

"Within a few weeks after I had given myself to him, things began to change. Maybe he sensed my own regret for having done what I did, perhaps the challenge of wooing me was all that had interested him.

"His visits became more infrequent until he hardly came around at all. I was already carrying his child the day he told me that his regiment was moving out. He left me with a handful of gold pieces and a promise to write and to come back for me after the war, but not once did I hear from him after he marched away."

She shuddered, as if the memories were too painful to bear. She surprised him by going on. “Lissybeth was born at the boardinghouse. The war ended and I waited for Jonathan to return. Finally, when the money was near gone and it was pretty clear that he was either dead or he’d lied and wasn’t coming back at all, I took Lissybeth and went looking for him. I used most of what I had left to get to Ohio, to the town he said he was from, only to find out that he had lied about that, too.

“By chance there *was* a man living there named Jonathan Smith, but he was in his sixties and no relation at all. I’ll never forget my humiliation when the old gentleman opened his door. He took one look at me and Elizabeth and called out to his wife, ‘Come see, Ma. There’s *another one* here.’

“It turns out I wasn’t the only woman Jon had lied to, nor was I the only one he had lived with during the war years.” Her words faded away and finally, dry-eyed, she looked at Dru again. “So you see, I gave up my reputation for a liar. I was a fool. He wanted nothing from me but . . . well, what he took. He used me and left me and did the same thing to who knows how many others.”

Unable to sit still any longer, Dru let go of Sara’s hand and walked across the room. “How did you get here from Ohio?”

“The Smiths helped me find work caring for an elderly woman who needed nursing. I received no pay, but there was room and board for Elizabeth and myself. When she died, her relations came in and sold off the house. I found work on a farm that spring. I started thinking about Kentucky and home and was sick of living off of charity. I saved and still had a bit of the money Jon had given me, enough to get me back here. I was at the lowest place in my life, Dru. I needed to talk to my granddaddy, to see my mama again.

"I wanted Elizabeth to have a real home, a place to live with family around her. I worked my way back to Collier's Ferry, but my daddy . . . well, as you know, he turned me away. I had nowhere else to turn but to Louzanna and thank God she didn't hold what I had done against me."

No wonder Sara was certain Smith would never seek her out and try to reclaim Elizabeth. The man had paid Sara off and walked out of her life for good. Dru thought of the good-natured, fair-haired child, pictured her sunny smile. She had been abandoned by her father before she had taken her first breath.

"Dru?"

He turned. She was lying back, exhausted and drained, waiting for his reaction.

What am I supposed to say? That I forgive her?

After listening to her he didn't know if he felt better or worse. He had a name and could imagine the man's face, but his raw and tattered heart was far from mended.

He ran his hand along his jaw. She was watching him intently, waiting for him to say something. There was such undisguised yearning for forgiveness in her eyes that he found himself tongue-tied.

She fought hard to smile, to lighten the moment, but her trembling lips gave her away. "I was infatuated with Jonathan, enough to throw away my good name when I went off after him without the benefit of marriage. I never, ever loved him the way I did you because I knew that kind of love could never, ever be replaced. By the time I was in Illinois, by the time I had slept with him and began to regret what I had done, it was too late to turn back."

31

THE TELLING OVER, Sara prayed she hadn't made things worse.

Dru's jaw was set, his shoulders rigid. More than anything, he looked sad and tired and had every right to be after what he had been through.

There was nothing for her to do but wait and see if Granddaddy was right. Maybe Dru would think of her differently now that he knew the truth.

Suddenly she remembered he was to see his first patient that afternoon. "Why don't you get some rest, Dru?"

"I need to see to Lou first."

"How is she?"

"Calmer, but still in bed when I looked in on her earlier. I'm having a hard time convincing her that you're not dead."

"If you'll get my nightgown, I'll go show her that I'm fine."

"You'll do nothing of the sort."

"I'd like to put it on anyway." Her cheeks burned like fire.

He started opening the chest of drawers, fishing for her nightgown. Clutching it in both hands, he brought the gown over to her and dropped it in her lap as if it were a hot coal.

Embarrassed, she stared down at the heap of white muslin. "I'm afraid I'll need some help."

His demeanor turned professional immediately but she could see him fighting for detachment as he came to her aid. For modesty's sake, she tried to hold the sheet over her with one hand. She glanced up, met his eyes, and was arrested by his nearness. He was so close, his warm breath caressed her cheek.

"Let go of the sheet, Sara. It's not hiding anything I haven't seen before." His voice was low, strained, and tight.

She lifted her arm, tried not to think about how close they were or how she was exposed to the waist. When the gown snagged on her elbow, he was forced to lean in closer to free the material. The rough wool of his coat brushed against her nipples and a small, barely audible gasp escaped her. His hands immediately stilled. His lips were a mere heartbeat away. He closed his eyes. She caught her breath.

Kiss me.

Kiss me and tell me everything will be all right.

A pained expression crossed his face. She couldn't quite believe that his hands, always so sure and gentle, had begun to shake. He gave the gown a tug and brought it to her waist. Then he stepped back.

"Thank you," she whispered.

He nodded, then looked toward the door.

"Help me stand up, please." She tried to smile, as if her shoulder wasn't on fire. As if her cheeks weren't flaming. Parts of her that hadn't tingled in a long time began to ache.

His gaze moved from the door, back to her face. "You stay put."

"Please, let's not argue, Dru. Louzanna has been nothing but kind to me. She needs to see me before she'll believe I'm all right." She tried moving without his aid, got herself poised on the edge of the bed, but she was afraid if she swung her legs over the side that they wouldn't hold.

She stared at him through a lock of hair that had fallen across her eyes. "I'm going with or without your help," she warned.

Despite his objections, Dru was beside her, brushing her hair back, palming her forehead to see if she was feverish, mumbling that she was being as stubborn as hell.

He wrapped an arm around her, helped her draw the sheet away, and supported her when she tried to stand. Before the hem of her gown dropped around her ankles he was tormented by a glimpse of her shapely thighs.

Finally, with his help, she stood. She clung to his arm and he held her tight, telling himself it was only because he was afraid that she would fall.

"Now, help me down the hall. Louzanna needs me."

"I'm against this, Sara."

"My hurt will heal. Lou's won't. Start walking."

What she managed was more of a shuffle. He knew she had to be in pain. It was a long, slow odyssey to Louzanna's door, but with his help, they finally made it.

He ushered her in, helped her to stand at the foot of Lou's bed. His sister was still buried beneath a mound of quilts. Only her eyes and nose and the top of her head were visible.

Sara whispered, "Lou?"

A feeble voice filtered past the mountain of patchwork. "I'm awake," Louzanna said fragilely.

"It's me, Lou. It's Sara."

Lou's eyes fluttered and finally opened. She stared at the ceiling for a few seconds before she raised her head.

"Sara? Is it *really* you? Are you *sure* you're alive?"

Dru kept his hand at her waist, afraid to let her go.

"Thanks to Dru, I'm still here," she said, smiling up at him.

"Come closer, let me see you." Lou's voice had already strengthened. "I want to make certain you are no ghost, like Mason. If anything happened to you, Sara, why, I don't know what I'd do."

"Oh, Lou." Sara urged Dru to walk her to the side of the bed, where she reached for Louzanna's pale hand. He could feel her knees knocking, knew that she was about to collapse. She clung to him like a new leaf clings to a tree in high wind, but her voice sounded sure and convincing.

"I'm alive and well and surely not a ghost. I think it's about time you got up, don't you? Jamie's here, but he's not staying forever. And from all the noise I hear coming from downstairs, I think Elizabeth needs you."

"Elizabeth needs me?" Lou pulled herself up to her elbows, causing a quilt avalanche. The pile listed; the two top quilts slid to the floor. "Who's watching Elizabeth?" Lou murmured.

"Jamie." Sara glanced up at Dru and seemed momentarily to forget where she was and what she was doing. She shook her head, recovered, and concentrated on Louzanna. "Please, try to get up and get dressed, Lou. I'm sure once you have some of your tea you'll feel much better."

Lou nodded. "I suppose so. Do you think I should get up yet, Dru?"

"I think it would do you a world of good." His patience with Louzanna was nearly gone, especially since she was helplessly clinging to Sara's hand, sapping her strength. Sara didn't seem to mind as she continued to encourage Lou, speaking softly and slowly, as if she was coaxing Elizabeth and not a full-grown woman. He could see how much Sara truly cared for his sister. He also saw that Sara was growing weaker by the moment.

He leaned close to her ear and whispered, "You've done all you can for now. I want you back in bed."

Sara hid a tremulous smile, gave a slight shake of her head. Just then, Lou pushed herself clear of the bed until she was standing beside it. Her nightgown was crumpled, her curls undone and mussed, so that her hair flared out around her head like dandelion fluff. Mason Blaylock's engagement ring hung around her neck like a millstone.

Louzanna muttered to herself as she searched for a slipper beneath the bed. "I still feel a touch of the hysteria," she warned. Her head and shoulders had disappeared beneath the bed. "Perhaps I need more tincture of zegonia?"

"What?" Sara turned to him for explanation.

Dru leaned close and whispered against her ear. "It's an old war curative."

"It's certainly one of the best I've ever had," Lou assured them after she wriggled out from beneath the bed with the missing slipper in hand.

Dru cleared his throat and then interjected, "I'm taking Sara back to bed." The minute the words were out, he realized what he had said and looked down at Sara to see if she would react; but her face was drained of all color now and she was so weak she could barely stand alone.

Rather than let her walk back to her room, he scooped her up into his arms and carried her down the hall.

"Thank you for that," he said softly.

With her arm around his neck, she turned to stare up into his eyes.

"Without Louzanna, Elizabeth and I would have been out on the streets and I might not ever have known that you were still alive."

The rest of her thoughts went unspoken.

32

LIFE UNFOLDED IN a state of fragile peace over the next month. The summer heat intensified, Sara's bruises faded, her shoulder slowly healed. One sunny July afternoon she took Elizabeth outside to play with Goldie beneath a glossy-leafed persimmon tree and sat beside them in a willow-bark chair.

Jamie was working across the yard in the garden plot. Before the war, Sara had come to admire his quiet strength and slow, even smile and now that he was back and seemed content to stay awhile longer, she had come to realize how much his presence soothed Louzanna's nerves. He was everywhere at once, calming Lou, snagging Elizabeth whenever she toddled into trouble, tending the garden, making repairs.

Sara watched Lissybeth straddle Goldie, clap her hands, and pretend to ride the dog as she lay contentedly on the blanket. Chuckling to herself, Sara got up and went to kneel beside Lissybeth to rescue Goldie.

Sara was pointing out a brown lizard scooting up the bark of the tree when the back door opened and Dru suddenly appeared. Every time she saw him, her heart quickened. She had grown used to the sudden heat that flared in his eyes when he saw her, and just as accustomed to seeing it quickly and carefully extinguished.

She didn't know how she was ever going to win him back when he wouldn't let her get close to him physically or emotionally. He spent most of his time at the office and when he was at home, they were always with Louzanna, Elizabeth, and oftentimes Jamie, too.

Since the day Dru had treated Pete's mother, patients began to trickle in for help. Just yesterday he had delivered a baby to a woman living on the outskirts of town. When Sara heard the news, she had been thrilled; her only regret was that she hadn't been there to help.

"You're home early," she said, smiling.

He glanced around the yard, waved to Jamie, and surprised her by sitting down in the willow-bark chair. When his gaze touched Elizabeth, his expression was telling. Sara guessed he was thinking of Jonathan.

Elizabeth stood up and charged over to him, threw herself at his knees, and babbled about doggie and 'izard as she cocked her head and smiled her fetching dimpled smile, trying her best to capture his undivided attention, perhaps gain a smile in return.

Dru didn't budge. As Sara's heart ached for them both, a boy of around ten years suddenly came running around the corner of the house. Dressed in short pants and scuffed shoes, one suspender hanging near his elbow, he ran up to Dru. His hair was tousled, his sunburned face bright with exertion. He looked frightened to death.

Dru gently extracted Elizabeth from his knees and waited as the boy doubled over, gasping for air.

Dru touched his shoulder. "Breathe slow and take it easy, son." After the boy caught his breath, Dru asked, "What's your name? What's happened?"

"Harold Junior. Harold Newberry is my daddy."

Sara recognized the name. Newberry had purchased Talbot Mill and hadn't made a payment to Louzanna since the Yankees burned him out.

"My baby sister's real sick with the croup and Mama's scared to death she's gonna die. Daddy didn't want to send for you, but Mama told me to come get you straight-away. I went to Doc Porter's but you weren't there, so I came over here." He looked at Dru imploringly. "You gotta come home with me. You just gotta, Doc."

Sara's heart was leaping like a drunken cricket, but Dru was cool and competent. Jamie ran over, hoe in hand. Dru asked him to hitch up the horse and buggy, then spoke quietly and calmly to the boy, reassuring him while probing for information about the sick child.

"Dru, wait." Sara grabbed Elizabeth and fell into step beside him. "Let me go with you." She not only wanted to help, but wanted to be alone with him on the drive back.

He didn't even break stride.

She quickened her steps. Going along suddenly became vital.

"I promise I won't get in the way. I'm a mother, Dru. I know what that woman must be feeling right now. Please take me with you."

There was a war going on behind Dru's eyes, his indecision almost tangible. Harold Junior hovered at his elbow. Finally he stopped and looked around the yard. His gaze lit on the barn, lingered, then scanned the woods beyond.

He turned to the boy first. "Run along and meet me out behind the barn, Harold. Tie your horse to the back of the buggy." When Dru turned back to Sara, his lips were firmly set. She held his unreadable stare and silently dared him to take her.

Elizabeth grabbed a stray lock of Sara's hair and began twisting it around her hand, tugging gently as she babbled to herself. Dru was silent.

Finally, as if it almost pained him, he said, "Be as quick as you can. I'll drive around front. Meet me there."

Sara hugged Elizabeth and ran inside to deliver her to Louzanna, afraid that if she didn't hurry, Dru would leave her behind.

A warm summer breeze was blowing heat through town as Dru drove the buggy through the streets of Magnolia Creek. The Newberry boy was tucked between them, and the old swayback mare the boy rode into town was tied behind the buggy.

Dru shifted the reins and stared at the road ahead. He tried to convince himself his decision to bring Sara along was solely out of concern for her safety, but he had hired Jamie to stay on until the end of summer specifically to guard the house and watch over her, so his excuse was just that—an excuse.

For some inexplicable reason, he hadn't been able to leave her behind.

Because you wanted to be alone with her.

The thought came to him out of nowhere, so obvious and so disturbing that he sensed he was losing control, and that made him angry. The farther they ventured from town, the more determined he became to prove he was immune to her charms.

Sara was hard to ignore as she tried to comfort Harold Junior all the way to the mill site. She asked about the boy's family, how many brothers and sisters he had, whether or not he had a dog. Dru listened while the boy told her all about the barn cat and her kittens.

She sat back on the worn leather buggy seat, her eyes on the road, stray wisps of hair blowing against her cheeks and lashes as they barreled along. Even with the boy wedged between them, Dru was aware of Sara's every move. By the time the Newberry farm was in sight, he was silently cursing his own mounting weakness.

Harold Newberry's home was on the far edge of town where the land opened up into wide fields once thick with rows of sorghum. The tall cane resembling cornstalks without ears flourished from Kentucky to the Gulf. Molasses was a household staple from milled and processed sorghum. Folks thought there was nothing better than dipping fresh biscuits—or anything else that was handy—into sorghum, which sold for about thirty cents a gallon.

Dru's grandfather had started the original sorghum mill on a small piece of farmland where he had planted the first crop in the area. As more and more farmers settled in and began planting more fields of sorghum, Grandfather Talbot purchased his own mill and began to charge the neighboring farmers to process their cane. Over time, he bought a second mill and expanded the business, eventually making what most folks considered a fortune.

Since the war, many of the surrounding fields lay fallow, overgrown with weeds and struggling cane sprouted from remnants of past crops. A handful of nearby farmers had cleared and replanted new crops, but with the mills down, the farmers were forced to take their sorghum into another county.

Dru kept his eye on the road as he turned up the wide

drive to the Newberry place and drove toward the old woodframe home where his grandfather first settled. He was struck by nostalgia as he viewed the two-story house and what was left of the huge old mill house and boiling shed beyond.

Mrs. Newberry, a common enough looking woman in her mid-thirties, waited nervously on the porch. She ran down the steps, quickly introduced herself as Dinah, grabbed Dru's hand, and thanked him profusely for coming to her aid. He picked up his medical bag as Harold Junior scrambled out of the buggy and untied the old nag before he ran into the house.

Sara took Dru's hand and gave him a reassuring smile as she stepped down from the carriage, then she hitched up her skirt and started toward the house with Mrs. Newberry. He followed the women through the sparsely furnished farmhouse into a stuffy back bedroom where Harold Junior stood waiting beside the crib.

A congested, feverish, year-old girl lay there fussing, exhausted from the croup. With every labored breath came a whistling, crowing sound. When she did manage a cry, it was no more than a hoarse, plaintive mew.

The child had sandy blond hair and blue eyes identical to her brother's. Small and helpless, she stared up at Dru so trustingly, he decided then and there he would rather treat a roomful of wounded soldiers than have the fate of one helpless child in his hands. Men who put their lives on the line in battle knew the consequences. This little girl was so young, so innocent. He hoped to God he could help her.

Dinah Newberry was wringing her hands, continually reaching out to palm the baby's forehead and brush back her fine curls.

"What's her name?" he asked softly, hoping he sounded more calm and confident than he felt.

"Violet." Dinah Newberry's voice was choked with tears. The baby was almost too exhausted to cry now and fighting hard for every breath. Despite the heat in the room, her mother had wrapped her legs in flannel.

"Have you given her an emetic to make her vomit?" Dru was already reaching for his bag.

"No, but I soaked her feet in hot water and I've been trying to keep them warm." Dinah moved up to his side.

Dru pulled out a bottle of emetic tincture of lobelia and some powdered bloodroot, and turned to her. "I'll need a spoon."

Sara looked about to comment when suddenly there was a commotion at the door and Harold Newberry Senior came charging in. The man cast a frantic glance at the crib, took one look at Dru and Sara, then turned on his wife. "Goddamn it, Dinah! I *told* you not to send for him."

Dinah Newberry burst into tears. Before Dru could react, Sara put herself between Harold Newberry and his wife. "I'm going to take Harry Junior into the other room, Mr. Newberry, so that the doctor can help little Violet. I think you best come along, too." She ruffled Harry Junior's hair. "Maybe you can show me where to find a spoon for the doctor."

Newberry turned on Sara before she could leave. "What right do you have coming into my home and ordering me around?"

Momentarily silenced, Sara didn't back down. Dru quickly stepped between them. "Look here, Newberry—"

Dinah Newberry grabbed her husband's sleeve. "Please,

Harold," she sobbed frantically. "I can't lose another baby."

The man quickly sobered. Helplessly, he stared at his wife, glanced toward the crib, then followed Sara and his son out the door without another word.

Dru had to work quickly to diminish the inflammation and irritation in the child's throat. Dinah Newberry's anxiety seemed to communicate itself to the baby, who began to croup and wheeze harder.

Sara returned with a spoon, saw Dinah hanging over the baby's crib, and put her arm around the woman's shoulders.

"The doctor knows what to do," she said softly, trying to reassure her. "I know just how you feel. I have a little girl of my own. She's almost two."

Dinah nodded, watching Dru measure out half a teaspoon of emetic. He tried to feed it to the child, but she started crouping harder, thrashing her head back and forth to avoid the spoon. Dru wiped his brow on his sleeve.

"Why don't you let her mama give her that?" Sara suggested softly.

Dru paused, willing to try anything, irritated that the idea had come from Sara and that he hadn't thought of it himself.

Dinah rushed around the crib and took the half spoonful of medicine that Dru handed over. She started cooing and coaxing and finally got the baby to swallow it.

Dru stood by while Mrs. Newberry crooned softly to the fussing child. They waited fifteen minutes before giving her another dose. Once Violet vomited until her stomach was empty and her throat clear, Dru asked Sara to boil another tincture, this one of half a teaspoon of cayenne and a cup of vinegar.

"My granddaddy has a cure for croup that never fails." Sara smiled reassuringly at Mrs. Newberry.

Dru interrupted. "Sara, if you could please just mix up the cayenne and vinegar—"

She stepped closer and lowered her voice to a whisper. "If Mrs. Newberry *thinks* we've got something that's surefire, then she'll feel a lot better, Dru."

"We're here to tend to Violet, not her mother. You promised not to get in the way," he whispered back.

She opened her mouth to object, but left with the words unsaid. A few minutes later she was back with the hot mixture, which she set on a side table. She then left the room. Dru called out, "Stay close by," and watched her walk away.

Then he turned to Dinah.

"As soon as the mixture has cooled enough to touch, dip a rag in it and rub it on her neck and chest for ten minutes. Then saturate some flannel strips and wrap them around her throat." He found working on the baby as nerve-wracking as it was heartbreaking. Sara's suggestion to have Dinah help had been an excellent one. The child was much calmer with her mother nursing her.

Time slipped away as Dru watched Dinah gauge the sound of the baby's cough. He couldn't say how long Sara had been gone when a gunshot broke the stillness.

He jerked away from the crib, broke into a cold sweat, tore headlong through the house, and rushed out onto the porch. There was no sign of Sara, Harold Junior, or Mr. Newberry, so he cleared the steps and headed off in the direction from which the shot had come—over near the barn.

"Sara!" he shouted as he ran. "Sara!"

Harold Junior came running out of the outhouse.

"They're out by the pigpen." He fell into step and jogged along beside Dru.

Dru's heart was banging away like a rock in an empty milk can when he rounded the corner of a lopsided hen-house and saw Sara standing beside a pigpen across the barnyard with blood running down her hands.

33

HER HANDS AND wrists covered with blood, Sara waved at Dru. He ran over, grabbed her upper arms, and swept her face with a hard gaze. His stare was intense, his face ashen.

"What's wrong? How's Violet?" Seeing the look on Dru's face, she was almost afraid to hear.

"What in the *hell* is going on?" He was furious, his mouth hardened with anger. Across the pigpen, Harold Newberry was huffing and puffing as he hauled a dead pig out by its heels.

"You don't need to shout, Dru." His hands were still clenched around her upper arms. Blood slowly dripped from both her hands and started to trail down her arms toward her elbows.

Dru hollered as if she were deaf. "Did he shoot you?"

"Of course not. Stop yelling at me."

"I'll yell if I want to. What are you doing?"

"I've got Mr. Newberry making a charm for the croup." She waved the man over, handed him the bullet she'd been clutching in one hand, and took the wet rag he offered in exchange. As she wiped her hands, she glanced at the dead pig and said, "You need to pound the bullet flat, then drive a hole clean through it with a nail."

"A *charm*?" Dru looked too mad to spit.

Sara stepped closer and lowered her voice. "You have to stop yelling, Dru. Mr. Newberry and I are getting along just fine."

She tried to sound confident, but she wasn't quite as sure of herself as before Dru had appeared in such a lather. "It's one of Granddaddy's surefire cures."

"A dead pig?"

Aware that both the young and old Harold Newberrys were hanging on to every word she told Dru, she said, "It's not the *pig*. It's the *bullet* from the pig. You have to dig it out, flatten it like a pancake, put a hole in the middle of it so you can thread a string through, and hang it around the baby's neck." She snapped her fingers. "Quick as lightning, the croup will be gone."

Dru looked like he was set to hog-tie her and put her in the buggy. He ran his hand over his hair and down the back of his neck, paced six steps away, and then came back. The noonday sun had slipped a bit but was still blazing. His shirt was damp with sweat. He had rolled up his shirtsleeves, exposing his corded forearms. His dark eyes were somber and piercing.

Sara lowered her voice to a whisper. "What's the matter with you?"

"Come back inside. Now."

"But . . ."

Without another word, he took her by the arm and led her across the barnyard and into the house. He didn't let go until they were in the small back bedroom again. Dinah Newberry was dipping a piece of flannel in the warm vinegar and cayenne mixture. She looked up as they crossed the room. The sharp scent stung Sara's eyes.

"Sit there." Dru pointed to an empty chair near the door.

"I don't—"

He wouldn't let her finish. He took two steps forward and leaned over her until they were eye to eye.

"Sit."

She knew when not to press her luck. She sat. Dru returned to Dinah's side and showed her how to massage the baby's feet with the warm flannel. He helped her wrap Violet's throat with the tincture-soaked fabric.

Sara finished wiping off her hands. Dru had prescribed remedies that were all well and good—they would do a lot to ease Violet's constricted throat. But Granddaddy took stock in old-time charms and though she was certain that it was the herbals that cured the body, the charms might just give a patient, as well as those around, peace of mind.

Dru spoke to Dinah as he finally rolled down his sleeves. "I think she'll be much better soon. She's breathing easier already. Keeping her warm shouldn't be a problem in this heat, but if it cools off, warm a stone, wrap it in cloth, and put it next to her feet. She should show some improvement by tomorrow. If she doesn't, then send the boy after me again."

Dinah Newberry grabbed both Dru's hands. "Thank you, Doctor. Thank you so much for coming. I don't know how we—"

Just then, Mr. Newberry walked in with the flattened, pierced bullet hanging from a piece of twine and held it out at arm's length. "All ready. Made it just like your wife said, Doc." He tried to hand the charm to Dru, but Dru merely looked at it.

Sara stood, went to Mr. Newberry, and smiled as he dropped the charm into her hand. Ignoring Dru's silence, she walked to the crib, gently lifted the baby's head, and hung the bullet around Violet's neck. She closed her eyes and then repeated a chant three times in a whisper loud enough for all to hear.

"Bullet turn the croup. Bullet turn the croup. Protect this child. Bind her to healing. Release her to health and let her breathe free."

When she opened her eyes, the first face she saw was Dru's. He looked mad enough to chew rocks into gravel.

"Maybe I should go wait in the buggy," she suggested.

"Wait for me on the porch. Stay *right there* and don't go anywhere," he ordered.

She objected to his overbearing tone, but since the Newberrys were hanging on every word, she held her tongue, turned on her heel, and walked out.

Dru watched her go, still furious that she had scared the daylights out of him.

Dinah Newberry thanked him profusely as he picked up his jacket and tucked it over the crook of his arm, then collected his medical bag. He followed Harold Senior into the parlor where he could see Sara through an open window. She was seated in a rocking chair on the porch, staring across the landscape with her arms crossed, her head against the backrest.

Mr. Newberry had slipped into a sullen silence. Given his own disagreeable state of mind, Dru was raring for a confrontation. He wasn't about to leave before he set things straight with Newberry.

"I know some folks find it hard to accept me because of what Sara did during the war, but if you're one of those who can't live with that, Newberry, then you're free to take Violet into Hopkinsville and have the doctor over there treat her."

Harold Newberry quickly shook his head. "It ain't

like we haven't heard the talk about your wife, what with that piece in the paper, but I can't hold a grudge. The way I see it, you and your sister have been more than fair to me. You could've run me and my family right off this land for failure to pay you what I still owe."

"Then why object to my coming out here? Why didn't you let your wife send for me before?" Dru wanted to know.

"It's not your wife I object to. Hell, she's trying to help. It's that I can't pay you for treating my baby girl." He lowered his head, flexed his work-worn hands. "I didn't want to call you out here 'cause I can't pay."

Dru knew how much it cost Newberry's pride to admit that he was flat broke.

"When a child's life is at stake there should be no talk of money. You know where to find me when you get square."

"It don't look like I'll have the mill up and running again anytime soon."

"What will it take to get it going?"

Now that Violet was sleeping a bit peacefully and the discussion of payment was behind them, Newberry appeared to be a bit more at ease. He scratched his thinning, fair hair. There was dirt and pig's blood beneath his fingernails. "I've got one of the mills repaired. I made new wood blades for the top and got the mule hitch fixed. What I sorely need now are new evaporating pans. The Yankees busted up a huge sectional pan and I need another one, otherwise I can't make more 'n one batch of molasses at a time. The second, bigger mill won't turn until I can find parts somewhere. The boiling shed needs to be rebuilt, too, and it's still hard to come by milled lumber that's not overpriced."

Newberry's frustration was understandable. By crippling his mill, the Union forces had effectively shut down commerce for miles around. Aside from the fact that the man owed him money, Dru hated to see the business his grandfather had founded come to an end. It was hard to believe Kentucky had gone Union, given what the Yankees had done to Magnolia Creek and other pro-Confederate towns in the state.

"I wish there was something I could do to help you rebuild," Dru told him. "If I had it, I'd be glad to lend you the money, but that still wouldn't get the supplies here any faster."

Newberry shook his head. "I owe you enough already, Doc."

"What about some of the sorghum farmers around here? Seems to me they'd be willing to help you build a new boiling shed if it meant they'd be able to mill their cane close to home."

"You'd think that, wouldn't you? But not many around here have their own places in order yet, leastways not so they'd have time to help me out."

"Maybe all it takes is a little organizing." Dru wished there was some way to help Newberry get the mill up and running before the sorghum crop was ready to harvest.

"I sure want to thank you, Doc." Newberry extended his hand. "I'm as embarrassed as hell not to be able to pay you anything right now, but how 'bout you and your wife stay to dinner? There's not much, but what we got, we can share."

Dru glanced out the window, watched Sara fold her hands in her lap as she slowly rocked the rocker.

"Thank you, Mr. Newberry. We'd like to stay but I've got to get back to the office."

Never mind that the office was empty. Dru was too upset at Sara to think about eating.

34

~

After they all spoke their good-byes, Dru led Sara to the buggy. He set his bag on the floorboards and then realized that she was waiting for him to help her climb aboard.

He steeled himself and took a deep breath before he reached for her hand. When their eyes met, she looked away first. As he helped her up, her breasts brushed against his shirtfront. The fabric of her calico gown stroked his hand. The edge of her lace petticoat teased his eye when it flashed white beneath the hem of her gown.

Frustration gnawed at his soul. He couldn't wait to get back to town, drop her off at the house, and go back to the office where she would be out of reach.

She made a show of arranging her skirt over the cracked leather seat as he climbed aboard. Dru turned back to touch his hand to the brim of his hat as they passed the Newberrys' and then they were off down the lane.

Without the boy sandwiched between them, he had to fight to keep his eyes on the rutted road and his hands on the reins. Locked in stubborn silence, they rode past open rolling fields, up gentle grades, and through sections of densely wooded ground without exchanging a word.

The air was hot and humid. Over the sound of the horse's even hoofbeats, he heard Sara say, "Dru?"

"What?"

"I didn't realize putting Mr. Newberry to work on that charm was going to upset you so much."

They had just crossed a trickling stream running through a wooded hollow where the road was shaded. He pulled the buggy to the side of the road, stopped the horse, and set the brake.

A blue jay winged its way past the front of the buggy, lighting on a nearby tree branch. He finally turned to Sara and saw concern flash in her eyes. She edged toward the far side of the seat—a movement that further irked him—and then she glanced around as if she was suddenly aware of how vulnerable she was out there all alone with him.

"I couldn't care less how many silly charms you dole out, Sara."

"Then what's got you so boiling mad?"

He took a deep breath, let it out, and stared at the patches of blue sky showing between the leaves of the tree tunnel arched over the road. His insides felt jumbled, his stomach knotted, his heart way off-kilter.

"When I heard that gun go off, I thought you were dead. Someone tried to kill you . . . or have you already forgotten?"

"I'm the one with the scar to prove it, remember? I think it'll be quite a while before I forget, but there was no reason for you to get so riled up."

"How in the *hell* was I supposed to know what was going on? You told me if I took you along you wouldn't get in the way."

"You're yelling again."

"You're damn right I am!"

"I can take care of myself, Dru Talbot."

At that point his frustration boiled over and he barked off a harsh laugh. "Sure you can. You got yourself knifed not a month ago. Your father smacked you in the face the day you came back to town. You got yourself *pregnant* and deserted by the first man to look at you sideways. Hell yes, Sara. You sure can take care of yourself!"

The minute the harsh words were out he regretted them but the damage was already done. Sara went pale and fell silent. Tears shimmered in her eyes, heightening the intensity of liquid blue. Dru felt like an ass.

He hadn't meant to lose control, but the gunshot still reverberated in his ears. Seeing her with her hands all bloodied; the still vibrant image of her falling over, bleeding upon the kitchen threshold; his own deep abiding fear that she would be attacked again—all of it had gotten the best of him.

It would be a cold day in hell before he forgot how she had nearly died. For all they knew, her attacker was still lurking out there, waiting to try again.

His tirade had obviously frightened her so much that she looked ready to bolt out of the carriage. Without making any conscious decision, before he even knew he was going to touch her, he pulled her into his arms. Before he could stop and think, he crushed her against him and covered her mouth with his.

When her lips parted in surprise he took advantage, deepening the kiss, plunging his tongue into her mouth. Her hands clutched the front of his shirt, gathered it into her fists.

He pressed her back against the black leather buggy seat, held her tight, and lost every shred of control he had left. Weeks, months, years of need exploded as he assaulted her mouth with his lips.

She moaned and tried to twist away. He wanted her too much to let go. He burned with desire as he slipped a hand between them and cupped her breast. Sara went completely still when he began to grapple with the buttons down the front of her gown.

The first came open easily, the second followed. The third button ripped away, pinged against the floorboard. She was kissing him back now, her tongue teasing his, her hands relaxed against his shirtfront, the warmth of her palm seeping into his heart.

His hand edged around the fabric of her gown, slid into the heated warmth between her breasts. The erotic feel of her satin-soft skin, its heat, his burgeoning need, all drove him past the turning point. He shuddered, nearly climaxed, forced himself to tear his mouth away.

Eyes closed, he dropped his forehead to hers as his breath came in ragged bursts.

No matter how hard he tried to deny it, no matter how much he lied to himself, absolutely nothing had changed the way he wanted her. Neither the lost years nor the things Sara had done could eradicate his desire. His heart was still bruised and bleeding and in the heat of the moment he had reacted to her nearness with the same lust and yearning she had inspired in him ever since the first time he laid eyes on her.

He hadn't planned to touch her, let alone kiss her. He hadn't expected things to go this far, but where Sara was concerned, his emotions had always spiraled out of control. As long as she was in his life, his reaction to her would forever be combustible.

Sara lay completely still in his arms, her breath coming

fast and shallow. Slowly he let her go, then leaned forward on the seat with his elbows on his knees and his head in his hands.

Sara's hands trembled as she pulled the front of her gown together. One of her buttons was missing. She glanced down, saw it on the floorboard, and started to pick it up.

Dru beat her to it, snapped up the bronze button. He stared at it in his open palm before he handed it back without looking at her. She fisted her hand around it, felt the metal warm to the heat of her touch.

She had wanted a chance to be alone with him—but not this way. Not this way at all. She had never seen this punishing, angry side of him, never knew he was capable of such anger. Had the war done this to him, or had she been too in love with him in the beginning to notice this side of him?

A quiet conversation, perhaps a gentle kiss. A new start. That's what she had been hoping for when she begged to come along today. Instead, he had kissed her relentlessly until she was ready to surrender all and then, just as suddenly, he had pulled back.

Clearly, he had made his point. She stared at his back as he remained hunched over, unwilling to look at her.

"Well, Dru, you proved how weak I am. Too weak to protect myself. Too weak to resist."

"I didn't mean for this to happen."

"No? What *did* you mean to happen?"

He faced her finally, unreadable, cold, assessing. Unforgiving. "Nothing. Nothing at all."

"I see."

The road that stretched before them yawned empty,

the leaves of the trees hung listless, limp, and silent in the summer heat.

"What now, Dru?"

She thought he was too angry to answer until he sighed heavily and said, "Now we go home."

35

Sara left Dru unhitching the horse, anxious to put space between them, hurrying into the house to take comfort in Elizabeth's bright smile and to focus on something other than what had happened on the road.

She hurried from the kitchen to the parlor, enveloped by the aroma of fresh bread that filled the entire house. The warm, homey scent did little to ease her melancholy. Whatever ground she had gained with Dru had been lost and now all they shared was a tense, silent wariness fueled by his anger and her embarrassment.

When am I going to learn?

When am I going to think before I act?

Dru was a man of honor. He had taken an oath and no matter what came between them, no matter how much he might hate her, he obviously intended to stand by his wedding vows; but surely his obligation was all that kept him from divorcing her. Why else would he let her stay on when he certainly didn't love her anymore? That was more than evident now.

As she moved swiftly through the house following the sound of her daughter's voice, she tried to convince herself that hanging on to a hopeless dream wasn't fair to any of them.

No matter what she did to prove herself, Dru might never forgive her and if he couldn't, then there was no place for her in his home or his life any longer. There was certainly no room in his heart for Elizabeth. What would she tell her daughter when Lissybeth began to notice his aversion to her?

The harsh truth started sifting through Sara's troubled thoughts during the tense silence they had shared on the ride home. If she stayed, all three of them would be miserable for the rest of their lives. If she released him from his obligation and asked for a divorce, then he would be able to move on and find happiness with someone else.

She loved Dru enough to want his happiness, even though she had no idea where she would go or what she would do.

The drawing room doors were open. Afternoon light sifted through sheer panels of lace at the windows, highlighting gilded picture frames and crystal teardrops hanging from the chandeliers.

"Mama!" Elizabeth called out to her but was content to remain in Louzanna's lap, playing with the opal ring. Louzanna's face was creased with worry lines, her hazel eyes filled with such concern that Sara feared the woman might be on the verge of another bout of jitters. Goldie got up and padded over to greet her.

Sara stepped farther into the room, petted the dog, then stopped dead in her tracks when she saw Billy, one of her three younger brothers, standing near the front window. She hadn't laid eyes on him since he was ten. Now, at sixteen, he was taller than she, lean and lanky with a shock of auburn hair falling across his forehead. Nervously, he pushed it back with fine tapered fingers, his hands more delicate than any of the other Collier men.

Musically inclined, Billy had taken to playing the fiddle early on. He wrote his own songs and kept the family entertained on cold winter nights. Standing in the Talbots' drawing room, he looked as out of place as a Baptist in a barroom, with his battered straw hat clutched in one fist, wearing his too-short pants and a mended shirt. Sara's heart sank to her toes when she noticed that his eyes were red-rimmed, his face colorless and sad.

"What is it?" Her voice was suddenly thready, so useless she could only whisper. "Granddaddy's dead, isn't he?"

Billy was shaking so fiercely his shirtsleeves trembled around his thin arms. "No. Granddaddy sent me to fetch you home."

Sara thought her legs were going to give out. "Mama? Not Mama!"

He crossed the room, took her hands. "No, Sara. It's not Mama, leastwise, not yet. Daddy's dead. He died this morning."

"Daddy?" She squeezed his hand and let go as she stared in disbelief.

Never in her life had she imagined Daddy dying. By all accounts, he was fifty-six. Folks who knew him always declared DeWitt Collier too mean to die, but her daddy had plenty of enemies. The Colliers had been feuding with more than one backwoods family for as long as anyone could recall.

"Who killed him?"

"Nobody. There's terrible sickness on the other side of the creek. Started a couple of days ago. Daddy looked as if he was getting better, then this morning he was bleeding from everywhere and then he up and died. Mama's beside herself. Jane's got it now. Fannie, too."

DeWitt Collier was often hateful, cruel, and intimidating; still, he was her father. He had provided for them and kept his family together in the only way he knew how—with a switch in one hand and the Bible in the other. It was up to God to judge him, not her. Right now, her concern was for the rest of her family.

"What about the others?" She was afraid to hear.

There were so many spread out over the backcountry—Donnie and Darrel and their families; Sue and Jo, her two older sisters, had married and gone long before Sara had married Dru; Ethan and Ray; Ronnie, who lived with Jo because their daddy had almost killed him once when Ronnie was twelve and he'd caught Ronnie wearing one of the girls' dresses. Agitated, Sara tried to concentrate.

"What about Granddaddy? Is he down, too?"

Billy shook his head. "Granddaddy's fine. He wanted me to come fetch you and he said to bring your man back with you, too." He slapped his hat against his thigh. When his lower lip trembled, he glanced over at Louzanna and then away, ashamed to let his feelings show.

Sara hugged him. Fighting for control, he didn't hug her back. Elizabeth wriggled off Louzanna's lap, ran over and tugged on Sara's skirt. Sara lifted the child, brushed her fair hair back off her forehead, and kissed her on the nose. Louzanna came to stand beside her and took hold of her hand.

"Don't go, Sara," Lou whispered. "Please don't put yourself in danger."

"Granddaddy needs your help, Sara," Billy urged.

"I'll come." She looked to Lou. "There's nothing else I can do. My family needs me."

"Death is out there waiting for us all." Louzanna

looked out the window. Afraid that Lou was about to get hysterical when she needed her most, Sara hid her own distress. She pasted a smile on her face and tried to sound calm.

"I have to go with Billy. Just for a day or so." She quickly handed Elizabeth over to her sister-in-law again. "I'll have to leave Elizabeth with you and Jamie again. Can you do it, Lou? Will you be able to watch over her for me?"

Louzanna wavered. Frantically she glanced over at Billy, then down at Goldie, and appeared about to protest until Elizabeth wrapped her arms around Lou's neck, touched her nose to Lou's, and said, "My Woo."

Lou straightened, looked Sara in the eye, and nodded. "We'll be fine." Fear danced around the edges of a taut smile, but she seemed to be calming. "Dru has to go with you this time."

"Go where?"

Dru stepped into the room and saw Sara standing beside a trim, fragile-looking young man with features so like hers that the stranger had to be a Collier. Sara's face was flushed, her eyes bright with unshed tears.

"What's going on?" Dru demanded.

Sara quickly introduced her brother. The youth nodded and shifted uncomfortably. From the look of the young man's disheveled hair and red-rimmed eyes, Dru didn't have to be told that something was terribly wrong at Collier's Ferry.

"Daddy's dead. There's sickness at home and Granddaddy sent for me." Sara's face was set with such closed, stubborn determination that Dru knew objecting would be a waste of time.

Now that her father was gone, they might never know whether DeWitt Collier had been the one responsible for the stabbing. That was his first compulsive thought, and it was swiftly swallowed by anger. He was still on edge, still furious at himself for what happened in the buggy and tired of worrying about her on top of everything else.

He'd grown weary of searching for Sara's attacker in the faces on Main Street, wondering if and when the man would strike again. He was sick to death of wanting Sara, fed up with torturing himself over her sleeping with another man and wondering if he might have prevented it all had he acted sooner.

Frustrated, he had spent hours from the very beginning doubting himself, her love, and everything she ever said or did. Still, he felt the need to protect her.

"You're not going back there. They wouldn't have you before. You don't owe them anything now," he argued.

Sara walked up to him. "They're my people, Dru. My family," she said softly.

"They threw you out. I'm still not convinced that your father didn't try to kill you. You aren't waltzing out of here without any more protection than that boy."

"You can't ask me to turn my back on my family."

"They turned their backs on you."

"Because Daddy made them. Now he's gone. It's Mama who needs me now, and Granddaddy's counting on me to come home. He wants you to come, too, but whether or not you do, I have to go, Dru."

He walked over to a low drum table, lifted the crystal decanter, and poured himself a shot of whiskey before he turned back to Billy Collier. "What are their symptoms?"

The young man started as soon as he realized Dru was

talking to him; then he took a step back. "What do you mean?"

"What's wrong with them?" Dru suspected cholera. Outbreaks during the war had been plentiful because of terrible sanitary conditions in the camps. The Colliers lived in bottomland that flooded in the spring and summer and drained improperly in the best of weather.

Billy glanced at Sara. She nodded encouragingly.

"Bad headache. Thirsty." The young man faltered. Swallowed. "Daddy turned yellow. At the end he was bleeding from his nose and mouth."

"What is it, Dru?" Sara asked.

Knowing that his sister was hanging on every word, Dru gave a slight shake of his head. To his relief, Sara picked up his cue and didn't press him.

"I'm not sure" was all he said.

"Whether you go or not, I can't wait any longer." Sara swung around and grabbed Billy's hand, ready to walk out. She crossed the room, towing Billy in her wake. Dru grabbed her as she walked by.

"Please, don't stop me," she murmured.

Without thought, he stroked her upper arm with his thumb. She was a fighter, his Sara, he would grant her that. However, he suspected the Colliers were facing something she couldn't fight, no matter what potions and charms she and her granddaddy concocted.

"What if it's yellow fever?" he whispered.

"I still have to go."

Dru knew that for the good of everyone in Magnolia Creek he had to go, too. As the only doctor around for miles, it was up to him to diagnose the disease and if indeed it was yellow fever, then he would have to demand the marshal quarantine the town.

Although there hadn't been an outbreak in years, he still knew enough about yellow fever to know not to lie to himself about the grievousness of the situation.

Sara was about to walk into hell and he wasn't about to let her go alone.

36

NIGHT CLOAKED THE land in coal-black shadows. Dru had no idea exactly where they were going, but Sara and Billy unerringly followed a maze of paths through the woods until they came to a small cabin in a clearing on the other side of Magnolia Creek. The mosquitoes were relentless in the lowland.

The stench of urine, feces, and death inside the mud-chinked log walls of the Colliers' one-room cabin nearly staggered Dru as he followed Sara and her brother inside. Greased parchment covered some of the windows. Spaces between the logs were daubed with crumbling clay. Dru reckoned the place had been constructed well over seventy years ago.

As he gazed around the cabin, it was hard for him to imagine a family of sixteen living in such a confined space. The main room was furnished with a long, hand-carved trestle table and benches, a bed, and other necessities. Against the far wall, an immense fireplace plastered with mud provided heat in the winter and a place to cook year-round. Two iron pots hung on a standing rod in the center of the open hearth. A spinning wheel stood nearby while a loom took up precious space near the back wall.

A loft covered half of the room; the only way up was

by a crooked pole ladder. Frayed edges of bedding dangled from the loft. The cabin was cramped, dingy, and depressing, with no sign of any conveniences, and Dru found himself unable to imagine someone with Sara's spirit having been raised in such a dismal place.

In a glance he clearly understood Sara's willingness to leave this place behind. She once told him that ever since childhood she had dreamed of another life for herself and that when Doc Porter had asked her to take care of Louzanna, it was an answer to her prayers.

Standing there in the middle of her former world, he suddenly became aware of the part he and his sister had played in taking her out of this life.

A thin, hollow-eyed woman bearing a vague resemblance to Sara ran across the dirt floor to greet them. Before Dru could stop her, Sara took her mother in her arms and held her close. The two women rocked back and forth, crying silently until Sara's mother was the first to pull away. She wiped her eyes on the back of her thin wrist and stared past Sara, straight at Dru.

"Is that him?" she whispered.

"Yes, Mama, this is Dru. He's come to help." Sara glanced over her shoulder and Dru's heart slipped a notch when their eyes met. She quickly averted her gaze. If Sara was still wary of him after the buggy incident that afternoon, he couldn't blame her.

Sara introduced him to her mother, Tessa Collier, who crossed her arms and clutched her elbows as if about to cave in on herself.

"Did you hear? Did Billy tell you?" Tessa asked Sara.

"Daddy's dead. I know, Mama. Has . . . has anyone else died?"

Tessa quickly shook her head. "No, but Jane and Fannie are down. They got it real bad. I sent Kittie and Arlo up to stay at Jo's."

"Where's . . . where's Daddy now?" Sara looked around as if expecting DeWitt to materialize.

"Donnie and Darrel buried him up the hill this afternoon." Tessa wiped her eyes again. "I can't believe he's gone," she whispered.

Dru couldn't tell if she sounded mournful or relieved.

"Mrs. Collier," he said softly, stepping forward with his medical bag in hand, "can I see the girls?"

She was about to lead him across the room when Sara's grandfather walked through the door. The only other time Dru had ever seen Daniel Wilkes had been on their wedding day, and the two of them had hardly exchanged more than a few words.

Wilkes was tall and straight as an ancient hickory and appeared to be just as tough. His face was the color of old leather, creased and dried by the sun. What arrested Dru most was the otherworldly color of the man's sky-blue eyes and the intense stare he leveled on them all as he took in Sara, her mother, Billy, and finally Dru.

Wilkes nodded in silent greeting.

"Sir," Dru said.

Sara ran straight to her grandfather's arms.

"I'm glad you came, Sarie. Glad you brought your man, too. Come with me." The old man led them to the only bed in the room, where two young girls lay side by side on a lumpy corn-husk mattress. They were covered with a darned sheet and a spread made of pieces of wool pants, jackets, and coats, all hand-stitched together.

Old Dan asked Tessa to bring the oil lamp closer. As her mother walked away, Sara leaned over the girls and

Dru grabbed her arm before she could reach out and touch the sister closest to them.

"It's yellow fever, Sara." He kept his voice low as his mind raced in a hundred directions at once. One look convinced him that the dreaded sickness had struck. He had to alert the town and have Damon Monroe set up a quarantine around Magnolia Creek. The ferry would have to be shut down and travelers contained until the threat lifted.

Dan Wilkes was watching him closely.

Tessa Collier returned. Because her hands were trembling, the lamplight was flickering madly. Wilkes took hold of the lamp and held it steady.

"How long have they been ill?" Dru tried to assess which stages of the fever the girls were in.

"Jane came down 'fore Fannie, about three days ago," Tessa said.

"Jane's thirteen," Sara told him. "Fannie's ten."

"Is that you, Sara?" The older of the two, Jane, spoke so softly they barely heard her.

Sara shook off Dru's hold and sank to the side of the bed, taking her little sister's hand. "It's me, Jane. I'm here."

"Have you come to stay?"

"For a while."

"I missed you, Sara. When you go, will you take me with you?"

Sara's voice was choked with emotion. "We'll see."

"I'm dying like Daddy."

"No. I won't let you."

"Promise?"

"I promise."

Jane fell silent. Beside her, little Fannie lay still as death, never even stirring at the sound of their voices.

Dru felt each of their foreheads in turn. Their skin was dry and hot and they were yellow around the eyes. He placed his thumb on the younger girl's chin, gently drew Fannie's mouth open, and heard Sara gasp. Fannie's tongue was almost black.

"Have they vomited recently?" He measured Fannie's pulse. She was so thin that he didn't hold much hope of her body putting up any fight.

"Not anymore," Tessa said.

"Is anyone else sick? How about yourself? How do you feel?"

Tessa shook her head. "I had yellow fever years ago, when Sara was just a mite. She had a touch of it, too, and so did a few of the older children, but they all got better." Her forehead creased. "I can't recall who else took sick back then. Some did, some didn't. I don't think DeWitt ever did."

At least, for now, Sara was safe. From everything he had read and all he had heard about yellow fever, it rarely, if ever, struck twice. But most folks didn't survive the first bout.

"How are you treating them?" Dru asked Wilkes. He was about to set his bag down when the elderly gentleman stepped close, raised the lamp, and looked down into Sara's eyes.

"What would *you* do, Sarie?" he asked.

Dru watched her forehead crease. She stared down at her sisters, lost in thought. Finally she looked up at her grandfather again.

"Vinegar rubs."

Old Dan nodded. "What else?"

"Pennyroyal and catnip tea. Keep the bed warm. Make them break a sweat."

Again, "What else?"

Sara chewed her bottom lip, thinking. "Chamomile. Boneset."

"Yes." Her grandfather tugged on the point of his long beard.

"Ground lobelia seed for emetic."

The fourth herb she named was the one Dru would have administered first.

"I tried 'em all," Dan Wilkes said. "Very good, Sarie. Very good."

Dru listened, impressed. Sara had just prescribed the same herbals and procedures he had been taught to use, but neither she nor Daniel had mentioned isolating the girls from the rest of the family or from the backwoods community at large.

The noncontagionist view of those who believed disease stemmed from conditions and not contagion was still widely recognized in the medical field. He leaned more toward germ theory, suspecting the moment they walked into the house that he and Sara had exposed themselves.

"Anything else, Sarie?" Dan was watching her closely, as if trying to divine her thoughts.

"Poppets for each. Prayer and a charm." Sara turned to Dru to explain. "A poppet is a doll, but it's also a conjuring bag of herbs—three, seven, or nine, mixed together. Added to that are things that belong to the sickly, a piece of hair, a fingernail. You stuff a finger-sized muslin bag and tie off one end so that it looks like a head, then sew up the top."

"Why don't you go on out to my lean-to and start makin' two poppets while I talk to Talbot." Daniel fell silent when Sara hesitated. She looked reluctant to leave.

Dru felt compelled to touch her. Gently, reassuringly, he laid his hand on her shoulder. Her eyes widened in surprise, her lips trembled with a heart-twisting, fleeting smile. His own heart ached with regret when he saw how much that one simple gesture meant to her.

"Go ahead, Sara," he said softly. "I'll see what I can do to help your grandfather."

"But—"

"Go on." He watched her hesitate and knew she doubted the healing power of the charms, but then she bent over her sisters, whispering to each of them, stroking her fingers through their long hair before she turned and hurried out the door.

"You agree with what she said, Talbot? All those things she suggested?" Wilkes asked.

Staring into the old man's eyes, Dru had the feeling the man already knew what he was going to say. "All but the poppet business."

"Poppets aren't child's play."

"I know you don't think so. There are other things I'd do before I put stock in a charm."

"Such as?"

"Curtailing this thing. Try to keep it from spreading. I'd wash the girls down, strip the bed. Keep my own hands clean."

"I got no more bedding," Tessa said mournfully. She had been so silent, so unobtrusive, that Dru had forgotten she was still there listening to every word.

He was certain DeWitt Collier had died in the very same bed. If it was up to him, he'd burn the whole thing. "Lay them on clean clothes, whatever cloth you have. That bedding should be burned. Anything the girls or your husband have worn should be burned, too."

Glancing around the pitifully sparse cabin, he thought of all the cupboards and the linen press at home overflowing with embroidered linens and piles of Louzanna's precious quilts. Most of the things were never touched, except when Louzanna refolded them to prevent fading and wear along the folds.

The old man's eyes took on a faraway look, as if he could see beyond the walls of the dilapidated, cramped cabin. "When I was young we used to always burn everything a body ever owned after he died so as to keep the devil from movin' in." He scratched his shoulder, rolled back on his heels. "Your town's got some bad times coming," he warned. "You'll be in the eye of the storm, Talbot. You think you're ready?"

Dru thought back to the battlefield tents, the deafening rounds of cannon fire, the smoke, the screams of the wounded and the dying. In aprons covered in blood, he had stood in field hospitals, shoved intestines back into abdomens, amputated so many limbs in a day that they were piled three feet high outside the medical tent. At times the only light to work by came from scooped-out turnips filled with oil and wicks.

"A man does what he has to do. What he knows he can do." He met Wilkes's potent stare and suddenly understood. "That's why you wanted me to come with Sara tonight, wasn't it? So I'd be ready."

Dan nodded. "A man ought to know his enemy."

Behind them on the bed the youngest girl, Fannie, coughed weakly. Dru, Tessa, and old Dan turned toward the sound. Tessa cried out and staggered, falling to her knees beside the bed. Blood trickled from the little girl's nostrils.

Dru wondered if that was why Dan Wilkes had sent

Sara out of the room. Had he known the child's death was imminent? For the second time that day, Dru was swept with overwhelming helplessness in the face of a child's fate. There was nothing any of them could do now but make the poor girl and her sister comfortable.

He shrugged out of his coat, draped it across a nearby bench, and set his bag down beside it. His heart broke for Sara. There was nothing further to be done for either of her sisters. No potion, no mixture, no magic poppet could cure them now.

37

SARA'S HANDS SHOOK as she stuffed finger-sized muslin cases with ground boneset, pennyroyal, and catnip. She added strands of the girls' hair she'd brought in from the other room. With a second string she tied off another section so that the tubes of muslin looked like armless, legless dolls.

Candles flickered on the small shelf lined with Granddaddy's conjuring things. She walked over to the altar, held the poppets tight, and repeated the Lord's Prayer three times before she began a chant.

"Fever, fever, be quick to leave her. Leave Fannie behind and go." She spoke the charm three times for each girl, holding the poppets tight, picturing the girls the way she'd seen them last, young and carefree, whole and healthy, playing in the clearing in front of the cabin.

When Lissybeth's image flashed through her mind, she quickly tried to banish it so that the illness would not jump to her daughter. Frightened, she started when she heard footsteps behind her and turned, expecting to see Granddaddy.

Dru was standing on the threshold watching her.

His gaze swept the tidy living area, the twine-bound bundles of herbs drying overhead, the altar with Granddaddy's candles and rocks, muslin, yarn, and bowls. His expression was solemn, his eyes bleak.

"What's wrong?" she asked, trying to swallow.

"Fannie just passed. Your grandfather's tending Jane. She's still fighting."

"I've got to go to them." Blinded by tears, she started toward the door. Dru blocked her way.

"Your grandfather wants you to go back to town with me."

His image wavered and blurred. She swiped the back of her hand across her eyes. "I can't leave now. There's the laying out to see to. My mama . . ."

"This is yellow fever, Sara. I've got to get back to see if any sickness has been reported and convince Monroe to set up a quarantine." His eyes searched her face. "I'm not leaving you here," he said softly, "even for a night."

There was something unspoken in his eyes, something besides anger that was so compelling her hands began to tremble around the poppets clutched in her fists.

"Because Granddaddy wants you to take me back?"

He shook his head, stepped closer. "*I* want you to go back with me, Sara." Lifting his hand, he cupped her face.

Her breath caught. She stared up into his eyes, watched him draw closer until he was so near she closed her eyes rather than be tempted to reach for him and be rejected. Her heart was beating triple time. A shock rippled through her when his lips touched hers. This time he kissed her with aching gentleness, the kind of tenderness she had been longing for before the disastrous affair in the buggy.

Afraid to move, afraid to break the spell, she parted her lips, let him trace them with his tongue. He did not embrace her, he simply touched her cheek and kissed her back. They swayed close, hearts drawn to each other until his shirtfront touched the bodice of her gown. Not until then did Dru lift his head and end the kiss.

More a declaration of doubt and need than of forgiveness or a promise of love, it was still a beginning.

Sara placed Fannie's poppet on Granddaddy's altar. She kept the other for Jane. Through her tears, she tried to smile, but failed miserably. Loss tempered her blossoming hope.

"We have to go back, Sara. It's too late to call a town meeting tonight, but early tomorrow I'll have to warn everyone and find out if there have been any cases in town."

"You really think folks can pass this fever to one another?"

Dru reached up and thumbed away her tears. "No one knows how it spreads for sure, but if it does travel from one person to another somehow, we have to stop it."

Her stomach dropped to her toes. She pictured the thing moving like a bad spell. She looked down at her hands, pictured Elizabeth again and the danger she might be carrying home. "I've touched the girls. You have, too."

"Your mother thinks you've already had yellow fever and so has she. Daniel may have had it, too. I hope to God she's right. Yellow fever isn't known to strike twice, at least not from what I've read. But we may be carrying it on our clothes. I can't say for sure."

"What will we do?"

"Go back to town. Wash ourselves down and stay at Doc Porter's house tonight. I'll wake Jamie and have him get us a change of clothes and burn these. In the morning I'll go to the mayor and the marshal."

"Maybe the fever is just on this side of the creek."

Dru squeezed her hand. "I hope so."

It was clear there was little conviction behind his hope.

Sadness was a heavy burden and tonight Daniel Wilkes's load weighed more than usual. In the space of twenty-four hours he had lost a son-in-law and a granddaughter despite all he had done.

Exhausted, Bible in hand, Dan walked over to the huge stone hearth and sat down beside a flickering oil lamp. He couldn't read as well as his grandmother, but holding the ancient, leather-bound text always gave him comfort. He knew his favorite verses by heart. His own granny had been the one to pass the old ways down to him, the charms and chants, the herbal lore. The secrets were always passed from woman to man and from man to woman. That was the order of things. None of the wisdom was ever written down. To do so would dilute its power.

He secretly wished he was Sara's age again as he coveted her youth, her vitality, her trust, and her belief in her own power to heal. He had made the right choice by deciding early on to pass his secrets to her. She was both quick-witted and graceful. She had a glow powerful enough to light up a room if one had the ability to see it.

Dru Talbot's attraction to Sara was so strong that it crackled like lightning as it arched between the two of them. Dan knew at a glance that his granddaughter and her husband were bound by more than vows. Strong, irresistible passion and desire drew them to each other, but there was also frustration, sorrow, and, on the man's part, a dark guilt as well as vexation. Their tumultuous past swirled like a vortex around them, one which might inevitably tear them apart.

As Dan stared from one to the other, he whispered a quick, protective chant in Sara's name, knowing she would soon have to face whatever came. There was no way to avoid a reckoning.

Sorrow tainted the very air inside the cabin where the women laid out Fannie on the table and gently washed her down. They stitched up a cloth shroud and prepared her for burial in the morning.

Poor Tessa's expression was empty, her mind safely flown elsewhere as she did work no mother should ever have to do, gently washing her child's face, hands, arms, and feet for the last time. Sara, not as stoic as her mother, cried silently for the lost years she might have spent with Fannie, the future they would never see together, and most of all for her mother. Now that Sara was a mother herself, watching Tessa suffer had to be that much harder. She must surely be wondering how she could live through performing the same heartbreaking task for her own child, a question that would be answered with the deepest pain of all.

Across the stifling room, Sara's husband had taken over Jane's care. The man's courage and stubborn refusal to give up both surprised and pleased Dan. Dru Talbot leaned over the bed with his sleeves rolled up, his brow glistening with perspiration, continually bathing Jane's arms and legs and pouring herbal concoctions down her throat.

Dan had already divined that Jane was going to live. He'd seen a change in her a few minutes after Sara had gone into the lean-to. Sara had returned and tucked a poppet into Jane's listless hand. With tears glistening on her cheeks, Sara had smiled up at him and told him confidently, "She'll live now, Granddaddy. Our Jane will live."

Dan waited until the last stitch was taken in the old horse blanket that Tessa had used for a shroud. He got to his feet and called Sara over, looked into her anguished eyes, and told her to go on back to Magnolia Creek with her man.

He didn't tell her that he could see what lay ahead for them in the coming days and nights, for he didn't know.

They would suffer a test of light and shadow, life and death, one that would either bind them together or tear them apart forever.

38

Well past midnight, Sara prowled the second floor of Doc Porter's house wearing one of Esther Porter's nightgowns, waiting for Dru to return. He had led her into a small shed out back, handed her a horse blanket, and told her to strip off her clothes and leave them in a pile on the floor.

When she was finished, he took her through the darkened backyard to the door, let her in, and told her where to find a lamp. He told her to wash herself thoroughly, then he set out to walk home, awaken Jamie, and enlist his help.

Sara carried the lamp as she wandered down the short hall separating the two small upper rooms. She chose the more feminine one for herself.

A portrait in an oval frame hung above the four-poster bed. She raised the lamp and studied the wedding couple smiling down at her—a young version of Doc Porter and his wife. The good doctor was dressed in his Sunday best. Clutching a bouquet of violets, his wife was dressed in a flowing white gown, primly seated on the arm of his chair. With the lamplight accenting the glow in their eyes, they looked so vibrant and alive that the idea that they were both gone weighed heavily on her heart. She wondered whether Doc Porter had already loved his wife as deeply that day as he had at the end of their lives or if his love had grown slowly over the years. . . .

A door closed on the first floor followed by the creak of floorboards. Sara turned her back on the portrait and set the lamp down on the bureau near the door. Light splashed out into the hallway, gilding the worn oak floorboards, pushing back the shadows. She walked to the edge of the ring of light, strained to see down the narrow stairwell.

"Dru?" she called softly, staring down into the yawning darkness. Her hand went to the open neckline of her borrowed gown, her fingers suddenly cold against her bare throat. "Is that you?"

"Yes, it's me, Sara. Go back to bed."

"Did you wake Jamie?" She waited, expecting to see him at the foot of the stairs, but he didn't appear. "Dru?"

"Get to *bed*, Sara."

"Is everything all right at the house? Did you bring back some of my clothes?"

"Yes." Then silence.

Why was he hugging the shadows, refusing to answer? She grabbed the handrail, started down the stairs.

"Don't come down."

She halted. "Why not?" She waited at the top of the stairs. "Was everything all right? How is Elizabeth?"

"The house was dark. They're sound asleep."

Sara wished this terrible night would end. Wished she could get home to her child and blot out the memory of Fannie's torturous last few hours, Jane's suffering, and her mother's intense sorrow. She needed time alone to mourn and to cherish all she held dear, to try to erase the memory of her mother's tears falling on the stitches of Fannie's shroud.

"Go back to bed, Sara," Dru insisted again.

"I wasn't *in* bed."

There was another long, silent pause, then a frustrated sigh. "I'm not dressed."

Her cheeks flared and she started to remind him that she had seen him naked before, but then thought better of it and walked back into the bedroom.

The stairs creaked in the way of an old, comfortable home as Dru came upstairs. Sara moved toward the lamp, waiting to turn it down until he passed on down the hall. When the sound of his footsteps abruptly halted outside of her door, her heartbeat began to dance.

Compelled by a silent force of magnetism, Sara slowly turned. Framed in the door in the half light, bare-chested, Dru clutched a towel around his hips with one hand while he raked the fingers of the other through his glistening, damp hair. A puckered scar, like the one at his temple, marked his shoulder, a forever reminder of the war. The intimacy of his near-nakedness elicited a rush of warmth that came with a need both fierce and desperate to cling to life.

Dru told himself to move, to walk, to *run* down the hall if he had to. Anything to break the spell. Backlit by lamp-light, Sara's voluptuous figure was silhouetted in alluring detail against the fabric of a flowing white nightgown; the enticing lift of her breasts, the gentle curve of her hip, the outline of her shapely thighs. Her auburn hair swept around her shoulders like a silken mantle. The blunt ends swayed around her waist.

After one glance, he found himself unable to pass by.

Nor could he think beyond the overwhelming urge to touch her. He knew her hair would feel like silk against his skin, that her lips would taste as warm and rich as expensive bourbon.

He fisted his hands. Despite everything, he still wanted her and no other.

Any other man would have taken her by now.

You aren't just any other man. You're still her husband.

All the more reason you're entitled to what you want.

He knew there would be no turning back when he stepped over the threshold. The drapes were drawn, the covers were turned down. The four-poster beckoned.

Nothing but your own stubborn pride is keeping you from having her. Pride makes a cold and lonely bedmate.

Six strides brought him directly in front of her. Suddenly he was staring down into those glorious, intense eyes. She met his stare without flinching, her eyelids red-rimmed and swollen from crying. Even knowing all that she had lost, all she had suffered that night could not temper his need.

Sara took a step back. When she bumped into the bureau her lips parted in surprise. A slight gasp escaped her.

He moved before he could talk himself out of it, dropped the towel and laid his hands on her shoulders, pulled her up against him. Then he slashed his lips across hers without a hint of warning or tenderness. It was her fault. She had driven him over the edge, forced him to lose control without saying a word, without even touching him.

He pressed her back against the bureau. After what happened on the way home from the Newberrys', he expected her to resist, but when she whimpered against his mouth, encircled his neck, and wound her fingers through his hair, he was lost.

The soft cotton fabric of her voluminous white nightgown teased his skin as he rubbed against her, seeking more. All the hunger he had suffered through the war years, everything he had denied himself these last torturous weeks of watching her, hearing her voice, aching to have her from the very bottom of his soul, all of it finally pushed him over the edge.

The kiss went on, long and deep, filled with more than words could ever say. He wanted her. He needed her. There would be no turning back from what was sure to happen in this quiet house on this sultry night.

In one swift move he broke the kiss, wrapped his arm around the back of her knees, lifted her high against his chest, and carried her to the bed. He pressed her back against the pillows and crushed her beneath him before she could draw another breath.

He wanted to be gentle with her but his lust overshot its bounds when she leaned into him and whispered his name.

He couldn't shut out the images poisoning his mind, images of her with another man. It was so damned easy to picture *his* Sara, *his* wife, in the arms of her lover—a man who didn't even deserve to breathe the air she breathed.

Dru pulled his mouth away and ended the kiss. A day's growth of beard scraped her soft cheek when he reached down for the hem of her gown and drew it up her silken thighs to her waist.

He edged his knee between her legs, opened her, probed with his erection. She felt slick and hot, willing and ready. Without hesitation, without any thought save one, he buried himself inside her.

You are still mine, Sara. You are still mine.

A burst of sound, a soft cry escaped Sara. She closed her eyes, bit her lips, wanting Dru, needing him, though she knew he was taking her in anger, not love. Discontent and indignation had finally gotten the better of him. He was punishing himself as much as her for the past and yet she sensed he was holding himself back, protecting her from his anger. He had the power to hurt her, yet he did nothing of the kind.

He thrust again and then went completely still, almost as if trying to stop what he had begun.

Tears slipped from her eyes, trickled hot and heavy down her cheeks. He raised his head, stared at her with eyes dark as midnight, deep as eternity. Then his lids lowered halfway, shielding her from a gaze as hot as his sweat-slicked skin beneath her hands.

Another tear leaked from the corner of her eye.

"You're my wife, dammit." His voice was raspy and tight. He sounded as if he was in pain.

She nodded, closed her eyes, and let the tears fall. She was his wife, and yet . . .

She slid her hands down his spine to his hips, then pressed her open palms against his buttocks, urging him to fill her. She wanted him too desperately to refuse even though it tore at her soul to have him take her like this, without love.

He sighed, a deep, telling sound of resignation, surprised her by tenderly kissing away the tears at her temples. She closed her eyes as he pressed his lips against her moist lashes, trailed feather-light kisses to her mouth.

Though she tasted gentleness, there was no hint of love. They both knew what they were doing and why. She raised her hips, silently urging him to move, but there were no tender whispers, no love words exchanged. Desire drove them to finish what they started.

Slowly he withdrew and then entered her again with such torturous precision that she was afraid she would scream. She tongued his ear, traced it. His thrusts increased in tempo until he reached around and beneath her, grasped her buttocks, kneaded them, and began to move with a wild, rapid beat.

Sara dug her heels into the bed, went with him. She panted, a harsh, breathy tattoo that matched his every thrust.

He drove into her, taking her to the brink of fulfillment, pulling back until she finally pleaded with him to bring her to the blessed release she craved.

Without warning he let out a groan and lunged. The headboard hit the wall. He arched and shuddered. When he released his seed, she shattered into fragments as fine as stardust. Drifting to earth again, all that was left of her was the beat of her heart and the echo of her ragged breathing.

The flame in the oil lamp sputtered and died. Dru was aware of little save the darkness and his heart pounding in time with hers. Sara lay unmoving, perhaps afraid to say anything to him. He tried to tell himself it didn't matter.

His arms and legs felt like deadweights. At last his body was at ease. Languid to his very marrow, he realized relief was only partial and temporary at best. His mind was still in turmoil.

Sara's tears had melted him, brought him to his senses,

soothed him so that an act begun in frustration and anger had dissolved into more tenderness than he had thought himself capable of anymore.

Slowly he eased off her, rolled onto his back, and draped the inside of his arm across his eyes. She moved beside him, drew her gown down to her thighs, and went perfectly still.

They lay side by side in an awkward, frozen silence, hip to hip, thigh to thigh. He dropped his arm, turned his head to study her shadowed profile as she stared at the ceiling.

He swallowed. He hated himself for his weakness but wasn't surprised by it. Where Sara was concerned, it had always been impossible to remain clearheaded.

"Nothing's changed, you know." The harsh sound of his own voice cut through the tense silence. He hadn't planned on taking her and certainly hadn't thought of what to say now.

"I know," she said numbly. "I understand."

"Do you?"

"Yes. A man . . . has needs."

"It was bound to happen sooner or later with us living under the same roof." He felt cold, almost dead inside. When and how had he become a stranger, even to himself?

There was a slight pause. Her voice crumpled as she admitted, "Yes. Yes it was."

"It was purely a physical release, Sara. Nothing more."

This time there was no reply at all, only silence.

Sara lay there aching with loneliness even though Dru was still beside her. Finally, he rolled off the opposite side of the bed. She heard him walk across the room and pick up his damp towel. It snapped as he shook it out. Eyes closed, Sara imagined him winding it around his waist, padding barefoot to the door.

"Your clean clothes are on the table in the hallway. I'll be going out early to see to the mayor and the marshal."

"If I went home, would Elizabeth fall ill?" She longed to retreat, to soothe her aching heart and soul.

Little more than a shadow in the doorway, he waited awhile before he answered. "I really don't know for certain."

"Then I'm not going home. I can't take that chance."

She realized she had inadvertently called the Talbot house *home*. It wasn't really her home, nor would it be until he could accept the truth and forgive her, but for now, while Elizabeth was there, it was the closest thing to a home that she could claim.

She would continue to do whatever she had to in order to keep Lissybeth safe.

39

Dru stood in the center of the Magnolia Creek Courthouse, a building his grandfather had commissioned thirty years before. It was an imposing structure made of brick resting on a limestone foundation. A Greek Revival portico, Doric columns, and octagonal cupola gave it an overinflated air of importance.

In emotional turmoil, worried that it was too late to halt an outbreak of yellow fever, he scanned the crowded room as the clock in the tower struck eleven. The fever might already be spreading among them, making this impromptu gathering a deadly one.

Inflated with his own importance, Abel Foster sat across the raised dais and nodded in greeting as more and more townsfolk crowded inside the hall.

"Know your enemy." Dru had taken Daniel Wilkes's advice and this morning before Sara had even stirred, went straight to Abel Foster and told the publisher that he intended to call upon the mayor and urge him to quarantine the town. He needed the *Sentinel*'s backing in the event there were objections to the quarantine. Abel readily agreed without argument and Dru suspected Sara's earlier visit to him was behind his change of heart. Abel claimed that he wanted to be front and center as the story unfolded.

Together they walked to Mayor Langston's office to explain the situation. Unwilling to set off a panic, the portly, balding Langston balked at restricting travel. He questioned Dru's diagnosis, his experience, and finally even his motive.

"Is this your way of getting back at the whole town, Talbot? Nobody I know is sick, let alone down with yellow fever."

"Have you been inside every home in town?" Dru asked the mayor. "Can you absolutely guarantee the lives of the townsfolk? If the fever strikes, will you be able to look people in the eye and say that you knew about this and didn't do anything to warn them?"

After a brief but heated discussion during which Dru reminded the mayor that Abel had come along to record their conversation, George Langston finally agreed. He personally walked Dru and Abel down Main Street to Damon Monroe's office.

As Dru, Abel, and the mayor passed the general store, Witham Spalding and his band of cronies fell into step behind them, piqued by the idea of doing something more exciting than sitting on a bench swatting mosquitoes.

The marshal deputized Witham and his friends, instructing them to go door to door and report back if they discovered anyone down with a fever. Dru told them what symptoms to look for.

No sooner had they canvassed the first block when word of the search began to spread like wildfire. Within an hour some citizens had rushed to Langston's home demanding a town meeting while others hurriedly packed up and left town in a panic.

Now the good folk of Magnolia Creek had either gathered, potentially endangering each other's lives, or were fleeing town, spreading disaster around the countryside.

Still war weary, the townsfolk demanded to hear what misery threatened them now. Courthouse Square filled with tense, anxious families. People crowded beneath shade trees seeking relief from already stifling heat. The doors to the hall had been thrown open to accommodate them.

Inside the packed courtroom, wooden chairs creaked. Murmuring children were quickly shushed by frantic mothers. Dru stood where his grandfather once dedicated the building and watched the already nervous crowd grow more restless. Seated in the front row, Minnie Foster refused to acknowledge him.

Finally Mayor Langston walked in. The man took his time, jovially greeting folks as he walked up the aisle. He stepped onto the dais and called the room to order.

"I'm sure you all know Dr. Talbot." Langston paused; the absence of what he left unsaid was deafening. There was a rush of hushed conversation and then stone-cold silence. Tension and anxiety were thick in the room.

Dru hid his emotions and faced the crowd squarely, silently daring anyone to say a word against Sara. *He* might not be able to forget what she had done, but he'd be damned if he let anyone else say anything against her.

Langston scanned the crowd. "The doc here says there's an outbreak of yellow fever over at Collier's Ferry."

Before he could say more someone shouted, "How's he know it's yellow fever and not cholera? There ain't been any yellow fever epidemics here for years."

The mayor hushed the crowd. Dru started to answer for himself, but Langston cut him off. "Talbot's been to medical college. I'd guess if he doesn't know what yellow fever is, then nobody does. What he's suggesting is that I quarantine the town until the danger's past."

"I got a bull to sell," a farmer shouted. "The roads haven't been this good since the war and I aim to make some money for a change. We don't need the roads closed."

An elderly gentleman stood up. "What good's it gonna do to shut down the town? If folks are going to get the fever, there's nothing to stop it. 'Sides, some have already packed up and left."

A strapping young man holding a four-year-old boy rose to his feet and slowly eyed the crowd. "Haven't we been through enough? If there's a danger to my family, I say we listen to the doc and close the roads until we know we're safe."

There were shouts for and against the quarantine. The farmer nearly came to blows with a middle-aged woman wielding a parasol.

Dru took the floor before Langston responded and let go a long shrill whistle that silenced the crowd. "There's no need to panic. I want to know if any of you have family members who've come down with a bad fever recently or if you've had any visitors passing through by way of Collier's Ferry."

Three families raised their hands and admitted to having had guests who had arrived via the ferry, but the longest anyone had stayed had been two days and none of them appeared to be ill.

Then another man raised his hand. "I'm Nate Dickens and I live down in the hollow. My son's twenty and he took sick a few days ago. He had a fever and a bad headache, but he's better this morning."

Dru's heart sank. Yellow fever struck, appeared to clear up, and then returned with a vengeance. Before he could comment, his attention was arrested by a slight movement at the back of the room. A woman appeared in silhouette, framed between the open double doors. He recognized Sara's lush figure the moment he saw her.

Sara had slept late and awoke to an empty house. She quickly dressed and then, too nervous to eat, she had walked out onto the porch where she noticed first one and then another family from across the street start walking toward town. By the time two buggies and a buckboard had rumbled by, all headed in the same direction, she decided something was going on and quickly left the house.

Now as she slipped into the back of the courthouse she was thankful that nearly all the people in the room had their attention focused on the men in front. Stepping in behind the last row of chairs, she saw an older woman frown and then sidle away rather than stand next to her.

Sara ignored the slight and concentrated on Dru. He looked so handsome, so strong and proud. A fierce frown wrinkled his brow. As he scanned the crowd, his dark eyes were shadowed with concern.

He stood alongside a heavyset man with hanging jowls and a receding hairline. Next to him was the town marshal, Mr. Monroe, and beside him, Abel Foster sat clutching a pencil and a wad of paper, looking as pompous and self-righteous as ever.

A sudden chill snaked down Sara's spine as she stared across the room at the publisher. Dru was in the middle of explaining the symptoms and stages of yellow fever when suddenly, a woman in spectacles stood up, grabbed her daughter's hand, and started dragging her up the aisle. Her expression was one of horror.

The woman's hasty exit didn't go unnoticed. Heads turned. Anxious glances were exchanged. People began to shift uneasily in their seats.

"The one thing we *don't* want is more panic." Dru's voice held steady and firm. Sara was proud of the way he controlled the crowd, especially with fear setting into every heart. He spoke in confidence to the heavyset man beside him, their discussion impossible to hear though the crowd hushed and folks scooted to the edges of their seats, straining to make out the words.

The butcher, still in his bloody apron but wearing a small bowler hat, shot to his feet. "How do we know Talbot's right? We've only got his word to go on. Why not call in another doctor and have him take a look at the folks over at Collier's Ferry?"

Dru was livid. "By the time we send to Hopkinsville for another doctor, the fever will have spread."

Someone Sara couldn't see yelled, "Right now, nobody in town has even got it!"

A woman's voice rang out loud and clear. "You were wrong about your wife, Dru Talbot. How do we know you're right about this? Maybe this is something you dreamed up so you can drum up some business!"

Shame nearly toppled Sara. She wished she could fade into the wall. If the insult affected Dru at all, he didn't let it show, nor did he back down. Instead, he moved closer to the edge of the dais.

"Leave my wife out of this!" he shouted back. "There *is* yellow fever over at Collier's Ferry, whether you believe me or not. Last night I watched a ten-year-old die and her sister wasn't far behind, but we may have done something to help her. If death is what you want for your families, there's nothing I can do to change your minds, so go ahead. Wait until someone's vomiting blood, *then* call in another doctor and get his opinion. You all have a hell of a lot more to lose than I do."

Embarrassment fired Sara's cheeks but her heart warmed her to her toes. Dru had just defended her before the whole town.

Witham Spalding shoved himself to his feet. "What are you gonna do, Mayor?"

The mayor turned to Dru and followed his political instincts. "I'm gonna let Doc here decide."

"First, I'm going to go over to Mr. Dickens's house and examine his son. If he appears to have yellow fever, I'll quarantine the house and demand Marshal Monroe close the roads."

A commotion went up the likes of which Sara had never seen or heard. While some folks rushed for the nearest exit, Marshal Monroe shouted for order. Others simply sat there in stunned silence.

Sara waited through the mayor's speech about how the good citizens of Magnolia Creek had always pulled together before and how he expected them to do so now, then the meeting was adjourned and the courthouse quickly cleared.

She watched Dru pick up his medical bag, step off the raised platform, and start up the center aisle. She didn't know if he had seen her come in, but when he reached the last row of chairs, he stopped and turned her way.

It was hard to swallow with her heart in the way. Her gaze traced his features, touching his lips, the scar at his temple, the sculpted line of his strong jaw. Raw sensation assailed her. His expression was unreadable.

"I'll walk you back," he said distantly.

She nodded, joining him in the center aisle. Together they stepped out into the sunlight. She squinted and raised a hand to shade her eyes.

When someone nearby whispered, "That's her," Sara raised her chin and stared straight ahead.

As if what had happened between them last night had never come to pass, she and Dru stood side by side in the thick, humid heat of the noon hour. She could still taste his lips, still feel his hands moving over her. She would never forget the way he had filled her, the way he had moved inside her. Last night intensified her desperate longing, her hope for the resurrection of their marriage.

He had defended her inside the courthouse—had even referred to her as his wife. She tried to tell herself that he must harbor some feeling for her after last night, no matter how cold he had been afterward. He couldn't possibly have put the act out of his mind so soon.

But as she took in his strong profile, the determined set of his shoulders, and the firm line of his jaw, she wondered if perhaps he *had* dismissed it as easily as he might have forgotten what he'd had for breakfast two days before.

Nate Dickens waited for them at the bottom of the stairs. The man gave Sara a quick once-over when she and Dru joined him. If he had any objections to her being there, Nate didn't voice them.

"I'll take you over to the house to see my son, Doc." He sounded hopeful when he added, "I sure hate to waste your time."

"I'd rather be safe than sorry, Nate. I've got my own buggy," Dru told him. "I need to take . . . my wife back to the office."

Sara leaned closer. "I'm going with you."

Dru looked as if he were about to object, then didn't. Dickens was hanging on their every word. They headed toward Doc's old buggy that was pulled up to the edge of the square. People had scattered across the park, gathered together in tight knots, and followed them with their eyes as she and Dru passed by.

He handed her up without a word and then climbed in beside her.

"You're going to need my help," she told him. "Granddaddy predicted it."

His mouth hardened. He worked the reins and the chestnut pulled into the street as they began to follow Nate Dickens down the road.

"What'll you do if his son does have yellow fever?" she asked.

"Set up a temporary hospital in the old livery down at the end of Birch Lane. Monroe said it's been empty since the war. We'll keep the folks who are sick away from the rest of the town and nurse them there if their families will bring them in. Some will prefer to quarantine their homes."

"You can't take care of everyone all by yourself, Dru. If this thing spreads quickly, you'll need me. Besides, if I can't go back to Elizabeth, I'll go crazy with worry. Please, let me help."

As he negotiated a turn, the muscle in his jaw jerked and his gaze slid over her. A long, tense silence stretched between them until he finally said, "Only if your presence doesn't keep anyone away."

40

Two weeks later, muggy heat swamped the kitchen as Louzanna held Lissybeth up to wave at her mother from an open window in the conservatory. Standing halfway across the backyard, Sara refused to get any closer.

"How much longer will the quarantine last, do you think?" Louzanna tried to shout over Lissybeth yelling, "Mama! Mama, come!"

"We don't know," Sara called back. "Three cases in one family came in two days ago."

Fear wrapped itself around Lou's heart and she found herself struggling to breathe, but she forced herself to be strong. There was Elizabeth to think of and Sara was depending on her. They all needed her to hold fast and not wilt like a shrinking violet or take to her bed. She was more bound and determined than ever to keep herself from falling apart until the danger passed.

Lissybeth struggled in earnest. With a whine and a grunt, she flopped over Lou's arm. When she finally started kicking and lunging up and down, Lou set her on her feet. The frustrated toddler threw herself against the back door and started slapping it with the palms of both hands, screaming for her mother at the top of her lungs.

Rattled, Lou pulled at her hair, trying to pin up the

raveled ends, but her curls were already a lost cause. Long strands straggled down her back. Her dark clothes stuck to her. The heat in the house was stifling.

Elizabeth started howling and gave the door one final slap before she crumpled into a heap, dropped her head to her knees, and sobbed pitifully.

Out in the yard, Sara was on the verge of tears. She wrapped her hands around the folds of her skirt and tried to call soothing words to Elizabeth and apologies to Lou.

"Don't worry about a thing," Lou called back. "She'll stop crying the minute you leave. We'll go into the parlor and draw the drapes to make it cool and quiet. I think I can get her to take a nap."

"Where's Jamie?"

"In the drawing room wiping down the high bookshelves for me. You take care of yourself, watch over Dru. We're all doing just fine."

Louzanna had come to think of Elizabeth as the child she would never have and, more often than not, found herself wishing Dru would soon see how very precious, how sweet, smart, and loving Elizabeth was and eventually come to love her as his own.

Lou watched Sara wipe her eyes with the back of her hand and then gather up the hem of her skirt and run out of the garden. After Sara left, Louzanna knelt down and scooped the distraught, sobbing child into her arms. When she turned around, Jamie was waiting for her in the doorway.

His strong hands were wrapped around a ladder he was hauling back to the barn. Anxiously, he glanced toward the conservatory windows. "Was that Miss Sara? How are they doing?"

"A few new cases of yellow fever have cropped up."

Lou sighed. "I just hope this will prove how important Dru is to this town. He and Sara are risking their lives to tend the sick over at the livery."

She knew if she let herself dwell on the precarious position Dru and Sara were in that she would come undone. As it was, she was hanging on to sanity by a thread.

Jamie shifted and extended his right hand. Lissybeth quickly stopped crying and started sniffling and flirting with Jamie when he wagged his fingers near her nose. Finally she hid her face against Lou's neck and giggled.

Louzanna felt her insides slowly settle and tried to smile. This solid, gentle man had been a part of her life for so long that she had taken his loyalty for granted. Suddenly it struck her that she had never thanked him for all he had done for them.

As he started toward the back door again, she reached out and touched his sleeve. "Please wait, Jamie."

He froze and stared down at her hand where it rested on his arm. "What is it, Miss Lou?"

"I just wanted to tell you how much I appreciate that you're still here. I know you planned to go back to New York and that you could have been safely away by now. Sara says we shouldn't worry, that there are fewer new cases of the fever every day—"

"Don't get yourself all worked up, Miss Lou. I'll be here as long as you need me."

Stunned and flustered by the unspoken emotion in his eyes, Louzanna watched him walk across the conservatory. As he negotiated the ladder through the back door, she reached for Mason's ring. Then, with an open palm, she pressed the opal to her heart.

* * *

For just over three weeks, Magnolia Creek found itself locked in the grip of yellow fever. Despite Dru's early fears that the town would rise up against Sara working by his side, objections quickly diminished in the face of helplessness.

Sara remained fearless, with a confidence and bravery that was admired by young and old alike. For the most part they worked alone in the livery, except for victims' relatives who refused to leave a loved one—most were mothers tending their children until they fell ill themselves.

The only other steady help came from an elderly woman named Lorna Pickering, who claimed she was going to die of one thing or another and that she'd rather take her chances lending a hand than sitting home worrying about it. Even now that there were only a half-dozen patients left to tend, Mrs. Pickering continued to work tirelessly beside them.

Hoping the worst was over, Dru glanced across the livery to be certain Mrs. Pickering was still on her feet before he let his gaze linger on Sara as she moved between pallets and cots, pressing her hand to a fevered brow, pausing to offer a drink of water, adjusting blankets, holding hands. She swabbed the patients with vinegar water baths and whispered encouragement.

Keeping the stricken patients isolated had not been enough to stop the disease, which sorely tested his belief in the contagion theory. Despite their efforts, the fever had rapidly spread until over fifty citizens had been stricken, many of them the first week.

So far, thirty-three had died. Dru kept a journal where he had entered the names and ages of the victims, carefully noting any relationships between them as well as their symptoms. The only thing he was certain of anymore was that very few victims survived the final stages of the disease.

Sara slowly turned, as if sensing his gaze. Her hands were full of dirty cloths, her eyes shadowed with fatigue, her face lined with a deep sadness that she rarely showed. When she noticed him watching her, the corners of her mouth lifted ever so slightly. She raised her arm to wipe her brow, then turned and walked the length of the ramshackle building and stepped out into the night.

The flickering light of a low-burning fire in back of the stable cast macabre shadows throughout the dim interior of the old barn. Day and night, the fire burned as they destroyed the rags, towels, and bedding they had used.

Dru looked around the livery at a scene reminiscent of temporary wartime hospitals. When surrender came he had thought the worst over, but now, as he drew a soiled sheet over the face of Elsie Jackman, his friend Keith's wife, he wondered if tragedy had somehow followed him home.

Poor Elsie would never see another dawn, never hold her children again; and yet to the bitter end of her life she had been one of those who had refused Sara's help. Dru walked to the front of the barn and looked across the street where Keith and his children awaited word. With his hands on his hips, Dru stood beneath the open night sky and took a deep breath of fresh air before he walked halfway across the street. Keith noticed him immediately.

A young boy stood beside Keith, holding his little sister in his arms. Dru tried to call out past the lump in his throat, but the finality of what he had to say choked him. All he could do was shake his head in defeat.

Keith's shoulder's slumped, his hands went slack at his

sides. His son turned his face against his father's hip and cried. Dru walked away, disgusted with the horrific, indiscriminate disease as much as he was with himself for not being able to do a damn thing but watch people die. He ached to stretch out somewhere and sleep and sleep until the plague ended. Instead he walked back into the huge barn where a seventeen-year-old who had missed her wedding day was crying out for water.

He waved Sara on and gave the girl a drink from a silver cup that her mother had sent along with other precious things she had packed for her daughter's final journey. Running his hand over the girl's dry brow, he slowly rose and went to wash his hands yet again. His skin was chapped and dry from lye soap.

He wandered out back where he found Sara staring up at the moonless, star-spattered sky, hugging her arms around her midriff, slowly swaying from side to side. Heat and fatigue had been their constant companions. Stepping up behind her, he was tempted to slip his arms around her, to comfort and hold her close. He hadn't touched her since the night they had returned from Collier's Ferry, the night he had taken her at Doc's old house.

"Are you all right?" He spoke over the crackle of the fire.

Sara whirled around. "I didn't hear you come out." She took a step toward him, then abruptly stopped. "Are *you* feeling all right?"

He nodded. "Just tired."

"All my bones ache," she said, rubbing her shoulder. She tried to smile.

He whipped around and pressed a hand to her forehead.

"I'm fine," she protested. "Really. I'm just tired."

"Why don't you go back to the house and get some

sleep?" When they had been too exhausted to stand, they took turns sleeping at Doc Porter's. Not once since the night they had been together had they slept beneath the same roof.

She shook her head. "I'll be all right for a while."

"There haven't been any new cases in the last forty-eight hours."

"I was afraid to say it out loud, but I was counting, too." She let go a long sigh. "You think it's almost over?"

"We can only hope and pray."

She looked so lost, so lonely, that his heart buckled. He knew how terribly she must miss Elizabeth. He thought of offering her his hand, but even that simple gesture would involve his heart and he didn't have the courage or the strength to let her crush it again.

"How do you do it, Sara?"

"Do what?"

"Stay here day after day, tend the sick, tote water, hold hands, trying to comfort and heal people who have turned against you?"

She frowned into the fire. "If you have to ask me that, then you don't know me at all."

She was right. He knew her body, craved it even now that his strength was nearly gone. At seventeen she had wanted nothing more than to be his wife, but he didn't really *know* her now. He didn't know the woman she had become.

Since his homecoming, he had been so full of anger and bitterness that he hadn't taken time to find out who she was or what she really dreamed of for herself and her child.

"I couldn't have done any of this without you, Sara." The words came easily, for they were true. Unafraid of the fever, she had given him the courage to go on when he'd been too tired to stand.

She seemed surprised by his compliment, which let him know how little she expected from him.

"I'm happy to help. It's what I wanted for us . . . back in the beginning." She continued to stare down into the fire and easily changed the subject. "I miss Elizabeth."

She rarely mentioned the child to him. Then again, he knew he had never given her reason to believe that he cared.

"I'm . . . sure you do." Too little, too late, he thought.

A barn owl hooted in the trees behind them and Sara shivered.

"What's wrong?"

"Bad omen. Granddaddy would throw salt on the fire to cut the bad luck."

"Bad luck?" He laughed, but it was a cold, hollow sound devoid of any merriment. "I don't see how things could get any worse."

"Maybe it's almost over."

Just then they heard a wagon roll up out front, heard the driver yell to his team. Dru thought of Elsie, remembered the pain and confusion in her eyes toward the end. He had made it a habit to ride with the undertaker to deliver the dead to a new section of the town cemetery where pine coffins waited beside open graves. He'd be taking Keith's wife this time.

"I'll be back shortly," he told Sara. He hated leaving her there at all, but after weeks without another attempt on her life or even a threat, and with most people unwilling to get within a block of the livery, he had gradually relaxed his vigilance.

"Go inside and take a nap if you need to," he said.

"Just don't walk back to the house alone. Wait until I get back and I'll take you over there."

"Thank you, Dru," she said softly, still staring into the fire.

"I'm not really the ogre you think I am, Sara." He rolled his head on his aching shoulders.

"You let me stay. That's more than most men would do."

"You're still my wife," he said softly.

"We could divorce."

His stomach tilted. "Is that what you want?"

She went very still. The owl hooted again. The low fire leapt and died back down.

She let him walk away without an answer.

Sara watched him go, aching to run after him, to take his hand and assure him that they would get through this somehow, that things would change and the last thing she wanted was a divorce, but she wasn't really sure of anything anymore.

Staring into the fire, she wasn't alone for more than a few minutes when a man rounded the corner of the barn and headed toward her. He was tall and broad shouldered and he walked briskly, bearing down on her without hesitation.

Her heart lightened for she thought that Dru had come back, until she realized it wasn't him. Alarmed, she took a step in the direction of the barn doors when Abel Foster stepped into the firelight and said, "Sara, wait."

Her hand went to her midriff.

"Dru's inside," she lied, edging closer to the building, glancing over her shoulder. She was ready to escape inside until Abel's words stopped her.

"I need your help."

Something desperate and unsettled altered his tone, something hesitant and uncertain and completely unlike Abel, which gave her pause.

"I need you to come home with me."

"Do you think I'm crazy?" She started to walk away.

"Sara, please wait. Minnie's taken sick. I'm afraid she's dying."

"I'll send Dru over as soon as he comes back."

"I thought you said he was here." He glanced toward the doors.

"He'll be right back. He left with the undertaker."

"Minnie wants to see *you*."

"I'm the last person on earth your wife would send for."

He shook his head, lifted his hat to smooth down his hair, and shoved the hat back on.

"She's been asking for you over and over."

"I can't do any more than Dru can."

"That's not what I hear. Folks have been telling me what you've done, how you helped some victims survive. They swear that you're a true healer, that you have a special gift."

Her heart was running wild. She glanced over her shoulder, praying to hear the rumble of the undertaker's old wagon returning, but it was far too soon. Mrs. Pickering certainly couldn't save her. She had to fend for herself.

Abel took off his hat, held it in his hands, pleading now. "Please, come with me, Sara. I'm afraid Minnie hasn't much time."

She wished she had Granddaddy's ability to see into a person's soul and know whether or not he was telling the truth. Her intuition had failed her with Jonathan Smith.

It very well might be failing her now, for she was beginning to think that Abel was telling the truth. His cheeks were flushed, his eyes bright. Worry was clearly etched upon his face.

"How long since she took sick?" she asked.

"Two days."

Her anger swelled. The woman lived right next door to Louzanna and Elizabeth. Abel had backed Dru in calling for a quarantine and yet he hadn't reported his own wife's illness, nor had he brought her in for two long days.

"What were you thinking, Abel? She should have been isolated at the first sign of fever."

His head wagged back and forth. "She didn't tell me that she'd been feeling poorly until this morning. She hasn't been out of the house since she took ill, though."

"Maybe it's not yellow fever."

"I'm afraid it is." Panicked, he was growing more impatient.

If he was right, Minnie would have to be moved or the house quarantined. There was no time to waste and Dru would be gone for over an hour. As much as she wanted to refuse, Sara knew her decision was already made for her. She rolled down her sleeves, smoothed a hand over her hair.

"Let me get my things and tell Mrs. Pickering where I'm going, then I'll be right back."

41

CLUTCHING HER BAG of herbs, Sara followed Abel through the dark to his buggy across the street. She kept telling herself not to panic, to take deep breaths and stay alert.

She climbed into the buggy without Abel's help and slid as far away from him as possible, determined to jump out if he tried to grab her. Clinging to the edge of the seat, she cast sidelong glances at him, reminding herself both Dru and Marshal Monroe had assured her Abel couldn't possibly have attacked her.

When Abel stopped in front of his place, Sara gazed longingly at the Talbot house next door. A lamp was shining in Louzanna's room upstairs, tempting her to go home and soak in a long, cool bath, to wear clean clothes and play with Elizabeth, to shut the door on all the horrors she had witnessed over the past weeks.

Instead, she climbed out of the buggy and cautiously followed Abel to his front door. The sound of their footsteps tainted the quiet, warm night air. Homes all along the street were mostly dark and as she stood on the porch waiting for him to open the door, Sara shivered despite the heat.

When it was time to step inside, she balked.

"Minnie's upstairs." He sounded nervous as he walked in and waited for her to follow.

Sara hesitated on the threshold, stared into the dimly lit entry that opened onto a parlor. A sweeping staircase stood off to one side. The glow from a lamp in the upstairs hall lit the upper stairs.

There was a silent hush in the darkened house, broken only by the ticking of a tall standing clock at the far end of the foyer. On the verge of walking away, Sara heard a weak voice cry, "Is that you, Abel?"

"It's me, Minnie. We're on the way up." Abel waited, sensing her hesitation. "You have nothing to fear, Sara."

Just then, Minnie pitifully cried out again. "Abel?"

Sara's decision was made for her. Her hand tightened around the herb bag as she walked in and started toward the staircase.

The Fosters' house was almost as beautiful as the Talbots'. A scarlet-and-gold Oriental carpet runner swept the length of the upper hall. Gas lamps lined walls papered with gilded paisley. Sara recognized a painting over a hall table, one that used to hang above the fireplace mantel in Lou's room.

Abel ushered her into a large bedroom and Sara knew without even examining Minnie that the woman had yellow fever. The air was heavy with the same putrid odor that lingered in the livery stable.

Abel took off his hat, dropped it on a chair near the door, then slicked his hair down with his palm as he walked to his wife's bedside. Minnie's riotous yellow hair looked garish against sallow skin as pale as paste against the starched, white linen pillowcase. Minnie watched Sara with huge and glassy eyes filled with fright.

"Thank God you came," she whispered, licking her dry lips.

So far her tongue hadn't turned black, so there was still hope. Sara set the bag on a bedside table and asked Abel to bring her some fresh water.

At first he seemed reluctant to leave, then he finally hurried out of the room. Sara lifted Minnie's wrist. Her pulse was erratic, her skin hot and dry.

"I'm dying," Minnie rasped.

"Not if you fight." Sara tried to be convincing, knowing she didn't sound as persuasive as she might have before she knew the power of the fever so well.

"I had to see you." Minnie grabbed Sara's hand and clung with thin, bird-claw fingers. "You have to forgive me for the things I did."

Sara was reaching for the herb bag but stopped, her hand hovering over the drawstring tie. It was hard to forget what Minnie had said to Louzanna.

Sara straightened and met Minnie's gaze. "I think the person you should ask forgiveness of is Louzanna. She considered you a good friend, Minnie."

Minnie shook her head and swallowed, a slow and agonizing movement. "That's not what I'm talking about. I'm talking about throwing a rock through your window and that night, the night I . . . the night I tried to kill you."

"Minnie!" Suddenly Abel rushed back in. Water sloshed out of the pitcher in his hands as he ran to the bedside. "Minnie, what are you saying?" He turned to Sara. "She's delirious. She doesn't know what she's talking about."

Minnie looked between the two of them. "Yes, I do.

You know it's true, Abel. I know you suspected that I attacked Sara all along, but . . . you didn't say a word."

Abel slowly set the pitcher down, his hands shaking. He glanced at Sara, then stared at Minnie, helpless to keep her from confessing.

"I saw you out by the barn with Abel shortly after we heard Dru was killed. I saw him kiss you," she told Sara.

"That wasn't my doing!" Sara protested.

"But he *wanted* you. It was more than I could bear and then, after you tried to steal my husband, you ran off with a Yankee. The Yankees killed my boy. I couldn't abide having you right next door under my very nose. I wanted to make you suffer the way I suffered."

Minnie winced and shifted. "I saw you leave that afternoon, then later I overheard Louzanna and Dru and knew he had gone to look for you. Abel wouldn't be home early, not with the press broke, so I watched and waited, pacing your yard in the dark. I was there when you stepped out of the woods."

Minnie closed her eyes. Her thin lower lip trembled. "You fought back and nearly knocked me out before I stabbed you. I thought you were dead. When I came inside, there was a huge bruise and a cut on the side of my face. When Abel came home that night I told him that I fell against the banister, but the next day, after Dru questioned him and told him that you hit your attacker . . ." She turned to her husband. "You suspected me then, didn't you?"

"Oh, Minnie," he said sadly. "I would have kept your secret forever."

"I've run out of forever. I don't want this on my soul," she whispered, looking up at Sara again. "Can you forgive me?"

Sara shivered and slipped her hand out of Minnie's grip. Unconsciously, she reached up and touched her own shoulder where the jagged scar lay hidden beneath her gown, a gruesome reminder of how close she had come to dying.

"Forgive you? When you would have robbed my daughter of a mother and left her an orphan?"

"The Yankees took *my* only child from me." Minnie burst into a fit of chills. Her teeth chattered while she was locked in the grip of the fever.

Abel gently eased Sara away from the bedside, then sat down and took his wife's hand. "Minnie, hold on. You'll be all right." He looked up at Sara. "You'll help her, won't you? If anyone can save her, it's you."

Sara ran her palms down the front of her skirt to her thighs and stared down at the woman in the bed. Fear and pain swamped Minnie's eyes, her expression no different than those of the others that Sara had tended. Many of them might have spoken ill of her at one time, too, but none of them had tried to kill her.

She reached for the herb bag on the table, wrapped her hand around the top, and then without another word, started to walk away.

She got as far as the bedroom door before she remembered something her granddaddy once told her.

"You're a born healer, Sarie. You're ready to do what generations of Colliers have done."

Minnie Foster was asking not only for healing, but for forgiveness—nothing more, nothing less than what Sara herself wanted from Dru. How could she refuse to give what she herself ached for?

She turned around, walked back to Minnie's bedside, dropped the bag on the table, and looked directly at Abel.

"You'll have to help," she said, opening the bag and searching its contents. "Pour a bit of water into that glass."

Minnie's mouth was lax, her eyes listless. "What are you going to do?"

"Well, Mrs. Foster, I've decided I'm not only going to forgive you, but I'm going to try to save your life."

The undertaker pulled up at the livery and let Dru off. Trips to the cemetery always took more out of him than fighting the fever. He had longed to be a physician his whole life, but never dreamed he would share duties with the undertaker.

Forcing himself off the high-sprung wagon seat, he jumped to the ground, took a deep breath, and filled his lungs with fresh air before he walked back inside the cavernous barn. For the most part, his remaining patients were asleep.

In a far corner of the room a man moaned in a husky voice. Mrs. Pickering sat in a chair beside the door, hands folded in her lap, head bowed, snoring as loud as a freight train. Dru glanced at her and shook his head, then realized Sara wasn't there.

Mrs. Pickering awoke with a sputter the minute he touched her shoulder. Still, it wasn't soon enough for him.

"How long ago did Sara leave?" he demanded. "Did she go out alone?"

"She told me where she was going, but I forgot what she said." Her brow scrunched into deep furrows.

"Did she go back to Doc Porter's to rest?" The butcher's wife was restless so he hurried over to her, wiped her brow, and then mopped spittle off of her chin.

"I believe she went someplace with a man."

"What man?"

Lorna Pickering rested an elbow on her opposite hand, then tapped her temple with her fingertip. "Tall fellow. I know him very well but right now I can't think of his name to save my life."

Dru dropped the wash rag into the tepid vinegar water.

She snapped her fingers, then rocked back on her heels. "I know. It was Abel Foster. His wife took sick. He drove Sara over to his house to see her."

42

"ABEL FOSTER?"

Dru's shout frightened a year off of poor Lorna Pickering's life.

She staggered back, clutching her heart. "Dear merciful heavens! What's wrong with you, Dru Talbot?"

"How long ago did they leave?"

She hesitated, studied the ceiling. "Oh my, let's see."

Suffocating panic slowly choked him while she debated. He gave up waiting, headed for the buggy. What did it matter how long they had been gone? A heartbeat was too long.

Mrs. Pickering trailed him through the front door. The street was quiet as death, not a soul in sight. "I don't exactly know when they left. Maybe an hour. Maybe more. Minnie seems like such a nice lady. Haven't seen her for the past few weeks."

Dru bolted into his buggy, grabbed the reins, and snapped them over the chestnut's rump. The horse took off, the buggy jolted, scarring the night stillness with sound.

He pulled up in front of the Fosters', set the brake, and leapt from the wagon. Panic fed his momentum as he ran up the walkway to the front porch, beat on the door with his fist, and then tried the latch. The door swung open and he strode into the softly lit interior. Through an archway on the left he saw Abel rise from a settee.

In seconds, Dru was on the man. He grabbed Foster's lapels. No surprise, no fear showed on Abel's face at all.

"Where's Sara?" Dru demanded.

"Upstairs with my wife." Abel sounded vague and exhausted.

Dru left him in the middle of the room, his long strides eating up the stairs. He charged down the hall, glancing into bedrooms until he found Sara. She was supporting Minnie's head and shoulders while the woman puked into a bucket.

"Sara." Her name shattered on a choked sigh of relief.

Wiping her hands, she turned. Her face lit up when she saw him, her expression giving away much more than he expected or deserved.

"Are you all right?" Without forethought he crossed the room until he was close enough to see the glow of lamplight reflected in her eyes.

"I'm fine." The hint of a smile traced her lips. When she glanced over his shoulder, he noticed Abel watching them from the doorway.

"How is she?" Foster glanced at the bed, waiting for Sara to answer, his anxious stance communicating hope.

Sara brushed her hair back off her face. There was a silver branch of candles burning on the side table, scraps of fabric and string beside her herb bag.

"I've done all I can. Now it's up to God and time. Give her teaspoons full of the mixture I'm leaving on the table," Sara instructed. "Don't leave her."

Abel ignored Dru and took hold of Sara's hands.

"You've done more than either of us had the right to ask. I hope you can forgive me, as well as Minnie."

"What's going on?" Dru looked from one to the other, then locked eyes with Sara. Minnie moaned and Sara hurried back to her side.

Abel met Dru's level stare. "Minnie confessed to the stabbing."

Dru's gaze shot to the bed and the feverish form of the woman lying there. Minnie Foster was a busybody, but it was inconceivable to him that the diminutive, seemingly harmless woman had tried to kill Sara.

Abel stared down at his shoes, his words weighted with embarrassment and shame. "Minnie hasn't been right since Arthur died. All of her sorrow and hatred centered on Sara. It didn't help that she saw me try to kiss Sara that day."

Dru still couldn't believe Minnie was guilty of the brutal attack, but if it were true, then they could certainly breathe easier. "Are you sure it's not just the fever talking?"

Abel nodded, fingered his muttonchop whiskers. "When I got home from the office the night Sara was attacked, Minnie had a terrible bruise on her face. She told me that she'd fallen, but after that she began acting strange. Every time I walked into a room, she would jump. She seemed to be spending more time than ever watching your house and she refused to go anywhere. God only knows what she was planning while I was at the paper every day."

By the time Abel finished, Dru was more angry than relieved. "You suspected she was a threat and you didn't tell me? Or the marshal? What if she tried to kill Sara again?"

"After that night, Minnie was afraid of her own shadow. When I saw Jamie back at your place and noticed he was never far from your wife, I figured you had hired him to protect her." Abel steadily held Dru's gaze. "Don't be too quick to cast stones, Talbot. When Arthur died it was almost as if a piece of Minnie's mind went with him. Surely you can sympathize with that. Look at your own sister. What if it had been *your* wife? Would you have rushed to tell Monroe, or would you have tried to help her?"

A few feet away, Sara was straightening the sheets and adjusting Minnie's pillow, unselfishly caring for the woman who had tried to end her life.

"Minnie confessed to Sara?"

"Yes, and even so, your wife has been fighting to save her life."

Your wife.

Abel kept referring to Sara as his wife. Dru continued to watch Sara whisper to Minnie and brush the woman's hair. Once Minnie was resting quietly, Sara backed away from the bed. Her eyes met his across the room. With an intense ache, Dru's heart contracted.

Sorrow flooded Sara's eyes, giving him a glimpse into her soul as she slipped the carefully wrapped packets of herbs back into the bag. The gift of seeds and powders from her grandfather had been invaluable to them both over the past few weeks. Finished, she walked over to his side.

"I've done all I can for now," she told Abel. "We can take her back to the livery with us."

Abel immediately objected. "I'd rather quarantine the house. I won't go anywhere until I'm certain she'll recover or . . ." Unable to go on, he covered his eyes with one hand, his long, ink-stained fingers trembling.

When Dru started to argue, Sara laid a hand on his arm. "What harm will it do to leave her here? There haven't been any new cases in two days and since she's been ill for a while now, that still holds true."

Abel dropped his hand and lowered his voice to a whisper. "I didn't even know she was sick until I came home this afternoon and saw that she couldn't get out of bed. I'll care for her myself. I promise not to let anyone inside. Nor will I leave. Please, Talbot."

"What about the paper? Are you willing to stay here and not publish the *Sentinel* until we know you aren't going to come down with this?" Dru wanted assurance before he would leave.

"There won't be a paper until this is over. I've spent far too much time there as it is. If I had been home more, maybe I would have been able to prevent what happened. At least I would have known that she was ill." Abel looked at Sara and then Dru. "If she lives, are you going to report Minnie to the marshal?"

Again, Sara touched Dru's sleeve, drawing his gaze. "It's over, Dru. Minnie's grief drove her to do what she did. She needs understanding and forgiveness, not punishment."

He hesitated. "Are you willing to take that chance?"

"People can change. If I'm willing to forgive and give her another chance, then surely you can, too."

Forgiveness. The one and only thing Sara had asked of him.

"All right," he told Abel. "I'll agree not to report the attack if you promise me that if Minnie survives, Sara's safety will be guaranteed."

Abel held out his hand. "You have my word."

43

LOUZANNA AWOKE TO the sound of Lissybeth fussing in the crib she had had Jamie move into her own bedroom. With a groan, she threw back the wadded sheet and slipped out of bed, nearly tripping as her toe caught in the bedclothes. When she stumbled, her ruffled nightcap had pitched toward one ear. She shoved it back up to the top of her head.

"What'samatter, baby?" Only half awake, she peered down at Lissybeth in the weak gray light of another dawn. The child was staring up at her, her fingers shoved into her mouth as she whimpered softly.

Louzanna began to massage Elizabeth's tummy in slow, soothing circles the way Sara had taught her. Through mists of sleep and bursts of wakefulness, she began to sense something was wrong. Lou rubbed her eyes and leaned closer to Elizabeth, felt her forehead. The child's skin was overly warm.

A buzzing filled Louzanna's head, shot down her limbs, and set her knees trembling. At first she couldn't move, then dread drove her to her feet and she ran to the window, called Jamie's name, then ran back to the crib. She touched her palm to Elizabeth's forehead again and then her own. The girl was definitely hot, feverish, and fussy.

Louzanna tripped over Goldie as she rushed to the armoire and began pulling out one gown after another, all mourning wear, all embellished with black braid or lace. Most were well-worn, many with turned collars and skirts. The contents of her entire closet were scattered across the bed like a billowing black storm cloud.

She ran back to Lissybeth's bed, then knelt beside the crib. Usually Lissybeth woke smiling, stood at the rail and called, "Woo! Woo!" until Louzanna got up.

The sun was already over the edge of the fields far beyond the wood. Light was shimmering against the windowpanes, slanting across the sills, but Lissybeth just lay there listlessly staring up at Lou with glassy eyes and a runny nose.

Louzanna threw her nightcap on the bed, then drew her muslin gown off and tossed it aside, too. She pawed through the mound of black, found a chemise, and threw it over her head. She picked up a corset, tossed it aside. No time to struggle with the ties. She began to pull on a gown, heard the stitches pop, and realized she was standing on the hem. Finally she shrugged into the sleeves and buttoned the bodice but not her cuffs.

She paced back to the crib, debating whether or not to pick up Elizabeth. The child was sound asleep again, so Lou gently felt her forehead and her heart sank. Elizabeth was still overly warm.

"Havetohurry. Havetohurry. Havetohurry." The words became a frantic litany. "HavetofindJamie. Havetofindhimnow." She whirled around, her gaze lighting on everything at once.

Impatiently she grabbed her shoes and slipped them

on bare feet, took another spin and looked around the room, then quietly edged out the door, locking Elizabeth inside with Goldie.

Lou ventured out the back door, past the water pump, the rain barrel, the outhouse, and the smokehouse. Jamie's cabin was yards away, still too far to go. Swaying onto her toes, she leaned forward, shouted his name.

No answer. With her hands balled into fists, she yelled once more and with a sinking dread recalled that some mornings he rose early to go hunting.

She shoved her fist over her mouth to stifle a cry. There was no way to get word to Dru and Sara except to go herself.

The thought of leaving the yard made her hands cold and clammy. Pins and needles attacked her legs, her breath came fast and shallow. The notion of searching for Dru was downright paralyzing until Elizabeth's sweet, trusting smile came to mind.

The child's life was in her hands. Lou whirled and started running around the side of the house before she could change her mind.

She skidded to a halt in the side yard, hovered in the cool shade of the house with her palms pressed against the wood siding. Mosquitoes whined near her ear. She swatted at them as she peered around the corner of the porch. The front yard was empty, the street beyond the fence deserted.

There was nothing out there—at least, nothing visible to the naked eye; but she knew better than anyone that death never showed its face until it was too late.

Lou glanced up at the second-story window, to the room where Elizabeth lay safely sleeping in her crib. She had to do something to save Lissybeth or she would never forgive herself.

As if in a dream, she began to move, one step at a time, one foot after the other until she was gliding along the stone pathway toward the front gate. She stumbled, caught herself, heard the sound of her own breath as it rushed in and out of her lungs. Fear magnified the drumming of her heart until it echoed through her mind, drowning out all thought.

She paused at the mended gate. Thanks to Jamie, it no longer hung there like a crooked rack of broken ribs. She hadn't touched the gate in fifteen years. Her stomach plunged to her toes. Her breath stopped. She saw stars as soon as her hand connected with the pointed pickets on top of the gate but she held on tight, swayed, and waited out the spell before she pushed the gate open.

Move. Start moving.

The summer heat was already close and humid, the eastern sky a riotous palette of color that she barely saw as she ran, fighting the unrelenting pull of the house, trying to outrun the dread of dangers both seen and unseen.

Exposed and vulnerable, Lou hurried through streets she had walked as a child. No one answered the door at Doc Porter's old place. Lou staggered back against the porch rail, shoved her hair out of her eyes with both hands, and drew a deep, shuddering breath.

She turned toward the heart of town. The old livery was at the far end—a terrifying thought, but she was beyond turning back.

Main Street looked much as it had the last time she'd seen it. There, in Courthouse Square, stood the old stone bench where Mason had proposed.

Run. Keep running.

On and on she ran. She now had blisters on her bare feet. Mason's ring beat against her breast. She was nearly blinded by panic. Storekeepers were opening shops, sweeping off the walk. She barely noticed. Someone called her name but she kept running, arms and legs pumping, skirt flying, revealing bare ankles and calves to the world.

She had been to the old livery with her father once, remembered watching a farrier shoe a horse there. The painted block letters over the door were so faded that they were barely legible. The tired roof sagged. Light from the new morning sky filtered through it where shingles and boards were missing.

She ran inside, escaped the bright light of the new day, blinded when she slammed into the darkened interior. She was staggered by the odor of illness and the lingering, ominous threat of death.

44

Folding an empty cot, Dru turned, distracted when a woman burst through the front doors. He barely recognized his sister with her hair streaming over half her face, her skin pale as ash. He couldn't believe what he was seeing, that the frightening sight was truly Louzanna. She looked completely mad.

He dropped the cot and hurried toward her as she started reeling across the floor with one hand shading her eyes.

"Dru?" She sounded as frail and feeble as a woman twice her age. "Dru, where are you? Sara?"

Louzanna collided with a cot, knocked her shin against it, and bent over to apologize to its occupant, an old man in the final stages of yellow fever. She took one look at his hideously darkened tongue, recoiled, and backed away.

"Lou, *stand still*!" Dru cut the room in half trying to get to his sister before she did any damage to the patients lying in her path.

Sara was nearly there, reaching for Lou as she careened into a crate piled with soiled towels and rags. Upending the crate, Louzanna crumpled onto the filthy pile like a wilted soufflé and lay there, too stunned to move.

Dru got there in time to help Sara extricate Lou from the pile of rags and lifted her to her feet.

Louzanna grabbed Sara's hands and held on for dear life. "You have to come home. I'm afraid Elizabeth has the fever."

"No. That's impossible." Sara spoke softly, her voice hard as iron. Her gaze flew to Dru, caught and held his eyes. Despite all they had been through, he had never, ever seen such a stricken expression on her face. She looked as if someone was cutting out her heart while she was forced to watch.

Sara was so pale he was afraid she would faint. He gently grabbed her arm, pulled her close, held on tight.

"I have to go," she said, trying to push away. Dazed, she glanced around, shaken, out of control. "I have to go, Dru."

He grabbed her arms, forced her to look into his eyes. "Take Louzanna out back. Wash your hands, arms, and faces. As soon as you get home, have Jamie bring you some clean clothes. Strip off these things and leave them someplace where he can set fire to them without touching them. Then wash again, very carefully."

Louzanna nodded absently, but he knew that Sara, despite her worry, would follow his directions implicitly.

Lou stared around the barn, her gaze lingering on each of the remaining patients. From the look of horror on her face, he knew that his sister could tell it was just a matter of hours for some of them. She was face-to-face with death, the thing she feared above all.

When her teeth started chattering he was afraid that if Louzanna didn't get home in the next few moments she might become irretrievably insane. Dru took hold of both women and led them outside.

He helped Lou climb aboard the buggy and then took Sara's hand. Before he helped her up, he took hold of her face and looked deep into her eyes.

"Elizabeth will be just fine."

"She has to be," Sara whispered. "She's all I have."

Before he could say another word she reached for the buggy and let him boost her up to the seat.

"Can you manage?" He handed her the reins.

She nodded.

Dru glanced over at Lou. His sister sat straight and tall, her arms wrapped protectively around her waist. He had a hunch she wasn't seeing anything, that she was staring at nothing.

"Don't forget what I told you about changing and washing clothes, Sara. I'll be home as soon as I can."

Sara helped Lou follow Dru's instructions to the letter, fretting, rushing so that she could get to Elizabeth. Jamie ran back and forth between the house and the barn gathering clothes, reporting back that Elizabeth was still asleep.

Once she'd dressed in a clean shirtwaist and skirt, Sara ran barefoot through the house, up the staircase, past the dogwood-patterned stained-glass window at the middle landing.

She opened the door to Louzanna's room and stopped short. The floor and the bed were littered with black clothing. She carefully picked her way through the mess to the crib.

Goldie was lying beneath the crib with her muzzle on her paws. Elizabeth was warm to the touch but still not overly feverish and she appeared to be sleeping peacefully. Too nervous to sit, Sara began to sort and hang up Lou's gowns and let Lissybeth sleep on.

Once the clothes were all put away there was nothing to do but wait. She paced the room from window to window, fearful of what the next few hours might bring. She had seen so many children die over the past few weeks that she had foolishly believed her heart numb, but this new threat had resurrected every ounce of dread.

Sara put her hand on the lace curtain at the window and was staring down into the yard when she heard a soft murmur behind her.

"Mama?" Lissybeth was standing in the crib, staring at her with a wide-eyed look of disbelief.

"Hello, baby." Sara rushed to the crib and lifted Elizabeth to her hip, pressing her cheek to the baby's forehead. Louzanna's diagnosis had been right; Lissybeth was slightly feverish. When Lissybeth started chewing on her fingers, Sara eased them out of her mouth.

"Let Mama see if you're getting a tooth." Praying it was so, Sara fingered the baby's gums and discovered the rough edges of a new tooth partially poking through the skin.

Instantaneous tears partially cleansed away her fear. Just then, Louzanna walked in with Jamie and stopped abruptly when she saw Sara crying. "Dear God, no!"

Sara shook her head and smiled. "I think she's cutting a tooth. I'm going to rub her gum with some whiskey to ease the pain and keep an eye on her, but I think she's just fine."

"It's not yellow fever?" Lou wrapped her arms around herself again.

"No, Lou. She's just teething." Sara set Lissybeth on

the bed so that she could put her arms around Lou, trying to calm and reassure her. "You were so very, very brave."

"I really did it, didn't I? I left the house." Lou babbled on and on, pale and shaken, but astonished. "I can't believe I really did it and nothing happened. Nothing at all. Elizabeth is safe."

Louzanna walked over to the bed and reached for Elizabeth's soft curls. "I didn't really need to go out, though, did I?"

"No, but I'm so very, very glad that you did. She could have been very ill. You've done another brave and wonderful thing for us and I'll never, ever forget it," Sara promised.

Lou smiled down at Elizabeth and then turned to Sara. "No matter what happened before, no matter what happens between you and Dru in the future, I'll always be your sister, Sara. Always."

45

THREE DAYS LATER, Louzanna was aware of dawn's light creeping across her room, but when she tried to open her eyes, a searing pain ripped through her head. She moaned, struggled to sit up, and failed. Every muscle screamed. Pain crushed every bone in her body. Chills rattled what was left of them.

She heard Elizabeth running down the hallway beyond the door. Images of Dru's poor, suffering patients filled her head. Ever since the night at the livery she had not been able to forget the terrible scene inside its walls.

Once again she tried to get out of bed, but she fell back against the pillows. It was time to start breakfast. Today was Monday. There was bread to bake and laundry to boil, but she couldn't move her arms and legs.

She heard Sara shush Elizabeth and lead her away from the door. Poor Sara. She had been so quiet and introspective since her return that Lou had prayed Sara wasn't contemplating leaving. Now that DeWitt Collier was dead, there was nothing to keep her from moving back to Collier's Ferry. Nothing but Dru.

Louzanna winced at the throbbing ache in her head. Concentrating on something besides the pain, she tried to think of a way to bring Dru and Sara together. The two people she loved most in the world deserved happiness, and in her opinion, their happiness depended upon the two of them reuniting.

She closed her eyes and drifted to sleep despite the sunlight that filled the room. She dreamed of Mason, saw him smile and beckon her to sit beside him on the weather-worn stone bench in Courthouse Square. She saw Sara and Dru watching a beautiful, grown-up Elizabeth walk down the stairs in an ivory wedding gown.

Lou tried to swallow, but her throat was parched. She slept fitfully, awoke later, and saw Sara standing at her bedside. At first she thought she was dreaming again until Sara spoke.

"You're usually the first one up, Lou. Are you all right?" Worry lines creased Sara's brow.

"Don't fret. I don't have the jitters. I ache all over."

Sara blanched, then Lou watched her force herself to smile. Sara pressed the back of her hand to Lou's cheek. There was no need for her to say a word. Louzanna knew by the stricken look on her face that something was terribly wrong.

The worst was over.

After weeks of fighting the disease and tending his last few patients—the butcher's wife had surprised him and lived—Dru finally went home. Magnolia Creek had weathered the epidemic as stoically as it had weathered the war.

Washed and dressed, his hair still damp and soaking into his collar, he walked through the garden toward the back door. A riot of blooms made a brilliant show of August color around the yard. He stopped to straighten an upset water bucket, admired the pastel sweet peas and bright red geraniums Sara had planted near the conservatory windows.

She had sent word that Elizabeth was fine and now as he walked into the house, he found himself listening for the sound of Sara's voice, but the place was suspiciously quiet.

He found Jamie in the parlor, watching Elizabeth. Healthy as ever, the little girl stood in front of Louzanna's favorite wing chair, teasing Goldie with a doe-eyed doll. The minute she saw him, Elizabeth picked up her doll and ran to him, offering it up for his inspection. "See?"

"Pretty." The brief exchange wasn't as awkward as it might have been a few weeks ago. He even found himself smiling at her.

Jamie jumped to his feet and tried to distract Elizabeth.

"Where's Sara?" Dru asked.

"Upstairs with Miss Louzanna."

"Is Lou all right?"

Jamie hesitated. Dru thought his sister's hysteria would have passed by now. "Don't look so worried, Jamie. She'll settle down eventually. She always does."

Elizabeth kissed her doll. Jamie said something Dru didn't hear. "I'm sorry." He turned to Jamie. "What did you say?"

"Miss Lou doesn't have the hysteria. She's got the yellow fever."

Dru found Sara at Louzanna's bedside sound asleep in a chair, holding Lou's hand. A shaft of sunlight fell across Sara's auburn hair, setting the deep red highlights afire. Her skin was as pale as cream. Shadows stained half moons beneath her eyes as she kept watch over his sister.

He crossed the room, knelt down beside the chair, and gently slipped his hand over Sara's so that their three hands were stacked together—Louzanna's on the bottom, then Sara's, then his own.

Slowly awakening, Sara raised her head and blinked when she saw him. "Are you really home?"

"How long has she been like this? Why didn't you send for me?"

"She just took ill yesterday. It hit her hard this morning, Dru. Real hard."

He looked at his sister's yellowed skin and tasted his own bile.

Not Lou. She never hurt a soul. She has barely lived. She doesn't deserve to die.

"Sit here." Sara got up and offered the chair. He started to decline, then he sank into it, suddenly as weak as old tea.

"What's going on downstairs?" she asked.

"Elizabeth is entertaining Jamie and Goldie in the drawing room." He took his sister's hand and shook his head, helpless. "Lou has never hurt a soul."

Sara's tears magnified the depth of blue in her eyes. "Louzanna risked her life to save Elizabeth. This is what's come of her bravery."

"Family members of victims came to the livery and not all of them took sick. I never took sick." Sighing, he leaned back in the chair, shoulders slumped, bone tired. He'd have to send Jamie to tell Marshal Monroe to extend the quarantine.

Sara was still beside him, standing near his shoulder. For a moment he thought she was going to touch him and he wished she would. But she simply sighed and said, "Maybe we'll never know where this terrible curse comes from or how it spreads, Dru. What we have to think about now is Louzanna. That's all that matters."

* * *

Sara wished there was something more she could do or say, but they both knew that Louzanna was fast approaching the last stages of the fever. There was a slight chance she would live, but the longer she lingered, the more the possibility faded.

"You look exhausted, Sara. Why don't you get some rest? I'm not leaving her," Dru said.

"I'll go start supper and see to Lissybeth. Poor Jamie's had to look after her for hours." She walked to the other side of the room, poured fresh water into a washbowl, and carefully washed her hands and forearms thoroughly, the way he had insisted at the livery. She felt him watching her, was disturbed by the intensity of his stare.

When she straightened and turned around again, he looked away.

"Minnie died the morning after we left her." Sara carefully kept her voice low, lest Louzanna hear. "Abel came by today and told Jamie. He's going to spend another week in the house, though he's still showing no signs of the fever."

Dru looked as if he was trying to will Lou to survive. When he smoothed out the lace on the pillowcase, his fingers came in contact with a poppet Sara had slipped beneath it. He held up the little muslin doll, turned it over and over in his hand, stared at the uneven stitches that held the herbs inside. Then he shook his head.

"You think me foolish, don't you?" Sara asked.

"No more than me. At this point I'm willing to believe in anything."

Sara went to him and when he didn't look up, she knelt beside the chair and laid her hand upon his arm. "Dru, look at me."

He turned his rich, dark eyes her way. There was anger brimming there, anger born of frustration and fear of an adversary that he could not fight.

"You've done everything you could, everything you knew how to do."

"Forty-one people have died. Forty-one of the fifty-two cases I've treated. What kind of doctor am I that I saved so few?"

"You're only human. Granddaddy says that no healing at all is a sort of healing. It's God's will that brings the final outcome, and we forget that. Nothing we can do is as powerful."

"Do you always see the good side, Sara? What if it's God's will to take Louzanna? Will you sit there resigned and philosophize her death away, too?"

Sara looked at Lou, her vision smeared by a rush of tears. Poor, frightened Louzanna. The only one brave enough to take in a fallen woman and her bastard child. She had loved Sara enough to call her *sister*, cared enough to stand up for her and let her stay on in the face of censure. Lou had been the only one to believe in Dru's return, the only one campaigning for them to be a family again.

As a tear rolled down her cheek, Sara sighed and wiped it away. She tried to answer as honestly as she could.

"I can't change the things I believe or the way I see life, but if the good Lord sees fit to take Lou, then I really don't know what I'll do."

46

When Lou battled the fever and came through the worst of it, they rejoiced. But her body, weak and ravaged by the disease, soon began to fail. Death was at the door again and Louzanna, more than any of them, was certain of it.

Nothing Dru said or did helped. No tonic Sara tried could shake Louzanna's own conviction that she was dying.

One evening at twilight Sara sat outside on a front porch rocker with Lissybeth half asleep on her lap and Goldie snoring heavily at her feet. Jamie sat on the edge of the porch, leaning against a post, watching the first stars come out. Neither of them spoke. Both were thinking of the woman upstairs.

Suddenly Dru's footsteps echoed in the entry hall. They turned to him at the same time.

"She wants to see you," Dru told Jamie as he stepped outside.

Jamie hesitated, then pushed to his feet and dusted off the back of his pants. He avoided looking at Sara as he walked silently past.

Dru hadn't slept more than a few minutes in days,

choosing to spend almost every waking hour at his sister's bedside.

He had lost weight again: not as much as he had during the war, but the strain and worry showed on his face and in his eyes. Sara wished she could smooth away the lines etched around the corners of his eyes and temper the deep grooves bracketing his mouth.

"How is she?" Sara asked.

"She's grown so weak. She hasn't much longer." A long sigh shuddered through him.

He hooked his thumbs into his waistband, walked to the edge of the porch, looked out over the yard. Lamps were already lit inside houses along the street. A few doors down, a small band of children ran between fireflies playing hide-and-seek in the gathering gloaming. Life in Magnolia Creek had begun to settle into a sort of normalcy again.

But would their lives ever be the same without Louzanna?

Sara rose, shifted the sleeping child to her shoulder. Unexpectedly, Dru stepped toward her. She was astounded when he reached for her daughter.

"I'll take her upstairs for you," he said softly.

Sara's heart tripped. "You don't have to."

"I know. I want to."

Carefully she transferred Elizabeth to Dru's arms. He lifted her high against his shoulder and patted her back when she stirred; she slipped right back to sleep. Lissybeth's fair curls looked like spun gold next to Dru's ebony hair. His hand dwarfed her back, yet communicated only gentleness.

Dru said nothing, yet Sara sensed he needed to hold Elizabeth for the exact reasons she had earlier. There was something about cradling the solid, perfect little form that soothed and comforted a heavy heart.

She smiled to let him know she understood. He stepped aside and let her go first. She continued up the stairs, aware of his presence behind her every step of the way. Once they reached her room, Sara lit a lamp, then replaced the globe and turned around in time to see Dru gently lower Elizabeth into her crib.

When he realized Sara was watching him, the heat in his eyes seared her. She was barely able to breathe as he crossed the room, his dark eyes boring into her soul, searching for and finding all her secrets.

Without a word he enfolded her in his arms and held her close to his heart the way he had Elizabeth. She slipped her arms around him and clung, offering him more than solace, silently offering him a lifetime of love, communicating without words that it was there for the taking.

Louzanna wished they hadn't propped her up against the pillows like a rag doll discarded amid the bedding. Slouched over to one side, she hadn't enough strength left to right herself.

There was a soft tap at the door, one she recognized as Jamie's. Her weakened voice failed her but the door opened anyway. He slipped inside, discreetly leaving the door open.

When he reached her bedside she motioned for him to sit in the chair Dru had vacated. Uncertain, he started to refuse, then he sat, his gaze lighting everywhere but on her face.

"Jamie, please, look at me."

When he finally did meet her eyes, Louzanna saw her fate in the undisguised sorrow on his face.

"Don't take on so, Jamie. Everybody has to die sometime. I'm just going sooner than later."

"Not you, Miss Louzanna. Not yet, anyway."

"Dru won't admit it, but I know I'm dying. He and Sara keep pretending I look better, but more often than not they can only sit here in an awkward silence that gives them away. No one will talk about my dying, even when it's right here under all our noses." She had to struggle to make herself heard, and waited until he leaned closer. "We've been together nearly all our lives, haven't we, Jamie?"

She reached for Mason's ring, felt the cold precious metal and the opal stone against her palm. "Help me get this off, will you?"

His bloodshot eyes swam with tears that began to trail down his cheeks. "You never go without that, Miss Lou. Why do you want to take it off now?"

"I won't need it anymore."

He shook his head. "Yes, you will. You're gonna be fine."

"Liar." She smiled, perfectly at ease. It was too late for anything, for doubt, even for the fear that had held her imprisoned for so long. She'd never been more certain of anything in her life, nor had she ever felt as courageous.

"Don't be stubborn. Help me, Jamie." He had been helping her all of her life. She was bound and determined to help him while she still could.

He slipped out of the chair, lowered himself to the edge of the bed, and gathered her into his arms long enough to raise her head and shoulders off the pillow. She mustered the strength to pull the chain over her head. Jamie gently lowered her again, righting her, plumping the pillow so that she was as comfortable as possible. Then he moved back to the chair.

She clasped the chain and ring in her hand, then held it out to him. The heavy opal dangled and revolved at the end of the gold links, catching the light, winking as if it knew a secret.

"I want you to have this, Jamie."

"I can't take it, Miss Lou."

"Yes, you can and you will. You still intend to go back to New York, don't you?"

"I do."

"You'll need a stake in the future. I can't give you anything else, but I can give you this. Sell it and buy whatever you need and think of me sometimes."

"I can't take it."

"Yes." She slowly nodded. "You can and should. Do you want to know something horrible?"

He didn't answer, but she went on anyway, pausing often to catch her breath.

"When Daddy died and the first thing Dru did was go to Hugh Wickham . . . to have your manumission papers drawn up . . . I was terribly upset."

Jamie sat up a bit straighter, his expression carefully guarded.

"It's true . . ." She nodded. "I was afraid that if you . . . had your freedom . . . that you would leave and I'd never see you again."

He dropped his head, stared at the multicolored starbursts of light coming from the opal as it twisted on the end of the chain, his shoulders sagging, tears flowing freely.

"That's why you . . . must have the ring, Jamie. Please.

I beg of you. To think I was . . . so selfish . . . that I would have kept you in slavery just so you'd always be . . . in my life."

"You didn't have to own me to keep me here, Miss Lou. All it would have taken was a word."

"I know that now, but it's too late. Mason was the one true love of my life, Jamie, but I think perhaps I wore this ring all these years because mourning him was a far cry safer than facing up to life. Maybe that's what kept me from seeing what I might have if I'd been stronger."

He reached out, closed his strong dark hand around hers, then he took the ring and chain. She let go and he carried it to his lap. The chain dangled between his knees, ignored.

"I'd rather you live, Miss Louzanna, than take this from you."

"That's not to be." She could barely hear herself now. She no longer feared death. Now her only fear was time running out before she said all she needed to say to those she loved so dearly.

"There's one more thing I want you to do for me, and then I'd like you to go get Dru and Sara."

Jamie listened carefully as she explained. Before he went to do her bidding one last time, she raised her hand. There was a long pause before he finally took it, but when he did, he held it with gentle strength and confidence until she bid him go.

Night had fallen and a gentle breeze had begun to blow through the old hickory out front. Leaves rustled outside the open window with a calming hush. Elizabeth slept soundly in her crib. Time seemed to stand still as Dru held Sara in his arms.

A deep calm came over him, the likes of which he hadn't known since before the war.

Throughout the yellow fever crisis he had barely enough time to think, let alone dwell on the future. Through it all, Sara proved herself capable of working beside him, proved the depth of her loyalty, her ability to forgive and to understand. She was loving and devoted to her child. She was his sister's best friend.

She was everything he had ever wanted in a wife.

He drew back so that he could look into her eyes and the longing he saw there took his breath away. He cupped her face, raised her chin, intent on savoring a kiss.

Just as he lowered his head, just as his lips were about to touch hers, there came a knock at the door. They quickly stepped apart. All thoughts fled, save one.

Louzanna.

Dru dropped his hands. Sara followed him to the door.

"What is it, Jamie?" It was clear Jamie had been crying. Dru reached blindly for Sara's hand, found it, and hung on. "Is she . . . ?"

"No. She wants to see you both." Jamie made no attempt to hide his tears as he stepped aside so that they could leave the room together.

Louzanna smiled weakly when they entered her room. Dru went immediately to her side, sat down, and took hold of her hand.

"Are you in any pain?"

She shook her head. "I'm tired. So . . . very tired."

He cursed himself. What kind of a doctor was he? He couldn't even save his own sister.

"I haven't much time left," Lou said softly, studying each of them in turn.

Irritation born of helplessness soured Dru's tone. "You don't know that."

"I know. I wanted . . . you all here, all three of you, so that . . . I could tell you how much you mean to me. You are my family, all of you. Not . . . not just Dru, but you, too, Sara. You've been like a sister to me, trusting me with Elizabeth, helping me do more than I thought I was capable of doing. And Jamie"—she looked up at him for a long while without saying a word—"Jamie, you . . . know what you mean to me."

"Louzanna, save your strength," Dru said, panicked, tormented.

"Whatever for?" Lou smiled a wistful, knowing smile.

Somehow Sara found the fortitude to sit down on the opposite side of the bed from Dru, take Lou's hand, and encourage her to be strong one last time. "Say whatever you need to say, Louzanna."

"I've . . . wasted the better part of my life inside this house, running from . . . from this very moment. Now that it's here, I'm not . . . afraid. I think of all that . . . time, all those years. I wish I could do it all . . . again. But this time I would really *live*."

Louzanna reached for Dru's hand. She held on to both him and Sara and slowly drew their hands together. Dru looked into Sara's eyes and held on to her hand even after Lou let go, their hands joined across Lou.

"Now you two must live," Lou admonished. "Share the love . . . you have for each other." She glanced at Jamie and then focused on Dru. "Sometimes love is standing right in front of our eyes and yet, for whatever reason . . . we refuse to see it. Don't throw it away because of what other people might think or say. Don't lose it because of stubborn pride, either."

Sara's hand tightened around Dru's fingers; her love was right there for him to see. Sara still loved him and always had.

Lou went on, "I've given . . . Mason's ring to Jamie. I want you, Sara, to . . . to have the ladies of my quilting circle each choose a quilt to remember me by. Save some of your own favorites . . . for Elizabeth."

"I will." Sara wiped her eyes. "I promise."

Louzanna took a deep breath. It appeared she hadn't the strength to exhale, but then she let go a long, deep sigh. "Now . . . I'd like to be alone with Dru."

When Sara leaned over to kiss Lou on the cheek, Dru had to turn away. He heard Sara whisper, "Thank you, Louzanna. Thank you for everything you've done for me and Elizabeth. I'll never forget you. Good-bye, sister."

Jamie had to help Sara from the room. Finally, alone with his sister, Dru looked deep into her eyes and admitted to himself that she knew better than he what was happening. She was at peace, ready to leave them.

"Don't take on so, Dru," Lou said. "I'm . . . probably calmer right now than . . . I've ever been in my life. I've nothing left to fear, you see. I'm done hiding."

"I'll miss you, Lou." His voice broke on the words as he thought of the last few years he had missed with her, regretting each and every moment they had lost.

"You . . . have Sara and Elizabeth. Don't wait too long . . . to tell her that you still love her. It's always been apparent to me, but she doesn't know it. You need to tell her . . . that you forgive her, too. Start your marriage over. Let go of the past."

Her breath caught, hitched. Her eyelids fluttered. Dru feared she was gone, but then she opened her eyes again. He was holding tightly to her hand when she whispered,

"I won't demand a deathbed promise . . . but what I'd like most in the world is . . . for you and Sara . . . to be . . . happy."

As her voice faded away, Dru kissed his sister on the cheek. They had been close their entire lives. She had believed in him long before he had ever believed in himself.

He held her hand, sat with her through the night, sat there until he could finally admit that he was alone and that his sister was gone.

47

FOLKS WOULD ALWAYS remember that the quarantine was officially lifted on the day of Louzanna Talbot's burial. On Dru's advice George Langston opened the roads and travelers and supplies began to feed into Magnolia Creek again.

Dressed in her mourning ensemble, Sara stood beside Dru at the grave, holding Elizabeth's hand. Almost as if she sensed the solemnity of the occasion, Elizabeth was unusually quiet as the Baptist preacher recited the Lord's Prayer and the Twenty-third Psalm over Lou's grave.

Sara glanced at Dru. Understandably, he had been withdrawn for the past three days, retreating to his room early every evening. The tenderness he had shown the night of Lou's death seemed to have vanished with his sister's life. He wasn't rude or sullen, but was simply absorbed in grief, avoiding the house, avoiding her.

Burdened with her own sorrow, confused about the future, Sara had sent Jamie around to invite Lou's quilting circle for tea and carried out her sister-in-law's wishes. The ladies put aside any ill will they might still harbor toward her long enough to come by and choose one quilt each from over thirty that had been stored in closets and trunks, or that were in use around the house.

Standing beside the grave, her thoughts everywhere and nowhere, Sara made it easy for Elizabeth to escape her hold. The child darted between her and Dru and then Elizabeth grabbed hold of Dru's hand. He looked down, surprised to see the curly-headed cherub clinging to him.

Elizabeth's finely drawn brows dipped into a frown.

"Woo?" She wanted to know where her friend had gone.

Her own heart aching, Sara started to reach for Lissybeth but Dru moved first, lifting the child into his arms and settling her on his hip.

Nose to nose with the little girl, he softly whispered, "Lou's not here."

"Aw gone?" Elizabeth fingered his collar.

Dru cleared his throat. "All gone."

The immeasurable depth of sadness in his voice broke Sara's heart. Whether he wanted her there or not, she stepped up beside him until they were shoulder to shoulder.

Absorbed by melancholy, Sara thought of all Lou had done for her and of their time together. Her thoughts drifted to her own family, Granddaddy, Mama, her old life in the ramshackle cabin across the creek. She thought of the little sister she had lost, and even her daddy. There had been no word yet from Collier's Ferry, so she could only pray there hadn't been more deaths.

The preacher closed his Bible and walked around the grave to shake Dru's hand. He offered sympathy and kind words, ointment for the soul that took away the sting, but could not cure the deep, forever ache.

It was time to go home, except that the house did not seem much like a home anymore. It was hard not to find Lou in the drawing room reading to Lissybeth or seated at her quilt frame. She would never again bumble around in the kitchen, nor would she hover at the conservatory windows to watch the seasons change.

Sara was fresh out of tears when she paused to glance at all of the new headstones in the cemetery. Without warning, her vision suddenly blurred. A soft, distant roar began to drone in her ears and gathered force until she couldn't hear a word anyone was saying. Her sight constricted to a pinpoint of light, then the world tilted, and everything around her faded away.

She was seventeen again, lying in the dark loft, dreaming of running through the woods to the old oak where the morning dew collected. She was anxious to bathe her face at sunrise, but unlike the first time, now she knew it wasn't just any man she wanted to charm—she would have her sights set on Dru Talbot.

Somewhere deep inside, she knew that before she could climb out of the loft she would have to work her way through the overwhelming darkness that engulfed her.

"Sara?"

She blinked, opened her eyes. The first face she saw was his.

"Dru." His name drifted on a sigh of relief. She wouldn't have to search for him at all; he was right there beside her where he belonged. His warm hands were on her shoulders, his face near her own. She could see into the depths of his rich, dark eyes. Once so full of hope and youth and the promise of a shining future, his beautiful eyes were stained with sadness.

She struggled to sit up and in doing so, realized that she wasn't dreaming. She was stretched out on the buggy seat and Dru was seated right there next to her.

A small crowd had gathered around the vehicle: the

preacher; Jamie, holding Elizabeth; Lou's quilting circle friends; Lorna Pickering. Sara rubbed her eyes, noticed she was wearing her black gloves. The buggy was drawn up beside the cemetery where a new grave yawned next to a mound of earth.

Louzanna's burial.

Time shuddered and settled back into place. Everything she had done and been and lived through came rushing back. She remembered how she had hurt Dru and all that they had endured over the last few weeks.

Embarrassed, she tried to ignore the worried onlookers as he helped her to a sitting position. She caught a glimpse of her hat and veil lying on the buggy floor. He carefully straightened the folds of her skirt. After a moment's hesitation, he smoothed down her hair, too. She tried to swallow around the lump in her throat.

"I don't know what came over me. I was thinking of Lou and suddenly, everything went dark."

"Have you been feeling poorly?"

"I'm just so tired. It's so hot out here."

Dru touched his palm to her forehead, searching for signs of fever. She shook her head. There was no pain, nor any of the aches that accompanied yellow fever.

About to assure him that she had never fainted in her life, Sara suddenly remembered passing out once before. At the time, she had been pregnant with Elizabeth.

"Sara?" He leaned closer, searched her eyes.

Sara swallowed, her mind racing back, counting the days, the weeks since she and Dru had been together at Doc Porter's house.

"I'm fine . . . really." She prayed that was true, hoped she didn't sound as shaken as she felt. Her hands were trembling so hard that she had to clasp her fingers together in her lap.

"Are you sure?"

She nodded, trying desperately to believe it.

"Any pain behind your eyes?"

"No. None." She shook her head.

"Muscle aches? Sore throat?"

"Nothing like that. Please, Dru, just take me back to the house."

After another silent appraisal, he slid a polite distance across the seat, cast a quick glance at the anxious faces gathered around the buggy.

"Just exhaustion. No yellow fever." The announcement ignited an outpouring of relief.

Sara sat by, dazed and speechless, embarrassed to be the center of attention as Jamie handed Elizabeth up to Dru and then went to fetch his own horse. He planned to spend one more night in his cabin before leaving for New York.

"Can you hold her?" Dru eyed Sara closely, hesitant to hand Elizabeth over.

"I'm all right now." Sara willed herself to stop trembling, reached for her daughter, and settled Lissybeth on her lap. She watched Dru negotiate the quiet streets as they headed back to the house.

Could I be carrying his child?

Her place here in his home was so tentative now that Louzanna was gone.

What if she *was* to have another child? How would she ever be able to support herself, Elizabeth, and a second baby?

How could she tell Dru? They both knew that any child they conceived that night at Doc Porter's had come out of anger, not love.

48

DRU WATCHED SARA run her hands along Elizabeth's sturdy legs all the way down to her shoes and then clap Lissybeth's feet together. The child giggled and the unexpected joy in the sound thawed a piece of his heart and eased the sorrow riding along with them.

There had been far too much pain in their lives, far too many sober moments over the last few weeks. He stole a glance at Sara, found her too pale for his liking. He didn't believe heat or fatigue responsible for her fainting spell. There were other hot, tired people gathered that afternoon, but only Sara had collapsed.

He reminded himself that she had been working tirelessly for weeks and since Lou died he had left everything up to her while he tried to deal with his grief, but no excuse answered the nagging question *why?*

She had nearly scared the life out of him when she suddenly crumpled to the ground without warning.

Shifting the reins, he glanced at her again. She might think she was fine, but he intended to examine her more thoroughly once they were home. If there was one thing he had learned from the war and the epidemic, it was that life, like time, was far too fragile and fleeting a thing to take for granted.

* * *

The house was quiet. Sara was upstairs tucking in Elizabeth. Alone in the parlor, Dru sat at the drop-leaf secretary with the family Bible open to the pages where the Talbot family history was recorded. A quarter of an hour earlier he had entered the date of Louzanna's death beside that of her birth. He hadn't moved since he noticed the date of his and Sara's wedding inscribed beside their names.

When the floorboards creaked in the hall, he looked up and saw Jamie step into the room. Dru closed the Bible, pushed it aside, and stood, relieved to vacate the small, hard chair that tucked beneath the desk lid.

"Are you all packed?"

Jamie hesitated, obviously working up to something important. Dru gave him time, dropping all pretense of servant and employer. He offered him bourbon, but Jamie declined, so he poured one for himself and settled into his father's wing chair near the cold fireplace.

Jamie closed the parlor doors behind him. "Miss Louzanna gave me one last job to do." He slipped his fingers into the watch pocket of his vest, pulled out a thin gold ring, and dropped it into Dru's palm.

"Miss Lou said that she hoped you would know what to do with this."

Dru stared at Sara's wedding ring, recognized the laurel leaves etched around the band. He had no notion of what she'd done with it, had thought perhaps she had sold it or traded it away during the war.

"This was my grandmother's wedding ring," he said softly, slipping it onto the tip of his forefinger, slowly spinning it round and round as he studied the engraving partially worn away by time.

Jamie paused, rubbed his hand over the back of his neck. "Miss Sara left it here with a note to Miss Lou the day she ran off. Miss Lou kept it safe until you could give it back to Miss Sara again."

Dru stared at the ring, pictured Sara on their wedding day, so young, so innocent. A constellation of stars had danced in her eyes that day. He'd been so in love, so proud to make her his wife, so certain he was doing right by her. He had taken a chance on marrying a girl he had only known for two weeks, a girl of seventeen, because the idea of marching off to war, of leaving to chance the possibility of their having a future together, had made no sense to him in the spring of '61.

He thought not only to give her his name but to protect her from the hardships that troubled times would surely bring. He went off to war with the memory of their wedding night, hoping that she might very well have been carrying his child.

Carrying his child.

Dru stared at the ring on the tip of his finger.

Is Sara carrying my child?

He shot up, pocketed the ring, and nearly bowled Jamie over on his way to the door.

"I'm going out. I've got to go back to the office." On the heels of a swift apology, Dru suddenly remembered that Jamie was leaving at first light. He stopped his headlong rush, extended a hand in friendship, refusing to believe that this was the last time he would ever see the man.

"Promise me that you'll find a way to let us know where you are."

"I will, soon as I'm settled."

"I can't thank you enough for all you've done for my

sister and me. And for Sara. I know your life wasn't easy, Jamie. I wish things could have been different—"

"As soon as you were able, you gave me the one thing that mattered most in my life. You gave me my freedom."

"I don't know what I would have done without you here these last few weeks. Thank you for agreeing to stay."

"I did it for Miss Lou. To make her life easier. I'da come back sooner, had I known she needed me."

"I know that. She knew it, too." Dru clapped Jamie on the shoulder and pumped his hand again. "Godspeed, Jamie. You'll always have a home here if you need it."

Sara closed the curtains in her room, made certain Elizabeth was asleep, and smiled when she heard Goldie snoring beneath the crib. She scratched the dog on the head and then sat in the rocker and counted back to that night at Doc Porter's house.

I could be pregnant.

She laid her hand upon her lower abdomen, tried to recall how she felt when she carried Elizabeth. She could only remember the latter few months, her aching back, swollen ankles, and a longing for butter. Tonight she had put extra butter on her bread.

Pushing up out of the rocker, she paced to Elizabeth's crib, drew a light sheet over the child, and then walked to the standing mirror near the dressing table.

Sara stared back at her reflection and wondered how any man, let alone Dru, could find her desirable now. Her eyelids were swollen from crying and there were dark smudges beneath them. She cupped her breasts through the bodice of her gown, winced at their tender fullness. Her nipples were even sensitive to the fabric of her chemise. Had she been aware of the changes all along but unwilling to admit to them?

She thought back to that night at Doc Porter's.

If she *was* pregnant, she could never keep something like that from Dru—but if she did tell him, he would feel compelled to do the honorable thing and keep her in his life just because of the child. He might never forgive her or love her again, but he would feel obligated to her forever.

Unthinkable.

And what of Elizabeth? How would Dru treat her once he had a child of his own? Lissybeth might forever be considered a bastard by Dru, her siblings, and everyone else in town.

Sara couldn't stand looking at her reflection any longer. Maybe if she went home to Collier's Ferry and stayed with her mother, if she talked to Granddaddy, she might be able to make the right decision.

With the quarantine lifted and Daddy gone there was nothing to keep her from going home.

Nothing but Dru and the truth.

49

DRU'S LONG STRIDES ate up the blocks as he walked back home from the office along the darkened streets. Before he jumped to any conclusions he had gone to read up on pregnancy in his medical journal.

> *"The usual period assigned to this process of development is nine calendar months, forty weeks, or two hundred and eighty days. General signs include cessation of the catamenia, morning sicknesses after the fifth or sixth week, heartburn, painful distension of the abdomen toward evening, demanding the loosening of strings and laces; indigestion, irritability of temper, longings, and fanciful desires."*

Among other complaints and ailments, *fainting* was listed—which disturbed him greatly.

The tome by Dr. A. W. Chase spelled out other physical signs and symptoms. Chase added,

> *"From the highly sensitive state of the nervous system in all women during pregnancy, and the remarkably susceptible condition of their minds and bodies, pregnant women should avoid all exciting scenes and be*

carefully guarded from the witnessing or hearing of any object of disgust or repulsion. They should avoid all risk of infection, for though they may escape the disease of which it may be the emanation, the child may be seriously affected by it in the womb and on its birth exhibit all its symptoms."

Sara had beheld all manner of disgusting scenes over the past weeks, more than any one woman should have to witness. She had been exposed to yellow fever over and over. She might not have contracted the disease, but the journal had him wondering what damage the exposure might have done to an unborn child.

As he headed home, Dru vacillated between anxiety and the pale, distant glimmer of hope.

There was only one light burning in the drawing room when he walked in. The kitchen was dark, the stove cold, the first floor deserted. He turned down the lamp and, guided by light from the upstairs hall, slowly ascended the stairs.

When he reached Sara's door, he heard her moving around inside and softly knocked before he could talk himself out of it.

She opened the door halfway, tugged the sash on a loose robe, and brushed her hair back out of her eyes.

"You're home." She looked startled to see him there.

And why shouldn't she? He had been avoiding her for days.

"I went to the office. There was something I had to do."

"Jamie plans to leave at dawn."

"I said good-bye earlier."

"I packed up some food for him to take along."

"Good. Thank you." He looked down at the floor, noticed her toes peeking out from beneath the hem of her robe. Her feet were bare, just as they had been on the day they'd met. Her long, auburn hair was unbound, cascading to her waist. He edged closer, picked up the scent of soap and talcum.

"Well, then." She glanced over her shoulder, then back up into his eyes. "Elizabeth is asleep. I was just getting ready for bed."

"Are you feeling better?"

"I'm just tired. I need some sleep, that's all. Good night, Dru." She started to close the door. He thought she spoke too quickly, sounded too defensive.

He braced his hand on the door to stop her. Her eyes widened in surprise. The door was open far enough for him to see past her into the room. Goldie was lying beneath the crib where Elizabeth slept soundly.

Sara's bed was still made. Elizabeth's little gowns were lying all over the quilt alongside a tired old satchel that was open. His gaze shot back to Sara's. Their eyes met and held.

"Going someplace?"

"To bed." She tried to close the door again, but he refused to let her shut it in his face.

Her cheeks blanched of color when he pressed the door open wider. She let go and backed into the room.

"You're leaving?" He motioned toward the bed, the satchel.

She clasped her hands. Her eyes widened when he took two more steps in her direction.

"I thought I'd go home and see how Mama's doing." She shrugged as if that explained everything. "I don't even know if anyone else in the family took sick or died."

"You were quick enough to get away from there back when Doc brought you to work here."

"I know what having family means now, even a family like mine. They're still my kin and when push comes to shove, family is all we've got."

Dru walked over to the bed, lifted the hem of one of Elizabeth's gowns, and absently fingered the neatly embroidered cross-stitch Louzanna had added. His heart jolted. Aside from Sara, he had absolutely no family now.

"Looks like you're packing for a long visit. Were you leaving for good this time?"

"I'm just going to visit my mother."

"What are you running from, Sara?"

"I'm *not* running."

"It sure looks like it to me. What are you hiding?"

"Nothing."

He shook his head and advanced another step. She was backed up against the bed with nowhere to go. Her hand went to her throat, settled in the hollow exposed by the open collar of her robe.

She licked her lips. "I thought that with Louzanna gone, you might want some time alone."

"Is that all that's kept you here? Louzanna and the quarantine?" He glanced over at Goldie, kept his voice hushed so as not to awaken the child. "Why the rush to leave now?"

"There's no rush, I just—"

"What are you hiding?" His gaze swept her body, the lush curves exposed by the thin robe. Were her breasts fuller? Or was he just trying to convince himself of something that wasn't true?

"Nothing. I'm not hiding a thing."

"You're pregnant, aren't you, Sara?"

Her mouth opened, then snapped shut without her uttering a word. He was playing a guessing game and never expected the truth to hit him so hard that his knees almost buckled.

"You *are* pregnant. Dammit!"

She whirled around, stared at the clothes on the bed, and frantically wiped away telltale tears.

"Sara . . ."

"I knew you wouldn't want this."

"What do you mean, I wouldn't want *this*? Were you going to leave without telling me you're pregnant with my child? I'm not Jonathan Smith. I would *never* let you take a child of mine away from me."

She turned to face him again. "I was going to Collier's Ferry to *think*!"

"About what? What is there to think about?"

Shoving her hair back with both hands, she let go a brittle laugh. "What's there to think about? Maybe the fact that I'm pregnant again, this time by a husband who can't stand the sight of me. I can't even *call* you my husband, can I, Dru? Because we don't have a marriage. You don't love me anymore. If you did, you'd be able to forgive me." She took a deep breath, let it out. "I don't even know you anymore. You're not the man I married."

"You're not the woman I married, either."

"I was just a girl back then."

Dru turned around, paced over to the dressing table. At first he simply stood there staring, his mind racing, his thoughts unfocused. Then he noticed four worn squares of paper laid out like a puzzle to form a rectangle and recognized his handwriting executed in even lines across the pieces.

It was his last letter to Sara, one she must have kept all

these years and worn out reading. A sudden calm washed over him, a peace so overwhelming that he almost had to sit down.

He turned around and walked back to where she stood watching him.

"I was a dreamer," he confessed. "I wanted a home full of children and a wife who loved me enough to stand by me through thick and thin. I wanted to settle down here in Magnolia Creek and live a quiet life as the town doctor. I wanted to walk down the same streets my grandfather laid out when he helped found this town, and hold my head up high."

"But I ruined it all," she said softly.

"The war ruined it all, not you." He stopped to catch his breath, fully aware that his entire future hinged on what he was about to say. "Since Lou died, I've been thinking that maybe we should try to get it right this time, Sara. Maybe we can both have everything we ever wanted."

"What did you say?" Sara couldn't believe she heard right.

"Maybe we can both have everything we ever wanted—if you want my child. If you really want to be my wife again."

He towered over her and yet she wasn't afraid, not even when he had forced his way into the room. What she was afraid of was hoping for another chance and having her heart broken.

"How, Dru?"

He reached into his watch pocket, feeling around for something. She watched him draw a thin gold band out of his pocket. Her heart tripped when she recognized the ring he'd given her on their wedding day.

"Will you wear this again, Sara? Will you be my wife again?"

She wanted desperately to slip it on. Her hand had felt naked without it, but she stopped, asking herself why his sudden change of heart. She suspected it stemmed from their unborn child more than from love.

"It's the baby, isn't it? You're just doing this so that I don't leave with your baby."

"You wouldn't really do that, would you, Sara? If so, then there's absolutely nothing left of the girl I fell in love with. There's no marriage left to save."

"You didn't fall in love with me, Dru." She wanted to hang her head in shame, but it was a night of truths and this one had to be told. "I charmed you."

At first he frowned, but then the corners of his lips lifted in a half smile. "You *charmed* me? What are you talking about?"

"The day we met, you didn't really have a chance. I used one of Granddaddy's oldest charms that morning. I washed my face in dew at dawn. Any man I took a fancy to would have fallen in love with me that day."

"You're saying that you set out to find a husband that day, and that it turned out to be me?"

She shrugged.

"But you've always said you don't hold as much stock in those charms as your granddaddy does."

"Why else would a man like you have fallen in love with a poor girl from the other side of the creek?"

"If you believe that, then maybe you really didn't love me at all. Maybe it was just the charm at work."

"Of *course* I loved you. I truly fell in love with you the day we met on the ferry."

He reached for her hand. "Just as I truly fell in love

with you, Sara, charm or no charm. I carried that love with me throughout the war and I've loved you to this day, to this very minute, but I let my stubborn pride get in the way."

"But—"

"It's not any old charm and it's not the baby, Sara. I didn't have any idea you were pregnant until a few hours ago when it suddenly dawned on me why you might have fainted. Lou gave Jamie your wedding ring to give back to me and the minute I saw it, I knew it belonged back on your finger and that we were meant to be together. I want you as my wife and I want that family I always dreamed of. I won't let anything stand in our way this time—not this town, not the past."

Her heart was already full, but she needed to hear him say it. "Can you forgive me, Dru?"

"I won't be the man you deserve unless you can forgive me, Sara. I'll understand if you don't want anything to do with me after I explain."

"You're scaring me, Dru."

"I woke up in the infirmary with no idea of who or where I was except on a ward with other patients who were sick in body and mind, but it wasn't long before I began to remember. I knew my name and that I was a doctor. Of course, I remembered you."

"You said it was six months before you got your memory back."

"I lied. I lied to you. I lied to the doctors and nurses in the prisoner-of-war camp. I pretended not to have any memory so that I wouldn't be eligible for a prisoner exchange. I didn't want to go back, Sara, not that soon. I'd nearly lost my life. I couldn't face all the wounded I would have to try and save and I wasn't ready to face those I couldn't."

He shook his head. "I had no idea that those stolen weeks cost me our marriage. If I'd gotten a letter out to you sooner, if word had reached you that I was still alive, then you would never have gone off with Jonathan Smith in the first place."

She closed her eyes, thought of all the weeks and months that she had suffered and mourned while he had been lying in a prison hospital pretending not to know his own name.

"I won't blame you if you can't forgive me," he whispered.

Sara shook her head, clasped her hands, and fought to understand. Until now she had seen only the physical scars he carried home from war, but for a man like Dru, a good, honorable, and unselfish man to have lied in order to steal a few months' worth of peace, then all he had seen and suffered day after day must have been a terrible burden to bear.

She wrapped her arms around herself, aching to hold him, aching to put everything behind them and start anew. The tables had turned and he was asking for her forgiveness, asking for her to say the words that would help them start over.

"Maybe," she said, reaching for his hand, "maybe it's time we forgive each other, Dru, and maybe if we forgive ourselves for the things we've said and done, then we can finally put the war years behind us."

He held up the ring. "Will you wear this again?"

She was about to say yes, but then she glanced over at the crib and hesitated.

"What is it?"

"Elizabeth."

"What about Elizabeth?"

"I won't watch her grow up in the shadow of brothers and sisters who are yours. The thought of her being the bastard—"

He cupped her face with his hand, made certain she looked into his eyes.

"Listen to me, Sara. Legally you were still my wife when you conceived Elizabeth. She may not be mine by blood, but through you, she bears my name. She's Elizabeth Talbot. She's mine as far as I'm concerned and she'll be mine from now on."

Sara was too stunned to say anything as he slipped the wedding ring on her finger and then pulled her into his arms. He kissed the top of her head, her forehead, her eyes, with exquisite tenderness.

"You're trembling," he said.

"I can't believe this is all happening." She thumbed the gold ring on the third finger of her left hand, not quite certain any of this was true.

"Believe it, Sara." He sealed the words with a kiss that started out slow but left her breathless. "I want you, Sara."

"Oh, Dru." She buried her face in his shirtfront.

"You're getting the front of my shirt all wet."

She was laughing and crying at the same time as she reached for his top button. "I think I can do something about that," she whispered.

"I wish you would."

Her hands shook, but she managed to unbutton his shirt and open it enough to slip her hands inside and run her palms over his corded rib cage. Her fingertips grazed his nipples and she heard him sigh. Before she knew it, she was in his arms, nestled against his bare chest as he carried her across the hall to his own room.

His door was already ajar when he kicked it open and carried her to the bed. Before he put her down, he looked into her eyes for so long, she started to melt inside.

"Is this what you want, Sara?"

"I want it all. I want to be your wife and have your children. I want to work beside you for the rest of our lives."

He lowered her to the bed, spread her hair across the pillow, taking his own sweet time as he raked his fingers through the auburn silk. Then he smiled down at her and her breath caught and held as he brought his lips to hers.

This time he took her gently, as if it were their first time again, as if she were a girl of seventeen and not a soon-to-be mother of two. He opened her robe, exposed her bewitching body, and worshiped her slowly, memorizing every curve and turn of her breasts, her hips, her waist before he pulled off his own clothes, threw them on the floor, and then joined her on the bed again.

"Kiss me, Dru," she whispered.

He acquiesced, his lips soft and warm. He explored with his tongue, tasted, teased her mouth, her neck, her shoulders. His hands were gentle and yet they were the hands of a strong, capable man, a man who could heal as well as fight, deliver a baby or hoe a garden. She treasured him for who he was, not what he could give her, for the precious gift of another child, for his love and forgiveness.

He loved her long and well throughout the night, sealing the promise they had renewed when he'd slipped her ring back on her finger. When they finally lay replete in each other's arms, too exhausted to move, Sara smiled.

The lamp sputtered and died, but not before he glimpsed her joy. "What are you smiling about?"

"I never thought I'd be this happy again," she whispered.

"I'm glad, then." He nestled her close to his side and threw his leg across her thighs.

"Sara?"

"Yes, Dru?"

"Promise me one thing, will you?"

"Anything."

"Next time someone tells you I'm dead, make sure you see the body."

50

AT EIGHT THE next morning, someone started pounding on the front door and all hell broke loose. Goldie barked and Elizabeth began to wail. Dru shot up, groggy, naked, and reached for his pants. Sara shoved her tangled hair out of her eyes. She was still in Dru's bed wearing nothing but her wedding ring.

Disoriented, she watched him hop across the floor on one foot as he struggled into his pants. Once he had them on, he grabbed his shirt and headed out the door without a word. She slipped out of bed, desperately rifling through the bedding for her robe. She shrugged it on as she crossed the hall.

Goldie deserted Elizabeth and ran after Dru. Sara heard the dog barking in the entry hall as she made her way to the crib.

"Mama's here, baby. Don't cry. It's all right." She scooped Lissybeth out of the crib and held her close, kissed her cheek, and swayed back and forth.

"Woo?"

Sara tightened her arms around Lissybeth, and remembered Lou was gone.

"She's not here, precious, but somebody's at the front door." She dreaded finding out who it was and what they wanted; she thought of Lou again and prayed that bad luck hadn't come pounding at their front door.

Sara jiggled Elizabeth up and down until she had her smiling, and then set her down. Voices floated up the stairwell. She heard Dru talking to another man and then a woman.

Her hands shook as she hastily pulled a burgundy print dress out of the armoire, praying that it fit. When she noticed her wedding ring, she paused long enough to run her finger over the band, and closed her eyes.

Is it true? Did last night really happen?

Her apprehension mounted with every minute it took her to dress. She had no idea what to say to Dru this morning, no notion of how to act. Life was never as simple as it ought to be.

Barefoot, shirttail hanging, buttons cockeyed, Dru whipped open the door and caught Hugh Wickham with his fist raised, ready to knock again. Anne and the two boys were beside him holding covered dishes.

"I hope to God you weren't still asleep at this hour." Hugh tried to see past Dru into the entry. "Up and at 'em, Dr. Talbot! The quarantine's over and the Wickhams have come to call."

The whole Wickham family swept into the house, the little boys leading the way.

"Are Sara and Lou in the kitchen?" Without waiting for an answer, Anne headed off in that direction, her sons close on her heels.

Dru barely got the door closed when he heard her exclaim from the other room, "Why, the stove's not even going yet. I'll stoke the fire and put on the coffee I brought along."

Hugh was still in the entry leaning on his crutches, slowly looking around. "Place looks about the same as always," he said.

Dru started shoving his shirttail into his pants.

Hugh cocked a knowing smile. "Hope you weren't in the middle of something. We wanted to come to call long before now, but the quarantine went up. We heard it was lifted yesterday."

"It was. Did anyone have the fever out your way?"

"Not that I know of. It sounded like you had your hands full, though."

Dru nodded. "We did. Magnolia Creek lost forty-two people." He took a deep breath and paused before he could finally say, "We buried Lou yesterday."

Hugh's smile vanished. He had always liked Louzanna, often made her laugh. "Dammit, Dru. We had no idea or we'd never have barged in here. If you'd like us to leave—"

"Not at all." Dru glanced up the staircase, wondering where Sara was and when she was coming down. He ran his hand over the stubble on his jaw.

Anne came in from the kitchen. "I've got the stove going and the coffee on. We brought fresh bread, too. I have a great crop of green beans so I cooked some up with bacon, and there's chicken all ready to fry for supper later. I hope Sara and Lou don't mind me taking over." She stopped long enough to catch her breath and noticed Hugh's expression. "What's wrong? Sara is still here, isn't she, Dru?"

"She's still here. She'll be down shortly."

Shortly was as good a guess as any. He had no idea when, or *whether* Sara would even come down. He had envisioned a quiet morning alone with her and Elizabeth, their first real day as a family, but obviously that wasn't to be.

Hugh saved Dru from having to tell Anne about Louzanna. She was both shocked and saddened by the news.

"Oh, Dru, I'm so sorry. We *shouldn't* have come." Anne watched his reaction closely.

Dru knew that the Wickhams would leave if he asked, but it felt good to see friends again, good to have the house filled with life. The two little boys were running around the dining room table terrorizing Goldie, but the old dog lay panting in the middle of the commotion with her tongue lolling, and Dru could have sworn she was smiling. The smell of coffee had begun to drift through the house.

Family and friends. That's all that mattered.

"I'd like you to stay," he assured them. "My mouth is already watering for that chicken."

"Do you think Sara would mind if I started some biscuits and gravy and cooked up a light breakfast? We got the boys up so early that they're already hungry again."

"Make yourselves at home," he told them. "I'll go up and see what's keeping her."

"If she woke up as tousled as you look, I imagine it'll take her a while to collect herself." Hugh laughed until his boys started arguing, and he headed toward the dining room to quiet them down.

Dru hurried upstairs, running his hands through his hair as he walked. As he expected, Sara wasn't in his room any longer, so he crossed the hall. Her door was closed. Awkward as hell, he knocked and waited for her to answer.

Elizabeth was in her arms. Sara was wearing a dress

he'd never seen before and the bodice strained over her full breasts. She'd already tamed her glorious hair into a prim braided coil wound at the nape of her neck.

Her cheeks were flushed bright pink. Her eyes were bright, her lips swollen from a night of kissing. But she wasn't smiling anymore and his heart sank.

Sara had never seen Dru this way, his hair sticking up every which way, his feet bare, his shirt buttoned crooked. Stubble darkened his jaw. His smile had slowly faded when he saw her.

"Are you all right?" he asked.

"Of course. What's wrong? Who's here?"

"Hugh and Anne and their boys. She's already making coffee. She brought food."

She hadn't seen Anne Wickham since shortly after the war started. Now the woman was downstairs making coffee.

As Dru's wife, *she* should be the one in the kitchen making coffee, offering the Wickhams her hospitality.

"What's the matter?" Dru was watching her closely.

"Everything," she said.

"What do you mean, *everything*?"

She rushed to the bed, set Elizabeth down amid the dresses and stockings still there from last night, and started taking off Lissybeth's nightgown.

She could feel his stare as she tossed Elizabeth's soiled gown aside. She closed her eyes and took a deep breath.

Dru followed her across the room. "Why? Are you already regretting last night?"

She whirled around so quickly, she nearly fell into him. Her heart was hammering, her mouth suddenly dry. "Are you?"

They stared into each other's eyes until Dru suddenly smiled. "We're not very good at this yet."

"At what?"

"At being married again."

She breathed a sigh of relief and smiled up at him. "No, I guess we're not."

"So what's wrong?"

"I should be downstairs making breakfast for our guests, not the other way around."

He shrugged. "Anne doesn't mind. She loves to cook."

"But—"

"They didn't know about Louzanna. I told them and asked them to stay. Let Anne help out. It'll make her feel like she's doing something for us." He touched her shoulder, ran his hand down her arms to her hands. "You look beautiful this morning, Sara."

She blushed and whispered, "You look like you just rolled out of bed. Why don't you get yourself pulled together while I go downstairs and see to our first guests?" Then she quickly added, "But don't be too long."

"You're nervous."

"I haven't had much practice at being a real wife to you, Dru. Everything's new."

He pulled her up to him and kissed her soundly until Elizabeth demanded attention again.

"You'll do just fine, Mrs. Talbot. After last night, I don't think we have anything to worry about."

They had breakfast and visited with the Wickhams. At eleven-thirty there came another knock at the door and this time Sara answered. Harold and Dinah Newberry, Harold Junior, and a thriving baby Violet—with the flattened bullet still hanging around her neck—were all standing at the front door. Harold Newberry was holding a huge ham. By one o'clock they were all at the table again sharing the noon meal.

Abel Foster showed up thirty minutes later. Dru warned the newspaperman that there were five children and a dog underfoot. Abel said he'd only be a moment, that he had something to say to both of them.

"I didn't mean to break up the party," Foster told Dru and Sara once they were alone in the drawing room. "I just wanted to let you know that I plan to run a piece on Louzanna, a memorial tribute. I'm going to give a bit of your family history and talk about what the Talbot name means to this town. It's the least I can do to make up for that editorial piece I wrote. After what you both did for this town during the epidemic and what you tried to do for Minnie, Sara, you both deserve more, but this is something I *can* give you. That and offer you both my sincerest apology."

Sara didn't know what to say except thank you. Dru thanked him, too, and shook the man's hand.

Sara walked back into the dining room and watched Dru take his place at the head of the long table and smile into her eyes. When she looked around at the Wickhams and their boys, the Newberrys and their children, and most of all, at Elizabeth—who was sitting contentedly on Anne's lap—her heart was brimming with so much emotion that she was afraid of bursting into tears in front of all of them.

She quickly excused herself and walked through the kitchen into the conservatory. Goldie followed along and lay down at her heels. Standing at the bank of windows overlooking the yard, the thriving vegetable garden and the summer flowers in full bloom, she felt Louzanna's presence more than ever and wished her friend was here to share her joy.

Sara was about to rejoin the others when she felt a calm sense of peace wash over her and sensed someone watching her.

She scanned the edge of the woods and saw Granddaddy Wilkes standing against the trees with his old flintlock resting on his shoulder.

She smiled and waved, and he waved back.

Before she could call out the window for him to come and join them he had already turned around and blended into the trees.

"See you soon, Granddaddy," she promised on a whisper, wishing he had stayed long enough for her to tell him that her future was no longer clouded by her past, that her long ago dreams were at last coming true.

But the more she thought about it, the more certain she was that Granddaddy already knew.

Read on for a sneak peek at Jill Marie Landis's breakout novel of contemporary women's fiction

LOVER'S LANE

On sale June 2003!

JAKE MONTGOMERY LEFT Long Beach before dawn on Thursday morning, leaving town a day early to avoid the weekend traffic headed up the coast. After three hours of driving, the dense population centers thinned and the land unfolded, spread out spring green and inviting. He drove past Santa Maria, cut over to old Highway One and followed the coast through Oceano and Pismo Beach.

As half owner of a private investigative firm he had founded, most of his days were spent not only enduring bumper-to-bumper traffic but L.A. road warriors venting their rage and the crowded, pulsing noise of city life as he gathered minutiae—details that among other things helped solve missing person cases, put an end to lengthy divorce proceedings, helped employers decide whether or not prospective employees had enough integrity to hire or promote.

Today the quiet solitude of the long drive helped ease the coil of tension in his gut, a coil that life in Los Angeles County tended to tighten deftly. This was the kind of getaway that his ex-wife used to talk about taking, but that was eons ago, back when they were still kids and newly married, long before they were consumed with their careers. Before there was no going back and the marriage had ended.

Lost in thought, he missed the turnoff to Twilight Cove. Cursing under his breath, he made a U-turn and followed Alamitos Canyon Road, a two-lane highway that wound down to the ocean alongside a creek of the same name. The gentle slope lined with low-growing chaparral ended abruptly after a sharp curve, and the picturesque town of Twilight Cove appeared suddenly, like a mirage.

The canyon road ended in the heart of a seaside village complete with a central plaza park with an old-fashioned, tiered Spanish fountain in the middle of a wide, grassy bluff overlooking the Pacific.

He slowed, checked out the various shops and stores, noted the location of The Cove Gallery before turning onto Cabrillo Road, which ran parallel to the ocean. Heading north, he found himself winding through residential sections of town, past wooden Craftsman-style houses. Most appeared to have been freshly painted. Many displayed flower boxes overflowing with alyssum, geraniums, and impatiens in delicate hues from white to pink to scarlet.

When he reached the point on the south end of the cove, he pulled into a scenic overlook, killed the engine and set the brake.

The moment he stepped outside his SUV, the onshore breeze kicked up, forcing him to zip his brown leather jacket. He walked to the guardrail. Even with mirrored sunglasses, he had to shield his eyes from the intense sunlight reflecting off the water. He watched distinct lines of swells form peaks offshore and counted six surfers in full wet suits cutting the waves on short boards. Then he turned full circle, taking in the view.

Lazy rolling hills covered in spring green grass and wildflowers tapered down both sides of the canyon to hug the cove. A few homes were scattered here and there on the hillside.

As he looked back toward town with its idyllic Plaza Park and avenue of historic storefronts, he shook his head. The place might look like Mayberry-by-the-Sea, but as long as real people inhabited it, Twilight Cove wasn't as bucolic as it appeared to be. He'd been in the investigative business long enough to know that.

The town still resembled the California dream of a hundred years ago—what so many other beach cities would look like if not for overdevelopment, smog, and too many rats in the maze.

The salt air was tinged with the sea and time. Standing in the cool breeze off the ocean, Jake easily imagined a clipper ship racing under billowing sails, her hold filled with wares to sell to the Spanish dons, Indians, and padres living in the shadow of the missions.

Steep steps and a narrow trail below the bluff led down to the beach. Limited parking and lack of accessibility to the cove kept the town from becoming overrun by seasonal tourists the way Monterey and Carmel were. Twilight Cove's small strand was still pristine. Only the hardy and the surfers didn't mind tackling the steps.

If it hadn't been for obligation and the driving need to see if a hunch would pay off, he would have lingered to inhale the fresh salt air and let the strong breeze whip through his hair and clear his mind. But he wasn't here on vacation. He'd come on what just might prove to be a wild-goose chase, but he was more than willing to risk taking the time if it meant finally winding up a case that had been open far too long.

He'd driven to Twilight Cove because he was a man of detail who hated loose ends, but most of all, he had come because of a personal obligation. He'd come to Twilight out of duty to a friend long gone, a friend as alive as ever in his memory.

The Cove Gallery was exactly as it appeared in the photos he'd seen in the *Budget Traveler* magazine. Uncluttered and open, with glossy golden oak floors and white walls, the interior was the perfect backdrop for the artwork displayed on the walls and free-form sculptures on platforms scattered around the room.

Jake had no sooner cleared the threshold when a slim young man sporting an artfully trimmed, pencil-thin beard along his jawline started across the room to greet him. He wore wire-framed glasses and was dressed entirely in black.

Geoffrey Wilson introduced himself, extended his hand in greeting, his smile both wide and genuine.

Jake shook hands. "My name's Jake Montgomery." He reached into his back pocket, pulled out a folded page carefully torn from a magazine, opened it. "I saw this article on your gallery in *Budget Traveler*."

The article stated that Geoff Wilson was twenty-nine years old, had moved west from Chicago three years ago after having grown tired of the brutal winters in the Windy City. The gallery had been open for a year and showcased local talent.

"Wonderful! I'm glad you stopped by. Go ahead and have a look around," Wilson invited.

"Actually," Jake pointed to the page that showed a

photo of Wilson standing in front of a painting. "I'm interested in the piece on the wall behind you in this photograph. The sunset seascape with the transparent figures in the foreground."

"An excellent choice, but I sold that a month ago."

"Who's the artist?"

"A local. Carly Nolan. Cove Gallery handles her work exclusively. She's one *very* talented lady." He started moving toward the far corner of the room. "Carly brought in a new painting just last weekend. I'm sure you'll find it equally stunning."

"So, she lives around here?"

Wilson paused, as if assessing Jake's character for a second. "She lives nearby, yes."

Jake followed him across the room, their even footsteps echoing in unison on the bare wood floor. The painting on the wall was of good size with a weathered frame that added to the tone of the piece.

The painting showed the huge dark boulders that ringed the cove and hugged the bluffs as violent storm waves crashed over them. The sky was gun-metal gray, dark and forbidding as the ocean. There were no buildings, no town above the cove, just wild grasses and two ragged junipers battered by the wind.

The artist had depicted a ghostly image of a young woman dressed in the style of the early 1800s standing at the edge of the bluff overlooking the water. Entirely painted in a sheer white, as if transposed over the painting, the woman stood with the fingers of one hand clenching the fabric of her long, flowing skirt. In the other hand she held a hat as if she had forgotten it was there. Long ribbons streamed over the brim, rippling just above the ground. Her hair was unbound, in wild disarray.

She was tall and lithe but her features were as subtly depicted as the rest of her, almost as if the artist wanted the viewer to wonder if there was actually a woman in the painting at all.

She could have been beautiful, or perhaps not. The artist left it up to the viewer to decide.

"This oil is of Twilight Cove from a different angle, one of the most dramatic pieces Ms. Nolan has done to date. Any work that showcases the cove tends to sell quickly. Visitors are so impressed by the beauty of this place that they want to take home a memory that will last a lifetime." Wilson rolled up onto his toes, settled back on his heels and smiled. "Not to mention the good investment that original oils become."

The Nolan piece was appealing in a haunting, ethereal way. Staring into the waves on the canvas was almost as hypnotic as watching the ocean. Not only that, but Jake found himself haunted by questions. Why was the young woman alone? Why had she gone to the edge of the bluff during a storm?

Except for a change of weather and time, it was a perfect rendition of the view he'd seen from the scenic viewpoint.

A label on the wall beside the painting listed the title as "Waiting." The price was more than adequate for a local unknown. The name Carly Nolan was printed neatly beneath the title.

"This one's a little dramatic for my taste," Jake said. "Do you have anything else she's done?"

Wilson's smile luffed at the corner like a sail losing wind. "Not at the moment. Are you staying in town or just passing through?"

"I was planning on staying until Monday, if I can find a place."

Geoff leaned forward conspiratorially. "Luckily it's the off-season. I can call a fine B and B right here in town."

"That'd be great."

Jake followed him to the counter to pick up a business card. Wilson picked up the phone and punched in a number. He held his hand over the mouthpiece and whispered, "This is a *wonderful* place. *So romantic.*"

Within two minutes Jake had a room reserved at the Rose Cottage a few blocks away. Geoff Wilson made a sticky note to himself with Jake's name on it with the reference—Nolan painting—and pressed it against the back of the counter.

Jake noticed a couple of tall baskets sitting near the cash register. One was stuffed with Chamber of Commerce maps. The other was filled with five-by-seven-inch cards printed with bios of the gallery's featured artists. Flipping through, he realized that all but Carly Nolan's bio-card showed photographs of the artists.

He picked one up and read the scant information.

Carly Nolan is a local artist new upon the scene. Her haunting paintings of Twilight Cove and the surrounding landscape peopled with ghostly figures from California's colorful past are quickly becoming favorites of collectors up and down the coast. Primarily working in oils, she has captured life in the very early days of the area using her own unique vision of color, style, and imagination.

"Please, take one," Geoff urged. "Actually, if you'd like to meet her, Carly may be working here this evening. I'll tell her you might drop by."

"Really?" Jake looked down at the card, at the blank spot where the artist's photo should be, and wondered if he'd hit pay dirt.

It was his partner, Kat Vargas, who'd found the article in *Budget Traveler*, not him. The painting in the background of the photo had reminded her of a small oil hanging on the wall above his desk.

Noting the similarities, Kat tore out the article, brought it in and slapped it on the desk in front of him. Then she had folded her arms, cocked her head, and asked, "Think it could be her? Your Obsession?"

Jake pulled his thoughts back, quickly thanked Geoff, adding that he wasn't certain he'd get by tonight but that he'd be in touch either way.

Before he left, he picked up a map as he turned to go and shoved both the biocard and map into the pocket of his brown leather jacket.

He had justified the drive up here by telling himself that he hadn't had a weekend off in so long that he couldn't remember when. But technically, this wasn't exactly a weekend off.

He was here on the off chance that Caroline Graham had finally slipped up. After six years, the young woman who seemed to have fallen off the face of the earth might have reappeared.

It was a long shot. In fact, it was downright ridiculous to think there might be only one artist using the same technique, but if Caroline Graham *had* surfaced, if she were still painting and now calling herself Carly Nolan, then he might have stumbled onto a woman who had managed to elude one of the top investigative firms in Southern California for years.